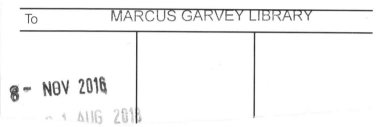

CARAF Books

Caribbean and African Literature
Translated from French

Renée Larrier and Mildred Mortimer, Editors

THE LEOPARD BOY

DANIEL PICOULY

Translated by Jeanne Garane

UNIVERSITY OF VIRGINIA PRESS
CHARLOTTESVILLE AND LONDON

Originally published in French as *L'Enfant léopard*
© Éditions Grasset & Faquelle, 1999

University of Virginia Press
Translation and afterword © 2016 by the Rector and
Visitors of the University of Virginia
Printed i

First pub lished 2016

9 8 7 6

LIBRARY

Picouly,

[Enfant

The le   ane.
        page   cm — (CARAF: Carib   translated
from Fre ch)
   "Origin lly published in French as L'Enfant léopard , Éditions Grasset
& Faquelle, 1999"—Verso title page.
   Includes bibliographical references.
   ISBN 978-0-8139-3789-2 (cloth : alk. paper)—ISBN 978-0-8139-3790-8
(pbk. : alk. paper)—ISBN 978-0-8139-3791-5 (e-book)
   1. Marie Antoinette Queen, consort of Louis XVI, King of France, 1755–
1793—Fiction. 2. Illegitimate children of royalty—France. 3. Racially
mixed children—Fiction. 4. Queens—France—Fiction. 5. France—
History—Revolution, 1789–1799—Fiction. 6. France—History—Reign of
Terror, 1793–1794—Fiction. I. Garane, Jeanne, 1960– translator. II. Title.
PQ2676.I274E6413 2015
843'.914—dc23

2015018038

CONTENTS

TRANSLATOR'S ACKNOWLEDGMENTS   vii

1. Dame Guillotine   5
2. Edmond and Jones   18
3. Rue des Moineaux   35
4. Sweet Victory   57
5. Haarlem   77
6. Moka   96
7. Sainte-Pélagie Prison   120
8. La du Barry   144
9. Zamor   167
10. The Marquise   194
11. Black Delorme   220
12. Marie-Antoinette   244

AFTERWORD   275
BIBLIOGRAPHY   291

TRANSLATOR'S ACKNOWLEDGMENTS

I am most grateful to Daniel and Odile Picouly for supporting this project and for a wonderful lunch at a bistro on Place de la Bastille in Paris, where I interviewed Daniel about the book. I would like to thank Series Editors Mimi Mortimer and Renée Larrier for their careful editing of the afterword, and special thanks to Mimi Mortimer and Susan Murray for their editing work on the manuscript. Thanks also to Cathie Brettschneider, Acquisitions Editor at the University of Virginia Press, for her patience and support. I am grateful to Allen Miller and Nicholas Vazsonyi, former and current Chairs of the University of South Carolina's Department of Languages, Literatures, and Cultures, for their support of this project in the form of research and travel grants, and for their recognition of translation as a valuable contribution to the Humanities. I would also like to thank the Provost's Office at the University of South Carolina for a Provost's Humanities Grant, and the African Studies Program in the Walker Institute at the University of South Carolina for additional support of this project in the form of research and travel grants. Thanks also go to Chris Higgins and Elizabeth Lowe, the codirectors of a 2013 National Endowment for the Humanities Summer Research Institute at the University of Illinois entitled "The Centrality of Translation to the Humanities: New Interdisciplinary Scholarship," where I was able to work on this translation and on sections of the afterword. I am also extremely grateful to the Poet Laureate of Michigan's Upper Peninsula, my old friend Russell Thorburn, who read drafts of each chapter and consistently returned valuable advice and encouragement. Many thanks also to Anny Dominique Curtius at the University of Iowa for her help with the translation of Martinican Creole in chapter 9. A special thanks goes to Amy Lahlou for the transcription of the first section of my interview with Daniel Picouly. Last but not least, I would like to give thanks for the continuous support of

TRANSLATOR'S ACKNOWLEDGMENTS

my husband, Garane A. Garane; my daughter, Shakhlan; my son, Gashan; my parents, Don and Mary; and my friends, colleagues, and students for their interest in this project and for their patient support and encouragement.

THE LEOPARD BOY

To Christian Mounier,
who spoke with such elegance
of Chester Himes's elegant style

Tutto a te mi guida
[Everything leads me to you]

— MOTTO OF MARIE-ANTOINETTE

1

DAME GUILLOTINE

The big, ruddy sailor pounds a gloved fist on the table. He seems to be trying to launch himself conscious.

"Citizen! Tonight I feel like chopping the dick off a little nigger kid. I'm tired of working on these aristocrats."

Groundhog immediately understands that he is the *little nigger kid* in question. He looks around. There is nothing else like him in the almost empty establishment. The citizen in question is so pink and blond she looks like she is doing it on purpose. Leaning on a cask, she reads a newspaper by candlelight and doesn't even raise her eyes to look at the sailor. In the room, there are only a few patriots bellied up to hot wine and a lone wood stove. All of it covered over with the fatigued silence of a bivouac and the ceiling pulled down for cover. No doubt about it, he's the only *little nigger kid* here.

The kid wishes he hadn't come to this tavern on Rue de la Monnaie. But it is late and he needs a little water and a saucer to get this devil of a dinky dog to drink some of this damned potion.

"Believe me, Citizen, it's when they're still little that you need to cut them short, these little nigger boys. Look, just to show you that I'm a good guy, I'll buy that one from you."

"He doesn't belong to me." Groundhog wishes that she had said, "He's not for sale!"

"So you don't mind if I skin his little piece of sausage?"

The Boss decides to pay no further attention to this hothead. She knows his type by heart. After two or three drinks, they try to cut the guts out of the first person they can lay their hands on; after four or five more, they ask for her own hand in marriage, and when they reach the bottom of the bottle, they fall into a drunken stupor. All she has to do is wait. She goes back to her newspaper. Meanwhile, Groundhog keeps Bigmouth in sight. Red-faced, he is strapped into what look like the staves of a broken wine barrel. His only glove is on his right hand, and the sword he carries at his side makes a clicking sound.

"Ahoy, there, Citizen! Is your rotgut liquor making me see double, or did your signboard get sunstroke?"

The sailor points to the slate plaque propped up on a wall shelf. It is divided into two parts. On one side is written in chalk, *October 15, 1793, Feast of Saint Theresa of Avila;* on the other, *24 Vendémiaire, Year II, Feast of the Amaryllis.*

"That's the new calendar voted in by our delegates. Get used to it, Citizen."

"That's too much change for me! Give me some rum to get me back on my feet."

The sailor stretches his gloved hand toward the small cask that the Boss has slung over her shoulder. Its rope has divided her ample chest into two parts, which still leaves a lot on either side of the rope.

"Hands off! These are my own personal reserves."

Groundhog senses that tempers are about to flare. Time to hightail it out of here. *Hey, pup, drink your brew! OK, it may be milky-looking and smell like saltpeter, but drink up!* Those people on Rue des Moineaux told him over and over . . . *You had better make him drink it at least one hour before you bring him here. If you don't, it won't work. And then the whole deal will be off.*

"Citizen! Is this a self-service establishment?"

The Boss ignores him impassibly. The sailor pulls his blade out of the blue. It gleams in the taproom. The sword could unmast a brig. With his single black glove and his protruding potbelly, the sailor looks like a half-dead pirate. Without so much as an en garde! he launches into the boy like a corsair forced to settle for the rowboat after the schooner has sailed away.

Groundhog sees the attack coming. He grabs the dog on the fly. The animal squeals. The saucer clatters away, and the potion runs down the buccaneer's snout. To hear him yell, the dog was right not to drink any of it. The Boss watches. The little black boy turns and jumps from table to table with the furious sailor in hot pursuit. The onlookers watch the scene with great gusto. Groundhog knows that this is no joke. He has seen this kind before. They'll run you through just to see what color you are on the inside. Beneath his hand he can feel the dog's heart race. Not to worry. This kind of cutthroat really likes animals.

"I'll stick that baboon! I'll stick him!"

The sailor traces bigger and bigger swaths with his sword, which makes him look like the windmill at Valmy before the cannons let loose. He leaves decapitated bottlenecks, pipes, and hats in his wake. The Boss wipes her mouth and hollers,

"Citizen Souse, if you don't cut it out, you'll get a taste of Sanson!"

Skewer-Wielder doesn't care. He should, though, because here, it's a good idea to know who Sanson is. In hot pursuit of Groundhog, Happy-Go-Lucky is still slicing through smoke in the void. Frightened, the dog tries to escape. Groundhog catches him and slips; the sailor traps him under a table, collars him, and pins him against the wall, the point of the sword stuck under his chin. This intensifies the street kid's insolent look.

"You're cute. A downright tasty chocolate mousse good enough to gobble up right here, right now!"

The eyes of Blade-Brandisher look like worn revolutionary rosettes that have run out of red. He stinks like the back end of a wine cellar. Groundhog feels that life is unfair. He was just about to turn thirteen in the newly named month of *nivôse,* and now he's already at the end of his part in the play. He's pushed up against an engraving frame that is hooked to his back. To bolster his confidence, he imagines that it shows a little monkey eating a ripe grenadine while perched on the shoulder of an elegant dame.

"That's enough, Sailor! You're going to ruin my Conqueror of the Bastille diploma!"

"So, Citizen! You say you're the one and only woman to receive the title of Conqueror of the Bastille! Or is it Conqueress! With all due respect, I'd always heard that it was that Charpentier woman."

Suddenly, a petrified silence falls over the tavern. If there is one name that should not be uttered here, it is the name Marie Charpentier. She's the whore who earned her diploma by straddling a delegate! Everyone knows it. The Boss has certainly proclaimed it often enough. Everyone hunkers down and waits for the storm. Here it comes. Citizen the Boss overheats and gets Sanson down from the wall. This clown is finally going to find out who Sanson is. And he will regret it.

Sanson is an axe. An immense tricolor battle-axe whose iron head and blade are painted blood-red. She seizes it like a lumberjack who has an account to settle with a recalcitrant maple and walks straight toward the joker. The sailor's gaze clouds over. Groundhog takes advantage of the cover. Throwing the dog in the sailor's face, he flicks the blade out from under his throat, grabs the picture frame, and breaks it over the sailor's head. Now the swashbuckler has what appears to be a shaving plate under his chin. Waving his sword in a blind rage, he whirls and roars,

"I'll cut you, you blasted little nigger!"

Instinctively, he jumps on Groundhog, the sword raised like a meat cleaver. The urchin ducks. The blade falls at exactly the moment that the Boss arrives with Sanson, armed and cocked above her head. She is about to be cut in half when suddenly, as the saber arcs downward, a set of yellow teeth chomps into the sailor's arm. The dog has pounced and has the sailor's wrist in his mouth. The swordsman is thrown off balance by the surprise attack. At the very moment of impact he latches onto a huge wine cask. Whack! The sailor's arm is cut off right where the dog has it in his teeth, and the barrel is pierced as if for a wedding feast. The fermented liquid spurts out. The amputee screams in a rather high-pitched voice. Incredulous, he looks at his stump.

"Vile Citizen, you've bled me!"

"Sorry, Citizen, that was just plain clumsy of me."

Amid these apologetic genuflections the gloved hand still gripping the sword passes by. In fact, it is running madly about the room. The dog has not dropped his prize. All of a sudden he leaps toward a half-open cellar window and escapes into the street.

"My dog!" Groundhog hastily gathers up his rags and rushes outside in a state of undress.

"My sword!" Wearing the frame like a ruff around his neck, the amputee runs into the street after the boy.

"Hey, Sailor! My diploma!"

The Boss hikes her skirt up to puddle-jump length, throws her cask over her shoulder, grabs Sanson, and rushes off after her patriotic certificate. The remaining patrons make the most of the situation by regaling themselves at the holes in the cask, slaking their thirst for free, and toasting the country.

Outside it's London and a thick emigrant fog. The few passersby on Rue de la Monnaie at this hour can just make out the shadow of a strange cortège. The crew is making its way up toward Rue Saint-Honoré. At the head of the procession, a dwarf dog bounds like a corsair, the sword between his teeth. A little half-naked black boy runs along after him in hot pursuit, followed by a one-armed specter galloping along behind him, his bloodless head laid on his shaving platter like a martyred Saint Denis. The pious man is trying to escape from a lewd fury, who, thighs exposed, is armed with a powder keg and a great bloody battle-axe.

It's a strange sight to behold.

Swaddled in this nippy October fog, Groundhog tries not to lose sight of the back end of the tiny dog as it scampers away. Luckily, the blade of the sword scatters sparks on the cobblestones as it races into the distance. Right behind him, Groundhog hears the vindictive death rattle of the one-armed man. He looks back. Blood spurts from the stump in regular beats, forming a kind of palm-tree pattern. Behind that, the clattering of wooden clogs draws closer. All of a sudden, whomp! It's the soft thud of a body as it hits the deck. The framed man is now sprawled on his back. His face wears the surprised look of a mortuary statue. No more blood beats from the wound. The palm tree has gone dry. The Boss shows up with her axe. Without stopping to catch her breath, she drives a huge kick into the ribs of the sprawled body, divests it of the diploma, generously settles accounts from its moneybag, and lets it slide into a ditch.

In the commotion, Groundhog can just barely see the sheaf of sparks as it rushes on, dead ahead. The dog! Bounding past another good one hundred street numbers on Rue Saint-Honoré, the animal suddenly slips through a half-open carriage gate next door to a boutique. Groundhog follows. A lantern's bluish light illuminates a corner of the courtyard. The dog is now sitting in a patch of it. Seemingly content, he releases the gloved hand, which in turn drops the sword. His lolling tongue is longer than he is. Groundhog takes the opportunity to better adjust his clothing. It's about time. The cold was beginning to close in on him from all sides. On the ground, the sailor's gloved hand looks like it's asking for a handout. Under the glove, Groundhog notices a bulge on the ring finger. It must be a big ring. He'll see about that later. He picks up the sailor's sword. Not bad either. True, it's pretty heavy. Groundhog tries giving it a twirl.

"What do you want with that dog?" The voice comes from a dark corner. There is plenty of darkness to be had tonight.

"I'm against cruelty to animals."

The shadow has a country accent and smells like a powdered wig. You should always beware of men who wear perfume.

"He's my dog, Citizen, I swear."

"My boy, if he was really your dog, you wouldn't have said, 'I swear.' Watch out, it's the little words that give you away."

Seated on his behind, the little mongrel watches the exchange as if it were a tennis match and wonders when somebody will finally get around to giving him a drink.

"If he's your dog, which I quite doubt, he will come when you call him. Otherwise you are nothing but a liar. Maybe even a conspirator. One of those traitors who are plotting in Paris this very night to help the Widow Capet escape from the people's justice!"

The sweet-smelling voice rises as if before a tribunal, then it suddenly falls and takes a watch from a vest pocket. It leans in close to look at the time. The lantern illuminates a face. Robespierre! Groundhog recognizes him and so do his legs. They feel like running away and leaving him behind. He catches up with them and promptly passes out. He'll try to leave later.

"It's fifteen minutes past ten."

Maximilien Robespierre is deep in thought. Over at the hearing they must be getting to the last witnesses, if that Hermann idiot isn't running late. What a stupid idea to have made him president of the Revolutionary Tribunal!

* * *

Hermann draws a line through a name on the list of witnesses. Only three left. The deal will be sealed by midnight. Maximilien will be happy.

"Take former police administrator Citizen Michonis away! Escort him back to La Force Prison. Citizen Fontaine is called before the bench!"

Marie-Antoinette gazes at her judges. For fourteen hours they have been sitting facing her without really seeing her. Fourteen hours in this dim room filled with the overpowering smell of sweat, tobacco, and oily lamp smoke. She can barely distinguish the masses crowded in before her. They are here to see her. The tricoteuses seated behind the railing taunt her.

"On your feet! On your feet, Capet!"

She obeys. Her legs are shaking and her stomach is churning, but she arches her back and lifts her chin. We shall carry out our queenly duties.

From behind the feather of his quill pen, Hermann watches Marie-Antoinette. No two ways about it, that dame can hold her own! Don't pity her, Citizen! The execution is set to take place in less than twelve hours.

* * *

Groundhog wishes he could be knocked out for good. But he doesn't have the guts. He tries to sneak out to the street. Robespierre blocks his path.

"Go on, Boy, call your dog. Let's see if he comes when he's called."

Call my dog! Groundhog breaks into a sweat. He thinks it over. Now what can I call this black, teeny-tiny, short-haired animal with a pug nose and a tongue that's too long? Marat, Victory, Fatherland, Equality, or . . . *Fido!* How idiotic! Of all names! It's ridiculous! The mongrel has just rolled up his tongue. It's all over. I'm headed for the guillotine, no ifs, ands, or buts.

"Now, Boy, that's what I call proof!"

Fido must like what he hears. He jumps into Groundhog's arms. Oddly, he seems to be wearing perfume. A light perfume that smells something like honeysuckle. Fido sets to licking his face as though it were the Fête de la Fédération, leaving him no time to think any further on the subject. The dog makes short work of it, given the extraordinary length of his tongue.

"Perfect, my boy! I don't know why, but this dog has decided to save your life."

There is a rapping at the door. Robespierre stiffens.

"Who is it?"

"It's me, Maximilien! I've got Brount."

Robespierre opens the door to a woman wearing a gray coat who slips into the courtyard. A big, black hulk of a dog follows her. The little mutt's heart starts to flip-flop.

"Maximilien, you shouldn't be waiting here. Someone could have recognized you. It's dangerous. Don't worry. Everything is going well at the trial. The city is quiet. The police are on watch."

"That's not what's worrying me, Eléonore. I was thinking about my dog. How did Brount do?"

"Good news! He did the deed."

"Did he do it well?"

"He did it in good quantity, with an even consistency and the right color. I would even say that he did his duty like a real Citizen."

"And his urine?"

"Fortunately, it was clear and abundant, resembling the Fontaine de la Régénération."

"Now I can rest assured. But I'm furious that I can no longer take him for walks myself, as was my habit."

"That time will come again, Maximilien. You will have made short work of your enemies. Soon, you will be the one to take Brount out. As was your wont, you will even be able to take him to defecate just under the Abbot of Sieyès's front windows."

They both laugh. She laughs more than he does.

"Consider this, Eléonore. What if the Revolution means nothing more than the right to take our dogs out to pee in peace?"

"Careful, Maximilien! What if Danton heard you?"

"There is no risk of that. While I'm here, that leech is out hiding in the countryside to avoid being around on the day that the people get rid of the Queen. Soon it will be his turn. Then, he'll get an earful from me."

Groundhog tiptoes toward the door. He swears he knows nothing. Nothing about God, nothing about dog pee, droppings at the abbot's residence or Danton, and especially nothing about Robespierre. So he can't tell on anyone. He just wants out. Maximilien and Eléonore continue their conversation without paying any attention to him. Great. Because that way they won't miss him much.

"Hey, Boy!"

It was too good to be true. But then, he knows how these butchers do business. Release the prisoner! You smile at the judges and then, bong! They knock you over the head with a log.

"Hey, Boy, you forgot your glove!"

Groundhog takes a deep breath. He thanks Robespierre and tucks the glove with the ringed finger into his belt. He wonders what kind of jewel could be on the ring. A diamond? A ruby? An emerald? Out in the street, he suddenly feels lighter, despite the dog in his arms, the sword on his back, and that hand that is slowly sliding down the inside of his pant leg. It stops moving. There! The treasure is now safe. Now Groundhog can go on his date with Louisette.

It's easier to talk about having a date with someone named Louisette than with Dame Guillotine. And yet, she's one and the same.

DAME GUILLOTINE

Groundhog reaches the end of Rue Saint-Honoré and starts down Rue Royale toward Place de la Révolution. He stops short and starts to shake. He has just realized that he has been following the exact same footsteps as the prisoners bound for the gallows. So this is their view from the prison wagon when they get here! This is what the Queen will see tomorrow. In the fog it almost looks like the entry to a harbor. The glimmering lights of the open-air camps set up over by the Tuileries Palace look like the deceptive lights of pirate wrecker decoys in the distance. A horn blares. Groundhog hears a rumble swell up through the night air. It is bearing down on him. It is almost on top of him. Thunder rolls inside his head. Huge teeth loom out of the darkness. Yaaa!

A whip lashes the gloom. Groundhog is cut in two. An enormous tip-cart just about runs him over. The wagon rattles by on wheels splayed out in four different directions. It spews golden-yellow straw as if it were spring sowing time. Groundhog watches the steaming donkey gallop through the fog. He can hear its bell jingling as it moves off. It almost sounds like a wedding horse carrying a bride away. The man with the whip blows into a shrill horn. He is delivering fresh straw to the prisoners of La Force, Les Madelonnettes, Sainte-Pélagie, and elsewhere. At the moment, "elsewheres" are not lacking.

Groundhog recalls that at noontime he saw one of the condemned pass by in a cart. He still had wisps of straw in his hair, like someone who had just taken a roll in the summertime hay. He was singing *Auprès de ma blonde*. It seemed to Groundhog that nobody would dream of cutting the head off someone with a wisp of straw still stuck to his lips.

The ruckus has passed. Groundhog is ashamed of having been so afraid. He has to get to his date. Louisette is waiting. She cuts a stark figure against a hole in the sky that looks like it was punched out just for her. Just be sure not to show her that you are terrified. Groundhog puffs himself up and faces the base of the guillotine. Way up there, the blade looks like a rotten tooth ready to fall out.

"If you want the tooth fairy to come, you'd better put that tooth under your pillow, Citizen!"

Dame Guillotine looks down at the little bitty black boy who has just awakened her from a sound sleep. Now that takes the cake. She's usually the one to throw the citizens off their straw pallets. Down by her feet, the kid looks like a smart aleck. His grin is way too toothy for his age. What is he doing running around in the streets at this late hour? He should be home in bed. Renamed *vendémiaire* or not, it's freezing as always in October. What good does it do to change calendars if the weather outside doesn't get any better? In this weather, you can catch a chest cold and end up dead. Especially given the way he's decked out! Let's have a look! Come over here. A light print calico cape . . . Hmm, let's see . . . worn over a pair of pants that seem to be going in opposite directions. He's as garish as a parrot. On top of that he's barefoot on the cobblestones! Where is his mother? And people wonder why so many boys from Bicêtre Prison leave there feetfirst. Groundhog sneezes. What did I tell you! What he needs is to have his chest rubbed, and then, off to bed! Cover up now! Oh, goodness, now he's got the sniffles!

"What do you care, Citizen? You'll never catch cold like me, with all the exercise you get!"

That little beggar, what does he know! He comes out here in the middle of the night, with no extra fat to carve off his puny little frame. He raises Cain, wakes the citizenry like a street vendor hawking his wares, and plays court jester. Is that any way to act? Does he have any idea what my work has been like lately? Head after head after head. And usually it goes on way into the night. I'm just lucky the blade knows its way down to the bottom so it can rest a bit before coming back up. But as soon as the last head has fallen between my legs . . . Poof . . . Everyone takes off and leaves. Just like a flock of sparrows! They tuck their knitting away, stow their sewing baskets, and fold up their newspapers. The good people go off to a bowl of soup, a club, or a café. Many a time, all I get in exchange for a hard day's work is to be left dripping wet all night long like a filthy whore. The time will come when I lay this blade down on Place de la Grève and go on strike . . . Stop this infernal cadence! They'll just have to dust off the torture wheel, the executioner's block, the rack, the garrote, and the gallows. Be careful not to aggravate her too much, she looks mad!

"Dame Guillotine, are you angry? Please don't be. Excuse me, I wasn't very nice just now."

All in all, this little bit of licorice is rather polite.

DAME GUILLOTINE

"Listen, Lady, I need to talk to you. I've got something very important to ask you. I wrote it down so it would sound better."

Groundhog searches himself. Here we go again! I just knew it! The little black boy is going to take out a scrap of paper. He has come here to sing my praises. As in,

> Oh, you, heavenly guillotine
> You shrink kings and queens,
> By your influence divine
> Our rights we have redeemed.

I know them by heart. Every Thursday, whole columns of schoolchildren file by here in republican ranks. Everything is explained to them—the height, the weight of the blade . . . *Teacher, who invented it?* "No, not Mr. Guillotin." *Is it true that it is actually an Italian contraption? And who built it? Teacher, Tobias Schmit, why is he German?* They want my nicknames, my measurements, and my price! *Teacher, is 824 gold louis a lot money?* Really, don't they teach children anything else these days?

"Drat! Hey, Lady, I can't find my scrap paper!"

In any case, I would be surprised if this little half-naked black boy knew how to read.

"I musta lost it, or someone stole it off me. I shoulda written it out on Revolution money. Because nobody wants it anymore."

"Don't say such things! Mocking our revolutionary currency is the swiftest way for you to wind up here and then, *chlank!*"

Chlank, why *chlank? Chlank* is not the sound that it makes when it drops. Now, what exactly does it sound like? She closes her eyes. Nothing. There is no way to recall the sound of a head being cut off. And yet, she has heard a lot of those sounds on this Place de la Révolution. Sounds like *flomp!* and *shlonk!* Recently, there has been much on which to train her ear. And of the finest quality! Counts, dukes, and barons! Nothing but finely embroidered linen. Even if she does miss Place du Carrousel, or better yet, Place de la Grève. The acoustics were better over there. On very quiet days, from twenty rows back, you could hear the wicker shudder when the severed head rolled into the executioner's basket. Now that was great art. But here, it is a veritable disaster for the connoisseur. There is no windier place than this in Paris. A squall from the Seine in the midst of an execution, and one loses track. At times, the head falls noiselessly because it's been reduced in size, like the Capetian head . . . *Louis Auguste de Bourbon! Louis XVI King of France! Louis XVI! From hence-forth Capet!* . . . Capet! Once your name has been shortened, the rest is not long to follow.

"Hey, Guillotine Lady! Lady! I have somethin' to say to you!"

What does that little black boy want now? He wakes her from her reverie. She can see him better now. He is not bad-looking and, for that matter, not all that black. More like a caramel color.

"Guillotine Lady, I'm here to talk to you about someone who will be coming to pay you a visit, tomorrow maybe."

"Visiting me doesn't involve maybes."

"Oh yes it does! Because I think I know some people who want to help her escape."

"Oh, for heaven's sake, be quiet! Do you want both of us to get caught?"

"OK, so I didn't tell you nothin'. So here goes. I was wantin' that, with her, you would be less, well, that, um, you would go a bit more gentle on her."

Poor child, the little citizens in the classrooms of the Republic will tell you: thirty pounds of metal falling from ten feet up, well, that just can't be very easy on a body.

"Citizen, I know her son. I played in the Temple Prison with him. He likes it when I play stick-and-hoop with him. It makes him laugh. Because him, he can't do it. His legs are sick. And tomorrow he'll be an orphan."

That little black boy is going to make me cry! What can I do about it? That blade just slips through my fingers.

"Citizen, can I just say that . . ."

He must stop calling me "Citizen." I prefer "Madame."

"Can I just say that, me too, I'm an orphan. But it's easier when you've always been one."

This caramel-colored kid is a real tearjerker! There's nothing left to do now but turn to rust!

"Well, now, that's all I came to say, Madame. I promised him I'd come and see you. Now, I guess you'll do what you can."

"I can't promise you anything, Kid. But I'll look after the blade on its way down and make sure the bevel is angled just right. As for the rest . . ."

"I found it! Guillotine Madame, I found it, my piece of paper. It was stuck in the glove with the hand and the ring."

Now what is that boy talking about? On top of having his

chest rubbed, he's going to need a good mug of hot milk and honey to clear his head.

"Madame, I'm leaving it here with you, my scrap of paper. You'll see, it's written down just like I said, but better. I can't tell a lie, I did copy bits of it out of books. But that's how I woulda said it. And on top of that, I put down the name of the lady, just so you don't get the wrong one."

There's no chance of that. I know who she is. Seeing as how they've sharpened me up, greased me down, and honed me across, the one whose turn it will be tomorrow is Marie-Antoinette. It's quite unpleasant when it's a woman. It's like giving birth with iron forceps.

"I'll put the paper here, Madame!" Groundhog tosses the piece of paper on the platform and takes off.

"Hey, Kid! I'm not the fountain of miracles. I do not grant wishes. Pick up your spitballs!"

The miniature dog comes to. He takes his flat muzzle from a fold of the cape. He considers the shadow way up there. So that's what a guillotine looks like! Big feet and a little tongue. Nothing to sneeze over. He yawns and burrows back into the warm cape.

"Halt, there, you little varmint!" A thin man dressed like a *sans-culotte* carrying a satchel over his shoulder and shorn to within half an inch of his scalp steps up. He waves the piece of paper that Groundhog has just thrown at the foot of the guillotine.

"My name is Groundhog, not Varmint."

"Don't try to change the subject. This yours?"

Never contradict a man who has crossed your path with a pike. Especially a finely wrought pike weighing at least eight pounds and decorated with a saucy ribbon. Groundhog says to himself that it is all well and good that eight pounds is equal to four kilograms in the new system of weights and measures, it still won't help the thin man run any faster. Groundhog fakes a dive toward the guillotine, ducks, and escapes in the direction of the Statue of Liberty. The man with the pike is stuck stock-still.

"That's not fair, Groundhog, you run faster than me!"

True, it's not fair, but Groundhog lengthens his stride even more. He waves at the cleaver. The bell will soon toll eleven o'clock at the Church of Saint-Roch. Time to take the dog back to those people on Rue des Moineaux. Dame Guillotine looks at the little black boy running away into the night.

"Put on some warm clothes, for heaven's sake!"

2

EDMOND AND JONES

"Come quickly, Sir! They're fighting!"

The Marquis d'Anderçon is oblivious to the panic-stricken valet who has just entered his study. Standing at the window, he watches for the two men he has summoned. As usual, they're late. The Marquis pulls out his watch. It is well past ten o'clock. The columned pendulum clock on the mantel has just struck. Since the death of his son Philippe, it only chimes on the half hour. It is strange to live time by halves. And yet, this is how his days unfold now. All the more so for the Marquise, who has retreated to her rooms upstairs. On the day of their son's execution, she had all of the needles in the household removed. It was like gouging out prying eyes.

"Sir, I assure you, they're fighting!"

The Marquis continues to scrutinize the area below his window. Because of the fog, he cannot even see the dome of the wheat market even though it is right down the street. Even if both men were walking straight toward him, he wouldn't be able to see them coming. And yet, they're big, with the massive, powerful builds of the itinerant window repairmen who carry entire panes of glass on their burly shoulders. Together they could fill the width of an entire street. The Marquis is worried. He wonders whether the two men will accept his mission this time.

"Sir, I swear, they really, really are fighting one another, Sir!"

The Marquis turns and finally sees his servant. He is even more disheveled than usual. His stockings are rumpled and his shoes have lost their buckles.

"Thomas, what is going on? You appear to be even smaller than usual today."

"The problem is my livery, Mr. Marquis, Sir. The color blue makes me look scrunched up. His Lordship will recall that I have already complained about it to him. A more flattering color would be bright red or light green."

"Now, Thomas, do you not know that I acquired this sky-blue color from Saint Louis himself?"

"And I, Sir, have inherited my short legs from my mother. One lineage is as good as another."

This servant is small, clumsy, and insolent. The Marquis suspects that he reads subversive newspapers and frequents useless political clubs. But he has two great qualities: he steals only the bad liquor and doesn't ask to get paid. As for the Marquis, it is all he can do to pay himself ever since he lost all of his money when the India Company went bankrupt.

"Let us leave our ancestors aside, Thomas. What alarm is this?"

"As I was saying, Sir, while you stand there staring out the window, they are beating each other to a pulp."

"Exactly who is fighting?"

If you're a dimwit, even wearing sky blue from the time of Saint Louis won't help you.

"They are, Sir!"

Thomas begins gesturing wildly to imitate one man the size of a Norman wardrobe cabinet and the other shaped like a Belgian sideboard. It's a good impression.

"Who do you mean, they?"

"Those two . . . I mean your two acquaintances, er, do you see who I mean? The two, er, Spades, citizens of the islands, men of color . . ."

This does nothing to clear the look on the Marquis's face. Thomas is furious. These days you don't know anymore what you can or cannot say. Before you open your mouth, you have to see which way the wind is blowing. One wrong word taken the wrong way and you lose your head. Despite the danger, he forges ahead.

"Sir, it's those black men. The ones that you sent me to fetch."

"To fetch?"

"Correct. It's them, all right."

The Marquis begins to relax. They're here. But he's worried. He seems to recall that the blue sitting room is one of the last in the house with any remaining furniture.

"And they're fighting with what weapons, Thomas? With swords, with pistols?"

"No, Sir. That's a bit too much to expect."

"Well, with what, then?"

"With their fists!"

And not just their fists. The Marquis contemplates the free-for-all in the blue sitting room. They are also using their feet, elbows, heads, and teeth. Body parts are flying in all directions. They're like those rabble-rousing medical students horsing around in the big medical amphitheater following Doctor Bichat's course on human anatomy. This is bad news. Pieces will be missing and the mess will never be straightened out. Whose tibia is this? Who is punching whose stomach? And those ribs sticking out of that knee?

"Sir, you must separate them, or they will slew each other!"

"Do you mean slay each other?"

"That's not much better."

There is no danger of slewing or slaying. It's black on black. The Marquis smiles. He observes. The two lads look to him to be in excellent condition, with bold movements and no measured breath. He does not even bat an eyelid. He sees that they are as they were when he last saw them. Neither of them will be the first to give in. These are exactly the two men he needs for his mission.

"Do something, Sir! If not for their sakes, then at least for the sake of Madame's furniture. You should intercede on their behalf."

"Just separating them will do. Thomas, when will you start using words your own size?"

"Sir, words are not like clothes. They come in one size only."

The servant seems quite verbose this evening. Aside from his vocabulary, he is correct as far as the furniture is concerned. The two raging bulls have just smashed one of the two armchairs with carved legs and blue Venetian velvet. A lovely piece, surely designed by Sené, now lying somewhere in the pile of debris. The Marquis now decides to save the remaining furniture.

"Attention!"

It never fails. The effect is instantaneous. The two entangled bodies immediately separate and divide their appendages and all the rest into equal parts. Which turns out to be two big, hulking men. They're as black as the islands, as Thomas would put it. The face of one of them shows signs of corrosion, and the other's is covered in dents. They straighten their clothing and pull on their long oilcloth slickers. When all is in order, they click their heels with a competent snap. They could illustrate the pages of the King's infantry training manual. Heels joined at the back, feet separated at the front, palms forward, the little finger held to the cloth of the breeches and the gaze focused on a point fifteen feet away.

EDMOND AND JONES

"Corporal Edmond Coffin, Sir!" He takes one step forward.

"One . . . !"

The parquet floor undergoes more battering under their rough heels. One of the two men steps forward. It's the corroded one. He's a head taller than the Marquis.

"What is the meaning of this?"

"Lieutenant, while we were waiting for you, we made the most of our time together by sorting out a little misunderstanding that will remain strictly private."

"Corporal Jonathan Gravedigger, do you confirm that this is so?"

"I do, Lieutenant, Sir. I confirm that this is strictly a private matter."

The Marquis has already heard about this "strictly private" matter that makes them break into a brawl every time they meet up here again. Because of an incident dating from their time together in the Americas, one of them thinks he was betrayed by the other, while the other thinks the first one incriminated him in some affair under false pretenses. Between swordfights, duels, hand-to-hand combat, and battles on horseback, nothing could bring them into agreement or convince them. The Marquis saved them from the firing squad in exchange for secret missions carried out behind enemy lines. In return, the two men insisted that they be given the inalienable right to beat each other to oblivion. This was the right they had just exercised in the blue sitting room. Too bad for the furniture.

"Is it therefore useless for me to demand an explanation here, men?"

"Completely useless, Lieutenant!"

They rap out their response in unison, their voices firm, their gazes still fixed on a spot fifteen feet away. Thomas shivers in his livery. He was not conscripted because he was too short for his rifle. He would nevertheless prefer to bust the parquet apart rather than scrub it down.

"Perfect, men! At ease. Dismissed!"

The two hulks fall into each other's arms. In military fashion, they tap each other on the back with blows hard enough to knock the dirt clean off a bull. The Marquis steps forward and shakes hands as their comrade-in-arms.

"Edmond! Jonathan! How happy I am to see you here!"

"And how is Madame the Marquise?"

Edmond just had to ask. That is what Jonathan was afraid of.

"You know, losing a twenty-year-old as we did with our son Philippe is devastating. But not to believe it and to deny it is even worse."

The Marquis says nothing more. It is useless to do so. The servant is sad. Nobody is paying any attention to him. The two hulks take notice and go to comfort him.

"Well, brave Thomas, still serving in the 126th?"

This is what they call the mansion of the Marquis d'Andeçon in remembrance of their regiment.

"Remarkably unremunerated common manservant in the household of his Excellency the Marquis, and Madame the Marquise, at your service!"

His complete title seems to have placed lifts in his shoes. He stands up straighter.

"You have the best position, Thomas. Look at us. Jonathan digs graves that are already full before he has even dug up the first shovel full of dirt. As for me, I cobble together measly little coffins for five-foot-tall citizens whose heads have already been removed and placed between their legs."

"Sure, but at least you have souvenirs from the army."

Jonathan could do without the scar on his back that irritates him when it rains and in times of trouble. As for Edmond, he prefers not to think about his own face, burned by acid in a little altercation, a memento from their last mission behind enemy lines. Even now the Marquis d'Andeçon still feels that he himself is to blame. He cuts the reminiscing short and starts playing the aristocrat.

"Men, will you have sherry or port?"

They were expecting something stronger, but the Marquis is already holding the promised libations.

"Oh, no, Sir! Don't do that!"

They have just enough time to glimpse the horrified look on Thomas's face. He dives at the tray as if the wines contained poison.

"Please, Sir, I beg you. You are not the one who should be pouring the wine. Else I am dishonored."

In his rush to intervene, the manservant gets caught on the foot of an armchair, trips, and grabs one of the carafes. The other one shoots from his grasp as if from a catapult. The sherry flies merrily across the sitting room and shatters into a plume on the wall. The stain is brownish red. The Marquis brushes himself off.

"Well, Men, I guess it will be port!"

Completely undone, Thomas backs out of the room. Perhaps he should kill himself . . . Like Chef François Vatel did when the fish for his big Friday banquet didn't get delivered on time. At least this is what Thomas yells out as his parting shot. But everyone knows that all he really does is listen to secret conversations from behind closed doors.

"Men, I have asked you to come here because I have another mission for you behind enemy lines."

Thomas is jubilant. "Behind enemy lines" sounds a lot better than "Go to the kitchen." All right, that does it. Tomorrow he will hand in his unflattering blue livery, join the Republican Army, and go fight for Vendée.

"I want you to know that you are free to decide. You have already repaid me by what you did for our son Philippe."

The two men mumble an embarrassed reply. Don't mention it. That was last year. They had sought out and found Philippe's severed head, which had been stolen following his execution. It was a strange affair.

"Men, the conditions are the same as they were last time. A weapon, thirteen gold louis, and a hat for each of you."

The Marquis never did figure out why Edmond and Jonathan were so adamant about the hats.

"And now, Thomas, who is behind that door spying on us, can go make the orange extract potion for Madame's bedtime."

The crouching servant jumps up. He wonders how his master knows that he has an ear to the keyhole. Masters certainly have extraordinary powers. Thomas dreams of becoming a fortune-teller instead of a soldier. He will set up shop across from the La Force or Bicêtre Prisons. Prisons and hospitals make people anxious to know the future.

"Men, here is your mission. It is simple. Locate a boy and bring him to me here within the next twelve hours."

The two men listen to the Lieutenant from their perches on the sides of the last remaining armchair. They seem ill at ease. Jonathan looks at Edmond from the corner of his eye. He wonders when he will open fire. Edmond has to be the one to inform the Marquis. He is of higher rank.

"Sir, we need to talk. But before that, don't you have anything stronger to drink?"

"I have some brandy here, men."

That will do. The Marquis pulls a bottle out from behind a curtain. He's even worse at serving drinks than Thomas is.

"Men, before I hear what you have to say, I want you to know that I have called upon you because . . ."

From behind their drink glasses, Edmond and Jonathan watch the Lieutenant at maneuvers. First movement, flatter the infantrymen.

"Only you two can carry out this mission."

Second movement, tempt them with mystery.

"It involves persons of the highest rank."

Third movement, tug at their heartstrings until they surrender completely.

"I know how attached you are to the Marquise."

Jonathan jumps up, looking embarrassed. He looks like he is about to propose to Edmond.

"Say no more, Lieutenant. We cannot accept this mission."

Chunks of plaster trim fall from the ceiling and onto the Marquis's head. He chokes on a couple of the smaller pieces in quick succession.

"Come, now! Men like you don't let a little danger get in the way!"

He's about to start in again with flattery, mystery, and sentimental heartstrings. Edmond stops him cold.

"We're going to America. To the United States!"

Happily, there is no more molding on the ceiling or brandy in the bottle.

"Lieutenant, Sir! We left the legion of the Chevalier de Saint-George three weeks ago when he was stripped of his command. In our opinion, to relieve the first black colonel of his duties as the commander of the only unit of black men in the Republican Army is high treason and an insult!"

The Marquis sees their point. The Chevalier de Saint-George is a friend of the Marquise. But he doesn't feel like telling them that. He's already calculating the time that is left.

"When do you leave?"

"Tomorrow. Jonathan and I are taking the twelve-noon coach to La Rochelle."

"What are you planning to do over there?"

"We'll be something like agricultural land managers."

"You mean farmers?"

The two rogues don't like his translation. The Marquis imagines them holding pitchforks. He bites the rim of his glass to stop from laughing out loud.

"Jonathan and I used our soldier's pay to buy land. In the Northeast. On the plains. There's good land, it's sunny, and enough water when you need it. With no tenant farming and no taxes, we'll be our own masters. Three hundred and fifty well-placed acres at the cost of ten gold pieces per acre."

Jonathan takes out a wad of papers covered with seals and signatures. He unfolds the sheaves of paper like a man turning dirt in a field.

"They're right in here!"

For their sake, the Marquis hopes that those acres are more than just pieces of paper. There are lots of poor sods these days who have been cheated by the many companies of the Americas mushrooming at the stock exchange and spreading like small-pox. He should know after losing his own shirt.

"Lieutenant, soldier to soldier, man to man, me and Edmond, we don't think there's a real future here for people like us. It's been four years and Parliament still hasn't found time to abolish slavery."

"Nevertheless, men, people are actively working toward abolition. Just look at what Mr. Condorcet accomplished at the Society for the Friends of Blacks!"

"It's a club for the well-to-do that costs two gold louis just to join! One hundred upstanding gentlemen. But what good are they next to the rich planters of the Massiac Club who buy politicians like bales of cotton?"

"You are harsh. And yet, my friends, there's been progress. The subsidy on slave trading was eliminated just last month."

"Lieutenant, Sir! If a battalion moved this slowly, you would give everyone a swift kick in the pants."

It was true, by God! He had often felt that itch. Yet, there was so much to do. There was the young Republic under attack at its borders. To the north, the Austrians and the Dutch; to the east, the Prussians; the King of Sardinia in Savoy; the English in Toulon, and of course there was also the region of Vendée. Suddenly, the door can hold no longer. It gives way, busting its hinges and gold trim. It's Thomas. Or what's left of him. He's in his shirtsleeves. Missing are his wig and his shoes. He looks worse without shoes than without his wig.

"You must come quickly, Sir! Madame is having one of her fits!"

The Marquis knows exactly what he means. Edmond and Jonathan give him a questioning look.

"Men, I have to tell you, ever since the Marquise discovered that I was charged with finding that missing child I was just telling you about, she thinks it must be our son Philippe."

Edmond and Jonathan recall Philippe's decapitated body laid out on the Marquise's bed. They remember the mysterious beauty of the black man with blue eyes.

"I haven't been able to get the idea out of her head. She's been looking for him in hospitals, sanatoriums, and even in cemeteries for over a year now."

Jonathan remembers seeing the Marquise haunting the graves, plunging her arms in up to her elbows like a washerwoman.

"Now, right here in this house, she performs the African rites passed down from her Yoruba ancestors. Rites I don't understand at all, and am not allowed to attend. Poor Thomas is the only one allowed to attend as her servant."

Not as her servant, but as her initiated apprentice. Let's keep things straight. Let there be no confusion. For Thomas, the distinction is important.

"Thomas, fetch a torch. I'll be right behind you."

"Lieutenant, let me go with you."

Jonathan seizes Edmond's arm. Not to retain him. Nobody can do that. But just to tell him that he shouldn't go. Edmond quietly frees his arm.

"Jonathan, you know of my debt to the Marquise. She was the one who saved my eyes when I got acid thrown in my face. You were there."

Jonathan says nothing. He had been really worried that night.

"Hurry up, Sir! Madame is in extreme danger."

The Marquis rushes after the servant. Edmond follows. Jonathan looks at the papers abandoned on the armchair. *The Scioto Company. This Land Deed Grants Exclusive Ownership to . . .* He gathers them up and stuffs them into his pocket. Jonathan feels as though he is crumpling a dream. There is a panicked galloping down the dark corridors ahead of him. Thomas is carrying the torch like an arsonist. He sets fire to a pair of drapery tassels as he runs by and scorches a pink Jouy toile fabric with a

fable motif. In passing, the flame illuminates the enormous painting that hangs at the head of the white marble staircase. On
the canvas, the Marquise poses in her white ball gown. The one
she wore for her son's twentieth birthday celebration. Her gaze
seems to follow the men who are running to find her. Her face
smiles as if to say, "Go right ahead! Keep on looking! You will
never find me!"

"To the crypt!"

On Thomas's command, the torch plunges into the black hole
that leads to the cellar. A spiral stone staircase takes them two
stories down and throws them into a damp earthen passageway.
They run right into an arched wooden door clad in iron filigree.
The men catch their breath and cluster under the torch. The Marquis doesn't move a muscle. But it's hard to hesitate for too long
under the spotlight. He pulls on the door. It opens into a dazzling
brilliance. A dozen steps below, a vaulted crypt is aglow with the
soft light of many tapers. The Marquise is there. She is lying face
down in the middle of the room. Her immobile black body forms
the X of a Saint Andrew's Cross on the floor, and her white satin
dressing gown is hiked up high. Edmond, Jonathan, and Thomas
avert their eyes. The Marquis rushes forward. With a single wave
of her hand she stops him cold.

"Do not cross the first circle."

That's when the Marquis notices the three concentric circles
drawn around his wife's body. A large white one, a blue one,
and a black one. The Marquise looks like a prisoner being held
hostage for target practice. Suddenly she sits up, wraps herself in
her dressing gown, and faces them, cross-legged.

"Thomas, come over here next to me."

The apprentice-initiate crosses the three circles and reaches
her, proud as a drum major. Edmond and Jonathan raise their
eyes and look at the Marquise. She displays the same majesty as
in the painting above the marble staircase.

"Gentlemen, from this moment on, you will be condemned
to search in darkness. You will seek a child. A boy. Remember
that the child is always hidden in a cradle. And that the darkest
cradle is his mother's womb. And that the wombs of mothers are
forever crowned."

Thomas makes a note of it. For the occupation of sorcerer you
need lots of candles and complicated, mixed-up sentences.

"Watch closely, Gentlemen!"

The Marquise stands up. With her heel, she traces compass lines through the three circles.

"You will seek this boy out. But there will also be others."

At the Marquise's signal, Thomas goes to a niche in the wall and takes down several small wooden dishes containing grains, beans, and powder, and retrieves a calabash filled with fluffy cotton.

"Some will try to find him in order to place him at the center of the circle, while others will try to banish him from it completely."

In each one of the compass sectors, she spreads coffee, cocoa, indigo, sugar, and cotton. The colors paint a strange map, where it seems that it would be easy to get lost. The Marquise approaches the men and stares at them in silence. They can smell her acrid perfume and sense the heart beating in her breast. Following an inaudible command, Thomas walks over to a panel on the wall.

"Memorize this map. Memorize this tracing and its colors. Because nighttime is about to make its entrance."

Thomas flips a latch on the wooden panel. A tremendous gust of wind surges into the vault of the crypt. It blasts along the walls and picks the circles up off the floor. It snuffs out the candles with the same joy as a kid munching on the meringue head of a candy Jesus at Easter. And then everything goes dark. Light footsteps are audible, then the rustle of satin, an accommodating latch, a door. And then nothing. In the space of a silence replete with the scent of every spice known to man, the Marquis becomes a lieutenant again.

"Thomas, go on and strike a light!"

"I'm trying, Sir, I'm trying! But above all, do not move. Under no circumstances should you step into the circles."

Trespass and you pass on . . . Thomas learned that from Madame the Marquise. To be a sorcerer, you have to make words go backward and forward.

"I've got the torch!"

There is a glimmer at the end of it. It illuminates the top of the vault. Little by little the men relight the tapers. Now there is enough light to see that the crypt is empty. The Marquise has disappeared. There is nothing left of her tracings on the floor. It could all be a dream except for the little pile of grains, beans, and powders all mixed up together against a wall. The men stay in the crypt for a moment trying to make sense of it all. Then they go back up to the Blue Room.

The Marquise is waiting for them by the fireplace. She greets them clad in a simple white dress. It is the same one as in the large painting. But now the painter has added a touch of fatigue and sadness to her eyes.

"My friends, I thought I heard a bell ring. I came down to see you, but you weren't here. Where were you? You seem troubled."

"It's nothing, my dear. Thomas thought he heard someone come in through the cellar door."

"Well, my friend?"

"A false alarm. Nothing but a nasty old draft."

The Marquis looks his wife straight in the eyes. He is looking for a sign of tacit reassurance.

"Is it also due to nasty drafts, my friend, that we owe this tasteless disorder?"

She is referring to the demolished armchair. Edmond and Jonathan hang their heads. They are prepared to sell a few acres in America in order to repair the damage. The Marquis saves them a parcel of land.

"Thomas forgot to close the window."

Tonight the little valet is happy to get paid for all the things he hasn't done. He'll make a fortune.

"So, my friend, that's why I was able to hear those awful barkers yelling out the latest news about the Queen's trial."

"Well, what of it, my dear?"

"Now they've gone and arrested Joseph Boze!"

* * *

Prosecutor Fouquier-Tinville rises to his full height. He seems to want to look like the carved griffons that adorn his table. His hat sports even more plumage than usual. He points at the witness and gets into position.

"Guards! Arrest Citizen Boze, former painter of the former royal court!"

An eager hubbub rises in the courtroom. Down in front! Down in front! We can't see! Judge Hermann's face wears a look of astonishment. He shoots an inquiring look at Prosecutor Fouquier-Tinville. Just what do you think you're doing? The accuser doesn't bat an eye. Marie-Antoinette takes advantage of the opportunity, closes her eyes, and takes a little rest. She plays a little harpsichord tune on her right knee. Destroyed, Boze looks around for help as two gendarmes take him away. Marie-Antoinette accompanies him with her eyes. The face of the one who had refused to alter the appearance of her children in their portraits is now haggard. *The truth is always more beautiful, Your Majesty!* No, that is not always the case.

"You're framed, you slapdash hack!"

The audience laughs as he walks by. Hermann scribbles a quick note. Does Maximilien approve? Fouquier sends a note back. *State Secret, Citizen.* His glare tells Hermann that he'd better drop the subject.

"Bailiff, go fetch the final witness, Citizen Jourdeuil."

The final witness. A collective shiver runs through the audience upon hearing the announcement. There is excitement, and already there is regret. As for Judge Hermann, he is not unhappy that this is almost over. He's getting hungry. Marie-Antoinette feels herself bleeding again. Life is making a half-hearted attempt to run itself out.

*   *   *

"But my dear woman, why in the world have they arrested Boze? He painted Louis XVI as well as Maximilien Robespierre."

"Do we need to discuss this in the presence of our friends here?"

Jonathan feels as though the Marquis and the Marquise are troubled by the news of this arrest. The Marquise moves in on Edmond.

"How are your eyes?"

"Splendid, Madame, thanks to you. But every once in a while there are things that escape their sight. Like what happened down there in the crypt."

"Forget that! You should be a lot more worried about what you can see than what you can't see. What about you, Jonathan?"

"Well, Madame, I feel like a man who is leaving tomorrow for the United States of America!"

"For America! What an adventure! Well, I understand. We were thinking about it at one point after our son's death. The Marquis even wanted to become another La Pérouse and to discover some new snow-covered route to the Pacific Ocean."

The Northwest Passage! The Marquis is sure he knows where it is. He got his information from the Alaskan fur traders he met during the War of Independence. But bankruptcy made him fold up his maps and put away his navigation instruments.

"But we gave up on that idea. We have to be here when our Philippe returns."

The Marquise laughs. A mother's protective laugh. She twirls around and executes a slow waltz step that swells her dress at the hem. This is how she plans to open the ball that will celebrate her son's return. She stops short in front of Edmond and Jonathan as though the music in her head had abandoned her.

"One can never give up on seeing one's child return home. Is that not so, Gentlemen?"

At that moment, Jonathan knows that Edmond will not be coming to America with him. *The Scioto Company. This Land Deed Grants Exclusive Ownership to* . . . He can feel the sealing wax on the deeds melting onto his heart.

"Edmond and Jonathan, I shall now take my leave. You have so much to say to one another. I wish you good luck on your adventure. I am sure that you will find what you seek."

The men bow. The Marquise leaves the room. Thomas goes with her. The door closes behind them. In the salon, there is a silence that seems to fall upon them from the chandelier above. It's a beautiful silence that rains down in crystal drops. Edmond and Jonathan exchange glances. Jonathan informs Edmond with a sign that he will speak for both of them.

"Lieutenant, I think that we will accept the mission."

Without a word, the Marquis fills three glasses. The men face each other. They raise their glasses in a toast.

"To the boy!"

They say it in unison. They toss their drinks back. The Marquis carries a candle to a corner of the room and feels around a piece of molding. A latch clicks. A door in the wood paneling opens to reveal a narrow iron safe. Hidden from view, the Marquis turns several keys and returns with a lacquered wooden box about a foot in length and with a much smaller one made of green leather.

"Come closer, Men."

Slowly, he opens the wooden box. One would think that it was holding the infamous necklace made for the Queen. But inside, it's even better. Edmond and Jonathan are struck by the sight of two jewels, stretched head to butt on the crimson velvet.

"Your pistols, Men!"

The two gawkers can't believe these toys are for real. Two veritable long-barreled silver fire sticks dressed with ebony handles lie there, engraved with their initials.

"Men, this model was only made in 1738; it was never equaled, never copied. They're called .38s."

Edmond and Jonathan raise the gleamers. This may not make them any stronger, but they are sure to be more feared.

"And your police badges."

The Lieutenant gives them two blue badges with the inscription, *To serve and protect.*

"I can fill you in a bit more now, Men."

It's about time.

"The boy you must find and return here, in what is now about twelve hours' time, according to my watch, is about fifteen years of age. He was taken from his parents. We do not know exactly by whom, according to my informants from the Forty-Third Division. The boy is currently being held in New Haarlem, in the neighborhood located behind the gardens of the Luxembourg Palace, in the triangle formed by the Rue de Vaugirard, the Rue de l'Enfer, and the Boulevard Montparnasse."

Edmond and Jonathan know that neighborhood. The Marquis knows that they know it. It was in Haarlem that they found his son Philippe's head. That is also where Edmond got his face burned by acid. Haarlem! Now they know why the Lieutenant has called on them. This triangle is also called Hell, the Negro Neighborhood, or the Black Ward. Before that, men from the Dutch city of Haarlem grew flowers with the help of the gardeners they smuggled in from their colonies. *The flowers faded but the blacks remained!* Free blacks and runaway slaves gathered around them in equal measure. In the West Indies, you head for the hills; in Paris, you live in Haarlem.

"Your informants didn't have any more information than that, Lieutenant?"

"No. That's why I need you."

"What else do we know about the boy?"

"This!"

The Marquis opens the green leather box. He takes out an oval medallion framed in gilded wood.

"This is the last portrait we have of him. He must have been about eight or nine years old."

Edmond and Jonathan look at the miniature. It represents a naked mulatto boy whose face and body are covered with large light-colored spots.

"Men, we call this a leopard boy!"

Edmond and Jonathan have already seen children like him, but they leave the explaining to the Marquis.

"I have nothing more to tell you about him. This portrait was done seven years ago. He must have changed a lot since then."

"And what about his parents, Lieutenant? Do we know anything about them?"

"Nothing that I can tell you, Men."

They will be told nothing further. They can feel it. The Marquis looks at his watch. Edmond and Jonathan feel as though they have been dismissed by the clock.

"Here are your thirteen louis apiece."

"And our hats?"

The Marquis returns to the iron safe and rummages about. It is perfect for hiding such relics.

"I couldn't find anything worse than these."

He pulls out two shapeless soft-brimmed hats made of a kind of dark felt. Edmond and Jonathan try them on like two coquettes at a milliner's shop.

"You never told my why you were so eager to get paid thirteen louis and a hat."

"Lieutenant, we also have our secrets!"

Jonathan lets the insinuation hang in the Blue Room.

"Perfect, Men! I'll expect you here tomorrow by noon, with the leopard boy. Good luck."

They salute according to protocol. The two men leave the room. They slam into Thomas who was listening at the door. He chides them.

"Gentlemen, you should knock before leaving!"

"Grab a light, Thomas, and follow us."

"Gentlemen, I do not follow, I precede!"

Once they arrive in the courtyard, Edmond and Jonathan stop and undress in silence. Each one piles clothing on top of Thomas so that he turns into a clothes rack carrying felt hats and silver-plated .38s.

"Gentlemen, you are not going to start fighting again! I'm going to have to turn you over to the Marquis."

"Right. Turn us in, and while you're at it hold the light up high."

"This won't take long, Thomas."

Edmond and Jonathan raise their fists like two boxers. They go at it again. Buried under the clothing, Thomas is having difficulty peeping through the pile. He can see nothing of their altercation. All he can hear are grunts and blows.

"Hold the light up high, Thomas, so that I can see the gnawed-up face of the traitor who sold out on America for the smile of a Marquise."

"My face, gnawed-up?"

The rest is no longer important. Edmond and Jonathan end up by getting dressed, more like brothers than they were before.

"Now, Edmond, I feel like calling you Ed. It sounds less like a lackey's name."

"And I'll call you Jones. So you won't think you're the master around here."

Thomas would be happy to be called Tom. But then again, that would make him shrink even more. Of course, it is not fair, not fair at all to be born black, but it's not fair to be born small, either. The deputies should take that into consideration when they start abolishing things.

At the window, the Marquis watches the two men stroll shoulder to shoulder down the Rue des Deux-Ecus. He pulls out his watch. Twelve hours! What a short amount of time for what they have to do.

From her first-floor balcony, the Marquise blows them a kiss. They don't see it. Perhaps they can feel it blow across the backs of their necks? Ed and Jones shudder.

"Tell me, Jones, in your opinion, who is the person with the most information about what is happening in Haarlem?"

"The owner of Sweet Victory."

"And who makes the best blood sausage and apples in Paris?"

"The owner of Sweet Victory."

"How about starting our mission there?"

"Think we got time, Ed?"

"From now on, Jones, time is us."

3

RUE DES MOINEAUX

Those people on Rue des Moineaux told Groundhog to show up with the little dog at the strike of eleven on the Church of Saint-Roch clock. He has plenty of time, but he hesitates. Should he stop by his place, a cellar in the Capuchin monastery? No! He knows better than that. If he takes a "little side trip" over in that direction, he'll just end up reading his book, *The Journals of Captain James Cook on His Voyage of Discovery*. He'll read one sentence, then another, and again another, and he'll end up being late! Reading stories is too dangerous—you're better off living in them instead.

Groundhog walks and talks to himself at the same time. What would happen if you didn't take the little dog to those people on Rue des Moineaux? Well, nothing much, but you would get to find out what happens next to the captain on his travels. No! Do not allow yourself to be tempted by the little green snake in your head. OK. You will head straight there by way of Rue Saint-Honoré, all the way to Rue des Moineaux. History can wait.

Rue des Moineaux. Remember, Rue des Moineaux, like *moineaux*, sparrows. They must think he's an idiot. It's in an alley, next to a shop selling tricolor rosettes. If you see a patriot's ribbon tied to the balcony, just keep on going. And don't come back, under any circumstances. That'll mean the jig is up. If you return the dog to You-Know-Who, then . . .

There is no ribbon. Just a bit farther up the street, a cabriolet waits with its lanterns extinguished. The driver is snoring. The street is on a hill. It would be easy to remove one of its wheels. All he would need is a jack, and that would do it. Groundhog has a whole collection at home. He'll see about that later if the cab is still there.

A light is on in the rosette shop. The owner must be getting ready for tomorrow. He's bound to make money as the Queen goes by. According to plan, the door at the end of the alleyway is not locked. Inside, it's so dark, you could get your throat cut and not even notice. The dog is sleeping on his chest. His warm breath calms him down. Groundhog realizes that he has not yet even had the time to thank the dog for saving him from Robespierre. He strokes his head. There is a rustling sound in the alleyway. Groundhog presses against his side of the door and waits. His heart is pounding. It's all over. Someone is out there! Someone is following him!

"You weren't tailed here, were you, Kid?"

The man with the lantern makes him jump.

"No, Citizen. I did just what you told me to do."

Sure he did. If he had followed their directions, he would have had to hug the walls, and then take a detour through Chaillot just to get here. That would be the same as going all the way to Clichy disguised as a street lamp!

"Where's the dog?"

"Where's my money?"

"I'll hold onto it for now. You'll see about that up there with them. Now get on up there!"

The stairway is as steep as the guard is stiff. At least the stairway has a ramp. The Citizen has his lantern, two pistols with grips shaped like pigs' feet, and a bunch of questions.

"Whose sword is that, Kid?"

"It's mine."

The door on the next floor up opens before he even has time to be surprised. A plump woman wearing a white apron is waiting. She looks like she is about to bake a cake. Instead, she executes an obsequious curtsey. It's such an honor.

"Follow me, my boy. Hang your sword on the coat rack, please."

At least some people aren't fazed by his instrument.

The guard stands watch at the door. Groundhog follows the woman, who is even more rotund from behind. The candle flame barely illuminates a long hallway lined with paintings turned against the wall. What a surprise. It's a gallery of ancestors in a bad mood.

"Come in. These gentlemen and this lady are waiting for you."

The chambers hold three of "these gentleman." Groundhog knows one of them, the Doctor. It's hard to say how old he is, even though his short beard is starting to turn gray. He is seated at the main table next to a delicate man sporting a short wig and wearing a high-collared, deep-purple coat. A viscount, it seems. The third man seated at the harpsichord pretends to play it. His long black hair falls to his shoulders.

"Say there, Commander, why don't you hammer us out a polka?"

The man doesn't answer. The woman wearing a shawl and beckoning to him stands next to the fireplace away from the others. She looks cold. She is accompanied by a young red-haired boy who keeps whispering in her ear. She is blind. He is her brown eyes.

Judging by the tobacco smell in the room, they have all been there for a while. Empty shelves line the entire room. The place looks like a library whose eyes have been gouged out. You can tell that a gilded bronze chandelier once hung from the hole in the ceiling. It's damp. In the mantel mirror, a haughty bust gazes back at itself.

Groundhog moves toward the woman, the little dog asleep in his arms. The three gentlemen get up and take off their hats together in a choreographed ballet. The movement has a certain flair to it. This time, he realizes that it is not because of him. They are all staring at the dog.

The Doctor takes him gently into his hands, raises him up over his head, and presents him to the others.

"Gentlemen, Madame, this is Coco, Her Majesty's pug."

There is a muted cheer. Their eyes are full of emotion. Even the condescending bust condescends. It takes Groundhog a few minutes to understand that Fido is actually Coco and that Coco is the Queen's dog. This means that the light perfume smell which is a bit like honeysuckle comes from her! Groundhog is sorry that he has already forgotten it.

"Doctor Seiffert, is there not a risk that the dog's disappearance from the Conciergerie Prison will be noticed?"

That does it. For Groundhog, Coco really does not sound royal at all.

"None whatsoever, Viscount. While this one is here with us, Her Majesty's jailers have been given an identical pug as a substitute."

The Doctor is purring. He seems happy about his subterfuge. Groundhog, too. He really likes the word "subterfuge." The Doctor is wearing glasses with tinted blue lenses. He places a leather satchel on the table and unfolds a length of white linen. On it he lays the pug, who yawns and stretches.

"Boy, did you administer the laxative potion that I gave you?"

"Just about an hour ago, Sir."

Groundhog remembers the tavern and the milky brew flung straight into the sailor's ruddy face along with the bowl it was in. So that was what "administer" meant.

"Excellent! Come closer, Gentlemen, we shall soon find out."

The Commander comes over to the table. He is huge, over six feet tall, with a ferocious bearing and very brown skin. Next to him, the Viscount seems like a priss. The woman with the shawl and the redheaded boy stay put. Out of his satchel the Doctor takes a collection of flasks, a pair of fine tweezers, a retractor, a tube, and a small silver bowl. He coats his hands with a yellow-ish unguent and begins to palpate the pug's abdomen. Ever since he found out the dog's real name, Groundhog doesn't think that Coco's face has as many lumps and bumps as it used to. The gentlemen are all leaning over the table. Gravely, they watch the pug as he lets himself go, paws in the air, tongue lolling like a bandanna around his neck.

"Gentleman, for propriety's sake I request that the operation on the Queen's pug be done away from the boy's sight."

"By God, Doctor, you are correct. We are only too happy to forget the existence of these little colored boys. We think of them as ornamental torch bearers, but this just makes it all the easier to spy on us and betray us. Commander, you who are Creole, you must be used to seeing that on your plantations in Saint-Domingue."

"They are not all like that, Viscount. Some of them would give their lives for me, as I would for them."

"I admire your soulful effusions, Commander, but I would prefer that this, er, individual be exempted from all of that. What is your opinion, Doctor Seiffert?"

"You are completely correct, Viscount."

When a viscount is correct, you get kicked out quick. Ground-hog lands in the corridor. He is immediately taken off to the kitchen.

"Come here, my boy! Do you like apple pie?"

Groundhog wonders how someone with the creamy voice of a milkmaid could also have a fist like a farrier. The plump woman accomplishes that without even changing her apron. The piece of pie comes before the answer to the question, and the smell of apple precedes the pie. No matter, his stomach doesn't have any particular order.

"I only hope they won't hurt him too much while they're retrieving the message."

Groundhog doesn't understand what the plump lady means by that. That's often the case when he's got his mouth full. She seems to be talking to herself as she stares at the cast-iron door covering the fireplace.

"It's my fault. I'm the one who told them that once, while playing with Her Majesty, Coco swallowed a pearl earring. He returned it the next day, in a manner quite natural, of course. That made Her Majesty laugh, and she called the jewel her little turd earring."

Groundhog finally gets it. The Queen has put a message in the little dog's belly. She had him swallow it in prison, and the milky potion was supposed to help him lay an earring turd. What a great idea! That's even better than using the mail coach. He will have to raise his rates. One gold louis coin for a royal pug isn't that much, but for a royal pug stuffed with a secret message, now that's highway robbery.

"I can hear them better over on this side. I wonder what they're doing to him."

The plump woman is crouched stiffly in a corner. She carefully opens a panel of the fireplace door.

"Come here, my boy, and tell me what they're saying. I'm just not as flexible as I used to be."

The fireplace connects with the other room. From his position on all fours, all Groundhog can see is a log sheathed in a silk stocking. It's not convenient to look out and see someone's calves. Luckily, he can just hear some of the shreds of conversation.

"Commander! Hang on to those front paws! No, that won't do at all. Boy, get the handcuffs out of my bag. Yes, those. I use them on epileptics." *Doctor, what do you plan to do with that tube? Go digging with it? Are you joking?* "Ow! The little beast bit me! His tail, Viscount, raise his tail!" *Except that he doesn't have one!* "Where are those cuffs? No, not on me! Madame, if you please, you are suffocating him! Get the salts, Boy! Not that flask! Careful—hold him down! I'm inserting . . ." *Watch out, or you will poke a hole in him.* "Where is the tube? I've lost it! I had it in my hand! Who took it! Get those handcuffs off me!"

This exchange is followed by a whole bunch of yapping, yelling, and untranslatable swearing.

"What are they saying, my boy?"

"That everything is going well."

Groundhog tries to interpret the minuet of mingling calves and bounding backsides.

"Gentlemen, I have tried everything. It's hopeless. I cannot reach the object. There is only one thing left to do! Operate!"

This is followed by a collective retching.

"Can't we let nature take its course, Doctor Seiffert?"

Groundhog wonders what the side effects are of having a bunch of words running around in your belly.

"Gentlemen, do not be alarmed! I had foreseen this problem. We shall operate! You'll see, it will be a rather pleasant undertaking!"

Groundhog had already seen barbers at work extracting teeth, letting blood, even doing an amputation in a tub full of milk one time. But never an operation. Over on the other side, there's a commotion. The gentlemen are removing their coats. They are calling for washbasins, boiling water, bandages, vinegar, garlic, bowls, a ewer, some candles, and a cake of soap.

"You want soap when it costs an écu a pound?"

The plump woman grumbles. The doctor proclaims.

"Gentlemen, I shall now proceed with the incision!"

There is a brief silence. The blade must be suspended over the pug's abdomen. Groundhog feels his navel twist. It's kind of his fault that Coco is lying there. All of a sudden, Eeeeiiii! A howl. A long painful howl rises up to the ceiling and pushes the men back. It's the little dog. He has just shot up over their heads like the cork from a champagne bottle.

"Good God, he's escaping!"

"Doctor, you said he was asleep!"

"Technically speaking, Viscount, he is!"

For something supposed to be asleep, Her Majesty's pug sure can run. The gentlemen chase him around the table in hot pursuit. Led by the redhead whispering in her ear, the blind woman is in on it too. *Catch him!* Suddenly, in midflight, the pug's petite derriere skids past the fireplace and slides elegantly across the parquet floor. In slow motion before his eyes Groundhog can see every detail of the anatomy that had been laid out on the table. As the dog skids by, he naughtily flicks his croup, lets out an irreverent little fart, and drops something that hits the metal panel with a clank. The mail coach is right on time. Coco has just delivered his secret. The Viscount dives at the dog and misses. His wigless head gets stuck in the firebox like an abandoned andiron. At the slightest touch, the metal panel could turn into a cleaver. October 15, 1793. Invention of the first indoor guillotine.

"I got it! Here, Doctor, is this it?"

The Doctor takes the little brownish cylinder from the half-conscious Viscount and holds it in his fingertips. He inspects it and sniffs it like an after-dinner cigar. His blue lenses light up.

"Gentlemen, this is it, all right. And it came by way of natural causes, just like I said it would."

There are three hip-hip hoorays, with hats thrown into the air and congratulations all around. The Viscount slips a word into Doctor Seiffert's ear and motions toward the fireplace. Groundhog can feel that he's been found out. Seiffert acts normal.

"Quick, Gentlemen, let's see Her Majesty's message."

The Doctor cleans the capsule and opens it. The Commander, the Viscount, the blind woman, and the redhead circle up around the tiny piece of transparent paper that the Doctor unrolls in front of a candle flame.

"Gentlemen, the Queen's pinpricks contain the entire future of our undertaking. Viscount, you bear the task of translating Her Majesty's message. You alone possess the Swedish code that she uses."

"It is an honor."

The Viscount sits alone at one end of the table with a quill pen, a portable inkwell, some pieces of paper, and a brown notebook. Doctor Seiffert retrieves Coco, who is lying forgotten under a chair with his tongue lolling. He takes him into the kitchen and hands him to the plump lady.

"You'll see, Sidonie, the incision is only skin deep."

She stabs the Doctor with her eyes. He backs out, furious. Groundhog thinks that Sidonie is a pretty name. Especially when she smiles at the pug while stroking his head.

"My little Coco, these men are nothing but barbarians. But you'll see, I'll embroider a little sweater for you in cross-point. It'll be quite chic. All of the little girl dogs will love it."

Groundhog wonders what kind of embroidery he could wear on his own belly so that the little girl citizens would find him chic. In the chambers, turmoil has returned. Groundhog goes back to his observation post.

"Viscount, have you finished decoding Her Majesty's message?"

"I have indeed, Doctor."

He holds out a simple sheet of paper.

"Read it to us, Viscount!"

Because his head is under the fireplace door, Groundhog has to turn down the last piece of pie. Pretty Sidonie has moved up next to him so she can hear, as though those words would never again be repeated. The Viscount raises, then lowers the paper. It is reminiscent of a decree from the county sheriff.

"Here, Gentlemen, is what Her Majesty has to say. I have translated the spirit of the message. The words themselves are more brief, as you can imagine. He clears his throat and begins to read, clearly moved.

> I give you my consent to do for me
> What honor dictates
> If misfortune were to strike your undertaking
> It would please me that
> On my route, He be exposed to me.

The Viscount rolls up the paper to signify the end of the message. Nobody seems to wish to add another word to those of the Queen.

"However, Gentlemen, I must specify that 'He' is written with a capital *H*!"

"A capital *H*?"

The Commander stands tall. He breaks through the silence with his large build. But his anger seems larger still.

"Her Majesty wishes to see the child. That's an outrage!"

"I beg you, Commander, control yourself!"

He bangs so hard on the table that it almost breaks.

"Doctor, how am I to contain myself, when our own Queen demands something as scandalous as that?"

"Commander, temper your words. It is Her Majesty's will."

"Are you certain, Viscount? All I can see are a collection of pinpricks on one side of a stinking piece of paper and some sibylline formulas on the other."

He rips the message from the Viscount's hands.

"Do you doubt my loyalty? If that is the case, while I do not possess your expertise in battle, I am nevertheless ready to . . ."

"Cease and desist, Gentlemen."

Doctor Seiffert separates the two men. Groundhog thinks that in case of a duel, he would bet the gold louis that he still hasn't gotten plus the two others that he deserves on the Commander. Groundhog wonders how the redhead manages to repeat it all in the blind woman's ear. Especially the dirty looks.

"I do not doubt your loyalty, Viscount, but to tell you the truth, it is the Queen's will that I doubt."

"How dare you, Commander!"

"Come now, Gentlemen, we are all aware of the Calvary Her Majesty has endured since being taken prisoner. The King is dead, she has been separated from her children, deprived of sleep, is allowed no personal care, and has no privacy. Her body can take no more. This is the woman who has written us, not the Queen that we once knew at Versailles."

"You speak nonsense, Commander. The Queen is still the Queen."

"Don't get carried away by your own talk, Viscount. There is no more Queen. Pretty soon there won't be a woman anymore, and there's hardly anything left of the mother. Did you see how the judges at her trial humiliated her and crushed her by accusing her of having unnatural relations with her own son?"

"What I saw above all was how Her Majesty moved the spectators to tears when she cried out, *I appeal to all of the mothers who are here!*"

"It's true, Viscount, I was there. It was both touching and unbearable. Because it's that woman who's asking after the boy. A mother whose own son abandoned her."

"That is sufficient, Commander! It is enough for me, a servant loyal to Her Majesty such as I."

"We are all loyal servants of the Queen, Viscount . . . in varying degrees."

"In varying degrees! Now that's a way to talk that is quite 'sibylline,' as you would say, Commander. And quite insulting, if you are referring to me! True, I concede that I do not possess the 'degree' of intimacy that you both have with Her Majesty. You, Doctor Seiffert, were the personal physician of Madame de

Lamballe, the Queen's closest friend. As for you, Commander, the 'degree' of your intimacy with the Queen was notorious."

A sudden tussle erupts. The Doctor stops the Commander from grabbing the Viscount by the collar and rumpling his outfit. The Viscount remains calm and readjusts the rattail on his wig.

"Gentlemen, that is quite enough!"

The blind woman brandishes her cane above the melee. Her voice is thunderous.

"Calm down. Are we here to save the Queen or are we just playing the game of knowing who was the most intimate with her? In the second case, my son and I have already lost."

So the redhead is her son! Groundhog just knew it. Having a blind mother is even better. That way, you always have her ear.

"As for me, my lords, except for Doctor Seiffert here, you don't know me at all. I am Catherine Urgon; my married name is Fournier. I was a lace maker before I gouged out my own eyes with a needle. I am called Dame Catherine. As for him, he's Pobéré, my fourteen-year-old, a shoeshine boy by trade. Neither of us knows the Queen. Maybe we've never even seen her. Nevertheless, we are going to save her."

Doctor Seiffert, the Commander, and the Viscount have all reconciled in silence. They are listening to the blind woman.

"Tomorrow, Milords, there will be five hundred brave partisans lined up along Rue Saint-Honoré, the Queen's route to the guillotine. That's five hundred people who don't know her any better than I do. There will be coalmen, laundresses, wigmakers, and cloth dyers. That's five hundred people armed with just two good pistols and some knives. They will be near the Red Porch, just up from the carpenter Duplay's house, where Robespierre has his lodgings. At the given time, they will overpower the guards, kidnap the Queen, and cross the Red Porch."

"And then what?"

The Viscount cannot contain his excitement.

"To find that out, Milords, ask Doctor Seiffert. He knows what we're up to. Better yet, come join us. A few minutes ago, you looked like you were ready to fight. Come with us! We will meet at the Red Porch one hour before the Queen goes by. You are welcome to help us save her."

"Madame, I find this an admirable undertaking. But please just answer one question. Why are you doing this?"

"What you really mean is, why aren't the others doing it? Others who have a greater stake in the outcome? Bah! Let's just say, Viscount, that I am repaying a debt. Doctor Seiffert is the only one who knows the whole story. But to get to the point, know that one man's generosity once saved my boy's eyes. And that man was the Duc de Penthièvre, the Princesse de Lamballe's father-in-law. So you see, this young man here constitutes a beautiful debt that I as a mother must repay."

Dame Catherine puts her arm around her son's shoulders as if to present him to the assembly.

"One last thing, Milords. Something only a woman would care about. If I were on the verge of passing over to the other side and I knew that somewhere in this wide world there was a child out there from my own womb, what I would want, above all else, would be to touch him and to hear his voice in my ear, if only just once! I would leave this world peacefully and I would take everyone who helped me find him to paradise with me. Good luck to the brave!"

Dame Catherine and Pobéré leave room. The mother allows her son to go first, his shoeshine box on his shoulder. Behind them there is complete silence. The Commander reacts first.

"See the state we're in now, Gentlemen. Here we have a lace maker telling us what to do about that supposed boy!"

"No, Commander. This is not just some 'supposed' boy; he exists!"

"Oh, I forgot, Doctor Seifert, you say you even know where he is right now."

"It's true. I can rely on my informant."

"Your informant! The infamous Zamor! That maharajah who squanders our money at the Jack of Diamonds and all the other sleazy dives in the black neighborhood."

Without knowing why, Groundhog feels that he had better remember *Zamor*, *Jack of Diamonds*, and *dive*.

"What mattered, Commander, was to know where the boy was while we waited for Her Majesty's decision. She has just made it known. The Queen wishes us to show this boy to her when she passes by. We had agreed—you, the Viscount, and I— to obey the Queen."

"No, Doctor! Count me out!"

The Commander bangs his fist on the table. The Viscount

walks up to him. The discrepancy in their heights doesn't seem to intimidate him.

"Commander, I find your change of heart quite serious and troubling for a gentleman. My only conclusion is that you must have personal reasons. Would it be because of your mixed blood?"

"What are you insinuating, Viscount?"

This time, Doctor Seiffert is not quick enough to stop the Commander from grabbing the Viscount by the throat.

"Come, now, Gentlemen, think of the Queen!"

The Commander reluctantly relaxes his grip and quickly calms down. He paces in front of the table.

"In fact, Gentlemen, I was hoping that the Queen's answer would end this masquerade and put an end to the grotesque rumor that she bore a child in secret."

"Commander, shall Doctor Seiffert and I therefore conclude that you withdraw the oath you took?"

Groundhog knows that's impossible. An oath is like a kiss; you can't take it back.

"Gentlemen, as far as I'm concerned, the child that Her Majesty seeks does not exist. There is only one Dauphin, one heir to the throne. Right now he's locked up in the Temple Prison. His nine years are our future. The time will come when he will accede to the throne of France."

Groundhog wonders whether the one who likes to watch him do cartwheels will remember him on that day. First Cartwheeler of the King. That's a pretty good title to have!

"On that blessed day, I hope we will be able to shout in unison, 'Long live the King! Long live Louis XVII!'"

Nobody else joins the Commander's cry. The other gentlemen exchange looks. He does not seem disappointed. He walks toward the door.

"Adieu, Gentlemen, that's all there is to say. I'm leaving now to carry out my duty. Be aware that from now on, I will devote all my faith and all my energy toward putting an end to this rumor, by any means possible! This is my final gesture as a gentleman."

Placing his hat over his heart, he salutes the Doctor and the Viscount.

"Every man for himself. May the best man win!"

Once the Commander leaves the room, it suddenly seems very empty.

"Well, Viscount, at least things are clear now. It's just you and I left to carry out the Queen's request."

Groundhog gets goose bumps down to the tip of his toes. He extricates himself from the fireplace. Pretty Sidonie wipes her tears on her apron.

"Well, Sidonie, my dear? Is Coco ready?"

Doctor Seiffert appears at the kitchen door. His beard hides whatever emotion he may be feeling. Pretty Sidonie hands him the pug. His inspection is almost obscene.

"What a miracle worker you are! You can't see a thing. We'll be able to send the response to Her Majesty by the same way, so to speak. The Viscount is now writing a coded message. As for you, young man, you know what you need to do next."

"What about my gold piece?"

Groundhog thinks he's pretty courageous for having the guts to ask.

"You'll get it when you take this one to You-Know-Who and bring the other one back here."

The Doctor returns to the library with the dog.

"Here you go, my boy, take this with you."

Pretty Sidonie plies him with an apple, some walnuts, and a small hot pastry filled with pâté. Groundhog wonders where the sailor's ring-and-glove-bedecked hand has gone.

"Take good care of Coco, my boy. He is everything to Her Majesty. As he is to me. But I have faith in you."

That's it. She doesn't even say, "He is the apple of my eye." Or, "for your trouble, when you get back, there will be lots of apples, walnuts, and little pâté pastries." Pretty Sidonie says nothing, but she does not need to. And she says "you" so kindly.

"There! The message has been posted."

Doctor Seiffert places the pug in his arms.

"You'll be fine, young man. I anesthetized him so he won't chew on his stitches. We're counting on you. You know what to do."

Doctor Seiffert pats Groundhog on the cheek. His hand stinks like antiseptic, and the smile in his beard doesn't smell too good, either. He returns to the library and joins the Viscount, closing the door behind him. Too bad. Groundhog would like to listen in again, just to find out a little bit more.

The guard with the two pigs' feet stuck in his belt pushes him toward the exit. He'd like to wave once more at Pretty Sidonie. There's no time. In the corridor, the pictures of the ancestors are still pouting. The guard keeps pushing him toward the back door. Slam! Now he's outdoors with three turns of a key in the back and a night as thick as molasses riding on his shoulders.

Both sides of the street are empty. Groundhog can't help trying to imagine the message rolling around inside Coco. Without knowing why, except that he likes to scare himself in the dark, he pictures the man with the pike and his stomach-piercing instrument. He could be anywhere. The smartest thing to do would be to wait here for someone to walk by and then to fall in behind. The only problem is that when you stand still, your fear grows faster. That's the one humor that's like poisonous sap. Coco's body weight is slightly reassuring. But just in case he has to start running, it would be better to lash the dog down in a makeshift hammock fashioned from his cape.

"Can I help you, Marmoset?"

The pike! And that beanpole is standing behind it. No matter how much he was expecting to run into him again, his heart skips out of his chest. It's going to be harder to shake him this time. He's cornered.

"I already told you, my name is Groundhog!"

"If you say so, but that name just ain't you."

"You already know what a Groundhog looks like?"

"No, but you don't look like one. Hey, don't try to mess with me. Now I want an answer: Are you the one who wrote this, yea or nay?"

He holds out a little wad of paper. It's got to be the poem he left at the foot of the guillotine. Groundhog pretends to think about it as he slides the sword over to one side. His idea is to try to grab the hilt under his cape without being noticed. Then, with a bold leap, he'll pierce the pikesman between the suspenders, right next to where he carries his game bag. Right in the belly! There's no chance of disturbing any royal messages there. Afterward, you're supposed to remove the blade with one foot on the sternum. The biggest challenge is to avoid getting blood all over the place.

"Who wants to know, Citizen?"

"Because I'm polite and you have piqued my curiosity."

"Well, if this is just a matter of being polite . . ."

Groundhog takes a bow. There. Thanks to feigned deference, he's almost reached the sword.

"Yep, it was me."

"So you know how to write."

"Course!"

Finally. Groundhog has just latched onto the hilt. Once he's stuck Spike the Pike, he'll tell him to go see Pretty Sidonie and get cross-stitched.

"And you know how to read, too, Groundhog?"

"It comes with the territory."

"I just knew it!"

Spike the Pike jumps him. Groundhog never saw it coming. Too late. The skinny beanpole takes ahold of him, lifts him up, and smashes him against the wall. Now that's cheating. Groundhog was not ready for hand-to-hand combat with a toothless old octopus that stinks like scurvy. This open sewer is going to smother him! The friendly bugger kisses his cheek. He should have known. Spike is a pederast, a child molester, a wolf in sheep's clothing, a sodomite, a worm-eaten rosette. He's out of words and he's out of breath.

"You know how to read! You know how to write! Now you're gonna teach me, too!"

Spike lets go of Groundhog who looks at him in a daze. Teach him how to read. So that's what he wants!

"Why me?"

"Since you're little and black, I oughta be able to do it, too."

With reasons like that, book learning won't be easy. Just pretend you agree with this escapee from Bicêtre Prison.

"Citizen, I'm warning you, it won't be easy to teach you all that in one night. Especially 'cause I have to get to the Pont-au-Change."

"I'll go with you, Groundhog."

A man, a pike, and a barefoot kid, now that looks more like a prisoner's escort.

"You know, Groundhog, all I need is to learn my letters! Look! I got the words!"

He opens his satchel. It's stuffed with bits of paper of every size and shape.

"Here. This is my latest prize."

"Moineau," that's the name of the street he was just on. Spike was following him.

"This one here's the longest. I found it on the ground."

With a smile, Spike proudly hands him "Logotachygraph." Next, it's "Convention," "Equality," "Bread." They walk on. Groundhog reads aloud. Spike hands him words as if they were so many delicacies. Groundhog looks him over. A word hunter in the streets of Paris! The first one he's ever met. Groundhog almost runs into an unlit streetlamp, as he holds the word "Opinion" in his hand.

"Why do you carry a pike around if you never use it?"

"So I can get by unnoticed. Everyone carries one."

Groundhog gives him his pâté-filled pastry without knowing why. Suddenly, a gang of torch-carrying loudmouths surges out of an alleyway.

"The Austrian is done for! Hermann and Fouquier have her. All bets are off over at the Tribunal. Now she's gonna get it! You coming with us?"

Spike shrugs his shoulders in regret. He points at Groundhog.

"We can't. He has to teach me my letters."

The gang laughs and moves off. A girl belts out a revolutionary carmagnole. The others sing along. Down Rue de l'Arbre-sec, lopsided shadows sing and dance by torchlight. It's the street that leads to the Revolutionary Tribunal. Groundhog and Spike continue on down Rue Saint-Honoré.

* * *

Marie-Antoinette finally looks up at the Commander. He is standing upright behind the balustrade. To get to that point, he had to bribe and push his way through the crowd in the Great Tribunal Hall. The rush for the spoils is obscene! In a few hours, the most flaccid body in this crowd will be more alive than that of the Queen.

How she has aged!

The Commander looks her over while her eyes are still closed. That white hair, that neck, emaciated but yet proud, the bosom that still tries to rise. The Commander admires the fierce will to instill nobility in the ruin that surrounds her.

Finally she sees him.

The first thing the Queen recognizes is the long black hair left untied about the shoulders. Her chest heaves. She wishes to stand. To go toward him. Brush the back of his hand with one finger as if by mistake. It happened last time while he was playing the piano in the apartments of Madame de Polignac. He was playing that piece by Glück so softly. The Queen can no longer remember which piece it was, but her hand remembers better. Shaking, she grabs the arms of her chair. Suddenly all is quiet. She can no longer hear the vociferous Fouquier-Tinville bellow out his closing speech for a prosecution that lacks conviction. The musical notes flutter in a flock around her lace cap.

All of a sudden, as if through an opening, the Queen sees the Commander's hand answer her from the balustrade. Now she remembers the musical code that they used in order to converse secretly with each other, right in front of everybody. *Tutto a te me guida*—Everything leads me to you. He reminds her of the motto she chose as a young girl. Why? Tapping his fingertips, the Commander asks her a painful question. Her heart aches. She answers him. The Commander insists with the passionate musical phrasing that she once so admired. But the Queen's hand remains firm. Yes . . . *It would please me that on my route He be exposed to me.*

Like a cover slamming down over a keyboard, the Commander removes his hand from the balustrade. He takes leave of her with his eyes.

At once, the noise in the room explodes through the temples of Marie-Antoinette. Her gaze follows his long hair as it leaves the room. The voice of Fouquier-Tinville thunders on.

"This is why, in the name of our country, we plead death to the Widow Capet!"

Marie-Antoinette turns white. The Commander has disappeared. He hides from her sight. He leans against a column so that she cannot see him waver as he listens to the sentence. How he would have preferred that he be the one condemned to death. They would have seized him, assaulted him, he would have resisted and been pierced with pikes and swords on the spot. This good fortune would have exempted him from committing the act that he was going to commit.

* * *

Groundhog and Spike walk side by side down Rue Saint-Honoré.

"So, tell me, Groundhog, where are we headed?"

"We're going to see a man about a dog."

"What dog?"

He opens his cape.

"This one."

"Are you going to make mincemeat out of him? There isn't much flesh on him."

"No, I'm going to trade him in."

"Trade him in for what?"

"For the same dog."

"I guess you won't be losing out that way. That's pretty clever. So, Groundhog, after you're done dealing with the dog, d'ya think you could teach me how to get the hang of these letters?"

Groundhog mumbles something that could mean, *OK, we'll see about that later.* Spike looks happy. En route, he catches street names, revolutionary banners, and handbills, and copies them down. His game bag is bursting. This is the first time Groundhog notices so many words jumbled together.

"So, tell me, Groundhog, where do you live?"

"In books."

"Inside 'em? How do you do that?"

"I built myself a hut."

"Where?"

"Between the Tuileries Gardens and Place Vendôme, in the old Capuchin church. They've turned it into a book depository. That's where they put all the ones that were confiscated from the convents they closed. There are thousands and thousands of them!"

"You read all of 'em?"

"No, only one, *The Journals of Captain James Cook.*"

"A pirate book?"

"Shh. Look!"

Groundhog points to a wooden wheel with yellow spokes. The most beautiful wheel ever. It's right in front of them on Rue Betisy. Its spokes are sun yellow, it sports a rag top, hitch, running board, driver's seat, horse, and coachman. And he's asleep. A drunk walks up and taps the cabbie with his cane.

"Rue Saint-Cyr on the double!"

"Hold on there, Citizen! Haven't you heard there ain't no more saints these days?"

"Right. Well, Rue Cyr, then!"

"Haven't you heard there ain't no more sires either?"

"Right. Well, if there are no more saints and no more sires, I give up! Here's two bits for your troubles, my good man."

The drunk walks away, and the cabbie goes on back to sleep. Groundhog and Spike head on down the street toward the Châtelet stronghold. Spike has just enough time to catch a few words, and they're right in front him on a painted wooden sign that reads "Café de la Barillerie." Spike likes it. So much the better. That's where Groundhog is supposed to meet You-Know-Who, for the pug exchange. Spike waits on the street.

"I like it better outside."

He's already gone off to hunt for more words.

Inside, the place is almost empty. Two men are dozing. The owner yawns. Seated behind an extra-large bottle, You-Know-Who waits, hiding under a coachman's hat. He's put on his all-purpose face and plays solitaire with a faded deck. As soon as he sees Groundhog, he folds his cards and gets up as if to stop him from coming all the way in.

"Hey, Chimney Sweep! You got the mutt?"

Groundhog doesn't like that name. The other guy knows it. He shows him the embroidered pug asleep under his cape. He's getting heavier and heavier.

"Come this way."

You-Know-Who leads Groundhog back out of the café and takes him through an arched doorway. Groundhog ends up in a paved courtyard. A tree that hasn't yet lost its leaves is planted next to the wall, wine barrels are lined up in a row nearby, and the moon is their streetlamp.

"Gimme the mutt."

"Where's the other one?"

"Which other one?"

"The dog that I gave you just a little while ago. You have to give him back. That was the deal. I'm the one who's supposed to return him to the Doctor."

"Do not name names! You were told, no names!"

It's no use getting all fired up. Doctor is not a name. Even Spike knows that.

"Ah, yes. The other mutt. Nope, that's changed. They said it's not worth it anymore."

"What about my gold piece?"

"What gold piece?"

His voice echoes in the courtyard.

"The one they were supposed to give me."

"You'll have to take that up with them. Come on, now. Hand the mutt over. I'm in a hurry!"

"First, my gold piece."

"That's enough, Chimney Sweep! Give him to me!"

You-Know-Who's dials his so-called face to furious. He pushes Groundhog away and snatches the dog from his arms. A shred of cape goes with it, the sword ricochets to the pavement, the nuts run out, and the apple rolls away. Plop! The glove-and-ring-bedecked sailor's hand falls at his feet. Groundhog feels completely naked.

"It's all over, Chimney Sweep. This is not child's play. From what I hear, you've heard way too much."

How does he know that already? That's all Spike's fault. He made him play hooky and go word picking all the way here.

"So, now it's up to me to deal with your mistakes. So let's get cracking."

You-Know-Who places the little sleeping dog on top of a cask. He looks like a miniature Saint Bernard who's gotten his kegs mixed up. The man pulls a bayonet out of his boot.

"Don't worry. This is my girlfriend. We do everything together. I want her to see this."

He drives it into a tree trunk and makes a coat peg out of it. Groundhog is scared. You-Know-Who is too quiet. His voice is too peaceful. It seems to be over already. Groundhog stands stock-still. The man grabs him around the neck. His eyes are smiling. He should yell. This guy intends to kill him. Groundhog unleashes the terror that courses through his body like a chimney fire. The blaze will take hold. Or maybe it won't. Two thumbs push into his throat, cut off his breath, and close his damper. A miserable dribble of spit bubbles up and trickles to slime on his lips. Hit him! Break loose! Groundhog holds on. He shakes his head no. No and no again! The guy laughs and lifts him up. His feet turn to ice. His head buzzes. A huge wheel with yellow spokes passes before his eyes. It starts to go dark. His eyelids flutter.

"Open your eyes! I want you to look at me!"

He drops him and slaps him. All of the darkness of the back courtyard surges into his chest through a gaping hole in his chest.

His body shakes. There's a scent to the air. Silver lime! That tree in the courtyard is a silver lime.

"Let's get this over with. I've got better things to do."

The man resumes his chokehold and gets back to work. There's no fun in it anymore. He's going to botch it. His fist is fast and furious. It's getting colder. The wheel with the yellow spokes rolls by again. *Still no takers?* It quivers and quakes. Groundhog would like to run after it, but he runs into the man's shirt. You're going to break your nose on this cotton, Nigger Boy! All of a sudden the white cloth rips and grows a big red poppy.

Bones crack. Blood spills.

The man looks at the pike that has just pierced his chest. What's that doing there! *Aeiii!!* He should have yelled out sooner, but it's good to hear it anyway, even after it's been delayed. Spike could copy it down. It's a good catch.

Curled up on the pavement, Groundhog listens to each part of his body returning to its rightful place. He's missing the lower half of his belly.

"Hey, Groundhog, lend me a hand!"

Spike has a foot wedged on the skewered man's back and is trying to dislodge the pike.

"It's not easy to dislodge eight pounds of spiked iron from this chunk of meat!"

Now that's a mouthful for a *sans-culotte* to say! The catch is speared through and through, but it finally gives up the ghost. Groundhog looks at You-Know-Who. Some of his face has finally returned so that he can die.

"That's one gold louis I'm never gonna see."

He's going to have to get back on track pronto or he'll be broke like John Law. While Spike rinses his weapon in the ditch, Groundhog crawls around looking for the ring-and-glove-bedecked hand. His treasure! He retrieves it from among the nuts and the apples. Now he'll buy wheels for hansoms, sedans, Tilburys, light gigs, and cabriolets. He carefully peels the glove off the slimy hand. Even a fat ruby could make him a man of means. Good Lord! Groundhog looks at the huge black pearl attached to the ring finger of the severed hand. It's a monstrous hairy pearl.

A wart!

It's a huge wart big enough to gnaw a man down to the bone. Groundhog has just enough time to run to the tree and throw up.

Gripping the hilt of the bayonet, he rids his body of the evening's unpleasant events. All this for one gold coin. *Next time, I'll take assignats.*

He retrieves his sword. Spike puts the pug on his shoulder as he would a sleeping fawn.

* * *

From his buggy, Seiffert watches the black kid flanked by the *sans-culotte* as they walk on down toward Quai de la Mégisserie. *The braggart blew it. Things could be worse. They still have Coco. He'll just have to get him back.* The Doctor opens a thin leather case. He takes out a scalpel that curves up into a fine point.

"Cabbie, follow those two jokers!"

* * *

"Groundhog, now that I've saved your life, you're gonna show me how to hook letters together."

"Nothin' doin'!"

"Come on! What else do you want?"

"A wheel with yellow spokes!"

4

SWEET VICTORY

Side by side, Ed and Jones stroll down Rue des Prouvaires, a blind alley whose vigilant façades stand waiting for the inevitable attack on the next poor sap who wanders in.

"Look out beeloowww!"

A yellowish plume spews from a second-floor window. Ed and Jones have just enough time to take cover before it lands on the pavement and splashes up onto their backs. No need to turn around to inspect the nature of its contents. The smell is enough.

"At least he warned us!"

"We should be wearing chamber pots instead of hats on our heads."

They are too busy scraping their boots on a nearby post to notice the hansom cab parked across the intersection over to the side of Rue Betisy. Two shadows hover around it. The cabbie would do well to wake up and crack that whip of his.

Each man ponders the mission that the Marquis has set out for them. Find a mysterious boy in the next twelve hours! Ed thinks he was an idiot for agreeing to do it. But that look the Marquise had given him! Jones tries to stop telling himself that her supposed black magic was really nothing but a bunch of mumbo-jumbo.

They pull up in front of a dimly lit eatery named Sweet Victory. Hanging over the door is a rusted tin cutout of the Bastille swinging on a gallows all its own. Sooner or later, that sign will decapitate someone.

"Tell me, Ed, didn't this used to be called Revolution Lunch Bucket?

"Yes, but the Boss changed the name in order to protest against an injustice."

"What injustice?"

"I think it was the injustice of cutting a little black kid's . . . Shh, quiet!"

All of a sudden, Ed drops down to a squat. He motions to Jones to take cover and slides his .38 from its holster. A flash of silver cuts through the darkness. Ed moves toward the entrance and places his ear to the door. He maintains the position of jealous husband for a moment, and then he begins to sniff around the keyhole.

"Hey, Jones. Smell anything?"

"Nope, not a thing."

"Right. That's just it. There's something wrong here. You should be able to smell something."

Jones waits for an explanation, but his partner just keeps playing the fox terrier.

"Smell something like what, Ed?"

"Like apples!"

Ed sends a signal that means, *Get ready to break and enter.* Jones heaves a sigh. The mission is off to a great start. They're smashing up a tavern door just because it doesn't smell like apples inside. Better not leave any other odors near Ed tonight.

"Ready?"

With one swift kick, they bash the door down and rush in, their .38s drawn and ready.

"Straighten up!"

"Count off!"

Ed and Jones bark their orders. Total silence. The room is empty except for the furnished jumble of overturned tables and chairs.

"What seems to be the trouble, Officers?"

The Boss pokes her head out from underneath a bench. She's on all fours, a lock of blond hair hangs in her face and the cask of brandy is strapped across her chest. She wrings a red rag over a bucket.

"Can't you knock like everyone else, Citizens?"

"Sorry about that, Citizen. We couldn't smell anything."

"That's because I run a clean joint here, Boys."

"Er, I mean it doesn't smell like apples. When it doesn't smell like apples in here, we start to worry."

The Boss pushes the hair up out of her eyes.

"Edmond Coffin! I didn't recognize you with that scarecrow's hat on your head!"

"Maybe it's my new smile."

"I gotta say, a little acid'll do ya!"

She inspects his face.

"Good work. I can tell that a woman took care of this for you."

Ed clams up. He doesn't feel like hearing the Boss talk about the Marquise. She knows it and adjusts her bodice with two demonstratively cupped hands. Her gaze lands on Jones.

"So you're here, too! The Dangerous Duo is back together again. Well, I guess that means we'll be seeing some action in this neighborhood."

"Well, Citizen, it looks like you've already had your fill of it."

Ed points to the upended room.

"Are you still hosting meetings of the Republican Circle?"

"I can't do that anymore. They've just outlawed women's political clubs. That takes the cake! They think I'm only supposed to serve drinks, not ideas. Especially not women's ideas. Apparently idea stains are harder to remove than red wine. But they'll find out that when you start trying to rub them out, they won't go away and they leave indelible marks. We already have our own saints: Madame Roland, Rose Lacombe, Théroigne de Mericourt. And, the author of our own . . ."

She points to the Declaration of the Rights of Women hung on the wall.

"Olympe de Gouges! They're sending her to the guillotine, even though she's pregnant! They'd never do that to a man!"

Jones would like to raise an anatomical objection, but when he sees the Boss twist her washrag as if it were a deputy's neck, he thinks better of it.

"I can see that the Terrible Two didn't come here to get me to sign a petition in favor of a woman's right to vote. The guillotine, yes! The ballot box, no!"

Jones thinks that with the Boss involved, a women's club meeting must get rowdy. She starts rolling a barrel toward the door. Ed stops her.

"Citizen, do you think we came here just to listen to you talk about your hen party? We don't have time for that. We've only got one night!"

"One night? That's enough for me, Edmond! Especially if it's an all-nighter. Fifteen hours of lovemaking. It won't be the first time we've done that!"

Jones had never really tried to find out what went on between Ed and the Boss. And he doesn't care to know what's left. But something sure was there. Ed stares at the Boss. Those eyes! If Ed had wanted it, today they'd be the owners of Café Procope, and the clientele would be calling her Madame.

"Hey, you two, I get it. Sit down. I'll pour you a drink."

The two of them clean up a bit and find a table. The Boss returns with two glasses and a dusty bottle of red wine. Ed recognizes the red sealing wax on the bottle. It's the good stuff. They got that wine together from the Réveillon wallpaper factory after they helped torch it in '89. Such great memories. The Boss slips him a wink.

"Let's talk, Boys. Last time I saw you, you were in Haarlem looking for the decapitated head of a blue-eyed black man. What is it this time? A baron's webbed feet in the King's gardens?"

"No, a boy with leopard skin."

The Boss bursts into laughter. There is a jiggling of breast.

"What did I tell you! The two of you should open an agency . . . Mercenaries for hire. We look for monsters and freaks . . . Sorry, but I can't help you there. Even though I see some unusual people come through here."

"As unusual as this?"

Jones holds up a miniature as if it were a policeman's badge.

"Poor kid!"

She blinked. Ed is sure of it.

"I swear, they must have thrown acid on him. Say, Edmond, is he one of yours? Hey, Jones, do you see the family resemblance?"

"Cut the crap, Citizen! Do you know him or not?"

Ed grabs her wrist and won't let go. He could nail her right then and there and not flinch. Just like she didn't flinch when he nailed her in bed. The Boss takes a swig straight from the cask. Ed swipes the brandy from her lips.

"Citizen, if you know something, you best say so now."

"We got no time to be gallant."

"That's never stopped you before, Ed. First, tell me what you want with the kid."

"We have to find him. As for the rest of the story, it's none of your beeswax."

"I ain't talkin'. You can slap me, jab me, or demolish this place."

"Too bad for you, Citizen. Now see this!"

Ed slaps his blue enameled badge down on the table.

"This means that we are official. You know the new law about suspicious characters. We have free rein to grab you by the hair and drag you before any old surveillance committee. You know the rest. It's the Tribunal, and then they'll cart you off to the guillotine. So, what do you have to say now, Citizen?"

The Boss stands up straight. She looks like she's going to spit in his face.

"What I have to say, Edmond, is that you are a dirty bastard. And that it is not just because you have the blue badge of a lackey that you're not a dirty . . ."

"A dirty what?"

Ed grabs her by the shoulders and shakes her.

"A dirty what? Say it! A dirty nigger? Is that it?"

That wasn't it at all. Her heart stops. That is not what she meant at all. And Edmond knows it. He knows her. He can't really believe that was what she meant. How could he have forgotten? She could just scream in rage. She had so wanted to have his little black babies. She would have borne many. A houseful of them. She had wanted them underfoot, running through the house, yelling and laughing like crazy. She had been ready to stay permanently pregnant, popping them out like a Statue of Liberty with a spatula in one hand instead of a torch.

"That's enough, Ed! Let go of her! You're going too far!"

Ed looks like he has just jumped out of bed. The Boss sobs quietly over her cask. Like an idiot, Ed starts wiping the table as though it was the one in need of consolation. Of course that's not what she meant, he knows that. But ever since his skin got acid burns, he's more sensitive about color. How do you say sorry in lummox lingo? Luckily, he and the Boss speak the same language. She accepts the apologies that he does not offer and noisily blows her nose into her apron.

"OK, you two goons, let's have at it. You asked for it. Sometimes, it's just better not to know. I'm telling you now. So don't come in here later and complain about my ragout. Especially not you, Ed."

The Boss has given them a chance. Nobody takes it. So she has at it.

"Two or three days ago, I was about to close up shop when someone came in clothed like a conspirator in a hooded cape. That person was looking for a boy. Showed me his portrait. It was him."

She points at the leopard boy.

"Who was it? Did you recognize him?"

"Yes. It was the Marquise d'Anderçon."

Neither Jones nor Ed seems surprised. Only stunned. Ed gets up and wanders around the tables. Jones takes a drink. The Boss watches Edmond. She is afraid of what he'll say.

"Go on, Citizen, tell us your story."

"It's quite simple. The Marquise came in . . ."

"Why did she come here, Citizen?"

"Are you going to let me talk, Edmond, or are you going to cut me into quarters like a dead rabbit?"

He can't believe how clumsy this woman makes him feel! How can he gain the upper hand? She always makes him feel like she's the one in charge. Jones gestures to the Boss to keep on talking.

"The Marquise told me about how she's looking for her missing son. She had placed him in a convent, but when the nuns were driven out, she lost track of him. She told me that all she has left is this portrait, that she's worried, and that she wants to find her son."

"That doesn't make any sense, Citizen. Why would she send her child off to a convent?"

"Because of his appearance. What with his skin disease and all, it wasn't too easy to show him off to society, this little leopard boy of yours."

"I can't believe the Marquise would do that, Citizen."

"Come on, Edmond! I thought the Marquise saved you from going blind. Now I just think she's blind herself."

"Hey, Citizen, knock it off!"

Jones pulls them apart. Their reconciliation sessions must have been something else. The Boss gets back to it.

"You have forgotten, my Dynamic Duo, that tales of hidden black children are a dime a dozen. If you ever took the time to read the newspapers, you would know that the tales start with Anne d'Autriche and continue with Restif de la Bretonne, not to mention the American ambassador to Paris, one Thomas Jefferson."

Ed and Jones wonder which newspapers they should get to find all that out.

"That Jefferson was the worst. He thought black people

smelled bad. But in Paris, he went everywhere with his slave Sally. You had to admit she was beautiful. Almost as much as the Marquise. They had a bunch of babies together, but she wasn't the only one he . . ."

Ed prefers not to try to understand what the Boss is implying, otherwise he would strangle her with the rope of her cask.

"OK, OK, Citizen! Let's get back to the boy in question."

"Unfortunately for you two terrors, this leopard boy is not a child . . . he's a god!"

Ed and Jones gasp.

"Citizen, I've always told you to stay away from the bottle."

"What kind of nasty dish are you cooking up for us now?"

"Cooking! That's a great idea, my Dynamic Duo. You came here for some of my blood sausage. And blood sausage it shall be!"

The Boss is already at her stove. Tin plates, pots, and pans are flying around her head. She has at least seven arms and ten hands. It seems that everyone is godlike tonight. Especially her.

"Yes, my dears, a god! A god for a bunch of maniacs who will tear you limb from limb if you try to get near them."

"What's the story on that?"

"You want the recipe? Choose someone special, neither black nor white, but both."

The Boss adopts the Stove Goddess posture. With one hand she peels her apples, with another she pours milk into a mixing bowl, and with a third hand she stirs her purée.

"But be careful. He must be quite tender. A boy. All innocence and purity. Perfecto. And it's no use getting worked up over it, you know the drill."

With a fourth hand she cuts a sausage into giant-sized bites.

"Then you add a little mystery. No one knows where this kid came from, or who his parents are."

She sprinkles the secret ingredients over it all with her sixth hand.

"Hey there, Boss, don't you even have a little teeny, tiny idea who his father and mother are?"

"You don't peek under the veils of the Virgin Mary. I learned that from the Sisters of the Order of the Blancs-Manteaux."

"You spent time with the sisters, Citizen?"

"Yes, Edmond, I've 'done my time.' The gardener gave me

my first communion in the tool shed. Now I got religion and a green thumb. On my seventh hand. That's the one I use on men to burst their blossoms. I guess you know something about that, eh, Edmond?"

He ignores her. Either he'll kill this woman or marry her. But she'll still be the one to determine how things turn out.

"To finish the recipe for a boy-god, you add misfortune to the mystery: the boy is mute."

Ditto for Ed and Jones.

With her eighth hand she tastes a mouthful.

"Voilà, your grub is served. Here's the plat du jour: a kid who heals all, brings about peace and brotherhood, and reveals the winning numbers for the Pont-Neuf lottery if you add a coin to the mix. All that without saying a word. If you can't fill the collection boxes with that . . . Careful, it's hot! The Boss's blood sausage and apple trio!"

She serves the food with her ninth hand and smiles with the tenth. Finally, the Boss adjusts a lock of her hair with the fifth hand that she forgot she had.

"And to top it off, here's a pot of real Maille mustard, a gift from an admirer."

This is met with the silence of blissful chewing.

"This is just delicious! I knew it would be delicious, but I'd forgotten just how delicious!"

"Memory is the worse hussy there is, Jones. She robs you blind, but you can't remember what she stole."

"You aren't joining us, Citizen?"

"I don't eat, I feed. That's good enough for me."

And in two hands she cups the parts that have visibly given already.

"So tell us, Citizen, do you know where this little Jesus of yours is living?"

The Boss crosses her arms under her monumental breasts.

"Jones, behold your partner, Sergeant Edmond Coffin! A model policeman. His mouth is full, his belly is bursting, his heart is stirred, but he can't help asking a routine question. Even while doing his patriotic duty, he can still ask questions!"

Jones tries to imagine the scene.

"Do you think that Sergeant Edmond Coffin would drop his investigation, even for a second, to say it's good?"

"It's good!"

The Boss separates the compliment from the blood sausage, the apple trio, and the burp in Ed's mouth. She smiles.

"To the man with the bad manners I respond by asking whether he has any idea how many gods currently live in the boardinghouses of Haarlem."

"I've heard that they have more congregations, churches, and sects than people down there."

"Don't laugh, Jones. We have our saints, our miracles, and our relics, with our bits of patella, tibia, and even foreskin."

Ed and Jones push their plates away. Suddenly the blood sausage tastes funny.

"Let's get back to the subject of the Marquise. You didn't tell us . . ."

Jones stops talking. Someone is rattling the door. Pushing on it, trying to open it. A bench is wedged against it. The knocking is tyrannical.

"We're closed, Citizen!"

The Boss belts it out from where she sits, without getting up. But the jiggling of the latch persists. Flushed, she jumps up, blows the wisp of hair out of her eyes, and grabs Sanson, in an apparent rage.

"When I say we're closed, I mean we're closed!"

She kicks the bench out of the way with her wooden clog and practically tears the door off its hinges.

"Are you deaf or what!"

"No, just blind."

The Boss finds herself facing two white eyeballs that stare sightlessly back at her. She stops just short of axing them.

"Now, Citizen, you won't keep a poor, ailing woman and her little one from warming their bones by the fire?"

"It's almost midnight. I don't want any trouble with the patrol."

"It'd just be for a minute."

"The blind woman enters authoritatively, followed by a young redheaded boy. The Boss lets them pass. Ed and Jones make their .38s, their blue badges, and the portrait disappear. The blind woman and the young boy sit at a table tucked into a corner of the room.

"Taverness, we'll have two mouniers!"

Jones intercepts the Boss as she whizzes by.

"What's a mounier?"

"Have you two terrors been living in a cave?"

"A mounier is one glass of wine divided into two glasses. You drink one for yourself, and then you drink the second one while thinking of someone else and saying, *To the one I'm thinking of!*"

The Boss starts to walk away. Jones grabs her by the sleeve.

"Tell me where that name come from."

"Say, Jones, what do you take me for, Le Moniteur?"

"Mounier drafted the first articles of the Constitution. Apparently he wanted one of the articles to be the right to drink alone and to remember."

The Boss blows the lock of hair out of her eyes and looks into Ed's.

"Hey, now I feel like having one. How about you, Edmond?"

Ed acts like he doesn't understand what she's getting at.

The Boss smiles and goes off to fill the orders of the new arrivals. The faster they're served, the sooner they'll leave.

* * *

The machete blade hovers over the Commander's head. He's on his knees, his cheek pressing against the chopping block. His long black hair has been pulled back and plaited into a single braid that is tied with a purple ribbon, the end of it anchored to the wood by a steel clamp.

"Do it, Jean-Baptiste!"

"Master, I cannot. Don't do this."

"Go ahead and do it, I said. That's an order!"

The face of the young mulatto holding the machete is shiny. He is sweating like a field hand.

"Do it, and you'll be free."

The machete blade strikes the chopping block and cuts the braid close to the neck. The Commander stands up and comforts his manservant.

"You'll see, with a few snips of the scissors and a shave it will look great. Let's go up to my study."

The Commander picks up the severed braid, slides it into a black velvet pouch, and leaves the kitchen with Jean-Baptiste.

In the Commander's study the leather blotter on top of the writing desk is covered with letters sealed in wax and bearing his insignia.

"If I have not returned tomorrow at thirteen hundred hours
. . ."

"Master!"

"Listen to me. You will take these to that good Mr. Deboval, my
notary on Place des Victoires. You've been there with me before."

"I remember."

"He will know what to do. One of these letters contains your
freedom. Don't cry! Not now. Not ever again."

Jean-Baptiste is not crying because he is free, but because his
master is going to die.

"There is also enough for you to live on like a gentleman, here,
or at home, whether it's called Saint-Domingue or is renamed
Haiti. History will determine that. For now, I need your barber-
ing skills."

The Commander looks at his shaved head in the mirror. He
needs this new face for the rest of the night. He goes to a door in
a corner of the room and opens it onto an altar. The Commander
lights a candle under a barren cross, kneels down, and begins to
pray.

"Jean-Baptiste, please help me to prepare now."

The Commander slips a dagger into each boot and shoves two
pistols into his belt. Jean-Baptiste helps him adjust the leather
quiver that he wears on his back over his vest. The Commander
goes to a rack on the wall and chooses a machete with a hand
guard. He inspects it and slides it into the quiver. He finishes
dressing.

"Don't worry, Jean-Baptiste, I'm just going out to raze some
bad cane."

* * *

The Boss serves the mouniers to the sightless old woman and
the red-haired boy. With a gesture, Ed informs the Boss that he
hasn't finished questioning her yet. She joins them. The three sit
together at a table looking for all the world like they are up to
something.

"We were discussing the Marquise and that line about her son
being held in a Haarlem sect."

"Do you buy it, Citizen?"

"I have to admit that at first, when I heard what the Marquise
had to say, I thought that she was . . . I hate to say this . . . a poor

woman who'd gone crazy over the death of her only son and who was trying to find a way to replace him at any cost. It's often like that, following the death of a child."

Ed watches the blind woman drink her mounier. The Marquise comes to mind. Without her help, he would be drinking blind with milky eyes like hers. The Boss goes on with her tale.

"That, you Deadly Duo, is what I said to myself, but later, I saw that leopard boy's color. He's light-skinned. So then I thought that his father must surely be white like the Marquis. But if it was him, he would have said so. Unless . . . he is not the father."

This time, Ed is sure of it, he'll look her straight in the eyes and strangle her with his bare hands.

"Taverness! Which way to the people's throne?"

The blind woman had crept up behind them without a sound. Had she overheard their conversation?

"It's the door behind that post, Citizen."

Dame Catherine and Pobéré leave the room with a candle in hand. The moment they reach the courtyard, the boy takes a map from the pocket of his pea coat and unfolds it.

"What does it say, Son?"

"It's just as we thought. In front of you and to the right are two tall buildings. There's no way to get through there. To the left is a wall that must communicate with a garden. From there we can get to the Rue de l'Arbre Sec."

"Verify. You must always trust but verify!"

The boy grabs a trellis and uses it to help him climb up and straddle the wall.

"I made it."

"What do you see, Son? Tell me what's over there behind . . ."

* * *

Ed's silence surprises the Boss and Jones. He sips the glass of wine to way past empty.

"Go ahead, Citizen, let's see you cook up another one of your sweet stories."

"Now listen up. The Marquis takes off to America with Lafayette in '77, to join the war against the British. And by the way, those Americans better not forget that France went to ruin liberating them. Two billion pounds it cost us! Without us they'd still be British."

"Quit raving, Citizen! This is not your club. Get back to the Marquise."

"I'm just sayin' . . . So, the Marquise is alone over here, and the Marquis is thought to be dead over there. That's true enough. He was declared missing and wasn't seen again until just before the siege of Yorktown in '81. He said something about how a band of trappers took him north with them after they had found him wandering around wounded with no memory of what had happened to him. So she goes and gets sweet on another man. A child is born. The Marquis resurfaces. She can't keep this forbidden fruit. She confines him to a convent."

Jones does a count on his fingers. The Boss's hunch would now be about fifteen years old. It adds up.

"The Marquis returns. The secret is kept. One day, the child disappears. It is thought to be God's will. There is praying and forgetting. Then all hell breaks loose. The guillotine comes to town. The one and only splendid son is lost. The search is on for the other one. Even if he does have leopard spots."

"That'll do, Citizen!"

Ed strokes the skin covering his ravaged cheeks. This is how he thinks things over. Never in a million years would he have imagined such an impersonal portrait of the Marquise. He can just make out the oval of her face.

"I gotta hand it to you, Citizen, your story holds water. But it's all the same to me and Jones. Where the kid came from is neither here nor there. Our mission is to find him!"

Kaboom! The tavern door blasts open. The latch rips free. Debris flies through the room. Tin dishes turn into carillon clappers. The door panel flies off sideways, hinges, ironwork and all. A draft floods the room. It's the second sighting of the comet of 1793! The fiery disk bounces off a table, smashes jugs and glasses en route, explodes in midair, and lodges in the ceiling beams above.

The Boss, Ed, and Jones look up at the contraption that now hangs over their heads. The flying object has been identified. It is a carriage wheel with spokes of buttercup yellow. She rather likes it and can already see it outfitted as a ceiling lamp.

"My wheel! Pardon me, Ma'am. Can I have my wheel back?"

Groundhog rushes in after the contraption. He tugs on the Boss's apron.

"You again! Haven't you already caused enough trouble?

You're hell on wheels! Why don't you go wreck someone else's place? You want their addresses?"

"Aw, come on, Ma'am, give me a break. You gonna give me back my wheel or not?"

I can't believe it! This little cupcake is trying to get on my good side, with that little heart-shaped mouth of his, and that impish grin. No way. Meanwhile, Ed and Jones are inspecting the little black kid who has just appeared out of thin air. They are looking him over, oval miniature in hand. He doesn't even see them. His eyes are clamped on the Boss.

"Ma'am, please give it back, if you please, Ma'am!"

The more the two of them look at the portrait, the more they think . . . Why not . . . You never know . . . With luck . . . Their mission would be accomplished in no time . . .

"Take off your clothes, kid!"

"What's wrong with you, Edmond, dear? Now you gonna eat the boy?"

"Don't be silly, Citizen! I'm just trying to find out whether he has any white marks on him."

Groundhog suddenly notices the two surly hulks who are trying to strip him naked. He can't believe his eyes.

"Ed Coffin and Gravedigger Jones!"

The aforementioned stand taller. They hadn't realized they were this famous.

"You bunch of traitors! You dirty rotten liars! You deserters!"

They don't hear the rest. Groundhog is upon them, pounding them with his head, fists, and bare feet. It's not easy to stop a raging street urchin. A citizen, now that's easier. Crack 'em on the nose with a gun butt, kick 'em in the ribs, and they quiet right down. But this spastic, snotty-nosed kid, first you have to get a grip on him. And it sure would be a lot easier if the Boss hadn't already gotten into the business of pulling them apart.

"Get your mitts off that boy!"

"Step aside, Citizen!"

Ed manages to flatten the Boss onto a tabletop. It's more like a reunion than an arrest. Jones has a bit more trouble with Groundhog, who won't stop hollering.

"Stop it! You'll start a riot!"

This gives the little pest ideas.

"Help! Calling all patriots! A child is being murdered!"

Jones gags Groundhog who puts up a furious fight before suddenly giving in. His body starts doing puppet twitches. He sobs against Jones's chest, clutching at his shirt. Jones looks at Ed and the Boss with shipwrecked eyes. What am I supposed to do now? Not a damn thing. The three of them stand around Groundhog in silence. It's a manger scene with a sniffling Jesus, a side of beef, and a dumbass. The Virgin Mary has returned in the form of a barmaid, while Joseph seems to be off rebuilding the door that the Holy Spirit blew down.

Over Jones's shoulder, Groundhog sees the blind lady leaving with the red-haired boy. They're from that gang on Rue des Moineaux! What are they doing here! Had they seen him? Oh, how complicated this night was getting! Groundhog is beginning to miss Captain Cook.

* * *

Out in front of Sweet Victory, six national guardsmen on patrol cross paths with an old blind woman and a shoeshine boy carrying a shine box on his shoulder. The Sergeant commands them to salute. The troop moves off.

"You see, Pobéré, tomorrow we might have to cut their throats in order to save the Queen."

"And so, Mother, we shall cut their throats."

"Come now. Before joining the others, we still need to check on that Rue Saint-Honoré business. That's more important than anything else."

* * *

Groundhog lets go of Jones and dries his tears.

"Why didn't you take me to America with you?"

Ed and Jones eye their little black interrogator. What is Snot-Face talking about? And yet, that little round kisser rings a bell. That's it! They finally figure it out.

"Groundhog!"

"Well, well, well! You've been through a real year's worth of changes. You're just a strapping young fella now."

The Boss can't believe it.

"You guys know this little troublemaker?"

"We've met, Citizen."

"He saved our lives."

She collapses onto a bench as they gush on. Ed and Jones tell Groundhog why they never went to the New World. Ten times over they tell the Boss how, a year ago, they had located the severed head of the Marquis's son in Haarlem. One hundred times over they describe how they snatched it from the clutches of Delorme the Black and his gang.

"Hey, you two bruisers, speaking of Delorme . . ."

"That's ancient history, Citizen."

Ed prefers to avoid the subject in order to keep his burned skin from reigniting. Mounted on a couple of chairs, Jones and Groundhog entertain themselves and reenact the carriage chase through Haarlem with Delorme and his mob of black uhlans at their heels. No, they did not abandon Groundhog. They just thought he was dead. They toast the resurrection with Réveillon wine and lemonade.

"And me, Ma'am?"

Spike the Pike sticks his head though the doorway. He's got the pug on his shoulder.

"Who's this character?"

"He's with me, Ma'am. He's my buddy."

"Well, come on in, Citizen. One more or one less won't make any difference."

"He don't usually go inside, Ma'am."

"And why would that be?"

"Says there aren't enough words for him to find."

The Boss doesn't even try to understand. This just isn't her night. That happens. She pours him a glass of wine. Spike copies the word "Amaryllis" off the slate. He shows it to her.

"What's it mean?"

"It replaces Saint Theresa of Avila in the almanac. It's a red flower. Its shape suggests the male apparatus."

"'Apparatus.' Would you write it out for me, Ma'am?"

"No, but I can show you."

"Citizen!"

Ed interrupts her. Hell. If you can't be bawdy in your own bar, you might as well close up shop. The dog takes advantage of the distraction to lick the glasses clean while the Terrible Two get back to being soldiers on a mission.

"Hey, Groundhog, you still got your wheel shop in Haarlem?"

"Yep. But with everything that's been happening these days, I gotta say, Mr. Jones, it's been kinda slow."

"Have you ever seen this kid in Haarlem?"

Jones shows the oval miniature to Groundhog. He looks at it with a distracted air.

"And what do I get out of it?"

"A beating! And after that, if you don't tell us, we'll drown you in a jar of brandy."

"And then we'll label it Stubborn Little Black Kid."

* * *

The president of the Tribunal continues to read the indictment.

"The French people hereby accuse Antoinette . . ."

How she loves to be called Antoinette! If Hermann knew that, he would surely stop. Toinette would be even better.

". . . all of the political events that have taken place over the past five years constitute a deposition against her."

Marie-Antoinette heaves a sigh. From the beginning, she has heard nothing but vague testimony, unfounded affirmations, pre-fabricated accusations, expressions of bad faith, and a general willingness to do harm. She has answered each and every one of them. They have been forced to resort to ignominy in order to bring her down. How dare they force her son to testify against his own mother? The Dauphin versus the Queen? To sully the sacred bonds that tie a mother to her child? To speak of incest? Poor little Chou d'Amour. You are so alone in your prison. They must be telling you that I have abandoned you so they can more easily convince you to betray me. Marie-Antoinette blames her-self. Betrayal! She wishes to erase this word, but Hermann's voice thunders on.

"Citizens, members of the jury, you will be asked to consider four accusations."

Antoinette crosses her hands over her abdomen. Could she be carrying a curse inside that afflicts the male line? The first Dau-phin died so young and now the second will die too. For what sin must she atone?

The jury rises.

My God! She has not even heard the accusations leveled against her. It is three in the morning. My, how this night has already toppled into the next day.

* * *

"OK, Mr. Coffin, I'll answer your questions, but promise to take me with you."

"Not a chance, Groundhog."

"The Boss is right. You're trouble on wheels."

"So just kill me now. I won't say nothin'. I won't even scream."

Groundhog takes the stance of a young Viala under attack by Royalist insurgents. The Boss thinks that with a character like that, this kid could be her son. With Ed as the father, she knows they wouldn't have to yell *Stop Thief!* as the three of them stroll around the Palais Royal munching on beignets.

"OK, Groundhog, I'll take you with me."

Ed shoots a complicitous glance at Jones.

"Go on, show us what you got."

"Swear? Spit on it!"

Ed and Jones spit on the floor. The Boss doesn't say a word. After the mess they've made, she'll be able to sell the place as a pigsty.

"The one in the painting, I know him. That's Pie Face. He kept the books for Le Mac in Haarlem. But you already know him."

They know him, all right. He was the small-time pimp who'd been found in possession of the severed head of the Marquis's son.

"He still there?"

"Nope, he took off at the beginning of the year. I mean back when the year used to start on January 1."

"And how long did he work for Le Mac?"

"No idea. Why don't you go ask him yourself?"

Sure, they'll go ask him, all right. Le Mac is at the top of their list of Haarlem prom dates. They'd been dreaming of taking a twirl around the dance floor with him for some time now. Ed and Jones feel their temperatures rise. The Boss tidies up the barroom a bit, but what she really needs is a fire brigade.

"What else can you tell us to help us find him?"

"That you better hurry up if you want to get into Haarlem without gettin' your throat cut."

Groundhog is right. Ed and Jones get their coats. Ed goes to the Boss, hat in hand. She's talking so he won't have to.

"I'm telling you, Edmond. Watch out, or you'll have a run-in up there with . . ."

"Don't worry about me, Citizen. Keep my thirteen gold louis for me. Take a few to fix this mess, Citizen, but don't get too handy with it while I'm away."

The Boss tosses the moneybag up and down in the palm of her hand. She blows a lock of hair out of her eyes and shoots him a sly look.

"Don't forget that I know how to keep the home fires burning. I'll wait 'til you come back to fan the flames."

She wonders whether Edmond knows that when the King gets married, he buys his wife for thirteen gold louis. Ed turns red. That's because his skin is lighter around the pockmarks. Happily, the others have already slipped out, just in time for the good-bye scene. From here, it's hard to watch the ensuing profusions. Jones, Groundhog, and the pug wait out in front of the tavern. Across the street, Spike is bent over a piece of old poster.

"There's a hackney cab, Kid. Call it. And above all, don't tell him we're going to Haarlem!"

"What do you take me for, Mr. Gravedigger?"

Groundhog walks to the middle of the street, the pug in his arms. The gray hackney draws up slowly, almost at a crawl. Groundhog scans it for spare parts, just in case. It's old and worn, sagging on its springs, rolling with its lanterns extinguished, its shades drawn, and the driver is bundled up like an abandoned baby. The cab stops right in front of him.

"Thank you, Citizen."

Perched up high on his driving seat, the coachman doesn't answer. Must be returning from a bad run. Groundhog opens the door. A shadow surges from its depths. It snatches the little dog away. A blade slashes at his throat. Groundhog ducks. Something hits him in the stomach. A kick. He glimpses the boot as he is thrown against a wall. His head smacks, the whip cracks, the coachman cries . . . yaahh! The rig tears away over the cobblestones.

"Stop him!"

It's idiotic, but that's exactly what Groundhog just said. Try stopping fifteen hundred pounds of iron-shod horseflesh hitched to a bone-shattering rattletrap launched into a strung-out gallop. That would be insane! Luckily, Spike fits the bill. He sprints away after the gray hackney, seeming to want nothing more than to copy a word off the back of the contraption. He carries his pike as though it were a javelin, leveled just above his shoulder. Suddenly, he cocks his arm back in the manner of the ancients and launches the spear into the air. It curves graciously up past the balconies above and lands with precise accuracy. The wrought-iron pike stabs through the roof of the hackney and becomes a ship's mast. As Spike steps back to admire his handiwork, Jones draws his .38, raises it above his head, and takes a shot at the cab.

"Hey, Slim! Hit the deck!"

Spike freezes. Bullets whistle by his Phrygian cap and ricochet off the top of the mast like blue lightning. In the darkness, the cab seems to be running on celestial electricity. On the roof, the pike sways back and forth. Finally, it clatters to the ground as the gray hackney turns toward the Church of Saint-Germain-l'Auxerrois and disappears from sight.

"What's going on out here?"

Ed walks out of the joint, lightning bolt drawn and ready.

"Someone stole the kid's dog."

Groundhog's stomach still has a dent from the incident. But above all, it was the odor that made him catch his breath. It smelled like medicine in the gray hackney. It was the same smell that was on Doctor Seiffert's hands when he patted his cheek back at the Moineaux gang's hideout. For now, the Boss has come running out with a bit of brandy to rub on his stomach.

"If your mother smells this on you, she's going to think you've been drinking."

"I don't have no mama, but I sure wouldn't mind a drink, just to prove her right."

The kid points at the cask. The Boss likes his answer. To kill the pain, he is allowed to take a great big gulp, his head cradled on her chest. Ed looks at the scene and thinks that Ohio is still very far away. He'd better get a hackney right away or he'll ask for a sip out of that cask for himself.

"Get going and make yourself useful, kid. Go find us a real cab."

"I'll get us a yellow one!"

"Why does it have to be yellow?"

"Because those are the only ones that even dare to drive into Haarlem."

5

HAARLEM

The driver at the reins atop the yellow cabriolet slings the whip over his head like David winding up against Goliath and lets his war cry rip.

"Yaîl! Ho! Kab!"

The bay horse rears. His hooves strike air, nearly knocking the rickety Sweet Victory sign clean off its hinges. On the doorstep, the Boss frets over her miniature tin Bastille cutout. The tip of the whip whistles in the ears of the restive equine. He doesn't seem to much like the sound of it. His hooves land hard on the cobblestones, and taking the bit in his teeth, he drags the cabriolet away at top speed. Inside, Ed, Jones, and Groundhog are thrown from the sagging leather bench. The jolt leaves them tangled against the walls of the cab. Out in front of the tavern, the Boss is waving good-bye with her apron. Ed tries to poke his head through the window and return the gesture. But with every heave and roll, he looks more like a drunken bird on a defective cuckoo clock. So much for long good-byes.

The rig rattles down Rue de la Monnaie at a gallop. They are headed straight for the Seine and Trouble with a capital *T*.

"Citizen Cabbie, stay away from the Pont-au-Change. There's already a crowd in front of the Conciergerie Prison."

A crack of the whip tells Jones to mind his own business. Yaîl! Ho! Kab! The clattering wheels and hooves rattle the storefronts. At the rate they're going, the cabbie will get them all killed before they ever reach the Pont Notre Dame. A framed certificate tacked inside the cab reassures them. Yes, the man who is driving the rig does indeed hold *Chauffeur's license number 91001 issued to said patriot Loïc Le Gallou in recognition of his civil vigilance.*

"What does 'civil vigilance' mean?"

Ed and Jones are too preoccupied to answer Groundhog as they are busy busting the bucking leather bench. Each has one hand clamped to the rough leather surface as the other hand waves in the air. The kid thinks he knows the story anyway.

Or most of it.

THE LEOPARD BOY

Following the King's escape to Varennes, a Breton representative to the National Assembly and member of the Jacobin club proposed a vote to have all cabriolets painted yellow in order to better identify those trying to emigrate. The Breton cab drivers created their own company. And a fierce brotherhood they were. Corsairs, they were. Sons of pirates, all of them. For a gentleman, rapping on the cab with a cane and begging for mercy was futile. To these cabbies, the poor sap was nothing but pirate's plunder. Now, when the cabs cut through the city, everyone gets out of their way. Yaîl! Ho! Kab! It comes from the Gaelic. It's their war cry. They run on insults, and they hog the road. When a yellow cab comes into view, that means, *Watch out, Citizen! Remember Varennes!* It's more than just a cabriolet rolling by, it's a memory on wheels. Or at least that's how Groundhog sees it. Give or take a few feet.

"Why is the driver crossing over the Pont Saint Michel a second time?"

Hanging on for dear life, Ed and Jones try to get the child to understand that this is not the best time to be asking questions. When your bronc starts to buck, you don't just sit back and wait to get dumped. You take charge of the situation. And they also need a little downtime to think about their mission. To think about this leopard boy. Maybe the Marquis is taking them for a ride. Maybe the Marquise is in on it. It's funny how "maybe" can make you feel like you're straddling a wild horse.

"Hey, why'd he cross the bridge twice?"

How can they explain to this annoyingly staid child that yellow cabbies have a nasty tendency to make their fares pay a surcharge on every bridge they cross. This drives them to invent new passages over the Seine and even over its tributary, the Bièvre, if they have to. But thanks to them, Paris looks like Venice, and you can even cure your hankering to see a canal by tossing your cookies out the window.

Groundhog wipes his mouth on the back of his hand. He has just barfed the Boss's rum into the wind. It must have been white lightning lit to 160 degrees! Ed and Jones are turning pale. They look like they've just gotten out of a bleach bath. As for Spike, he's opted to stay safely perched up on the seat outside.

The cabriolet rolls on lickety-split. It disappears down Rue de la Huchette like a sweep's brush down a chimney. Almost without slowing down, the rig hangs a left into Rue de la Harpe and bogs down amid a procession of men, women, and children carrying lanterns and torches. They are walking down to the Seine through the mist. Groundhog sticks his face out the window and questions a mustachioed *sans-culotte.*

"Hey, what's happenin', Citizen?"

"We're going to the pantomime play! It's not every day that a queen gets cut down to size."

"That's it, then? It's all decided, they gonna guillotine Marie-Antoinette?"

"That's it!"

* * *

In an isolated chamber, Marie-Antoinette waits alone. She wonders what the jurors can possibly be saying about her. They are still next door, in the Grande Chambre The gendarme who is guarding her hands her a glass of water. How cool it is! It's almost as sweet as the water from Ville-d'Avray. Just for that, in bygone days, she would have made this lieutenant a colonel of the dragoons and paid him fifteen thousand francs. He is quite civil and very amicable, without shirking his duties. She hands back the empty glass. Lieutenant de Busne! He smiles graciously at her. Come now. We mustn't shirk on favors. We shall make him brigadier general with twenty thousand francs and the rank of baron. The office will hardly cost the treasury a thing.

Marie-Antoinette hears a row in the Grande Chambre. She trusts the jurors. During the entirety of these last two days, nothing serious has been leveled against her. At worst, she'll be sent away with her children. There is that horrible Guyana, but the air over there would be too harmful to the complexion of her poor little Chou d'Amour. Now that would be a crime. An abbey would suit her wonderfully, as long as there were a music director of quality.

The president's bell rings in the Grande Chambre. Marie-Antoinette shivers.

It is Judgment Day.

* * *

The yellow cabriolet rolls on at a crawl. It cuts through the crowd, pushing against the tide of people headed toward the

Conciergerie. Sunk in a corner, Groundhog is now silent. Ed and Jones look over at him. Strange how when this child is sad, he could almost be holding his beloved dog in his arms.

"Just what gives them the right to kill somebody else's mama?"

The Dreadful Duo is dumbstruck. The boy looks back at them with saucer-sized eyes.

"Just tell me."

"They aren't killing anybody's mama, they're bringing a queen to justice."

"So when you get to be a queen, you ain't nobody's mama no more?"

Ed and Jones suddenly wish that the lurching, yelling, and whip cracking would start again. Then they wouldn't have to answer any more questions containing the word "mama."

"I say that once you start being somebody's mama you don't ever stop."

Groundhog hugs his saber and rubs the handle against his cheek. The yellow cabriolet reaches the top of Rue de la Harpe. There's a bonfire lit on Place Saint-Michel. A mob carries an effigy capped with a lace bonnet ready to burn. Women and soldiers sing together. The horse sneezes. The coachman bellows.

"First stop, Hell!"

It's his way of announcing Rue de l'Enfer, which leads out of the square. The yellow cab slides along the Luxembourg Palace until they have passed the Rue Saint-Dominique. Across from the entrance to the Feuillants des Anges Convent, he bears right and passes beneath a stone arch. A hail of stones immediately rains down on the yellow cabriolet.

"Yep, this is Hell all right!"

Ed and Jones show themselves at the window with their engraved, nickel-plated .38s. The deluge ceases immediately.

"Corner of Lenox Avenue, formerly known as Les Noix Avenue, and 125th! That'll be seven fifty."

"Does that include the price of the horse, Citizen?"

The cabbie gives him a dirty look from atop his perch. This Mr. Le Gallou is no pushover. Ed holsters the quip and pays up. For the price of the fare, Spike gets thrown in for free. Weapon in hand, he leaps from his seat. Groundhog wants to throw himself into his arms. Ask him what new words he has found along the way. But he shoots him a grin instead. It's better that way. Ed and

Jones stretch as if they had just gotten off a long-distance coach. The yellow cabriolet grinds away over the cobblestones. Yaîl! Ho! Kab! Now they're all alone in Haarlem.

"At least it won't be too hard to find our man!"

Ed points to an enormous red lantern engulfing the entire top floor of single building. From two blocks away, "King Mac's Burger City" is visible in yellow letters three feet high.

"Well, well, well! Looks like King Mac's burger joint has made some dough since the last time we saw him. Let's go pay him a little visit."

With Ed and Jones in the lead, the company heads up 125th toward the red lantern. The street is lit brightly like Versailles, with the nightlife of the Pont-Neuf.

"Hey, Groundhog! Why are the streets numbered on a grid?"

"Back in the day, Haarlem used to be a garden with flowers in rows. They kept the layout."

In spite of the late hour, all Haarlem is in the street. Divided into three orders like the Estates General, it's a pickpocket, hired gun, and harlot convention. People have gathered into groups on Haarlem's front stoops. As they vent, they keep an eye out for gold chains, patsies, or paying customers to tempt. Spike doesn't know where to lay his eyeballs or place his pencil. It's all Groundhog can do to keep him from being had at every step.

"If you wanna do it with your spike, it'll cost ya double! But it's free for the kid!"

"Hey, Groundhog, let's go! These ladies are nice!"

"Keep walkin'!"

Spike is crestfallen. He makes do with what he can get and stuffs it all into his bag. *New love is in the stars! Get into the lottery of love!* Peddlers loaded down like porters hawk their wares. *Pictures, pictures, get a load of these pictures! It's the Brooks! The unbelievable but true reproduction of a slave ship and its human cargo! Pictures, I got pictures for sale! Two bits for the real deal!*

A little round man, completely swathed in gold cloth, runs after Ed and Jones in hot pursuit, business card in his outstretched hand.

"Moka! Moka's the name! Citizens, I must have a word with you!"

The pockmarks on his face and hands make them want to walk faster in the opposite direction. Ed and Jones make tracks. They are now in front of a sign that reads, "Chez Mac, King of Burger City."

Two grinning plaster lawn jockeys guard the entrance to the restaurant. Each of them holds a tray covered with bits of paper touting a special tooth powder of some kind. Spike takes a couple for his collection.

"I'll stay out here and start copying."

Spike sets up shop outside. Ed, Jones, and Groundhog go on inside. The room is decorated in ribbons and rosettes. A series of still-lifes representing various kinds of burgers are displayed on the walls. The Marat Burger. The Equality Burger. The Homeland Burger. Customers eat them standing up. There is no place to sit. Nothing but high pedestal tables.

A long counter forms a barrier to the kitchen, where an army of workers dressed like *sans-culottes* busy themselves at the ovens. Others chop, assemble, and wrap, singing work songs as they go.

Ed and Jones approach the counter. Slightly troubled, they listen as the workers sing their ditties from the Antilles. A young waitress smiles at them, notepad in hand.

"Can I take your order please, Citizens? This week every meal includes your choice of either a Voltaire or Rousseau action figure. Which one would you like?"

"We want your boss!"

They flash their blue shields. The young woman stops writing, pencil in midair. Ed whispers in her ear.

"Go tell King Mac that Officers Ed Coffin and Gravedigger Jones wish to have a word with him."

"But before that, give us a Voltaire or a Rousseau for the kid."

The waitress takes his order and disappears into the kitchen through a pair of double doors.

"Hey, Groundhog, where'd the kid in the portrait work?"

"Back there."

Pointing at the back of the kitchen, he shows them a kind of dividing screen made of sculpted wood.

"How'd you happen to see him?"

"I used to come in the back way, where they deliver the wine barrels."

"And just what were you doing back there?"

Groundhog fumbles around for a suitable answer. King Mac makes his entrance just in time.

"Well, if it ain't my old friends Ed Coffin and Gravedigger Jones!"

King Mac has gone through a makeover since they last met. He is still muscularly plump, just like in the old days. But his mouth is loaded with even more Peruvian gold than before. Now his smile twinkles like a treasure chest. As for his skin, it has turned two shades lighter, thanks to Windward Island Skin Serum. A vintage wig à la poodle sits on top of it all.

"Hey, Mac, we're takin' a gander at yer joint."

"Joint, you call this a joint? Ed Coffin is harsh. King Mac is currently at the head of the biggest fast-food restaurant in all of Haarlem. In all of Paris, even."

Ed and Jones realize that King Mac is still just as proud of himself as ever, even in the third person.

"Truth be told, King Mac has come a long way since last we met."

"Let's hope so! Last time we were here, we found a severed head that almost got made into Fraternity pâté."

"Along with that dead white stiff that landed head-first in your bun bin."

"Shut your traps, you troublemakers! Someone might hear you!"

Somebody already has. The jaw on a tall man the color of café au lait drops open as if the meat on his Double-Equality burger had suddenly begun to squirm before his horrified eyes. King Mac grabs Ed and Jones and pulls them out of earshot.

"Let us let bygones be bygones, my friends! Let us go to the upper room and celebrate our happy reunion with a glass of my Special Wicked Delicious Elixir."

"Keep your filthy concoction to yourself!"

King Mac adopts an offended, pedantic look.

"You should know, my friends, that King Mac's Special Wicked Delicious Elixir is a distillation of rare plants from the Americas whose medicinal qualities are known to combat stomach afflictions and phlegm. It has a pleasant flavor and is pleasing to the palate. Hence the name. Behold! My Special Wicked Delicious Elixir is so good it can return the shine to gemstones and the polish to silverware and pewter cups."

Jones cuts the pitch down a size.

"Speaking of which, how about we go back behind that screen and take a gander at your silver?"

On the other side of the screen, they find the table, portmanteau, and document cabinet just as Groundhog had described them. By candlelight, an elderly gentleman is busy with a quill pen entering numbers into a ledger. His crown of curly white hair and his feverish eyes make him look like a Templar knight.

"Trinité, would you kindly leave King Mac and his companions alone for a moment?"

Without saying a word, the old man takes his computations outside.

"Know this character?"

As soon as they get behind the screen, Jones pulls out the portrait of the leopard boy and shows it to King Mac, who pretends to be thinking hard under his wig.

"Nope, never seen him before in my life."

Ed grabs him by the scruff of his frock coat. The fine cloth is expensive to the touch. He forces him down into a chair.

"Wrong answer. That is not what people say when they see a face like this for the very first time."

"What am I supposed to say, then?"

"How's about, "Gadzeeks!" Or, "Goodness gracious!" Or, "Yikes, what happened to him?"

"By the way, what did happen to him?"

Blim! Blam! Ed can stop neither the forward nor the backward stroke of the slap across that face.

"He used just a little bit too much of that Windward Island Skin Serum."

"See what's in store for you, King Mac?"

"Yikes! Good God! Gadzeeks!"

He squeezes his cheeks to make sure that his skin is not peeling off his face in shreds. For now, it's just his molars that are loose.

"So you've never seen him before. What if we told you that he used to work here?"

"Right where you're sitting now."

King Mac looks under his chair as if someone were hiding there.

"It is simply not possible. We really do not believe that. Well, perhaps. But King Mac thinks it is simply impossible for us to get to know all of our employees."

Ed resumes the smackdown.

"King Mac! This is for talking about yourself in the third person! That is for saying 'us'! And this is for using the royal 'we' instead of 'I'!"

Crouched in his chair, King Mac begins to wonder just how many more personal pronouns his face can take.

"Since your memory is so faulty . . ."

"We're going to have to make a few adjustments."

Jones goes out and gets Groundhog. Enraged at the sight of him, King Mac clamps his golden trap shut and charges. Ed cuts him off at the pass and sends him flying back into his chair.

"What is that little baboon doing here! He's stolen enough hamburgers from King Mac to feed the entire Northern Army on campaign!

Groundhog looks the other way and plays army on his thigh with Voltaire and Rousseau.

"He says he's seen the kid in the portrait at your place."

King Mac takes out a diamond-studded pince-nez and raises a candle to the oval frame. The glimmer seems to send the light straight into the leopard boy's eyes.

"Oh, yes, now I remember! Yes, I think he may have temped here once or twice."

Ed grabs an enormous account registry and waves it over King Mac's head.

"Hey, hands off the books! . . . OK, OK, King Mac does know him. He would be happy to discuss him, but not in front of this little conniving, double-crossing, thieving chimpanzee."

Groundhog gets the message. On his way out he grabs enough grub from the kitchen to make a copious meal for Spike, who is waiting outside.

"Take another look at his portrait."

"OK, King Mac does recognize him; he did employ the boy here. But since his papers were iffy, King Mac did not wish to stir up trouble for him."

"What do you mean, 'iffy'?"

"King Mac can only recall that his papers said he was 'Indian.'"

"Indian! Now that's a horse of a different color! They said he was black."

"Black? My friends, that is so passé. There are no more blacks in Haarlem today."

Ed and Jones contemplate the diners in the restaurant. Funny, they look black.

"No, my friends, there are no more blacks from the Coast, nor any Negroes from Guinea! Just Indians. Their papers all say they're from the Indies! It's the latest fad. Pretty soon, in all Haarlem there will only be the sons of maharajahs, and sacred cows will amble down Fifth Avenue on their way out to graze in the fields near Notre-Dame-des-Champs."

"Stop trying to change the subject. We know you."

"I'm telling you my friends, we even have BPWs."

"BPWs?"

"Blacks Passing as Whites."

Ed and Jones would like to hear more, but not right now.

"Back to the kid. How old was he?"

"He said he was seventeen. King Mac thinks he was younger than that."

"You're still trying to pull the wool over our eyes. You want us to believe that you turned your account books over to a mere boy?"

"Listen up and listen good, my friends. You should have seen him juggle florins, pounds, marks, sous, and liards. As far as King Mac is concerned, he had a machine in his head. My wife Félicité even thought he was inspired by an archangel. Did you know that the Archangel Gabriel could tell the number of feathers on a bird just by watching it fly?"

"Speaking of which, what is good Félicité's latest scam?"

"Last time we saw her, she was cooking assignat notes in a wood stove and turning them into gold louis."

"That's over and done with. You have King Mac's word! Now she's hosting a Republican Chat Salon up on the second floor."

King Mac points up at the ceiling. Ed tries to visualize all three hundred pounds of Félicité's chatty self. Jones looks up at the ceiling support beams. Suddenly, he gets an idea.

"By the way, where did the kid live?"

"Out of the kindness of his heart, King Mac found him a room on the fifth floor."

"Can we see it?"

"Trinité lives up there now."

King Mac points at the feverish Trinité bent over his columns of numbers. He is pretending not to hear. But Ed and Jones are certain that he has been listening since the very beginning. They exchange questioning glances and then come to an agreement. They must see the room. But for now, they continue to force King Mac to spill his guts.

"Just when did the kid leave your place?"

"King Mac is still wondering that himself. One day, the room turned up empty. He just wasn't there anymore. I never saw him again."

"And that was when?"

"Just a short time after your last visit."

Ed slams his two fists down so hard that the table cracks. King Mac jumps out of his chair. Ed curbs his urge to cleave him down the middle. He chooses life.

"Pardon my outburst. But you will see the reasons for it when I summarize what you've just said. Here we are, in the middle of the night, on an urgent mission to locate a person of the highest national interest. Five minutes ago you didn't even know him, and now you're telling us that he kept your precious books, lived in your cozy little room, and disappeared from one day to the next just after the last time we were here?"

"Do you see why this might make us just a bit short-tempered, King Mac?"

Put that way, it made sense, but Jones's backhand isn't so sensitive. It sends his loose molars flying and costs him a fat lip.

"Talk straight or I'll beat you to a pulp. Where'd the kid come from? How'd he end up working for you?"

"He came by way of one of my suppliers. A brother who has a farm in Beauce. A potato grower."

"Give us the details."

"Now, you know that as far as King Mac is concerned, anywhere below 110th Street is savanna land."

"So what's the name of this black farmer?"

"Zamor! Another one of the kind who say they're from the Indies. He even dresses like a maharajah."

Jones notices Trinité slipping away from his account books, as though the name "Zamor" had suddenly given him a republican urge.

"If you call him a farmer, he'll gouge your eyes out. He's a lord. To hear him talk, he was at Versailles, at the court of Louis XV."

"Where can we find this Zamor?"

"Ask my lovely wife Félicité. He's one of her clients now. She's got a connection with this maharajah. And he talks nice, too."

From the bitter tone of King Mac's voice, it's not hard to guess that while this Zamor used to be his potato supplier, his wife is still receiving deliveries. Considering Félicité's three hundred pounds, that's a pretty good deal!

"We'd like to speak with your fair Félicité."

King Mac takes out a gold watch, which is only a bit smaller than the clock at the Conciergerie.

"On Thursdays, she hosts a séance on animal magnetism."

"That a voodoo scam, or what?"

"Nope, voodoo's on Mondays."

"No problem. We'll take what we can get."

A skinny, frog-eyed kitchen aide raps on the divider and pokes her head in.

"Citizens! It's that white guy, your pal with the spike who's been waiting outside. Says it's urgent. Says some citizens are trying to stuff him into a sack and toss him into the Seine."

Ed and Jones leap to their feet.

"King Mac! You stay put!"

Ed deals him a final blow to keep him from leaving the scene. King Mac spits a bloody tooth into his palm. Taking out his notepad, he scribbles, *Heard they're making teeth from porcelain . . . check it out . . .*

The Deadly Duo leaps over the counter. They split the room and its John Does like a couple of axes on dry pine kindling. This spatters burgers, paper goblets, and a blackish liquid all over the walls.

"Citizens! I must have a word with you!"

It's that Moka fellow again. The golden man with the pockmarked face blocks their path. Ed and Jones run him over as he offers them his business card. Moka is launched against a wall. Ed and Jones rush from the restaurant. In front of the entrance, Spike is surrounded by a gang of leering drunks. Groundhog seems to have left the neighborhood. The Terrible Two muscle through the circle.

"Where's the kid?"

"He was following that old black man with the white hair done up in a monk's doo."

"Which way'd they go?"

"They went down that little alleyway behind the building marked 'Novelties.'"

Jones could kick himself for not following Trinité. That damned old monk has all the trappings of a fanatic. The kid is bound for trouble. They have to get rid of these hotheads.

"What's going on here, Spike?"

"I was doing tricks for the kids when the one with the rabbit fur draped across his shoulders started riling the crowd."

Ed and Jones spot the troublemaker. They step up, show their weapons to daylight, and shout.

"Line up!"

"Count off!"

The stunned crowd takes a collective step back when the two nickel-plated parade .38s come out.

"And who are these two bozos?"

Fuzzy Rabbit gets the answer when Jones smacks him across the muzzle. Gravedigger skins the Rabbit with a left hook to the backbone and throws a one-two punch at the chin. Two broken teeth go flying, the lips bust open in solidarity, and the nose tries not to follow.

"Cool it! Everyone calm down! We're Ed Coffin and . . ."

"Gravedigger Jones, police officers!"

They show their blue shields. Cries and whispers riffle through the crowd. They're cool like that.

"Hey, Boss, it's not our fault. It's that Big White Guy. He's a warlock. He puts weird ideas into our heads and then he pulls them out of our ears and even out of our hats."

The stocky fellow with the low brow has nothing to complain about. Where else is he going to get his ideas?

In a live demonstration, Spike pulls a scrap of paper out of Ed's nose with the message, "New love is in the stars!" He keeps it up with Fuzzy who watches horrified as the words "Love," "Money," "Health," and "Fidelity" issue from every bodily orifice. The crowd steps back. Fuzzy starts shaking in terror and goes into a trance. He starts spinning and swatting at himself as though he were suddenly covered with bugs.

"Words! Words! They're everywhere!"

The possession dance draws a street crowd that grows rowdier by the minute.

"You'd better put a stop to that, Jones. That's how riots start in Haarlem."

"Look over there!"

Spike points to a gray cabriolet crossing at the corner of Lenox Avenue.

"This is not the moment to be watching passing cabs!"

"It's the one we just saw. Its top is ripped."

Spike is right. It still bears the marks of his weapon. Ed launches into pursuit of the cab. But the circle closes again into a gallery of stony faces and pointy instruments.

"Look out, Brothers! They're gonna get away!"

In chorus, the crowd starts chanting, *Look out! Look out!* and begins to clap slowly to the beat.

"It's gospel time, Jones! And you know there's hell to pay when it's gospel time in Haarlem!"

* * *

Doctor Seifert lifts a corner of the curtain from inside the gray cabriolet. He observes the two black jokers and the gangling goon with the pike in front of King Mac's place. The gang of thugs that has them surrounded appears poised to raise hell. These are indeed the same characters he saw earlier at Sweet Victory when he had gone to pick up the pug. The little black kid is missing. But if they are all here together now, it can only be because that little brat must have already told them what he knew. The Doctor is furious with himself. The Viscount had proved that the little bastard was spying on them through the double fireplace door. He really should have gotten rid of him a long time ago.

The Doctor bids the coachman to make haste. According to plan he will wait for Zamor at his gaming club. The Jack of Diamonds is on 115th, not too far from here. Seifert thinks about the Commander. The man is dangerous. All the more so if the Viscount is right about his mixed-race background.

* * *

It is hard to tell by reading his eyes whether the Viscount is right or wrong. Even though they are wide open. As is his mouth. It looks like that wad of paper stuffed down the back of his throat choked him on a secret too big to swallow. That's what the Commander thinks. The Viscount shouldn't have raised the question of mixed blood in front of the others.

"Yes, Viscount. I can confide in a dead man. I will leave nothing in my wake that could lead to any conclusions regarding black blood in my lineage. Nothing whatsoever. Not even you."

The Commander rifles through some papers lying inside a mahogany secretary. He retrieves a couple of passports, and some military command orders. The Viscount was a skilled counterfeiter. The only thing he couldn't forge was his own death. The Commander flips through the book he had found lying on the desk. *The Journals of Captain James Cook.* When he had entered the room for his unannounced visit, the Viscount had been translating a coded letter. He had been doing it with the help of the book, where certain passages had been underlined. The Commander knows that the Queen had been reading these *Journals* in her cell. This book had become a kind of rallying point for her loyal subjects. He himself had once owned one. He had burned it that very evening before leaving home. Had the Queen been using this book as a means to communicate with the outside world? The Commander will never know. He had suffocated the Viscount with the map of Captain Cook's first expedition. The one that had left Norfolk on January 22, 1768.

Bon Voyage, Viscount!

* * *

From the first-floor window, King Mac gazes down on Ed Coffin and Gravedigger Jones, who are surrounded by a gang of singing and clapping thugs. He looks like a piece of soft dough in hot oil. King Mac smiles through his remaining alphabetically ordered teeth. On his notepad he writes, *Sidewalk entertainment in front of restaurant: great idea.*

"Jones, you ready to break through?"

"Ready!"

Spike stops them and shows them a piece of paper with writing on it in Groundhog's hand. They read it with a doubtful air and shrug their shoulders.

"What do we got to lose?"

"Nothing it all. Anything is possible."

"After all, we're in Haarlem!"

They say it together. Two pistol shots punctuate the phrase. Two shots fired from the long-barreled, nickel-plated .38s. Jones waves the message from Spike.

"It's free! Citizens! Citizens! It is our pleasure to announce that . . ."

"For the next fifteen minutes, King Mac is giving out free hamburgers! But hurry!"

"Only while supplies last!"

For a split second, disbelief registers on the faces in the round. Suddenly, there is a hue and cry from the crowd, reminiscent of the clamor at the Battle of Valmy. A horde descends on the restaurant. Four teens sporting red hats turned backward take advantage of the distraction to embark the plaster statues that once stood at the entrance. The two lawn jockeys leave feetfirst, ready for a Haarlem statuary race. Still at his window, King Mac scribbles, *Free food: a dangerous but effective concept.*

Ed, Jones, and Spike do not have time to savor the joy of not being torn limb from limb. The golden man is standing in their way. He is still holding out his card.

> Moka
> The Living Memory
> 245 Lenox Avenue, Haarlem

"Citizens, it is I. I really must have a word with you."

"Sorry, but we don't have time for that now."

"Citizens, I assure you, this will be brief . . ."

Ed and Jones are already on their way toward the alleyway. Spike precedes them.

"It's back this way. It goes behind the restaurant."

Judging from the smell of warm bread, Spike seems to be right. They slip behind a wooden palisade into a dark courtyard populated by rats and encumbered with wicker baskets mounted on wheels. Some are empty and others are filled with round buns ready for delivery.

"I followed Groundhog until we got to the ladder. After that, he told me to come back and tell you. But I was doing my magic tricks and . . ."

Ed and Jones would really like to give Slim a thrashing, but he seems sad enough already. The ladder leads to a kind of wooden catwalk that rises level by level up the entire front of the building.

"Spike, stand tall. Your job is to skewer anything that tries to get by."

"And this time, don't move!"

Spike gives them his word. Ed and Jones start climbing. It wobbles and sags. From what King Mac told them, they know that they have to get up to the fifth floor. A window is open. They press against the walls on either side of the window, .38s drawn and ready. The room is dark. They can hear a soft scuffling somewhere inside. Ed gestures to indicate that he will go first. He steps over the sill and slips inside. The smell of incense and snuffed candles fills the darkness. Ed releases his silhouette from the window frame. He lowers himself to a crouch and cocks an ear. Too quiet. Not even the rats are breathing. Someone is in the room. Someone who is completely motionless, who is holding his breath and steadying his beating heart. But the guy is not afraid. Fear has an odor. Above all, don't move. In this game, the first one to blink is a dead man. The other guy is thinking the same thing with a knife laid flat on a thigh. He may be just within reach. He can just distinguish his profile. He is going to pop him on the back of the neck.

"Ed! Are you OK?"

No answer. Jones will understand. Ed feels around on the floor for a piece of furniture or a wall. Reconstruct the room so as to dive toward that glimmering white splotch that he has just identified. His hand meets what feels like a candle, then a leg. A body is lying on the floor. Ed jumps. It moved! The white splotch comes straight at him, a light silver lightning bolt surges from below, and Ed throws himself to the side. A sharp pain shatters his shoulder. He rolls. The shadow leaps through the window.

"It's up to you now, Jones! He's getting away!"

"I'm on it!"

Ed tunes into the confused scuffle playing out along the length of the catwalk outside. Laid out flat, he fumbles around and strikes a light. The glimmer lands on a pair of bare feet.

"Groundhog!"

Ed has discovered his motionless body, whose head and torso are under the bed. Outside, a shot. A pane bursts into a star formation before it shatters. There is a long scream followed by a dull thud. Ed lurches to his feet.

"That you, Jones?"

"You disappoint me. Who were you expecting?"

"Cut the crap. The kid's in here. I think he might be dead."

They get a better look by the light of an oil lamp. Ed and Jones pull Groundhog's body out from under the bed. Blood trickles from one ear. He's still holding Voltaire and Rousseau in one fist. His face looks angelic in the lamplight. The hearts of the Terrible Two begin to crumble. Jones palpates, taps, and pats. And yet, the body shows signs of life. The kid must be a bad liar. A couple of smacks open his already worried eyes.

"Where my army men at?"

"Look down."

Groundhog smiles when he sees Voltaire and Rousseau and winces when he touches his head.

"Don't sweat it. It's nothing but a flesh wound."

Jones might be trying to make him feel better, but Groundhog still sees red.

"Ed, was Trinité the citizen you went after?"

"Yep. He was pretty sharp with a knife for an old quill pusher. The quill's what got 'im. He must've thought he could use it to fly with but he took a five-story nosedive instead."

"You hurt, Ed?"

"It's nothing. Just a little shoulder pain."

Jones looks around. His scar is itching. Something is wrong. But he can't say what.

"Hey, Ed, don't you think there's something strange about this room, with all those candles lined up on the floor around the bed and not another stick of furniture in here?"

"That Trinité really did live like a monk. What do you think he was up to?"

"No idea, Ed. All I know is that the name "Zamor" made a big impression. Let's go pay Félicité a visit so she can tell us more about that maharajah. We're on the right track now to find the leopard boy. I got a hunch."

"OK, Jones. But first we're going to have to frisk the corpse of wingless Trinité."

"Trinité came in for a landing. And a soft one at that. Landed right into the bread bin. Now he's rollin' in the dough and headed for Bicêtre. That's what's stamped on the side of it. Lying in his wicker basket he looks like a missing pilot cut down from a hot-air balloon. Jones dives into the buns, and Groundhog plays with

Voltaire and Rousseau. Spike hangs a lantern on the end of his pike and scribbles, *Bicêtre, home for foundling boys.* Ed sews up his wound in vivo with tools from his army field kit.

"This is all I found in his pockets."

Jones reports on the loot. It's a gold chain with a blood-spattered medallion containing the barely visible image of the leopard boy.

"Ed, I think we've run into a fanatical leopard boy worshipper who's turned his old room into a sanctuary."

"That is not good news. This means that the Boss called it right. It's a god we're looking for."

"Félicité's the only one who can help us with a scam like that. According to King Mac, she's in the middle of an animal magnetism séance right around now."

6

MOKA

Animal magnetism!

For Jones, there's no point in saying anything more. That would be useless. The reason lies just behind this padded door. Spike and Groundhog are waiting downstairs in the street. Spike likes being outside, and Groundhog has a head injury. At least that's what he told them. In fact, inside that cracked skull a plan is hatching. First, he'll find the gray cabriolet that he saw driving by King Mac's place. Then, he'll look for Doctor Seiffert's pug. After that he'll take Coco back to Pretty Sidonie, just as he'd promised. And then he'll score a huge hunk of pie. As for Ed and Jones, their plans haven't changed. They'll just have to see how it goes. They get a servant girl to show them upstairs.

"Down there. That hallway. A door. Got bars on it. Madame. She ain't gonna open it."

Word Chopper got it wrong. Félicité opens up. It goes without saying that before that, Ed and Jones had to hold their fine .38s up to the peephole, explain how they'd blow the lock off the door even though they would regret the adverse effects that their forced entry would have had upon the clientele. Félicité is convinced. She opens the door wide on her three hundred pounds of gleaming ebony and that special way she has of perpetually looking twelve months pregnant. She appears in court dress, her bosoms swathed in pink taffeta and trying to push their way out. Félicité is swollen with fury, and her whisper gives the distinct impression that she has sprung a leak.

"Ed Coffin and Gravedigger Jones! Someone's already been up here to tell me that you been at King Mac's and caused a ruckus. I'm warning you that if you make any trouble up here . . ."

They flash their blue shields. This keeps Félicité from mentioning her influence with the Committee. Her attitude softens, and she shows them into a kind of boudoir done in Chinese gold dragons on black-and-red lacquer. The walls are laden with a confused jumble of mirrors, patents, and certificates. One reads, *The Savant Energy Society.* There are pages from Diderot and d'Alembert's *Encyclopedia*. The place feels like a bordello turned junk shop. Jones takes out the little oval portrait of the leopard boy.

"Tell us about this individual and a guy named Zamor."

"And don't try to tell us you don't know him, because that's just the kind of thing that can cause a ruckus."

"Shhhh! I'm not saying I don't know him. Problem is, I'm right in the middle of a séance for the unification of the phlegms. I simply cannot abandon my patients at this sensitive moment."

"You mean your sick people."

"You shut your mouth, you miscreant! There is no such thing as sick people. There are only patients who are victims of divided energies. I cannot leave them alone. The teachings of Dr. Mesmer are categorical on this point. Their vital fluids run the risk of wandering outside their bodies. It could kill them. Come with me. I've almost finished, and then we can talk."

Ed and Jones follow her through a mirrored door into a pitch-black room. Somewhere someone is playing a drifting melody on a pianoforte. Gradually, they begin to distinguish an oval-shaped wooden mass about twenty cubits in length in the middle of the room. The shape is vaguely reminiscent of a tubby rowboat.

"Ah, so this is the famous Mesmer baquet!"

"That's what his enemies—like that Freemason Dr. Guillotin, who'd rather decapitate than re-capacitate—call it. In fact, this is a magnetism concentrator."

Jones apologizes for the error. He examines the machine in detail. At regular intervals, pliable bent rods protrude from the lid. Patients seated in armchairs have applied their tips to various body parts. They resemble castaways clinging to a raft for dear life. A small nightlight dimly illuminates a group of well-dressed men and women. Félicité moves around them in a royal procession all her own. Ed and Jones follow close behind like a couple of courtiers. The only sound they can hear is the rustling of her dress and the muted melody of the pianoforte. She enunciates with the voice of a priestess.

"*Remember! There is only one illness and only one cure! Let go of your phlegm . . . Allow your fluids to rise up within.*"

Félicité alternates with ease between exhorting her patients and whispering to Ed and Jones.

"*Observe! Your magnetism is dispersed . . . It will not be easy* for you to reach the child in the portrait . . ."

"You know him?"

"It's the leopard boy ... *Now we shall gather it together* ... Everybody in Haarlem knows who he is ... *Take each bit one by one* ... But nobody will talk about him."

"Why not?"

"In Haarlem, a god is born every week ... *Feel your personal magnetism regenerate!* ... I've seen a steady stream of messiahs, marabouts, and prophets come and go ... *Feel it!* ... But this child is different. *Feel it rise!* ..."

"How can you say that, Félicité?"

"Con games are my specialty ... *Hold on to it a little longer* ... For a while there, I was going to get into the Savior business, like Catherine Théot, the Mother of God. It's good money. She even has Robespierre as one of her clients ... *Hold it in* ... The leopard boy has nothing to do with all that. He's the real deal!

Ed and Jones realize that they are witnessing a historic event. Félicité is being sincere!

"And this Zamor character who claims that he was at Versailles, at the court of Louis XV ..."

Jones whispers this like Félicité.

"It's true. He was du Barry's sex slave. *Expel your phlegm!* ... The King's favorite! *Make way for the essential fluids!* ..."

"You seem to know him pretty well. Heard he's a client of yours."

"Let's just say that he's worried about his ... man tool. He's experienced a couple of malfunctions lately ... *Careful! Do not allow it to rise too quickly!* ... So he comes in here to get a tune-up ... *You must maintain your control* ..."

"Is it working?"

"Better than any sex aid I know of. Would you like a free session, Ed? ... *Breathe deeply!* ..."

"What we really want to know is whether this Zamor character is here tonight."

"*Now you can begin to let go* ... That's him over there in the middle!"

Félicité points to a kind of maharajah wearing a turban and a pearl earring. Ed and Jones should have known. Snugged into his armchair, Zamor is full of animal magnetism. He's bent over a flexible metal rod, groaning, hips thrusting, eyes rolled back.

"*Now concentrate! The magnetism is taking effect!* Don't talk to him until the session is over. Or at least not until he's paid up! Go easy on him! . . . *The humors are uniting. Feel it!* . . . And don't you mess him up, now, hear?"

"Why not Félicité? He yours?"

"Let's just say I get to benefit from his surplus animal magnetism, on those off days when I don't get it anywhere else . . . *Now liberate all of the humors that you are holding inside . . . Do it! . . . Do it! Again! . . . And again! . . .*"

Félicité exhorts the assembly like a midwife attending a birth. That's when Ed and Jones notice that the rhythm of the piano has intensified and that other members of the group are emulating Zamor down in their armchairs. The groans and convulsions multiply. Pliable rods are passed around and fluids flow freely. Ed and Jones now understand how the former madam was able to move so quickly into the baquet business.

"Do it! All together! Now! . . ."

Dong! Dong!

The walls quiver and the floor quakes. There's a final, fevered frenzy. And then, an explosion of ecstasy! The collective moan ranges in intensity, from the tocsin's low tolls to the high tinkling of servants' bells. Vocal registers will vary! Hallelujah! . . . The patients gaze dumbly at one another. Never before has any of them experienced a visitation like this one.

Dongggg! . . . Dongggg!

The assembly comes to. Those really are bells ringing. Real, live bells. They recognize the bells of Saint-Zita, whose tower is practically right next door. Some Easter Day when the bells fly off to Rome, they'll split the building in two on their maiden voyage from the tower.

Donggg! . . . Donggg!

They can hear shouts rising up from the street.

"Death! She got death!"

Félicité opens the drapes. Daylight surprises the patients as they reposition their flexible tips, readjust their magnetism, and run to the windows. In the church courtyard below a mob has gathered.

"Death! The verdict is death! . . . To the Conciergerie!"

In a single motion, the impatient and disorderly troop rushes to the door, knocking Félicité over. The mirrored door explodes into a million times seven years bad luck.

"Jones! Our man is getting away!"

In this fire-alarm panic, Zamor is not one of the slower ones. He slips out like a volunteer on his way to fight the blaze. Jones charges after the maharajah but bogs down in the boudoir bottleneck. It's hopeless. Ed fishes Félicité's three hundred pounds from the prow of the energy concentrator. She looks like a whale that has been rammed by a rowboat.

"Those damned freeloaders just found an excuse to vamoose scot-free!"

Ed and Jones go over to the window. According to the Saint-Zita bell tower, it is four o'clock. They get it. Over there, beyond Haarlem, across the Seine, over the wooden balustrade, the verdict is death to the Queen.

* * *

"The penalty is death!"

Marie-Antoinette is not sure that she has heard them say it, but she understands the meaning of it. With her heart, with her belly, with her suffering flesh as it throbs in her extremities, she understands. Antoinette feels faint. There is nothing frivolous about this sudden languor. No perfume. Only the body as it gives way. Not here. Not in front of these people. Fouquier-Tinville's voice seems foggy and distant.

". . . That the defendant be sentenced to death, according to article one, section one, of title one of part two of the penal code . . ."

It seems to her that they want to reduce her death to a simple paragraph. But that does not suffice. Now they are trying to dismember her. Trying to tear her limb from limb.

"And also according to article eleven of the first section of the first title of the second part of the same code."

In how many pieces do they want me? When she arrived at Versailles, she was the one they used to call *the tasty morsel . . .* , and now here she is a part of the leftovers. Please make it so that those who love me do not see me dismembered like this. Especially not you, my children. All of my children. My thoughts go out to your souls. What a bad mother I am to pass on before you do!

"Antoinette, do you have any complaints regarding the application of the laws invoked by the public prosecutor?"

Complaints! How vulgar! As though it were simply the matter of a whim at the milliner's shop . . . *Madame Bertin, I have some complaints to make about this dreadful puckered shoulder seam* . . . Her heart aches. Let it at least be said that I did not make a spectacle of fighting for my life like a coquette arguing over a piece of ribbon.

"In accordance with the unanimous declarations of the jury, the Tribunal, acceding to the indictment of the public prosecutor, in accordance with the laws heretofore cited by him, condemns Marie-Antoinette, known as Lorraine of Austria, widow of Louis Capet, to the penalty of death."

Marie-Antoinette steps off the dais. She can neither hear nor see her surroundings. Her step does not falter. She looks at the gate of the balustrade. It is beyond that point that now it all begins.

* * *

Ed and Jones are busy struggling to get the magnetist back on her feet.

"Félicité, you think your friend Zamor spotted us?"

"The way you look, that wouldn't be too hard. In any case, his kind of citizen knows he'd better act first and ask questions later. He's always watching his back."

"And what's he looking at back there?"

"Gambling debts and jealous husbands."

"Félicité, do you think there's a connection between the leopard boy and Zamor?"

"Moka could tell you that better than I can. As soon as a black man is in the picture he knows it all."

"Moka? The Gilded Fool? The Living Memory?"

"That pockmarked maniac who keeps running after us?"

"Show a little respect now, Gentlemen. When he was a kid he got cannoned on a slave ship."

Ed and Jones knew that when there was a slave revolt, the crew would shoot at them with dried peas so as not to mar the merchandise too terribly much.

"And where can we find this Moka?"

"He'll find you."

"OK. For Moka, there's no rush. As for this Zamor, you must know something about the man in question, Félicité."

"Citizen, I am a licensed magnetist with the Savant Energy Society, not a fortune-teller."

About that, there's no doubt. Otherwise, she would have predicted what Ed and Jones would do next. They grab her under the arms and tote 150 pounds each of her bad attitude over to the baquet. Jones lifts the lid.

"How about a little sitz bath?"

"No peeking. That's a patented trade secret."

The trade secret looks more like a row of thick apothecary jars placed on a bed of iron filings. The magnetist looks down in horror as the hidden mechanism of her art is laid bare.

"Listen, Félicité, we warned you. This is how we end up making a ruckus."

"You don't really expect us to believe that you've been soaking up your maharajah's magnetism without a little pillow talk on the side."

"Don't muss my dress. I'd be happy to fill you in, if you'll just leave."

"Pique our interest and we'll scram."

Ed and Jones release Félicité. It's like letting go of a life buoy.

"With Zamor, it's hard to tell, 'cause he likes to brag. One thing I do know is that he was du Barry's personal stud. But not too long ago he had a thing with some woman writer by the name of Olympe de Gouges. She's one of those kind who thinks she knows all about black people just 'cause she wrote a play about slavery."

Olympe doesn't seem to be too dear to Félicité's heart.

"She cast a spell on him. She made him shine. For the first time, everyone was more interested in the turban on top of his head than the tip of his you-know-what. But then she got tired of him. As far as I'm concerned, she's the kind who needs a black man so she can write about blacks, and a horse so she can write about horses. On top of that, after she sent him on his way like some servant, once she got put in La Force Prison, she called him back to get her pregnant so she could escape the guillotine."

Ed and Jones pretend not to be shocked by what Félicité is saying.

"But it didn't work. Long story short, Olympe has it in for Zamor, and he thinks she dried him up. That's why he comes to my séances."

"And what does the leopard boy have to do with all this?"

"Zamor was looking after him for awhile, and then the kid disappeared."

"And then what happened?"

"I already told you, nobody in Haarlem is going to talk to you about him. Except for Moka! Go pay him a visit! That man knows it all. On top of making the best coffee in Paris, he's got a whole library in his head."

Ed and Jones drop Félicité, who plops down into the baquet like a drunk in front of a bottle. Ed and Jones go back to Mac's restaurant. Groundhog and Spike have left the premises.

"What do we do now, Jones?"

"We wait for Moka."

"I'm not going to hang around here like some subaltern army orderly. The least we can do is pretend to be on the march."

"Don't bother. Look!"

The little golden man emerges from the edge of the crowd. Moka is headed straight for them, card in hand.

"Citizens! Citizens! If you please! I'm . . ."

Ed stops him before Living Memory can recite all of his titles.

"Don't wear yourself out, Moka. We're ready to talk to you now."

Without even realizing it, Ed and Jones tip their hats to him.

"Really? . . . Citizens, what an honor. Wait. Let me get my color wheel out."

The little golden man pulls something from his bag that looks like a fan made of paper tabs in varying shades of brown. He holds several of them up to Ed's face and then Jones's face.

"Just what do you think you're doing, Moka?"

"I'm trying to see what color you are."

* * *

Groundhog has slipped under a gray cab parked on 121st Street. The vehicle is empty. It is standing in front of a gambling establishment called the Jack of Diamonds. It's Doctor Seiffert's carriage, all right. It's all there—the tear in the top, the odor of medicine. Groundhog puts his ear to the door. Perhaps the Doctor left Coco in the cab. Meanwhile, Spike is trying to distract the driver.

"Citizen, can you tell me how to get to 121st Street?"

"You're standing on it, you moron!"

Try as he might, Groundhog can't hear anything inside. The mutt isn't in there.

"Don't get upset. I'm just trying to find 121st Street."

"Hey! Jackass! I'm gonna help you find the end of my whip!"

Groundhog motions Spike back. They get behind the carriage and stake out the entrance to the Jack of Diamonds.

"Hey, Groundhog. What makes you so sure your Doctor's inside?"

"Because I'm using deductive reasoning."

"What's deductive reasoning?"

"I took something you said, that the gray carriage often passes by Mac's restaurant, and another thing I heard while I was with the Moineaux Street gang . . . *Your informant! The famous Zamor! That maharajah who's squandering all our money at the Jack of Diamonds* . . . And I put two and two together."

"That's deductive reasoning?"

"No, that's a more like a double merger. After taking these two things into consideration, I said to myself . . ."

"You supposed to talk to yourself in deductive reasoning?"

"Yep. 'Specially if you talk to yourself like you didn't know yourself. Then you see if you understood yourself or not."

"I don't need nobody else for that. I don't understand myself already."

"Don't mix me up, Spike. Now where was I? The carriage . . . the Jack of Diamonds . . . Zamor . . . the Doctor . . . Hang it all! Now my reasoning's all mixed up! I'll have to do it all over again."

"No, you won't, Groundhog, 'cause your reasoning just turned up right across the street."

Spike points at Zamor, who is leaving the Jack of Diamonds dressed like a maharajah and headed straight toward them. Then Doctor Seiffert comes into view. He's running after Zamor. In a flash, Groundhog and Spike hide behind the gray carriage. The two men engage in vehement discussion. They must have lost big. The Doctor pushes the maharajah inside.

"Listen up, Zamor! I need that kid."

"Doctor Seiffert, I already told you I was on it."

"You really think you're going to get the kid back while you're gambling at Thirty-One, playing at passe-dix and losing?"

"Calm down! First I have to go see La du Barry in prison. But the warden at Sainte-Pélagie Prison told me to wait until seven o'clock tonight."

"And your Countess is still up for it?

"She has no choice. She needs money. And lots of it, if she's ever going to reach your colleague Dr. Belhomme's private clinic in Charonne."

"Zamor, if I've told you once, I've told you twice. Belhomme is not my colleague. He's nothing but a carpenter who's now making a living helping the people who can pay a fortune to stay in his clinic escape the guillotine."

"Right. And the Countess is broke."

"So what they're saying in Paris is true? There's nothing left of the famous coffer of jewels that Louis XV gave her?"

"Correct."

"Zamor, everyone says you played a significant role in emptying it. Especially since the Countess was put in prison and you were given the task of overseeing the sealing of her estate in Louveciennes."

"If that were the case, Doctor, why would I go to all this trouble to get La du Barry out of prison?"

"That's what I would like to know. I really cannot believe that you have any feelings for this woman. She really humiliated you. No, it's something else."

"Doctor Seiffert, I am shocked, shocked, at your doubts about my feelings for her. Do you not recall that people thought the same thing about you regarding the Princesse de Lamballe? And when I say 'people,' you know who I'm talking about."

Seiffert feels like slashing Zamor's face with his scalpel. This maharajah has no business reminding him of that day in October 1787, when, on orders from Marie-Antoinette, the Princess abandoned him in England and went off to join the Queen. He will not forget it now, and he will not forget it ever. He will make Marie-Antoinette pay!

"Drop it, Zamor! It's better that way. Since we have the time, why don't you explain instead how your Countess can help us with the child, given that she has nothing left to her name."

"She has nothing except for one thing, Doctor, and it's a treasure. A treasure that can save her life. It's the Maréchal de Saxe's Black Pearl!"

Doctor Seiffert heaves a sigh. One hundred times over, Zamor has explained the story of the unique pearl that Louis XV gave to the Maréchal de Saxe following his victory at Fontenoy. The Maréchal later gave that same pearl to one of the uhlans in his corps of black guards as a reward. This uhlan was Black Delorme's father. Later, under circumstances that the Doctor could not recall, the pearl had been taken away from the uhlan and offered to La du Barry by Louis XV. In memory of his father, Delorme wants it back at all costs. Now the Doctor needs explanation one hundred and one to finally get the story straight.

"In fact, it's elementary, my dear Doctor Seiffert. Three of you are involved here: Delorme, La du Barry, and yourself, Doctor."

Zamor draws a triangle in the condensation on the glass window of the carriage.

"Each one of you has something the other one wants. Delorme has the child. La du Barry is in possession of the Black Pearl. As for you, Doctor, you hold La du Barry's freedom in the palm of your hand."

"That's a bit of an oversimplification, isn't it?"

"Doctor, you alone can obtain an order for La du Barry authorizing her transfer from Saint-Pélagie Prison to the Belhomme Clinic. Then we'll be in business."

Zamor returns to his window-fog diagram. Seiffert pretends to follow along.

"Look! We make La du Barry trade the Black Pearl for her freedom. We give the pearl to Delorme, and he gives us the child. It just a plain, old, everyday *échange à trois*."

Doctor Seiffert stares at the window-fog diagram. He hopes that reality will be easier to read than the diagram.

"OK, Zamor. But what if I can't get La du Barry transferred to the Belhomme Clinic?"

Zamor wipes the window with the back of his sleeve. All that's left is a gray hole. That clarifies things. This time, Seiffert gets it.

"The time has come, Doctor! Off we go to Sainte-Pélagie Prison to see La du Barry!"

Groundhog and Spike slide under the carriage. They haven't quite understood the story of the pearl, the Countess, and the boy, but it makes them want to hitch a ride even if it means an uncomfortable trip hanging from the axles.

* * *

Ed feels the skin on his face twitch with rage.

"Say what, Moka? You want to look and see what color we are? Ain't it obvious?"

He doesn't quite know how to go about shooting piercing looks at the little Gilded Man who's full of pockmarks already.

"Can't you see we're both black like you?"

"It's not that easy, Brothers! Now look here Coffin Ed, you're . . ."

He flips his color wheel in front of Ed's face.

"Let's see . . . Kettle Black . . . And Grave Digger is . . . hmmm . . . more like . . . Charcoal Gray . . ."

Ed and Jones look as if they're seeing each other for the first time.

"What? Moka, is this some kind of a joke?"

"Brothers, this ain't no joke. It's scientific. Seventy-four different skin tones in blacks and mulattoes have been named and observed. I need to identify the one hue that corresponds exactly to your skin color so I can make an action figure out of you."

"What action figure?"

Ed and Jones now think that Moka is even more pockmarked, even more gilded, and even crazier than they had first thought.

"Brothers, I thought you were already in the loop. I'm talking about the little figurines that come in my packets of coffee. I already got Mirabeau, Louis XVI, the Princess of Lamballe, Marat, Voltaire, and Rousseau. And there'll be more!"

Ed and Jones think that he's in no danger of running out of models.

"So, Moka, are those the action figures we saw at Mac's?"

"Right on! But given the demand for them in Haarlem, I've decided to start a series with heroes of color! I've already chosen the Chevalier de Saint-George, one of the best minds of our times, General Alexandre Dumas-Davy, who's in the army right now. Of course, there are the leaders of the revolt in Saint Domingue, Biassou and Toussaint, and others still . . . and . . . yourselves! Ed Coffin and Gravedigger Jones, the first black police officers in Haarlem."

Ed and Jones turn a light "proud to be me" hue that is probably not on the color wheel.

"What about Zamor?"

Jones thinks that he has done a fine job of shining light on that particular figurine.

"He'll be included too. He'll be formally recognized as the official lover of the Countess du Barry, favorite of King Louis XV. And let's not forget his affair with the playwright Marie Olympe de Gouges . . ."

"And Delorme? You gonna make his action figure?"

"Done."

"Under what pretense, Moka? As one of the assassins of the Princesse de Lamballe, or as the one who burned my face with acid?"

"Gentlemen, it is not my job to put him on trial. I just make the figurines. History will do the judging."

"You're nothin' but a cop-out! You sit around making miniature figurines while everybody else does the dirty work!"

Suddenly Moka stands stock-still, removes his spectacles, and looks Ed straight in the eye.

"Take a good look, Edmond Coffin. You know how I got these pockmarks all over my face and body?"

"We heard you got shot on a slave ship."

"You heard right. With rotten coffee beans shot from loaded cannons. On the *Apollo,* a slave ship under the command of René Auguste de Chateaubriand. I was already fifteen years old when they came to Africa and stole me away from there. During the voyage there was a mutiny. And we didn't just sit back and let them get away with it. That's how I ended up looking like this!"

Moka points to the pockmarks forever imprinted on his skin. Ed feels like apologizing. But he doesn't know how.

"It's been about forty years now, Gentlemen, and the pain has never left me, not even for one day. When I got my freedom, I wanted to go back and see the captain, just to show him the marks that were left on my body. Brittany was a long way away. When I passed through Saint-Malo, I was proud. How rich and clean it was! A little because of us. But when I got to Combourg, at Mr. de Chateaubriand's country manor, and when I saw that beautiful estate, I was ashamed. I wasn't ashamed of him, I was ashamed of myself. I was ashamed of being there, of being dirty, raggedy, tired, and poor. I was the slave who was ashamed in the presence of the master! I spent the night crying in a ditch and then I came back here. That was the day I decided to start making action figures, so that we would never forget."

Ed and Jones feel like awkward and ungainly clods. Regardless, Ed has a question.

"So what ever became of the ship's captain?"

"René Auguste de Chateaubriand? He's dead. And his son, François René, is starving in London. One of these days he'll come back here and write about things that he don't know nothin' about. Then I'll make an action figure outta him!"

Moka explodes into laughter. It's a laugh to burst all subcutaneous coffee beans. Ed and Jones laugh too. My, how laughter clears the air! They end up stopping in front of a sign that reads, *Moka, Coffee Roaster Since 1632.* They hadn't noticed that Moka had been leading them there.

"My factory, Gentlemen!"

"It's a church!"

"It's Saint Zita, Patron Saint of Lost Causes. I acquired it when the holdings of the clergy were being liquidated. I've been paying for it with assignat certificates that are losing value every day. The longer I wait, the less it costs me. Six months ago, a one-hundred-pound assignat certificate could be had for thirty francs. Today you can get it for ten. So now, I just wait."

"So you're a speculator, Moka?"

"Time is the speculator, not me."

Ed and Jones prefer not to think about the daily depreciation of their soldier's pensions.

"You'll see. Inside my workshop in Saint-Zita, there are some characters who'll interest you."

"Like who?"

"Like you."

* * *

Lying flat on his belly, the Commander watches the next visitor through the glass roof. He hums a Spanish lament from back home. The Song of the Caiman. A song of foreboding . . . *Hoye que te coge ese animal. Y te puede devorar* . . . Run, because this animal will catch you and devour you . . . But the object of his attention will not have time to run away. It's an old man with long white hair. He is bent over a naked body stretched out on a stone table. It's the slender body of a boy. Next to him, at hip level, sits an hourglass that the old man turns over. Immediately a scalpel makes an incision in the lower abdomen at the groin. The opening is small and clean. The Commander admires the blade work. In spite of his age, Norcia still has a quick and steady hand.

As for the rest of the operation, the Commander knows all about it. You have to act fast, otherwise putrefaction will blacken the insides all the way down to the bone. Norcia slides his first and second fingers under the skin. He probes the entrails. He finds the cord and the testicles. He pulls, cuts, and ties. Voilà! It's done! He turns the hourglass back over again. All he has to do now is sew it up. This is how they've been doing it for centuries in Italy—that's how the barbers back home in Lecce create the castrati who will either die in the days following the operation or who will become princes, idolized in all of Europe. Except that today the young boy being castrated is a cadaver, his head has been chopped off, and Norcia is the only one doing any singing.

The old Italian still has his falsetto voice. That way he'll have something to take with him when he dies! The Commander checks to make sure that the blade of his machete slides smoothly in and out of its sheath. He lifts a panel and drops down from the glass roof. He lands just behind Norcia. The old man does not flinch. He calmly picks up the scalpel from the dissecting table and turns around. Norcia looks as impassive as Il Dottore, the stock character from the Italian Commedia dell'arte. He doesn't even seem surprised.

"Commander! Itsa . . . beena longa time."

Norcia has also retained the idiosyncrasies of the Italian accent. He points to the headless cadaver.

"Did you see my operation? Yes, you did. Of course you did. You were hiding up there. You are just like a black panther. Now you see him, now you don't and, pfft!"

The old man mimes a wild animal batting at its prey. The Commander thinks that Norcia still has some life left in him. He'll have to keep his guard up. The Commander backs up to one of the dusty glass cases encumbered with medical instruments and vital organs of painted plaster.

"You saw me! I beat the hourglass, eyes closed! I can put my fingers into a man's belly and they do the walking all on their own."

Waving his hands as if they were a couple of Sicilian mari-
onettes, the old surgeon palms the scalpel and slips it up his coat
sleeve. The Commander doesn't miss a thing.

"Anda you, Commander, what have you been up to since the
last time you needed my services? Youa still living on your islands
with your lovely black beauties? You keep them satisfied, no?
You are a stud, yes? It's a little bit thanks to me, no?"

Arms crossed, the Commander continues to watch the old
man and says nothing.

"Ah, si. Itsa true. Always so mysterious. The silent type. *Co-
mandatore que dice niente!* . . . I should have operated on your
voice, not the boy's."

The old surgeon stops short. He senses that the blade has cut
the flesh too deeply. He pulls the steel back out. Too late.

"Norcia, you brought the boy up, not me. Keep talking."

"I was wrong! For this boy, I have already been punished.
Look! People have turned away from me. I used to be Norcia da
Lecce! Today, I'm just the Norcia who is forced to practice on
leftover cadavers from the guillotine."

"And whose fault is that, Norcia?"

"Mine, of course. But remember, Commander! For you, I restored much more than just your voice. That's something no man
can ever forget."

Norcia stares the Commander in the eyes. He has the look of
a moneylender come to collect on his IOU.

"I don't owe you a thing, Norcia! I paid in full for that job."

"That job? That's what you call the privilege of being able to
love women without running the risk of making bastard babies?
You think that job was some kind of vulgar condom made from
animal intestines?"

The Commander says nothing.

"I know you. Since you're not talking, that must mean you
have come here to kill me."

"You are probably right."

"*E la vita!* . . . But before that, you will of course accept to
have a drink with me."

"Only if it is Amarone."

"Follow me."

Norcia and the Commander leave the laboratory, each keeping a close eye on the other. They walk through jumbled corri-

dors and end up behind a red velvet curtain. They pass through it and find themselves on the stage of a tiny theater built in the Italian style. Placed at its center, as on a set, are two armchairs, a low table, four wine glasses, and a bottle of Amarone.

"You see, Commander, I was expecting you."

* * *

Ed and Jones look around at Moka's studio. It resembles the workshop of a santon statuette maker. The fire burning in the brick oven fills the room with dancing shadows. The shelves are crowded with a dusty army of white terra-cotta figurines.

Moka gives Ed and Jones their miniature likenesses. Each man places one in an open palm. They are firing their .38s into the air. How does Moka know them so well? Ed and Jones feel that any minute now they will hear themselves yell, *Straighten up! Count off!* It's a strange feeling to hold yourself in the palm of your own hand. Moka continues the tour.

"I set up shop in one of the caves beneath Saint-Zita's. The church was built over an old quarry. It's hard to believe, but right under our feet are huge caverns and a dried-up branch of the Bièvre River."

"Now, Moka, we know that you didn't bring us all the way here just to tell us the story of Saint Zita!"

"Chill! Take a look!"

The Gilded Man lights a copper chandelier adorned with three emerald opaline oil lamps that he raises to the ceiling by pulling on a chain. The light falls on the felt cloth of a billiard table.

"As is often the case in Haarlem, this cellar must have served as a storeroom. That's where the table was. As you can see, I've re-created a replica of the parishes of Paris and placed it on top of this table."

On this field of green, the city appears to have been transported to the countryside. Ed and Jones didn't know that there were so many saints scattered around Paris.

"As you can see, I've placed a few historical figures here and there, some of whom should be of interest to you."

Ed and Jones recognize Marat in his bathtub, Charlotte Corday with her ebony-handled knife, Camille Desmoulins holding an oak leaf, and Fouquier-Tinville standing behind his table. Ed and Jones come to realize that a man is recognized by his accessories. They'll have to remember that when they're ready go down in history.

At the miniature Conciergerie, Marie-Antoinette is alone and somewhat isolated. Jones seems more intrigued than anyone.

"Moka, how do you know so much about what's goin' down?"

"I have a whole web of informants. I call them my spiders. They hide in the tiniest holes in the walls while weaving a web that covers the entire city. I stand at the center of it. All I have to do is wait."

Jones is incredulous. He really wants to check out Moka's web.

"So let's see you tell us where Zamor is on your little replica here."

"There he is right there. He's between 121st and the old Sainte-Pélagie convent."

He points to the figure of a turban-wearing maharajah. On its base, Ed reads the inscription, *François Sébastien Zamor (1751–)*.

"Gentlemen, your Zamor is going to pay La du Barry a visit in prison."

Jones examines the Countess: *1743–* . The blank space haunting her birth date is not very reassuring.

"Moka, if you really want to help us, now would be a good time to show us where the leopard boy is."

"You got a figurine of him?"

"And under what pretense, Gentlemen, would I have made the child's likeness?"

If they had the answer to that question, Ed and Jones would not be here playing army with him. Moka looks down at his tricolor watch and counts on his fingers.

"Sorry, Gentlemen, but I got to go. It's almost time for me to make my Posterity rounds. But before that, I'm going to give you a little help."

Moka takes the action figures and places them on the billiard table mockup of Paris and moves them around with a roulette rake.

"First, we'll place the ladies. Marie-Antoinette and La du Barry are already waiting for us. Let's slide the Marquise d'Andeçon home."

Ed thinks she's the most beautiful of them all. He doesn't dare imagine that he could actually pick her up and take her into his hands.

"That's it for the ladies. Let's move on to the gents. This won't take as long. This is a story that's all about the ladies."

"Cut the crap, Moka! Why don't you give us a straight answer?"

"Because, simply put, Gentlemen, you have to earn action-figure status!"

"We don't want to be made into action figures! We want to find the leopard boy, return him to the Marquis d'Andeçon, and become farmers in Ohio!"

Moka bursts into laughter.

"Farmers in Ohio? Is that all you're after?"

"Yep! With pigs and chickens and cows!"

"Well, if that's all you want, then here! I'll give you your leopard boy!"

Moka pulls a wooden box from a shelf and opens it out over the billiard table. A torrent of figurines cascades on to the map of Paris. They are thrown down in a jumble, bounce off one another, and mix together without breaking. The biggest one falls over Haarlem and lands in a heap. They even seem to hear a horde of giants pounding on the roof of Saint-Zita.

"Gentlemen, here's the leopard boy! He's all yours. I'm off to make my Posterity rounds. They're waiting for me at Sainte-Pélagie."

"What's this about Posterity rounds?"

"Posterity doesn't seem to interest you two gentlemen. All you care about are cattle!"

Moka picks up his bag, places his gold-plated hat on his head, and leaves through the stairwell that leads up to the church. Ed and Jones are taken aback by Moka's abrupt departure and are at a loss before the figurines lying in disarray. The Boss is chatting with the Marquise, while Zamor, under La du Barry's watchful eye, is pushed up against an indifferent Marie-Antoinette.

"Hey, Jones, does any of this make any sense to you?"

"It sure does, at least according to what the Marquise told us while we were down in the crypt. We're in Haarlem, so anything's possible!"

Gingerly, Ed pulls an action figure from the pile, as if he were afraid of waking the others.

"Who's this guy? He looks like a sugarcane cutter, armed with that machete."

"And this old woman? Doesn't she look familiar?"

Ed and Jones remember the blind woman and her son in the Boss's tavern. And who's this? And who's that? Now Ed and Jones paw at the action figures with the excitement of a couple of treasure hunters.

"Here he is! I found him! Look. I have him in the palm of my hand! It's the leopard boy!"

They move the figure so that he appears to be seated on a throne.

"Hey, that's not him! That's Groundhog!"

Jones takes a closer look. It's true. The kid is holding his sword and looks like he's made a fool out of this citizen.

"What's he doing in this story, anyway? It doesn't make any sense, especially since I found this lying next to the Queen."

Ed opens his hand. Seated in his palm is a little dog with a great big tongue hanging out of his mouth.

* * *

Groundhog and Spike cling to the carriage chassis. They watch the pavement slide away behind the clatter of its wheels and the creaking of its body. Any minute now, the next bump will break this crate to bits. They imagine Zamor chatting with the Doctor, both seated comfortably above them.

"Hey, Chipmunk! How would you describe the sound of horses' hooves?"

Groundhog tosses off an onomatopoeia. Clippityclop!, Clippityclop! Spike likes it, and sure enough, the horses copy the sound right off the bat. Clippityclop! . . . Clippityclop!

His belly aching, Groundhog thinks of Coco. He promised Pretty Sidonie that he would return him to her. But first he must take him from the Doctor and escape. When he's running, Groundhog is unbeatable. The carriage slows down and comes to a stop. Groundhog sticks his head out from under the carriage. It's Sainte-Pélagie Prison. He and Spike poke at one another. They're both still in one piece.

* * *

Ed and Jones drop the figurines on the billiard table, climb the stairs leading up to the church, and run down the nave.

"Moka! Wait up!"

The church is full. The rows are peopled with well-behaved negroes made of painted plaster. They bear torches, play guitars, hold candelabras, or act as clothes racks. Moka is seated in a pew. His spectacles perched on his nose, he is busy sorting through a sheaf of yellow papers piled on top of his satchel.

"What seems to be the trouble, Gentlemen? Have you lost your cows?"

Moka does not even bother to look up from his papers as he flings the congenialities that echo through the church. Ed and Jones do not want to admit that all those action figures have made them dizzy and that they need Moka to help them make sense of it all. They would rather change the subject.

"Say, Moka, what's with the statues?"

"The youth of Haarlem have organized a Front for the Liberation of Domestic Negroes. They snatch them up whenever they see one of these humiliating plaster black men . . . That's how they put it. Then they release them into the forest at Bondy."

Ed and Jones are stunned. They never imagined that there were so many blacks in captivity.

"Come, Gentlemen. We'll have to go through the rectory to get my car and take it to Sainte-Pélagie."

La du Barry's prison! That's how Ed and Jones think of it. The very idea of meeting the Countess ignites all kinds of strange desires inside them. They arrive at the rectory.

"That your car, Moka?"

"Sure is!"

Or it might have been at one time. But the contraption parked in front of the gate is now something else entirely. Hitched to the horse is a kind of hearse. The passenger compartment has been raised and now perches atop a protuberance that makes the vehicle look like a giant package of coffee. Painted gold and black down to the horse's blinders, the rig flaunts the motto, *Moka rex Arabica Company, Founded 1632.*

"Is this a family business, Moka?"

"Not in the least. But people like to think that what they eat and drink is old-style, so . . ."

Ed and Jones get into the hearse without saying a word. Moka climbs up to the driver's seat and launches the apparatus onto the pavement.

"Keeping memories alive is all well and good, Gentlemen, but I gotta make a living!"

The golden hearse draws away from Saint-Zita and exits Haarlem through the stone arch. In Rue de l'Enfer, a mist still lingers with the night, but already the warm smell of coffee rattles on through it.

*　*　*

Seated at her table, Marie-Antoinette rereads the beginning of her letter . . . *This October 15, at half past four in the morning* . . . She feels that nothing has happened since she left the courtroom. Back in her cell, a deluge of thoughts had assailed her and it had been necessary to put them in order. Writing them down had seemed of the utmost urgency. She has almost forgotten that there is a quota on everything, including her paper and her candle. To write! She must! To write, but to whom? Madame Elisabeth, of course! That devoted soul, her good Louis's sister. She will act as her messenger. But what to say, how to order her thoughts, and where to begin?

This October 15, half past four in the morning . . . Dear God! She has written the date in the old way, and she is mistaken. Today is the 16th. The trial has made her lose her sense of time. If she is not careful, she'll die a day too soon. Marie-Antoinette corrects the error. She turns and gazes at Lieutenant de Busne, who is sleeping in a chair, his head pressed against a corner of the cell. Poor man! He must be exhausted. The good man must rest. He was a worthy escort when she left the courtroom, and he lent her a steady arm as she descended that dreadful staircase in Bonbec Tower.

In his sleep, the Lieutenant makes the sounds of a child who has difficulty breathing. Like the first Dauphin. She thinks back to that night in Meudon when she had not even been allowed to keep a vigil over her son's body. Ah, the rules of etiquette! She often thinks that the child had the good grace to leave just in time and to avoid having to face all of this. How well advised he had been!

Marie-Antoinette returns to the letter addressed to Madame Elisabeth. She must hurry. Her quill is so slow . . . *I am calm, as one is when one's conscience is irreproachable. I feel profound sorrow at having to abandon my poor children; you know that I existed only for them and for you, my dear, sweet sister* . . .

THE LEOPARD BOY

The quill crosses the paper under a candle's dim light. From time to time, Marie-Antoinette stops and ticks off the words in a diagonal line across the page, then counts on her knuckles. Will Elisabeth remember their secret code? She must be the only one to understand this confession. Her censors, Fouquier-Tinville and Hermann, will read it. Will the letter even reach her? She must at least pretend to believe that it will. Let us continue.

. . . *I must tell you of a matter that causes my heart much sorrow. I know how much this child must have distressed you. Forgive him my dear sister. Think of his age . . .*

Marie-Antoinette rereads the end of the passage that she has just written. She shudders. Is it too obvious? Scratching it out would make it look even more suspicious. Her hand trembles as she dips the quill into the inkwell. A blotch! A blotch would be her fault, as it was on her wedding day when she signed the register. But who would have imagined the existence of this child? She, his own mother, had not even known of it. The candle flickers. Her hand begins to write again, more steadily.

. . . *and how easy it is to make a child say what one wishes him to say and to make him say things he does not even understand . . .*

Marie-Antoinette lifts her eyes to the tiny window of her cell. She is waiting for dawn. It is through that window that it will come. But not yet. She continues to compose her letter . . . *I sincerely ask God to forgive all of the misdeeds that I may have committed over the course of my existence. I hope that in His bounty, He will mercifully hear my final prayers, as well as those longtime and ever constant prayers asking that He receive my soul into His goodness and mercy.*

She watches as the candle consumes itself. Antoinette recalls how impatiently she would wait for the candles to burn down during those tedious concerts by Lulli. Instinctively, her fingers tap the table. Glück! She recalls the Commander's determined face at the Tribunal. How rigid he was! In his day, at the slightest touch of a hand brushing across the keys of a harpsichord he would have bid her to leave the court for his sake.

I forgive all of my enemies for the evils they have done to me. I bid adieu to my aunts and to all of my brothers and sisters. I had friends.

Her heart aches. She thinks of Fersen. And yet she had decided that he was to be forbidden to her. That tender heart! He must be furious with himself for not saving her. Even she had not been able to come to the aid of her dearest friend, the Princesse de Lamballe. She hears the shouts of the crowd, back in that month of September '92. My God! It has already been a year. She remembers the King's troubled voice.

"No, my dear, do not go. It is Madame, Superintendent of the Royal Household. How horrible!"

Below her windows at the Temple Prison, where they were being held, her powdered head was being paraded around on the end of a pike. Why had the Princess returned to France? She had come to join her in Paris. What folly! At the time, she had not understood the note that the Princess had sent her.

Madame, I am returning to Paris. Because here, there is someone of your own blood who will be most dear to you, over whose well-being I have watched in your name ever since he took his first breath and who is in great danger of savagery.

Now she understands. Secretly, Madame de Lamballe had taken this child into her protection. How ungrateful and unjust she had been toward the Princess! How she now regrets her cruel and futile games with Madame de Polignac, who had so quickly abandoned her.

There is movement behind her cell door. She must finish her letter.

Think of me always, I embrace you with all my heart, along with those poor, dear children. My God! How heart-wrenching it is to leave them forever! Adieu! Adieu! Henceforth, I will attend to nothing but my spiritual duties.

Up above her, it looks as though Sunrise cannot wait to peer through her cell window.

7

SAINTE-PÉLAGIE PRISON

Sunrise had decided that every morning he would shine his light on a different woman. Today he had chosen Sainte-Pélagie Prison, corner of Rue de la Clef and Rue du Puits-de-l'Hermite. In the middle of that gray stone façade, up on the second floor, just behind the lower corner of that fifth window, is the infirmary. Inside, Madame Roland wants to die.

She is seated on the edge of her straw mattress, holding a sheet of paper. Her long black hair falls unfettered to her waist. With a few well-aimed rays, Sunrise tries to revive her will to live. He goes to her and moves softly over her long neck and face, to bring back the feel of a caress. But she chases him off. He returns, runs across her arms, brushes her inner thigh and knee. The woman does not even quiver. He falls at her feet. She ignores him. So he relents and sheds his light among some scattered leaves on the ground.

Sunrise is annoyed with himself. He should have chosen the Queen. Perhaps it is not too late. Hastily, he dashes off and takes flight. But when, winded, he appears, the Queen has her head in her hands. Her letter is already finished. It lies on the table, and the candle is still flickering. He thrums the window, in an effort to attract her attention. *Tap! Tap! Tap! . . . Madame! Madame! . . . It's me! I'm here!* The Queen will see him. She will be surprised. *Oh, my God, you have finally arrived! I almost missed you . . .* And so she will add to the bottom of her letter . . . *Postscriptum . . . The sun is rising.*

But Marie-Antoinette does not even look up at him. He's out of luck. He will rise neither for Madame Roland nor for the Queen. As humans say, this is just one of those days. And that's just too bad. Sunrise decides to be democratic and goes off to shine his light on a nobody.

* * *

"Oh my God, I've missed it!"

Marie-Antoinette is angry with herself. She allowed the moment when daylight entered her cell to slip by. That single moment. Never again will there be another. This thought tears at her heart. Even so, these times are nothing more than a procession of final days. Her husband, her children, her sister. And yet, it is this tiny instance of time gone by that makes her realize that from this point on everything else will also slip through her fingers.

Marie-Antoinette startles. Suddenly she spies a man leaning against her cell wall. The man is looking her over. It is not Lieutenant de Busne. Never would he have taken such a careless pose. This is a different gendarme altogether.

"Please excuse my reaction, Monsieur, and please do not take offense. I had not seen you."

The man does not respond. His gaze is one that she now knows well. It is the gaze of those who have filed past her cell day and night, here or in the Temple Prison. There were those who had come to see "the Austrian," "Madame Veto," or the decadent "Empress Messalina." If she really tries hard, she can read the nickname in their eyes. This fellow, with his head cocked to one side, is a kind of horse trader. He evaluates her haunches and measures her bosom like a knacker squeezing a mare's teats. He finds hers to be a lot smaller and sagging much lower than he had expected. He is disappointed. At the tavern tonight, he will proclaim . . . *I do believe that Madame Deficit will not be leaving us much recompense!* They will laugh.

Marie-Antoinette thinks of her body. She hopes that in the hours to come, it will stop bleeding. It is not this female blood that they want. They want the blood of a queen. Otherwise they would feel cheated.

"Tell me soldier, has Lieutenant de Busne gone away?"

"He has been arrested, Citizen."

"For what reason?"

"I am not authorized to share that information with you, Citizen."

She imagines the reason why. The mere offering of a supportive arm in a stairwell could lead to death as easily as dancing the minuet. Marie-Antoinette shivers. When will misfortune cease to strike those who come near her? Especially the men. She will end up believing in the curse of the rotten tooth. Many times she had been told that, on the day of her birth, her mother, the Empress Maria Theresa of Austria, had had an extremely decayed tooth pulled while in labor during the birth of her fifteenth child. One tooth less, one daughter more. Such a bad omen on that November 2, a day when Masses are said for the dead.

Her mother had been right. Marie-Antoinette does bring bad luck. She wishes she had not encouraged the plans of those who had tried to save her. This afternoon, even. During the interruption in the debates. Instead of her dear Rosalie, a heavily made-up woman that she did not know had come to bring her some broth. The woman had whispered, *Be ready. It will happen just across from number 400, right after you pass Robespierre's lodgings. At the Red Porch!*

From that moment on, Marie-Antoinette keeps repeating, *Opposite number 400. Robespierre.* It will be on Rue Saint-Honoré, then . . . *the Red Porch.* She cannot stop her heart from fluttering in her chest. How credulous it still is!

*   *   *

Dame Catherine and Pobéré take Rue de la Vannerie and enter the Cave des Charbonniers, the Coalmen's Wine Cellar. They go directly up to see the wine merchant on the second floor. In the low-ceilinged room, straw is strewn on a floor piled with empty crates while cookware hangs from the ceiling beams. Two men and a woman wait silently seated in a circle under a lantern, playing a game of piquet. Off in a corner, a fellow with shoulders the size of an ox yoke nurses a lamb with a baby bottled fitted with a brass nipple.

When the blind woman arrives, they make room for her. She stands in front of them.

"I hear a suckling sound. Are you still playing nursemaid, Merlin?"

"You have to understand, Dame Catherine, they had to slaughter his mother. Since then, he won't leave my side."

"Are you planning on giving him to the Queen?"

The assembly emits a kindly laugh. Merlin looks sheepish.

"Are you all here, my brave hearts? Speak up, so that I can see you!"

Everyone has something to say. Jean-Baptiste, Guillaume, and Elisabeth.

Dame Catherine gestures with her hand. They set to work. Pobéré unfolds a map on top of his shoeshine stool. Forgoing any preliminaries, the blind woman begins to speak.

"It will take place at the Red Porch as planned. Right . . . here!"

Pobéré points to a red X placed at the end of Rue Saint-Honoré, near Rue Royale.

"On the odd-numbered side of the street, across from number 400, past the Duplay house. He's that wood seller who fattens and houses Robespierre. The porch is red, the color of beef blood. We will act when the Queen's carriage passes. It will arrive on Rue de la Monnaie."

"What do we know about who is in her guard?"

"Wait, Guillaume! Before reviewing the details of our plan, I need to know the answer to a question that has been on my mind. What about the executioner?"

A collective shiver runs through the little group. The word "executioner" cuts the murmur to its own measurement.

Dame Catherine continues.

"You know that this Sanson is even more gigantic and even stronger than his father, the one who cut Louis XVI down to size. He's a real piece of work. He's young, but he carries his two hundred pounds and seven-foot-tall frame strikingly well."

The murmur becomes one of admiration.

"And that is not all. You need to know, my brave hearts, that the executioner's rules require that 'in the event that the condemned is in danger of escaping his or her punishment, it is the executioner's authorized duty to carry out the sentence by any of the means required by the state of emergency.' Which means . . ."

The brave hearts need clarification.

"That Sanson can strangle the Queen when we attack. And then all would be lost. Therefore, Sanson must be eliminated first. And to take him out, we need a Charlotte Corday. You! Elisabeth! Are you still ready? If you don't want to do it anymore, just say so. Nobody here would blame you for that."

Elisabeth straightens up and stands tall. The look in her eyes is enough to say that she has not given up on the idea. The knife she pulls from her skirts says it all.

"I will plunge these seven inches into Sanson's heart. I swear I will do it for the Queen, with no hesitation whatsoever!"

Guillaume squeezes her hand. It is obvious that he is proud of his wife. Dame Catherine goes to her and embraces her.

"Thank you, Elisabeth. I was sure of your woman's heart. My braves! As soon as you stab Sanson, you will seize the Queen, but not before! And you will spare his assistant. He is still a child."

"There shall be no pity for the executioner's offspring!"

"Jean-Baptiste! I am blind. Will my son be blind too?"

The group concedes. They vote to spare the assistant.

"As soon as you have seized the Queen, you must bring her all the way here!"

Pobéré points to the spot on the map.

"To the Red Porch! There are just thirty feet separating the cart from the porch. But it will be a mad dash. That is where you come in, Merlin!"

"I'm ready, Dame Catherine!"

"You'd better be, my brave, because everything will be riding on you! Sanson has just been stabbed by Elisabeth, the men rush the cart, they put the Queen on your back and you head straight for the Red Porch. You must think of nothing other than that door. If Marie-Antoinette goes through it, they will never be able to catch her again. Not ever!"

They all stare at the tiny space through which it will be necessary to take a queen.

"Once you get beyond the Red Porch, you cross a courtyard, until you reach a garden shed. Once inside, there is a well that connects with an underground network of tunnels and sewer pipes that will take us to the Quai des Tuileries. The route has been marked with white crosses. While we're in the tunnel we'll take the time to disguise the Queen as a chimney sweep. It will be perfect with her hair cut. Once we reach the Quai, we'll go down to the Port aux Huîtres. That is where the Queen will board a sailboat, brought there by Pobéré. Anyone who hasn't slipped behind the Red Porch will have to fall back through the tavern, as agreed, on Rue de la Monnaie. We checked it out."

Pobéré circles the site of Sweet Victory and with his finger follows the route that leads to the Church of Saint-Germain-L'Auxerrois.

"Brave hearts, this time our plan is unstoppable. We cannot fail."

* * *

Norcia and the Commander raise their wine glasses. In unison they shout, *To the one I'm thinking of!* They drink slowly, eyes closed. Norcia takes the cork from the bottle and sniffs it emphatically, his face deeply moved.

"Hummm! Masi Amarone! *L'amarone della valpolicella.* The best wine in the world! *Virilita e grazia* . . . This is the wine used for casting spells. It can hide the most powerful potions. It reveals the soul and regenerates the body. Truth be told, Commander, I think of Amarone as the true blood of Christ."

"Thou shalt not commit blasphemy!"

"Are you worried that I will pass from this world in a state of mortal sin? But tell me again, why am I going to die? Can you remind me?"

Norcia holds out his glass to the Commander.

"You're not going to die, Norcia. Because as far as I'm concerned, you're already dead. You are dead because you castrated this boy."

"Castrated this boy?"

Norcia rises from his armchair and laughs through the trills of his falsetto voice.

"Who told you that tale?"

"Do you deny having worked him?"

"You must know, Commander, that at one time, I 'worked' a lot, as you say. I was the Padrone of Privates! To men, I returned fertility and virility, and to women I restored virginity. People came from all over Europe and entrusted themselves to me. Blue bloods, even."

"Such as the poor Prince de Lamballe?"

"It was too late for him. He already smelled of rotting flesh, devoured as he was by smallpox and half-emasculated. Luckily, it's sometimes a more pleasant task, such as mending the Countess du Barry. Or more secretly, when it concerns the royal family. Louis XVI! Before his operation, he spent seven years without being able to be the Queen's husband. As for the Dauphin, he crushed a royal attribute in the Temple Prison. And the Queen . . ."

"Watch it, Norcia! I will not allow you to sully Her Majesty's honor."

"In that case, *il eût fallu que vous l'interdissiez,* you should have stopped it! Would that you had declared her off-limits to yourself!"

The Commander lowers his head.

"Oh, French language, how I adore your imperfect subjunctive! How disarming it is! Yes, Commander, you were one of the Queen's lovers at the time!"

"Your assertion does not even merit a reaction."

"Are you ashamed of it? No, I rather think that you are afraid. Afraid of the consequences. You are afraid, Commander, that this child is the proof that there is black blood in your lineage."

"And for that, Norcia, I will kill you!"

"What, Commander? You have already killed me. You are not going to proffer more death threats now!"

"So be it, Norcia. You speak in pleasantries and I bow to them. But let us hear how you justify castrating a child. Because that is where we left off."

"I will justify it, Commander, as easily as cutting the leg off a runaway slave on your plantation in Saint Domingue can be justified."

"I exercise the right to apply the law governing slavery as specified in Le Code noir. Are you the type who blames the executioner?"

"Certainly not. But the surgeon in me is curious. When you cut off a limb, do you do it with a machete? The very idea fascinates me. How high up do you make the cut? Above the foot? Above the knee? Do you smash the kneecap before that? What do you do for the pain? Do you use rum? Cocaine? Opium? And how do you treat gangrene? And I have another question. At what point do they scream the loudest?"

The Commander paces back and forth on the stage, hands clasped behind his back.

"You see, Commander, we are almost in the same business. We could even talk about our dexterity. Me with the scalpel, you with the machete."

"That's enough, Norcia! You are desperately trying to change the subject and make me forget about the boy."

"Forget about him? How could I? I remember perfectly the day when they brought him to me. It was for a phimosis. The foreskin was too tight and would not retract. Just like what Louis XVI had. The circumcision went off perfectly. He had returned for a check-up. I was monitoring the healing process. Everything was going wonderfully until the day when tragedy struck."

Norcia strikes a dramatic pose.

"The child was eight years old. It happened right here on this stage. Right where you are now, Commander. The boy used to love to come here after he learned that the Chevalier de Saint-George had played one of his violin compositions here. Suddenly, it was the most extraordinary event of my entire miserable life. It was also the most tragic one."

"Why? What happened, Norcia?"

"The child began to sing. Suddenly, I knew that I had just encountered the most beautiful voice that anyone had ever heard. That does not sound very original I know. But what else can I say? It was truly a miracle! I was in a state of profound beatitude and at the same time, I was terrified."

"Of what?"

"That this treasure would disappear. That the boy's voice would change. Never again would such a unique voice be heard. So, at the very moment when I heard him, I knew that I would make him into . . . a castrato!"

* * *

Moka parks the gilded hearse outside the entrance to Sainte-Pélagie Prison. He checks his tricolor watch: it took fifteen minutes to get here from Haarlem. *Not bad at all,* he muses. Outside the prison gate, men and women stand in a long line. Ed and Jones cannot believe their eyes.

"Visitors this early, Moka?"

"Nope. These are the caterers, wigmakers, barbers, cleaning women, and valets who are here for when the pistoleers wake up."

"The pistoleers?"

"Yeah. The ones with money. Ah, gentlemen, you are true policemen! You throw people into prison, but you don't want to know what happens once they're inside!"

Ed and Jones do not like the word "policemen" because they consider themselves to be soldiers. Moka jumps down from his seat.

"Help me unload my cart."

From the trunk of the hearse, Ed and Jones extract a kind of three-wheeled dray. To this, Moka affixes two round copper drums, each one fitted with a spigot and topped with a row of tin cups hung on a rack. A plaque announces, *Moka rex arabica. Coffee fortifies the limbs, makes the entire body smell good, brings on women's monthlies, and cures scabies.*

"Come on. We're going in. But leave everything to me. If you show your badges around here, they might balk. In here, this is your best bet."

The gilded man tosses a money pouch up and down in his

palm. He hands the pouch to Jones and gives his writing case to Ed. He throws a brown canvas bag over his shoulder and rolls the dray up to the prison gate. A collective grumble rises from the rank-and-file. Moka ignores it. He announces his arrival. The heavy knocker strikes the gate like a warrant being served. The lattice on the Judas window slides back.

"Well, now. If it ain't good old Moka, the purveyor of poison! See that line? Go stand in it!"

Moka shows him the pouch and the canvas bag. On the other side of the Judas window, an eye lights up. This is followed by a rattling of bolts and latches that give way to the keeper's halitosic breath. The man is as rumpled and creased as a night spent curled up on a prison cell floor. Moka slips him a coin to help lift his lids and authoritatively trundles the dray into the narrow entryway. He places a gray canvas bag next to the door and walks up to the barred window. Ed and Jones follow close behind.

"They're with me. My assistants."

The suspicious keeper scratches his cheeks and looks both of them over. He locks the door even more securely and sticks his nose into the contents of the gray canvas bag.

"I thought I told you that when it comes to tobacco, I only like the Brazilian kind!"

The weasel grunts his displeasure. Ed and Jones feel like two magi bearing gifts of leather pouch and writing case. They look around. On this side of the bars, the place stinks like a fishing net full of foul bait. If anyone calls for the guards, they won't have a chance. The keeper drops the bag of tobacco and comes to glare at them up close.

"What's wrong with him? You better not be bringing small-pox in here."

The jailer raises his hand toward Ed's face.

"Mitts off!"

Ed grabs his wrist in midair, twists his arm like a skeleton key in a lock, and secures it to the shoulder backward. This could make the arm break at the elbow. With the crisp, dry sound of a latch being snapped to, the bone could splinter, pierce the flesh and the cloth covering it, and cause fresh blood to spurt out onto the flagstones. But Ed stops short of that and merely jabs a knee into the keeper's kidneys as he muffles his yelps with one hand. He throws him up against the prison bars. The keeper grunts, groans, and begins to drool when he bites down on one. Ed shoves the blue badge in his face.

"Have I made myself clear?"

The keeper tries to practice his diction with the bar between his teeth. What he would really like to say is, "Yes! Perfectly clear!" But his enunciation is slightly impaired. Ed releases him. Moka rushes over to dust the keeper off with a look of false distress. He takes the coin and puts it back into his own pocket and picks the conversation up where it left off.

"What's the news in this can, Citizen?"

"Yesterday, we topped one hundred and fifty prisoners."

"Wonderful. I'll have to get some more cups."

"Those theater ladies have been complaining again. Have you given any further thought to denouncing them? Things are getting out of hand!"

Moka eludes the question, waving his hand as though he were chasing away a fly.

"That it?"

"Uh, don't know. Moka, do you think you could use the council hall today? Because there was a counter-interrogation last night."

"You mean there was an orgy. Aren't they done yet?"

"There are a few stragglers."

"Well, that's just too bad. I need that room. That's the only place where I can fill my barrels. That all, Citizen?"

"Oh, and the football fanatics are organizing a match against Saint-Lazare in the courtyard at nine o'clock. You'll get lots of people then."

"Thank you, Citizen. See, you can be really nice when you want to be."

Moka picks up the gray canvas bag.

"And you're right. Brazilian tobacco is the best. I'll try to find you some."

With his good hand, the keeper opens the gate. He tries not to look at Ed and Jones, who are standing in his way.

"Where can we find Citizen du Barry?"

"Cell number five in the Ideas block, Captain."

"And just where is this Ideas block located?"

"On the upper level. That's where we keep the ones who've had a few too many. Ideas, that is! The floor below that is for the

Players. Those are the thieves and the whores. And below them are the Scarecrows because all they get to sleep on is straw. Same thing on the men's side."

Ed continues on with the investigation.

"Where are the women kept?"

"Come see for yourselves, Citizen Captains."

The keeper bows so often that the keys on the chain around his neck jingle and swing like cowbells. He leads them to a narrow courtyard flanked by two long buildings that stand facing each other.

"This is the women's side and that's the men's side."

"But they're right across from each other!"

"How do you keep them from communicating?"

He shrugs his shoulders in resignation to indicate that it's useless to even try. To prove it, he points to an open window on the Ideas level of the men's side. A prisoner stands completely naked before a mirror shaving with one hand and keeping himself company with the other. This must be what "communication" means.

"By the way, Citizen Captains, I forgot to mention that this used to be a convent. Back then, there wasn't much going on in front of the windows. Saint Pélagie herself used to be a lady of the night before she converted to what used to be known as God."

"While we're at it, who is that Citizen with shaving cream all over himself?"

"He's a general—the Duc de Biron—he used to be called the Duc de Lauzun, so in here he's called the Double Duke. The ladies love him. Did I mention that he was one of the Queen's lovers? He's an eccentric who has the means to satisfy his fantasies."

Ed and Jones admire his means. They are not alone. Across the way, the women's prison is waking up to the magnificent view. Moka joins Ed and Jones, his gold plating slightly tarnished.

"Let's get a move on, Gentlemen! I have my rounds to make! It's almost . . . seven. Give me a hand! I'm going to set up my cart in the council hall so I can start making the coffee. No matter about the orgy. I'll just remove my pince-nez."

They enter the hall.

Moka sets up his machine. He removes the lids from the drums and fills the funnels with ground coffee beans. Meanwhile, Ed and Jones scrutinize the end of Thursday's counter-interrogation. Just as the gatekeeper had predicted, there are stragglers. Enough gray light filters through the window to allow Ed and Jones to locate each other. They gaze though the half light at what seem to be a series of paintings done in shades of gray. They recognize the various obscene postures that would be on display in a philistine antiquities collection. But here, there are no delicately carved, translucent cameos. Instead, the picture is drawn in bold lines. People cavort in unions, indifferent to the idea of mutual consent. A grunt signals an agreement that is finalized on a table, bareback. There is so much shaking that a drawer rattles loose, emitting a series of high-pitched squeaks. Across the room, a poor, defrocked priest is selling off his possessions to the highest bidder. He presents some miserable baubles to a group of bidders who snatch at them voraciously. Elsewhere, patriotic sentiments animate and inflame arduous bodies as they seek to re-create a series of edifying tableaux. Easily recognizable are: Liberty Seated on Tyranny Brandishing his Vigilant Trident, a full-breasted Fountain of Regeneration, flanked by her majestic Circle of Attendants, Blind Justice Weighing Evidence through Touch, Naked Truth, and many more.

Suddenly, Moka strikes a light, igniting a ramp of oil burners lined up under the kettles. The hall is filled with a glow that brings the figures into focus.

"And, gentlemen, voilà! Café de Moka! Take a look. This here is a portable machine for making hot coffee! I have a water supply, a heat source, an alembic coil, a spout, and boiling water that I drip through this fine powder filtered through a silk stocking. It'll be ready in five minutes."

Moka sits down behind the table and looks at his tricolor watch while counting on his fingers. Jones finds this to be a strange habit.

"Why are you always counting on your fingers when you check the time?"

"It's these dang newfangled watches where a day is ten hours long, an hour lasts one hundred minutes, and minutes last one hundred seconds. Some reform! If I didn't have my fingers, I would never know what time it is."

Moka looks at the time again and suddenly slams the cover of the writing case shut.

"Ladies and Gentlemen, I now declare this orgy over!"

* * *

In front of Sainte-Pélagie Prison, Groundhog and Spike are still hiding under the carriage drawn up in front of the prison. They've been there for a while, waiting for Zamor and Doctor Seiffert to get out of the cab. Finally! The two men walk along one of the prison walls. The Doctor is carrying his big black bag. Groundhog thinks that Coco must be hidden inside. Poor dog! He'll suffocate. Zamor and Seiffert walk up to a door so green it looks like it must lead to a garden. The men stand talking in front of it. Their conversation is still just as animated.

"Why have you brought me here, Zamor? This isn't the entrance to the prison."

"This is where the warden who can take us to the men's quarters is waiting."

"I thought we were going to see Madame du Barry."

"Not right away. It's too dangerous."

"Watch it, Zamor, don't try to play any tricks on me."

"Calm down, Doctor! You seem nervous. You could have waited for me out of the cold in the cab."

"Let's get one thing straight, Zamor! I need you, but I don't trust you. I'll not let you out of my sight until I have that boy!"

Seiffert grabs Zamor by the scruff of his maharajah suit. Spike and Groundhog wait until they start pounding on each other to move in closer by skirting a small hillock. It's not yet light enough for them to be seen. The green garden door swings open. They watch Zamor and Seiffert go through it.

Groundhog and Spike run up to it. Too late. It's locked. Spike harpoons the top of the wall with his pike. Groundhog uses it to climb up and straddle the wall. Spike isn't as limber. He huffs and puffs with his tongue hanging out. He looks like a giant tricolor lizard. Sweating, he ends up next to Groundhog, rather more red than white or blue.

Without taking the time to catch their breath, the two clamber down the wall with the help of some ivy. They land with a flourish on the opposite side. On the ground, voices congratulate them.

"Bravo! Good job, Men!"

They look up to see a pumpkin and its zucchini sidekick.

"But if you're trying to escape, you're going the wrong way."

Someone grabs them from behind. Upon closer inspection,

they realize that they are under surveillance, not by a squash
and its companion, but by two other varieties of plant known
as *gendarmes*, who were waiting down below in the dirt. The
garden looks more like an exercise yard in a penitentiary than
a vegetable plot. Near a covered well, Groundhog notices a girl
about his age dressed in a sailor suit, sitting on a swing and reading a giant picture book. She has long, golden locks and big blue
eyes. Groundhog thinks that there are some very pretty things
growing in this garden, in spite of it all.

* * *

"Ladies and Gentlemen! I repeat that Thursday's orgy is now
over!"

Moka's announcement echoes like a gun fired into a tree full
of crows. There is hustle in the patriotic scenes and bustle in the
edifying tableaux. People run from the room, hiding their faces.
Among the refrocked, some engage in male posturing. Ed and
Jones put a stop to that with their blue badges. A young woman
with perfectly arched brows stands completely naked and alone
in the middle of the hall. From underneath a table, she picks up
a curly blond wig, covers her breasts with it, and exits without
uttering a word.

"It's always like this on Thursday nights. That's why I wanted
you to come with me."

"Moka, we're not your bodyguards! Let me remind you that
we're carrying out an investigation here."

The golden man does not have time to answer. A skinny
woman bundled in a black shawl appears before him.

"Did you bring the opium?"

"No, Ma'am! I already told Madame Roland that I refuse to
procure her any."

"She wants to die anyway, so what difference does it make?"

"I do not have the right to change the course of history."

"Well, Mr. Moka, if anyone could get away with that, you
could."

"Drop it. No means no. Case closed. Tell her I'll be up to see
her in the infirmary."

"Well, have you at least found anything interesting to leave
her for posterity?"

Moka rifles through a sheaf of yellow papers, extricates one, folds it in half, seals it with wax, and gives it to the woman in the shawl.

"Have her read this and tell me what she thinks of it."

The woman moves away. It is obvious that she is itching to break the seal.

"What's in those yellow papers, Moka?"

"I already told you, Gentlemen. Posterity! Come along with me on my rounds and I will explain. And you'll see that when you have coffee with you, people like you a whole lot more than they otherwise would."

* * *

The Commander is now standing on the stage. Upon hearing Norcia utter the word "castrato," he shrinks back in horror like a tragic actor in a melodramatic play.

"A castrato! Norcia, you admit to having castrated this boy. By what rights?"

"By the right to great art! That right that confers the imperious obligation to save a *chef d'oeuvre* from oblivion. This boy's voice was one of those works. You should have heard it. He sang several times on this stage. All alone. Without an audience. Because of his appearance, he couldn't stand having people look at him. Those who came to hear him stayed on the other side of the curtain. They've all been marked by this voice that had something both animal and childlike in it."

"But you did not save that voice, Norcia. To the contrary."

"True. That's my fault, I'll give you that. My hand was shaking. That was a first for me."

"And you turned the child into a mute!"

"How little you know, Commander! After the operation, the child refused to sing. He even refused to speak. But the child isn't really mute. I am sure of it. I could make him recover his voice. But he was brutally snatched from me and taken to England, with that Doctor Seiffert. I only uncovered his traces again last year when the child was alone in Paris with no protection. He! That absolute masterpiece, a shopkeeper's assistant! All because the Princesse de Lamballe was stupid enough to return to Paris and get herself slaughtered."

"The Princesse de Lamballe! So she's the one who kidnapped the child!"

"O, Dio! This Amarone is making me forget my lines! Let's just say that it was a dramatic turn of events, Commander."

"Norcia, you just said that the Princesse de Lamballe cared for the boy. Is she his mother?"

"Not in the least! So sorry to disappoint you, Commander! The Princess is not his mother. She took charge of his care as soon as he was born. Thanks to her fortune, she was able to ensure that the child would have the most secret and the best of educations. The Princess succeeded. Today, he's almost fifteen years old, and he's an accomplished young man in literature, the arts, and in combat. He's already the equal of the Chevalier de Saint-George, who was his teacher and who is his model. There are so many similarities that I sometimes wonder whether the Chevalier isn't his father."

"But the Chevalier de Saint-George is a mulatto."

"So is the child you are trying to kill, Commander."

* * *

"Citizen escapees, Welcome back!"

The two gendarmes throw Groundhog and Spike into a cell. It doesn't take long to land on the other side since it only measures about ten feet by ten feet. And those feet are little. The uniformed Pumpkin and his Zucchini partner are already occupying half the space.

"Wait here for the police to come and question you. Upstairs, room and board costs fourteen pounds a month paid in advance. It's not prorated, and it's all due on the first of the month."

"That's why they carry out executions on the second day of every month!"

The gendarmes snicker. Pumpkin's belly shakes like jelly, and Zucchini's voice box rises and falls in his neck like the slider on a toy trombone. They allude to the abundance of "domestic help" at their disposal and to the magnificent food service at hand. Groundhog translates this into "cockroaches" and "watery soup."

"Enjoy your stay, Citizens! Above all remember to have someone bring you some cold, hard cash."

"Otherwise, you won't last long."

The gendarmes exit, leaving the door wide open. Groundhog goes out to inspect the long corridor that runs along a row of cells. A turnkey passes him, opening the locks one by one. *We've got to get some air in here!*

The corridor is lit by a set of windows that open on to the courtyard. In the building across the way, women are chatting in front of the cells on the different floors. Groundhog looks around for Zamor and Doctor Seiffert but can't find either of them. Yet, they said they were going to meet the Countess du Barry. Groundhog thinks about the little girl on the swing and the loose ribbon on her dress. When you can only remember one thing about a girl, that means you've fallen in love with her. Great. It just had to happen right at the moment when he gets thrown in prison.

* * *

Zamor is leaning on a windowsill on the second floor of the men's wing of Sainte-Pélagie. He is gazing down at the prison courtyard. Doctor Seiffert is pressed against the wall next to him, out of sight.

"Hurry up! Your jailer friend gave us fifteen minutes and no more!"

Zamor tries not to let the Doctor's nervousness overcome him. He is speaking to the Countess du Barry, who is in the building across the way. In order to avoid unwanted attention, the trick is to give the impression that he is conversing with someone else in the courtyard below. Both of them developed this skill through their extensive experience dealing with the love triangles of the salons and woods at Versailles. They never dreamed that it would come in handy in prison.

"I have news about your son."

From the building across the way, the Countess du Barry plays the same game and answers him by addressing another prisoner located in the same general direction.

"My Petit-Louis, 'e is fine, Darling?"

"He is progressing very well and is talking more and more."

The Doctor listens and tries to understand.

"Zamor, who is this Petit-Louis?"

"He's my parrot. Now pipe down!"

"I asked you to bring me a big ball of wool so zat I can knit a sweater for my Petit-Louis. Did you bring it?"

"I brought the knitting bag to carry it in."

The knitting bag! Seiffert doesn't find that very flattering at all.

"Zat's all well and good, but without ze ball of wool, I cannot knit a sweater vest for Petit-Louis and 'e might catch cold and even die."

The Doctor pulls on the hem of Zamor's frock coat.

"What is the Countess saying?"

"She is saying that without the large sum of money she requested, any information she has about the boy is out of the question."

"Tell her about our agreement. I promise to get her out of Sainte-Pélagie in exchange for the Black Pearl."

Zamor relays the message.

"A sweater vest is useful when it is cold out, but a long walk outdoors in ze fresh air is much 'ealthier. Zat's what makes boys into vigorous and . . . 'andsome men."

From the tone of her response, the Countess du Barry seems to like the idea.

"She agrees to go to the Belhomme Clinic. She says that she will give us the Black Pearl in exchange for a written order requesting her transfer to that clinic. And she needs it by noon today."

"By noon today! She's out of her mind! No matter, Zamor, tell her that it will be done. I just hope you're not putting me on with your ridiculous mumbo-jumbo. If you are, you'll be wishing you were under the guillotine yourself."

Zamor relays the message to the Countess du Barry but replaces "guillotine" with "scarf."

"Let's go, Doctor. We can leave now."

"First we have to get the dog."

Back in his hovel, the jailer is letting the pug play with his keys. Zamor and Doctor Seiffert try not to show their impatience.

"Ain't he just the cutest thing with that flat little pushed-in nose! My daughter'll love him. Belle-de-Nuit just loves animals."

"Belle-de-Nuit. What a pretty name."

"It's not just a pretty name, Citizen, it's a Republican name. She was born on 16 Vendémiaire, which is named for the mirabilis flower, also known as belle-de-nuit. If she'd been born on the 17th, she'd be named Pumpkin. Now what breed is your dog?"

"He's a pug, Citizen."

"It's Citizen jailer. A patriot should be precise."

Down the corridor, a prisoner in a powdered wig, silk stockings, and silver buckles on his shoes watches the scene from over the top of an open book, *The Journals of Captain Cook*. Zamor is intrigued by his behavior. The man has a feverish look to him. He gives Zamor a bad feeling. The man in the powdered wig pretending to read is watching the dog with a strange look in his eye. Zamor jabs the Doctor in the ribs.

"Yes, Zamor. We're leaving!"

The Doctor takes his medical bag from the jailkeeper's hole and reaches for the dog.

"Don't do that, Citizen! You'll kill him. I'll carry him to the door for you. We'll go through the courtyard of the condemned. That'll be more discreet."

Zamor, the Doctor, the pug, and the pug carrier descend the staircase single file. The man who was reading the book follows them at a distance. He keeps his eye trained on the dog, who is licking the keeper's ear.

At the gate to the courtyard of the condemned, the keeper hands the pug over to the Doctor.

"It's a cryin' shame. I woulda kept him and fed him for my little Belle-de-Nuit."

At that moment, the man with the book comes up behind them and lets out a shrill whistle.

"Coco!"

The pug yelps and jumps into his arms. The man takes hold of him, hugs him to the point of suffocation, and deeply inhales the scent of his fur.

"Her perfume! It's her. I can smell her perfume!"

His face displays a strange ecstasy. After his initial surprise, the enraged jailkeeper rushes to retrieve the pug. But the man fights him off and pushes back. The keys fly into the air, and Zamor and the Doctor are thrown against the bars. The keeper dashes into his hovel, grabs a sword, and brandishes it under the throat of the man in the powdered wig.

"Gimme back that dog!"

"He's not yours. He belongs to our Queen! He is wearing her perfume. You are not even worthy of touching him."

"You better call her the once and former Queen, Citizen!"

"She is our present Queen and Queen she shall remain. Your words will not change that."

"You better say 'former' Queen! That law was decided by the Convention."

"The Convention, ha! But I thought, you once and former man, that in these new times, there weren't any more conventions."

"Say 'former Queen'!"

The keeper pushes the point of his blade into the carotid artery of the man in the powdered wig.

"Say it. Or I will skewer you!"

"Don't bother. I'll do it myself."

In a flash, the bookworm tears into his own neck with the blade. Blood trickles from his sliced Adam's apple. With his hands holding his throat, he crumples to the floor with a sorrowful look in his eyes.

"Please forgive me for splattering blood on you."

"That aristocrat bastard! He never did say it!"

The keeper retrieves his sword and his keys. Zamor wipes his shoes. Prisoners walk by not daring to look at the body of the dead man. His blood has run onto the open book, drawing a kind of large dark map on its pages. Doctor Seiffert takes the pug into his arms.

"No, Citizen. I think that you will be giving him to me as a gift for my little Belle-de-Nuit. She'll really likes his scent."

The keeper rattles his keys. The jingling sounds like a gift.

Behind them, Zamor and Doctor Seiffert hear the cries of a street vendor. *Java, get your hot Java! Come and get some Moka rex arabica!* They won't say no to that. They could use something strong and hot. Zamor and the Doctor exit the prison by way of the courtyard of the condemned.

Moka reaches the Scarecrow section with his portable coffee kettles. *Java! Java! Come and get your hot Moka rex arabica!* He is immediately overrun by a group of women dressed in flamboyant clothing. It's coffee for the French Theater troupe! There is a mad rush to the coffeepots. Ed and Jones once again find themselves pressed into service.

"Master Moka, where did you find these two characters? We'd like to have them in for a private audition!"

This is followed by coquettish laughter. As in ancient classical drama, the roles seem to have been divided between the Chorus Members and the Chorus Leader, the Coryphée.

"Maestro Moka, you absolutely must write that letter about Madame Grelis! This is a serious matter!"

"That is simply out of the question! I refuse to denounce any actress belonging to your troupe who has done nothing wrong!"

"But we haven't done anything wrong either! Isn't that so, ladies?"

Cries issue from the Chorus of the Virtuous.

"Understand our despair, Maestro Moka! We have already been separated from our male players, who are locked up in the Madelonnettes Prison. This has seriously impacted our repertoire. And now, they won't even let us have Madame Grelis, whose skill at playing Andromache cannot be replicated! Isn't that right, Girls?"

Herewith a Canticle of Praises.

"One little denunciatory letter to the Committee for Public Safety is all it would take to get Madame Grelis back into our troupe. Then our theater season would be saved!"

"I said no! I'm interested in preserving posterity, not your theater tour."

Forthwith issue Songs of Lamentation.

"That is simply not fair. The football fanatics denounced Mr. Fontaine so that he would be transferred to their prison squad, all because of his ability to execute precision footwork. And what about us? We are not allowed to have Madame Grelis. Now, I ask you. Does football have more value today than the French Theater?"

Ensue Complaints of Indignation.

"So be it, Maestro Moka. We shall go elsewhere. Snitches are not lacking in this establishment. Now let us see those tirades you've brought us."

Moka pulls a sheet of yellow paper from his bag. The Coryphée takes it from him and reads it aloud to the Chorus.

"Ahem. The title reads, *Testimonials, or, A Selection of Goodly and Truthful Last Words Reserved for the Use of Theater Women Who've Been Condemned to Die on the Guillotine.* What a way to go!"

Taken aback, Ed and Jones give Moka a questioning look.

"That's right, Gentlemen. I trade in last words, guillotine speeches, historical citations, and witticisms. This is what I mean by Testimonials for Posterity!"

"Quiet, please, everyone! The curtain has been raised."

The Coryphée strikes her pose.

"Attention, Ladies. First and foremost, you should know that the entire work is ingeniously presented and neatly categorized by genre, in the manner of Diderot and D'Alembert's *Encyclopedia*. One can chose among entries classified under 'witticisms,' 'colloquialisms,' 'philosophical musings,' 'religious murmurings,' 'vengeful utterances,' etcetera."

Murmurs of admiration issue from the Bluestockings.

"Let us proceed directly. Hmm . . . I choose 'witticisms'! This entry reads, Situation: An unfortunate woman faces the guillotine neck hole."

> For Heaven's sake! Why
> This hole to whisper cues by?
> My talent is such that I
> Have no need to rely
> On this vulgar mnemonic device!

Applause breaks out in the ranks.

"And another, also written in verse!"

> Oh, public!
> Forgive this, my death!
> For I shall not be able
> To re-create it forthwith!

"How admirable, Maestro Moka! Now hear this one from the section called 'colloquialisms'! On the scaffold:"

> Here lie before me
> Such mournful planks as to die for.
> Suffer that with my blood
> I gaily paint them red.

"Now that is simply divine!"

The Coryphée embraces Moka as though in the closing finale of a reconciliation scene.

"Ladies, I have an idea. Tonight, we shall perform *The Testimonials of Master Moka*. However, we shall call this diversion quite simply, *Testimonial Tidbits*."

Accolades ensue, and a clapping of hands.

The troupe becomes as cheerful as a roomful of schoolgirls, as they wave the yellow sheets above their heads. Already a band of Scarecrows has come to take their place. They are demanding words to go with their coffee. Ed and Jones extricate themselves from the mob.

"Moka, we'll leave you to posterity. We're going up to question La du Barry."

* * *

Marie-Antoinette waits for Rosalie. Her servant will soon return. She had asked her to be there by eight o'clock. At least the young woman will be able to serve as a kind of barrier to shield her from the eyes of the gendarme. She feels that the lower half of her body may have begun its effusions again. She dares not rise from her chair for fear of appearing soiled.

How frivolous! These are perhaps her last solitary moments. She should be dedicating them to thoughts about her dear ones, and to the examination of her own conscience. But here she is, completely caught up in worrying about being seen with stains on her clothing. She reproaches herself for being so foolish. Perhaps she really is the "featherbrain" who was so ridiculed in the newspapers.

She no longer has time to set her thoughts in order and to respond to all of these questions.

"Citizen Corporal, could you please tell me what time it is?"

"No, Citizen, I cannot do that. I have my orders."

"Why? Are they worried I will fly away like time itself?"

The gendarme does not respond. He keeps his eyes trained on her. No matter, she is content with her words of wit. Sometimes that was all it used to take, when a soirée at the Princesse de Lamballe's would begin to lag. Poor dear heart! Why does she come to mind during her hours of boredom? Is it because of the boredom or is it because of the blood?

* * *

Ed and Jones climb the stairs to the prison's highest floor. They are on their way to meet La du Barry as if it were a lovers' tryst. In the stairwell they pass columns of women in various states of undress. Chamber pots in hand, towels over their shoulders, in relaxed attire or formally dressed, their servants at their heels. Unmitigated billows of stench mingle with the scents of various perfumes. *Make way! Make way for the personal attendants to Madame de Prinon!* A wigmaker in white gloves accompanied by his powdered assistant prance past them holding a platter bearing a silver bell. *Make way! Make way!*

On the upper Ideas level, Ed and Jones start down the corridor to one of the cellblocks. Jones stops and points Ed toward a woman standing a few feet away from them. She is poised in front of a window that opens onto the courtyard.

"You think that's La du Barry?"

"Who else would know how to look that good half-naked?"

8

LA DU BARRY

Ed and Jones walk down the prison corridor without for a moment taking their eyes off the so very undressed woman whose back is turned. A few steps ahead of them, a slender young woman hefts two buckets of steaming hot water. She enters cell number five.

"Citizen du Barry?"

"We would like to ask you a few questions."

The so very undressed woman does not respond. She lets Ed and Jones stew in the scent of her perfume. A faint odor of night-withered bergamot rises from her hair like burnt ash.

"Citizen, it is in your best interest to answer all of our questions."

Ed waves his badge in front of the Countess's eyes as though it were a bell to wake a sleepwalker.

"Gentlemen, do you take me for a trout ready to rise for a shiny bait? Per'aps you 'ave 'eard zat I adore all zat glitters of silver and gold, but I am not as 'ungry as all zat."

Ed and Jones had not even imagined that her voice had a sound, or that it could be so high-pitched, or even that she had a speech impediment. No one ever thinks of the voices behind the portraits. The Countess turns toward them with a grace that is not quite in tune with her body. They expected her eyes to be of an emerald green, but they stop at hazel. They thought she would be adorned with jewels, but her ears, neck, and hands are bare. They expected that her features would retain the traces of the King's favorite, and they do. Above all, there is that bitter line that pulls down on the corners of her mouth. Perhaps the Countess bears more resemblance to a trout than she would like to think.

"You are indeed the Citizen du Barry?"

Smirking, she fakes a curtsey. Ed and Jones have never seen so much fabric displayed on someone so scantily dressed.

"I am She. Jeanne Bécu, Countess du Barry! Removed, but only temporarily, from my estates!"

"Ed Coffin!"

"Gravedigger Jones!"

They, too, are temporarily removed from their land in America.

"Mercy! I 'ave been sent zese two 'andsome 'unks from the Indies. I see zat my tastes in men are well known."

La du Barry looks them over, progressively unbuttoning each one with an appraising eye. Ed and Jones are ill at ease with the idea that this gaze has also contemplated Louis XV as nonchalantly as they themselves would consider their own clothing when draped over the back of a chair.

"Gentlemen, if you 'ave come 'ere like everyone else to ask me about my jewels, you are too late. Zey 'ave already been stolen."

"That is not why we're here, Citizen."

"We are looking for a boy."

"A boy? In Sainte-Pélagie Prison? Yes, it is true zat many are being conceived day and night. Zere's even an impregnation room for escaping ze guillotine by way of ze belly. My age 'as prevented me from taking advantage of zis possibility. Otherwise, I would 'ave tried many times to escape."

"This is the boy we are looking for."

Jones hands her the oval portrait. La du Barry takes it and walks over to the window to look at it in the daylight. She tilts it back and forth as one would a precious stone.

"Do you know him, Citizen?"

"Of course I know 'im."

"Who is he?"

"'e is my child!"

* * *

Groundhog looks out the window. He is disappointed because it does not open onto the prison's fake vegetable garden, or onto the girl on the swing. He would have enjoyed watching her swing, just to see the blue ribbon around her waist float in the air.

"Groundhog! Come here and see what I done."

Spike pulls him into their cell, which is now decorated with words pulled from his satchel. The word "canopy" is tacked over the bed; "Nevers" is stuck to the earthenware jug made in that city. That makes sense. But he has also placed "fraternity" in the bottom of the chamber pot, "demagoguery" next to the transom, and "guillotine" in the doorframe. It is as though a gaggle of giddy words got mixed up and lost their way.

"Groundhog? You think we'll be stuck in here for long?"

He is wondering instead how he is going to find Coco again and take him back to Pretty Sidonie. Maybe he'll be at the Red Porch that the old blind woman was talking about. She said it was behind Robespierre's house. Groundhog knows where it is now. But there's just one troublesome detail. The Red Porch is outside, in the open air. Spike needs to find the word "escape" in that satchel of his. Even if the word is too dizzy to walk, it'll do the trick.

* * *

Dame Catherine and Pobéré make their way down Rue Saint Honoré toward Rue de la Monnaie. They are driven to the side of the road by two charging horses pulling a clattering cannon on wheels. The yelling, the clattering hooves, and the general racket more than fill their ears.

"Those young men sure seem to be in a big hurry! Son, pay close attention to the position of each vehicle and the name of each unit as it goes by."

"Already did that, Mother!"

"These night rides and crack patrols at this late hour are not a good sign. Our ten o'clock appointment might not show up."

"You think somebody has betrayed us?"

"No, but if I was on their side, that's what I'd do. Always think like the other guy, son."

"You mean like how I'm your eyes for you?"

"You, my little Pobéré, are not the other guy. You're a part of me. You're my baby boy."

The blind woman holds her son to her breast and tousles his shocking red hair. He makes a show of trying to get away, but her touch feels good to him.

"Mother? Why has the Duc de Penthièvre been so good to me?"

"One day, I'll tell you why. But now is not the time for that. All you need to know is that the time has come for me to thank him for it. For the moment, we have to get to that tavern on Rue de la Monnaie. I have a meeting with Jean-Baptiste."

Jean-Baptiste is already sitting at a table in Sweet Victory. The young man is nervous.

"Dame Catherine! I have good news! We have twenty new recruits who've come over to our cause from Vanves, all of them packing two pistols each."

"Good for you, Jean-Baptiste! And how many have you recruited all on your own? Doesn't it come to about five hundred, my brave boy? For that, the Queen will give you a baron's daughter in marriage."

"Not so fast! I haven't even turned nineteen yet, and I'm nothing but a wigmaker in another man's shop!"

"Don't you worry about that! Once you get married, the wigs will be powdered and delivered directly to your head! You're doing good work. The Queen will be proud of you."

The blind woman squeezes the young man's shoulders. He is solid and full of energy. And yet she feels a tightening of the muscles hardening the back of his neck. Jean-Baptiste is hiding something. She ponders this as she listens to him walk away from her and out of the tavern. No sense in upsetting her son.

"Listen to me, Pobéré. I'll wait here while you go find out the exact time that the execution is scheduled to take place. It's very important."

"Who cares about the time, since we're going to rescue her before that?"

"Go find out anyway. And bring me back a cart."

"A cart? For what?"

"So I can play queen, that's what."

* * *

Marie-Antoinette is lying on her bed. The gendarme keeps a vacant eye on her. His thoughts seem to be elsewhere. Maybe he's just hungry. Maybe he'd just like to smoke his pipe or take off his boots. Marie-Antoinette smiles. They must look like an old married couple, bourgeois and bored. Eyes turned to the light, she thinks of her son. Her baby. Did the infamous Simon, his Temple Prison guard, wake him up to tell him that his mother is going to die? With what insults? Will the poor child repeat them like a patriotic compliment in exchange for a glass of wine? There is no attack more abject than the desire to sully the image of a mother in the eyes of her son. Tears roll onto her hands, even though she had promised herself not to cry. But her strength is running out. The waning day and the waiting are bleeding her dry. She jumps. The noise of a key turning in the lock startles her. Already? Good God! How her stomach turns, all of a sudden! What time can it be?

"It's me, Madame."

It's that beautiful angel, Rosalie! How well the girl has understood that from now on, she will need to be reassured like a little child, at the slightest noise, at the least alarm. Her voice trembles, but she wears her beautiful heart on her sleeve as she enters the cell.

"Madame, you did not eat last night and ate almost nothing at all yesterday. What do you wish to have this morning?"

God, how her time is now conjugated in this simple question. How she would have liked being asked which slippers she would like to wear . . . tomorrow.

"My dear, I no longer need a thing. It's all over for me now."

Now why did she say that? Was it to ravage poor Rosalie's heart? All is not yet lost. Out there, people are working to snatch her from her fate. Marie-Antoinette repeats, *Robespierre's house, the Red Porch* to herself. She must have faith in them. She must regain her strength in order to be ready for them when the time comes.

"Madame, I have been keeping a hot broth on the stove for you."

A broth! This almost brings her to tears. A broth for her! She had recoiled at doling it out to the needy while surrounded by her entourage. Now she was the needy one who would be receiving it from Rosalie's hands as a kind of Last Supper, and she would never be able to reward her generosity with anything more than a smile. Confused, Rosalie begins to weep. She must think I've lost my mind! She must think that I am laughing at her, that I was mocking her offering. How detestable is the old Hapsburg arrogance that must now be visible in the shape of my mouth! Those little folds of skin and bone where others think they can see your soul. Rosalie is retreating. I have offended this generous heart.

"Come back here, my dear!"

Dear God! How her beautiful face brings tears to my eyes. How pleasant it would have been to endow her with a title. To see her mingling, joyous and gay among her friends at the Trianon Palace. She would have upheld her rank. What does it take, really, to be a princess?

"Rosalie, do bring me your broth!"

The servant exits and reenters the cell so quickly that it is as though the oven were heating up just outside the door. Marie-Antoinette is now sitting up on the bed. Her legs barely support her. The repeated openings and closings of the door convince her that they will be coming for her anytime now. She had once found comfort in locks and latches. But she had cared little for the concerns of her poor Louis and had mocked him when he had ordered that a deadbolt be installed on their door to keep them safe from the public. The Committee for Public Safety. The words twist in her stomach. No thank you, my dear! Swallowing another spoonful of this broth is simply out of the question.

"What time is it?"

The Queen has managed to whisper her question just at the moment when the servant's body shields her from the gendarme's prying eyes.

"It's just after seven o'clock."

"Rosalie, I'm bleeding again. You will bring me another shift."

"Yes, ma'am."

"Ho there, Citizens! No talking, or I'll have to report you!"

Men can tell when women are whispering, but they're usually too late to hear anything.

"You will also bring me . . ."

"Citizens! I just told you to watch your mouths, or I'll report you!"

Mr. Reportyou. That's a perfect name for a gendarme. He's made an impression on this dear little Rosalie. She is shaking. Her heart aches. She had better let the girl go.

"Rosalie, you will return at around eight o'clock to help me dress."

"As you wish, Madame."

At the hour of Rosalie's return, she will only have two more hours to live.

* * *

"Citizen du Barry, are you saying that the boy in this portrait is yours?"

Without saying a word, the Countess turns on her heels and disappears into her cell, taking the portrait with her. Ed and Jones follow her in.

"Welcome to my Louveciennes palace!"

The Countess shows them in with a gesture meant to invoke the highest of ceilings.

"Admire my bath!"

La du Barry points to a tub with copper claw feet whose rising steam pushes them away and closer to the vicinity of her straw mattress.

"It's my only luxury! I 'ave nicknamed it 'Marat,' which is not a luxury but an act of insolence. In zese times, insolence is ze only remaining luxury. Is it not?"

She laughs and tosses her hair. Ed and Jones exchange surprised looks. La du Barry does not seem to have noticed the presence in her cell of the water bearer, who stands rooted in front of a small notice pasted to the wall, her face ecstatic.

"Ninon! That is enough! You will ruin your eyes! And 'urry up. Marat is not yet full!"

As though awakening from a dream, the young woman gathers her pails and departs. The Countess seems to feel that she owes them an explanation.

"She's a good girl, but penniless. In 'ere, zat's ze kiss of death. In return for 'er services as my water bearer, I allow 'er to read about my jewels."

She points to the notice. Ed and Jones step forward and read:

Reward: Two thousand gold louis in exchange for the return of lost diamonds and precious jewels.

The following diamonds and precious gems were stolen from Madame du Barry's Louveciennes Palace near Marly: a ring set with one oblong gem weighing about thirty-five grains, mounted in a hoop setting . . . a ring case, of green copper, containing between twenty to twenty-five rings, in one of which is a large emerald, an openwork pendant weighing about thirty-six grains, of a fine color but very opaque, having much depth . . .

"Watch your steps now, Gentlemen! You are ruining my straw."

"All of this was stolen from you?"

Jones taps the notice, which goes on ruining them line after line for many generations to come.

"My memory 'as also stolen some of it from me."

Ed and Jones move away. They are beginning to worry that the notice might empty their pockets.

"Citizen du Barry, you have just declared that the boy in this portrait is yours. Do you reconfirm that statement?"

"Yes, I confirm it. What else do you wish to know?"

"We just want to know where he is."

"But I 'aven't the slightest idea!"

"But you are his mother!"

La du Barry bursts into laughter. A genuine simper-free belly laugh that finally results in almost completely disrobing her.

"I, ze mother of zis child! . . . And w'o did you think was 'is father? 'is Majesty Louis XV?"

Now she explodes into peals of laughter. It rings out over the entire Ideas block, trickles down to the level of the Players, and finally drips onto the heads of the Scarecrows.

"Please, Citizen, this is no joke!"

Suddenly she regains her composure. Her face is almost serious now.

"Gentlemen, when I speak of 'is Majesty, I do not joke. I remember!"

The Countess buries her face in her hands. Her tears bubble up in small affected sobs. Ed and Jones had not expected this. In fact, they had not expected anything whatsoever. Jones extends a hanky large enough to rub down a Percheron draft horse.

"Thank you, but I 'ave my own."

From her cleavage, La du Barry unfurls a delicate lace handkerchief and an embroidered smile to match.

"Do not be fooled by tears, Gentlemen. Because zen, you would 'ave to believe in women too."

Suddenly, all Ed and Jones want is to become farmers in Ohio, to believe in the changing of the seasons, in the rising of the grain, in the falling of the rain, in tears, and in women who are truly women.

"Once and for all, Citizen, are you or are you not the mother of this child?"

"Gentlemen! Look at me and then look at this portrait. With w'om would I 'ave been able to procreate such a prodigy?"

"With Zamor!"

La du Barry lets her lace handkerchief drop to her feet. Neither Ed nor Jones moves to pick it up. They lock eyes with La du

Barry. Her gaze has become ferocious. How quickly the weather changes on this face!

"Touché, Gentlemen!"

Suddenly, two jailers wearing caps shaped like cock's combs burst in. Their raptor eyes search the cell.

"Citizen du Barry, you seen the suspect?"

"What suspect?"

"A good-lookin' recalcitrant in a curly wig. Citizen Devey. She's supposed to move down to the Scarecrow ward, but she's hiding."

"Leave 'er alone! And get out of 'ere!"

"Watch what you say, Citizen!"

"Clear ze decks immediately, or I'll 'ave you beaten by my lackeys!"

The two roosters take a gander at Ed and Jones. Well now. These two lackeys are mighty big. It makes sense to go and look elsewhere. Ed observes La du Barry as she pats her neck and chest with a damp cloth. She seems genuinely moved. Jones pores over the notice like a kid staring at pastries through a bakery shop window. He is wondering what an antique Bacchus carved in relief upon burned carnelian might look like, but especially what a slave-collar necklace with a double row of pearls and its matching pendant might resemble. Ed brings Jones back to the interrogation.

"So, Citizen! Are you or are you not the mother of this child?"

"Gentlemen, I can tell you quite plainly zat . . . No! I am not 'is mother and Zamor is not 'is father."

"And yet, Citizen, you and Zamor were . . ."

"Yes, everyone knows it's true. And I am not saying zat at one time, if we 'ad let ourselves go, we wouldn't 'ave been able to paint such a portrait. But, Gentlemen, in my position as the King's favorite, it would 'ave been a disaster for my interests if I 'ad gotten with child. All ze more so if I would 'ave painted it with zat color. Can you imagine the scandal at Versailles?"

"So why did you say that he is your child?"

"In a manner of speaking, 'e is."

"In what manner of speaking, Citizen?"

"Zat I 'ave a role in the existence of zis child. Let us just say zat I learned, by pure luck, of Madame de Lamballe's little secret."

"How was that by luck, Citizen?"

"By pillow luck, Gentlemen! Ze pillow is ze luck of kept women. I am able to speak of zis luck because I think zat 'e is already dead. In any case, 'e should be dead by now. 'is name was Norcia da Lecce. 'e was an Italian surgeon 'ose greatest talent was to turn babies into angels. Which comes in 'andy when nature dares to take precedence over ze King's pleasures."

That's just a nice way of saying that children are thrown to the wolves because His Majesty gets impatient in bed.

"Zis Italian was ze protégé of Madame de Lamballe, 'is compatriot. The Princess was of ze noble Carignan-Savoy line from ze great House of Turin. It was zat Norcia da Lecce who operated on ze Prince de Lamballe."

"For what?"

"You'll understand when I tell you zat after zis operation, 'e was called Ze Prince Sans Balls!"

Ed and Jones understand how at Versailles, such a nickname could kill just as easily as a surgeon could.

"Where can we find this Norcia da Lecce character?"

"If 'e is still alive, 'e'd be in an outbuilding to one of ze lodges at ze King's Garden."

"You mean the Botanical Garden, Citizen."

"Au contraire! For me, a king will never be replaced by a collection of plants."

The Countess imagines that the Norcia da Lecce fellow could prove to be a tantalizing lure for these two hulks.

"Norcia da Lecce, Gentlemen, took great care of zis child. But for some unknown reason, ze Princesse de Lamballe decided one fine day to remove 'im from 'is care and to place 'im in ze care of 'er personal physician. "'er very personal physician, if you get my meaning."

"Can you give us the name of this very personal physician, Citizen?"

How foolish of her! Now they're following a more succulent fly. And she's the one throwing out the bait!

"Doctor Seiffert. 'e was German. But you will not 'ave 'im in your confessional. 'e is in London. 'owever, Norcia da Lecce is not far from 'ere."

The Countess points in the general direction of the King's Garden, which happens to coincide with that of the cell door. Ed and Jones suddenly find this gesture to be all too familiar.

"Let's get back to the child, Citizen. You are saying that the Princesse de Lamballe, of royal blood, heiress to the Penthièvre fortune, one of the largest in France, has taken it upon herself to educate a child who is not only black, but ill? We don't get it."

"Is the Princess his mother?"

"What an idea! If zat were ze case, ze Duc de Penthièvre would 'ave moved 'eaven and earth in order to get zat child back and make 'im 'is heir. Don't forget zat ever since ze death of 'is eldest son, 'e 'as but a daughter to carry on ze family name."

"Aw, come on now, Citizen! Who's ever heard of a black prince?"

"Gentlemen, when you add a couple of million to your name, you're not black. You're rich!"

Now there's a shade to add to Moka's color palette! The pithy quip reduces Ed and Jones to silent pondering. La du Barry savors its effect while visibly pretending not to. Suddenly, Ninon the water bearer reenters the cell. She is sans pail, wearing a dogged look and dangling arms.

"Madame Countess! They're after Aurore Devey!"

"I knew it! Zose bastards! Where are zey now, my dear girl?"

"In the impregnation room. Er, I mean, in room number eleven."

"Gentlemen?"

"We're on it, Citizen."

"Just show us the way, Little Miss."

Ed and Jones sprint down the corridor behind Ninon.

"Down there!"

She points to a cell door at the end of the hallway. It is guarded by two plumed roosters. A couple composed of a pumped-up peacock prepared for a nuptial parade and a woman in a pink riding hood languish in a corner, waiting. The peacock is complaining.

"This is a most inconvenient delay in the action! We wait, we wait, and we deflate! I'm not a bubbling spring! We had a reservation! But clearly, some people around here take precedence over others!"

Ed confronts the bird guarding the cell door. Even with his crest raised, he ain't pretty.

"Just what kinda precedence we talkin' about here?"

"Interrogation of a suspect, Citizen."

The bird snickers and gives Ed a complicit wink. But that winking eye never sees what comes next. Ed smashes it shut with a sucker punch direct to the socket. In its momentum, the slug embarks a part of the nose, folding it over. The septum deviates, the head snaps back and knocks on the door. Nobody answers, "Who's there?" but Ed and Jones go in anyway, shoving the bird along in front of them as they go.

"Git outta here, Norbert! I told you to wait. Can't you see I ain't done yet?"

The guy who ain't done yet is a bird of another feather. Bare-assed, he is on his feet in front of a table, his breeches sagging around his ankles. His buttocks flap as he pants out a series of stiff, short cries.

"You're done, all right!"

Ed rushes him, throws a kick into the curving small of the back, grabs the man by the shoulders, pulls him off, and throws him against the wall. Ed uncovers Aurore Devey. She is lying face down, belly to the table, dress pushed up, wrists and ankles bound.

Jones covers her with his raincoat, unties her, and leads her out of the cell. In front of the door, the frustrated peacock is still complaining.

"And none too soon! This might stop me from being able to perform now!"

Jones boots him out of way with a kick that confirms that the performance is now cancelled. The Peacock ceases and, bent double, limps away with Little Pink Riding Hood following close behind.

"Hey! Come back here, Mister! Gimme my money back! I want a refund!"

Inside the cell, Ed doesn't give Breechless a chance to recover. He breaks his teeth in with a head butt. In a two-armed embrace, Ed takes him by the waist and shoves a knee up into the groin. *How's that feel? How about that?* The man chokes, coughs, and drools. Ed crunches the vertebrae and whispers in the man's ear.

"You like that?"

Ed doesn't. Ed throws the human wreckage down onto the table and flattens it into the same position that Aurore Devey had been forced to take. Ed takes the other guard bird between his fists.

"I didn't do nothin'!"

"Well you got some catchin' up to do then!"

When Ed leaves the cell, Ninon is standing right outside the door. There is just enough time to glimpse one feathered cock fluttering atop another less feathered one. Ninon smiles and hands Ed a glass of water.

"As you'll soon see, Sir, the water is nice and cool."

Ed returns to La du Barry's quarters. Jones has preceded him. When he enters the cell, a look from Jones tells him not to mention the tussle. The Countess simply says, "thank you."

"Gentlemen, where were we before zis, er, interruption?"

"You were saying that with a pension of two million, there is no color. But you were also saying that if you had had a child of color you would have been banished from the court. Isn't that a bit of a contradiction?"

"Not at all! You must know zat in ze eyes of ze world, ze King's favorite is nothing but a whore and zat everyone is just waiting to let her know it. My day arrived on May 10, 1774. 'is Majesty Louis XV lay dying. Life as I 'ad known it was over."

Ninon returns with two pails of water that she empties into the bathtub.

"Gentlemen, 'ow do you know when a king 'as just died at Versailles? From ze noise! It comes from ze stampeding feet of courtesans rushing down ze main staircase in order to be ze first to prostrate zemselves at ze feet of ze new sovereign."

Ed and Jones have the distinct impression that La du Barry can hear it even as they speak.

"At zis very moment, Gentlemen, zat little red-'eaded snob named Marie-Antoinette is becoming queen, and I am now nothing. She is not even twenty years old, and I am over thirty. Everyone abandons me, just when ze King decides to keep 'is most insane promise.

"Which one?"

"To turn himself black!"

Ed and Jones are dumbfounded. La du Barry casually dips her fingers into the bath water. She nods to Ninon. Yes! It's perfect! With a pail in each hand, the young woman immediately becomes reabsorbed in reading the notice concerning the missing jewels.

"The King was a little jealous of Zamor. In fact, 'e was royally jealous. Zat is to say zat 'e commanded me not to think zat 'e was. One night, 'e said to me, 'Zis young man seems to give you much pleasure, Madame. If your satisfaction is at zis price zen I promise you I'll turn black myself!'"

"Sire, zis constitutes a challenge equal to your stature. It would be far easier for me to become a virgin again."

"I will take you at your word, Madame. I will turn black if you become a virgin again. For a wager like zis, something substantial should be at stake."

"Sire, I propose the Black Pearl that is now in the possession of the Maréchal de Saxe. It is said zat zere is none other like it. And its color seems most appropriate for our wager."

"And so it shall be, Madame. I will 'ave it returned to me and in turn bestow it upon you."

La du Barry seems to be reliving the entire scene and sees the Black Pearl pass before her very eyes.

"I won our little bet, thanks to a visit to Norcia da Lecce. 'e remade me into a ravishing virgin! 'e was a master in zat domain. 'e's capable of restoring ze virginity of others who are a lot more virginal and a lot more . . . royal zan I am."

Ed and Jones make a mental note of that last allusion. They tell themselves that the Countess has the gift of making one think that she is just chatting when in fact she is making serious talk.

"I won ze bet and spent an unforgettable wedding night with ze King. You see! I was destined to be a virgin. Unfortunately, I was born in Vaucouleurs where virginity was only for ze likes of Joan of Arc. After what 'appened to 'er I got disgusted so I turned myself loose. I became a whore."

The Countess seems to be repeating this last word over and over again in order to tame it.

"On 'is deathbed, ze king also kept 'is promise. Smallpox 'ad completely covered 'im with dark pustules. Louis XV 'ad turned black . . . for me, at least."

La du Barry strokes the surface of the water in her bathtub.

"Perfect! My bath is ready. I apologize, Gentlemen, but I must ask you to leave now."

This is the second time that the Countess has tried to dismiss them.

"We'll do nothing of the sort! Ed asked you a question, and this time you will answer it."

"What 'appens if I don't?"

"You'll be taking your next bath in the Conciergerie Prison."

La du Barry pales. She thinks about the little redhead who will be sent to the guillotine. This is a vengeance that she has been waiting for, ever since she was humiliated in front of the entire court. The date was January 1, 1772. *There are many people at Versailles this evening.* The Countess has sworn to make the Queen pay for that sentence. Just for that, every day at the exact moment of Marie-Antoinette's execution, she will thread a new red bead onto a necklace. La du Barry does not wish to be deprived of this pleasure.

"Very well, Gentlemen. I agree to respond to your questions, but I will not allow my bath to get cold. Turn around. Ninon, you may leave us now."

The young woman swipes a few more jewels from the poster with her eyes and goes out. Ed and Jones turn around, pushed from behind by the sound of the Countess's remaining clothing as it slithers to the floor. They can hear her rummaging through her wooden chest. Out of the corners of their eyes, they are able exchange a quick look, one just quick enough to tell each other the same thing. Jeanne Bécu, Countess du Barry, favorite of Louis XV, is naked back there! They suddenly get the urge to make a few babies just to be able to tell them the story later on when they've grown up.

"Gentleman, zis is ze better part of life."

They think so too. Especially when it is accompanied by a series of indiscreet lapping sounds, the cause of which can only be left to the imagination.

"Citizen, don't you dare try to take advantage of this awkward situation in order to avoid answering our questions."

"Imagine what would happen if we are forced to turn around."

"Some things are better left to the imagination, Gentlemen. I'm an old lady now, now fifty years of age. The picture you paint of me will always be more flattering if you do it from memory. Oh! 'ow clumsy of me! Come back 'ere!"

La du Barry curses to herself. A yellow leaf of paper flutters by Ed and Jones and lands at their feet.

"'ey! Could you two 'oney buns please 'and me my notes? Zey 'ave blown right out of my tub!"

Jones picks up the paper and hands it to the Countess backward.

"Thank you. Er . . . Zis comes from my memoirs. I 'ave decided to write mine as well."

Ed and Jones smile. They recognize Moka's yellow sheets of paper and his notary's script. The Countess is suddenly more energetic. It is obvious that she has just remembered her lines. Her memories must have been locked up in that chest.

"I 'ave just as many stories to tell as zat gloomy visionary Madame Roland, who is always going around saying zat she wants to die. She writes it so often zat she won't 'ave anything left to do but to put her life into a post-scriptum."

"That's a Moka, all right!"

"What, Gentlemen? What's zis about your Moka?"

"He's a friend of ours who traffics in words on yellow sheets of paper just like this."

Suddenly, they hear thunder roll behind them accompanied by a theatrical metallic rumble. The Countess is pounding on one side of the bathtub.

"Oh, what ze goddamn 'ell use is it all, anyway?"

Now that definitely is not a Moka. It doesn't taste or smell like one either. Ed and Jones stand there listening, shoulders hunched, eyes caught on a stray crack in the wall. All of a sudden, lightning strikes.

"Yes! 'ell! Yes! 'e is the Queen's child!"

* * *

Eyes closed, Norcia slowly drinks a glass of Amarone.

"Commander, although this child is a mulatto, given the unorthodox skin condition that afflicts him, I do not know to this day whether he is white or black. This wouldn't surprise a Creole such as yourself. You are familiar with the vagaries of racial mixing. Pigmentation fades and disappears only to reappear sometimes several generations later."

"I am aware of that."

"It must be a constant worry for someone like you, Commander. One is never certain when darker skin will resurface. How can one ever be certain of one's ancestry?"

"You never give up, do you, Norcia? You seem to enjoy insulting me by calling my bloodlines into question!"

"It is not I who have cast this doubt, Commander, it is you. Otherwise, why would you have asked me, fifteen years ago now, to prevent you from being able to have any children?"

"That is my business alone. But keep it up, Norcia. Now that you have made the incision, you'll have to operate."

"I'll say it again: I think you want to kill this child because he could be living proof of the existence of black blood in your veins."

"Go deeper, Norcia! Ever deeper! Even though I don't see the connection between me and that boy."

"Well, there is one, Commander. And that's the Queen! Although you deny it, you were Marie-Antoinette's lover and that boy is her son. Perhaps even your son!"

* * *

In the carriage now leaving Sainte-Pélagie at a slow trot, Zamor and Doctor Seiffert are silent. They have asked the driver to drive slowly. They both need time to think. The Doctor wonders what he is going to do without the pug. For the masterminds of this operation, the dog functioned as a kind of royal seal. Once again he recalls the distressed look of that prisoner. He remembers the look in his eyes as he inhaled the scent of Marie-Antoinette's perfume that still lingered on the pug. The former Queen! To think that he gave up his life for refusing to utter the word "former."

Doctor Seiffert also thinks of Marie-Thérèse, the Princesse de Lamballe. She also died for a word. She refused to swear hatred for the Queen to her torturers. So they slaughtered her. The Doctor's heart withers. No harm would have come to her if Marie-Antoinette had not recalled the Princess to Paris just when the riots were at their peak. Seiffert runs his hand over his beard. He has sworn not to shave until he has avenged her death.

Zamor is satisfied. Everything is proceeding according to plan. Doctor Seiffert will gallop off to the Belhomme Clinic in order to procure the documents authorizing the Countess du Barry's transfer.

"Just why do you insist that these orders have to be blank, Zamor?"

"It's simply a safety precaution. If by some misfortune you were captured, Doctor, it would be easier to defend yourself. But with the name 'du Barry' on the papers, it would be the guillotine, no doubt about that."

He is absolutely right. Even so, Doctor Seiffert does not trust him. He can tell that the maharajah is trying to trick him, even though he can't yet figure out how.

Zamor knows why he wants the orders to be left blank. It's because the name "du Barry" is not the one that he is planning to put on them.

* * *

Marie-Antoinette presses her hands to her belly. The pain has returned. In spite of the fact that she stayed in bed after Rosalie left with her broth. Hopefully that brave heart will remember to bring her a clean gown! Hopefully they will allow her to wear it. That would be the final infamy, to force her to go sullied to her death. Why is her female belly being such a tyrant? On this, of all days. That belly that had finally become so cooperative. That belly that had finally learned to give birth. With half-closed eyes, she thinks of each birth as if it were a road back through the past.

The birth of Louis-Auguste, her youngest, her Sweet Baby Boy, had been as smooth as silk. But with poor Louis, the first Dauphin and heir to the throne, it had been as though he were wearing a crown of thorns! But how much joy he had brought to the eyes of the King! And that feeling of finally being Queen! The joy of erasing the phrase that haunts her still, *It's only a girl!*

Marie-Thérèse had just been born and had almost killed her in that vicious chaos sanctioned by court etiquette at Versailles. She remembers the blackened face of that little chimney sweep in his stocking cap. He had perched himself atop a chest of drawers and had watched her, head tilted to one side.

Suddenly, her belly emits a sharp pain, as it does each time she thinks of that birth. And yet she cannot quite recall it. Half-conscious, feeling as though she were slipping away, she had been suffocating. People had bustled about as if they were trying to extinguish a fire. Through her fog, she had just been able to glimpse the signal that she had arranged with Madame de Lamballe signifying . . . *It's not a boy.*

Marie-Antoinette no longer recalls where that phrase of disgust, *It's only a girl*, had come from. It felt more like a ringing in her ears. It was a reproach from the entire court.

The Queen had just given her first child to the world, but for her as well, it was as though it were nothing more than the extraction of a decayed tooth. The child had no value . . . *It's only a girl*. The curse remained the same! She had felt ready to give up, to let herself die, and yet, she could still feel a strange sensation inside her. She had felt as though her belly had not been entirely delivered. That it was still inhabited by a presence of some sort. She had been told that she had been delivered of an undeveloped fetus. An undeveloped fetus! She remembers the incident ten years prior at Fontainebleau when that awful carriage door had struck her in the abdomen.

There is a rapping on her cell door. The gendarme opens it. It is eight o'clock. Marie-Antoinette must now get dressed.

* * *

The Commander drinks his glass of Amarone. He raises it to Norcia.

"A toast!"

"Commander, I find your tranquility most strange. I have just told you that the child that you seek to kill may be your own son and still you sit here drinking."

"Remember this, Norcia. In my eyes, you are already dead! Perhaps I was drinking to your health. To your memory. Because none of the things that you just spoke of exists any longer. The Princesse de Lamballe was murdered, the Countess du Barry is not far from here. As for Doctor Seiffert, he already knows too much."

"What about me?"

"For you, Norcia, *E finita la commedia!* The curtain is closing on your play! It's time to leave the stage now."

"That's too bad, Commander, because I enjoyed being like Scheherazade in the *Thousand and One Nights,* always telling a new tale to put off the hour of my death."

"You've put it off long enough, Norcia."

The two men exit stage left. Seconds later, Norcia rips a scalpel from his sleeve and strikes at the Commander's throat. The blade scrapes his cheek. The Commander has already drawn a dagger from his boot. The scalpel hisses at the eyes and excavates the heart. The hand is keen, the eye is peeled. The jaw is slightly tense. The entire body is arched. Too aggressive, Norcia! The throat, the eyes, the heart! Too much anatomical pondering. Too much desire to cause pain. Kill, Norcia! Kill! Just do it! Like this. Without saying a word.

The Commander plants his dagger in Norcia's stomach.

The old surgeon cries out in a high falsetto. It's like an ache that cannot truly be expressed because the correct tone is lacking. He drops the scalpel and looks down at the dagger now stuck in his body. The man smiles.

"Excellent job on the incision, Commander. It's just a tad short."

Norcia holds the dagger between his hands, climbs back up on the stage, and defies the room with his eyes. The Commander thinks that he is going to salute and fall over with a theatrical flourish. But all of a sudden, he disappears behind the red curtain. The Commander rushes after the surgeon. In the time that it takes to break free from the curtain folds, Norcia has reached the laboratory. He stands before the stone table, where the naked and headless cadaver lies. The old man's bloody shirt is lifted above his belly. One hand supports the blade of the dagger inside the wound. The other seizes the hourglass that had been standing next to the body.

"No, Norcia, no! Don't do it!"

"I'll do it for the boy. I owe it to him!"

The surgeon turns the hourglass over. Immediately he pulls down on the dagger, making the incision slightly longer. He doesn't flinch. His hands work quickly. Two fingers palpate the flesh inside the wound, making it look like a puffed-up pouch. Blood spatters the movements and the body. Suddenly the mask begins to roar. The hands pull a bloody cord and a bulging mass of viscera from inside the abdomen. Norcia takes a short-bladed knife from the pocket of his vest and lets himself slide down so as to sit with his back pressed against the foot of the stone table, legs spread wide apart. He pants and rails. Above his head, the hourglass is running out. Norcia steadies his hand on the knife handle and pushes it down. He shudders and jolts, his mouth opens wide as it struggles to utter a voiceless cry. The torso collapses overtop the belly parts that are now strewn on the floor between his legs. Norcia gazes dumbly at the part of himself he now holds in his hands. He whispers.

"Norcia . . . da Lecce!"

The Commander takes the hourglass and turns it over. One little grain of sand teeters on the brink.

"I've won again, Commander."

* * *

Ed and Jones wonder whether they have quite understood what the Countess has just shouted out. But there is no doubt about it. She repeats it as she pounds on the copper bathtub like an obsessed metalsmith.

"If I've said it once, I'll say it again. Zat is ze little Red'ead's child. Marie-Antoinette Queen of France! Zat angel of virtue, zat patched-up virgin. Right from 'er arrival at court, she despised me, 'umiliated me, ignored me! She refused to speak to me! Spoke one single sentence to me in two entire years! *Zere are many people at Versailles this evening!* That sly lass. Now she'll see! Pretty soon zere will be many people on Louis XV Square!"

Ed and Jones can feel her fury blowing at their backs. The crack in the wall just got wider.

"Yes, Gentlemen! Ze boy zat you are searching for will soon be an orphan."

"Careful, Citizen! What you are saying is extremely serious business, and the consequences are immeasurable."

"Do you have proof of this claim?"

"In fact, I do 'ave proof and I'm ze only one w'o does."

"Citizen, you better hand it over pronto!"

There is an empty silence behind them.

"Citizen! Did you hear what we said? We need that proof on the double!"

No answer. Ed and Jones exchange worried looks. Together, they turn around at exactly the same moment. The Countess has disappeared. Her hair floats on the surface of the water. Ed rushes over and grabs her. Jones plunges his hands in without looking where they're going. They fish out a beaming Countess who is snorting like a sailor. What do you do when you have a Countess in your arms who is naked, wet, and heavy but pretends not to know it? Answer: you turn yourself around and face the schismatic crack in the wall again.

"Thank you, Gentlemen! I 'aven't done zat since I was a little girl. Zat demonstration was intended to show you, I 'ope, zat I will only furnish zat proof to the one w'o'll get me out of 'ere."

Moka enters the cell with a mug of hot coffee. He removes his gold-plated hat and kisses the back of the Countess's hand.

"Maestro, I 'ave several complaints regarding your so-called Posterities."

"What, Countess, are they not to your liking?"

"To ze contrary! I find zem to be pleasant and quite witty. In fact zey are extremely 'elpful when I need to shine before an audience full of gentlemen w'o like to pretend zat zey are a bunch of fools."

She shoots a complicit glance at Ed and Jones.

"What I don't like are ze sheets of paper zat you 'ave given me."

La du Barry leans hardily over the side of the tub and picks up a sheaf of "Posterities."

"Zis yellow color is quite comely and useful for keeping track of zem. But zeir excessive length makes zem impractical and even indiscreet. Perhaps zey could be made smaller by folding zem into a fan, like so."

She shows Moka the result of her handiwork.

"They truly are easier to handle. But the title no longer reads 'Posterities.' Now all you can see is 'Post it.'"

"Post-it! Zat's perfect! And it even sounds like an English word, doesn't it? Post-it! Gentlemen, you shall bear witness to my invention, if anyone should come along and question its . . . paternity!"

She winks at Ed and Jones again. Perhaps she is trying to tell them that she also knows who the boy's father is.

"Countess, here is the most recent collection of 'Last Words for the Scaffold' that I have prepared for you at your request."

Moka hands La du Barry a sheet of yellow paper.

"Hmm . . . let us peruse these precious morsels . . . *Display my 'ead to the people. It may be a pain, but it's worth it! . . .* Zat one's a bit short. . . *Oh, Liberty! What crimes are committed in zy name!*"

"Madame Roland really likes that last one."

"Let 'er choke on it, zen! 'ow about this . . . *Give me one more minute, Mr. Executioner! . . .* Oh come now! Zat one is really too undignified . . . *Shit!* Now zat one's really daring!"

"The Duc de Biron gets that last one."

"I'll 'appily leave it to 'im. It's fitting for a general. Zis next one would also be quite suitable. Turning toward ze executioner, 'e 'ands 'im a glass of wine: *Drink zis! You could use a good stiff drink, given ze job you 'ave!* 'ere's another one zat includes ze executioner. It is said zat posterity is shared with one's executioner. *I 'ave tread on your toes. Pardon me, Sir, I didn't do it on purpose.* Zat one is rather airy and pleasant. But zere are one too many *'aves'* in zere for me to say. 'ave you noticed, Gentlemen, zat ze only *h* zat I can pronounce correctly is ze one in 'have you found my jewels?' For the scaffold, I need something to zat effect. I cannot allow my speech impediment to be 'eard when I am about to die. Zat would be undignified."

Moka rifles through the post-its. Ed and Jones wonder what they themselves would say at that moment.

"Here's one, Madame. Upon seeing the neck hole on the guillotine, you declare, 'What? Is this to be the last necklace I'll ever wear? Fortunately, my taste was better while I was still alive!'"

"Come now, Maestro! I expected better! Is zat all you 'ave for La du Barry at 'er death? I must maintain my rank!"

"Alas, Madame. My stock is continually depleted these days."

The Countess rereads the yellow paper with an indecisive pout.

"No. Really, none of zese appeal to me. Well, too bad. Since I cannot determine what my last words will be, I shall simply forgo dying!"

The Countess laughs and claps her hands.

"Excellent! May I write that one down, Countess?"

"Things are really backward these days, Maestro. Whores proffer puns and queens bear bastards."

Ed and Jones try to make sense of all of La du Barry's allusions. Moka is disappointed and grumbles as he puts his post-its away. Vexed, he leaves the cell after a quick kiss on the hand and a tip of the hat. Ed and Jones turn to face the Countess, who, wrapped in a sheet, is shivering.

"Citizen, Jones and I are going to go and check out your story about this child and the Queen."

"For your posterity, it would be a good thing if you haven't lied to us."

"In my position, Gentlemen, I 'ave ze luxury of not needing to lie. It is one of ze only luxuries in life zat I 'ave not abused. And I didn't get zat line from Moka!"

Ed and Jones leave La du Barry with the feeling that they will never see her again. They requisition a gendarme to stand guard outside the Countess's door.

"It is absolutely forbidden for anyone to enter into contact with the prisoner. Otherwise, it'll be your head, Citizen!"

"And don't even think of peeking through the keyhole. She just might try to seduce you."

9

ZAMOR

Down in the prison yard a prayer bell clangs. Ed looks out the window. The football fanatics have begun a match. Jones tugs on his partner's arm.

"There's no time for that now, Ed. We've got to go see the Marquis."

"Just a minute! Take a look!"

Down below, it's a courtyard scrimmage. The players run helter-skelter between the two wooden gallows that have been raised at each end of the playing field. Jones doesn't see anything interesting. Ed thinks that the Sainte-Pélagie Blue Shirts maneuver better than the Saint-Lazare Yellow Shirts thanks especially to their sidestepping maneuvers at the flanks. The open windows along the corridors are now filled with spectators on every floor. The Scarecrows cheer, the Players make wagers, and the Ideas make comments. Moka comes in. He has abandoned his mobile coffee cart and has donned his pince-nez, demonstrating that he is deep in thought.

"Gentlemen, have you succeeded in grasping the symbolic value of this confrontation?"

Moka develops his point before they even have time to open their mouths.

"In fact, these men are not playing a game. They are engaged in mortal combat. That ball figures a severed head. It symbolizes the horror that must be trampled underfoot and kicked aside in order to protect the Self by directing aggression toward the Other. Because the Other must die. And why must it be by the foot, you ask?"

Actually, Ed and Jones haven't uttered a single word.

"The use of the hands would seem to be more obvious and more comfortable. But the hand, Gentlemen, is a tool for working. Calluses are the stigmata that prove it. To have white hands is to possess the privilege of saints and aristocrats. To use the feet in play is to appropriate this privilege and this grace!"

Ed and Jones look down at their hands. They could use a little more privilege and a lot more grace.

"See that? Observe that admirable gesture!"

In front of the Sainte-Pélagie gallows posts now under siege, the Double Duc de Biron brandishes the ball between both hands.

"Here he is adopting the stance of the executioner when he raises the severed head to the crowd. The object of fear has now been exorcised. The object of desire is now erected in its stead!"

Ed and Jones think that Moka may have drunk a bit too much mocha.

"And who gestures thus, Gentlemen? 'Tis the goalkeeper! The only one among us with the right to hold the ball in both hands! The only one with the right to raise horror above the heads of the crowd! Indeed, t'was the Duc de Biron who inaugurated this transgressional practice upon declaring, 'I prefer to hold my privates out in public!'"

Ed and Jones now recognize the man who, by the dawn's early light, had been shaving naked by a window while holding a private part in one hand.

"There is so much more to say here! This game carries great meaning and has a long future ahead of it. Observe the enthusiastic crowd!"

At the windows, the separate floors are now indistinguishable because of the mass of people. Everywhere, the same shouting, cheering, booing, and singing floods the prison and flows over its walls.

"Someday this game for fanatics will replace the guillotine. Entire crowds will come to watch it."

All of a sudden a roar rises up inside the prison. The Sainte-Pélagie Blue Shirts have just scored. The players are slapping each other patriotically on the back and there is a general kissing and hugging all around. They seem to be playing for no other reason than to gather together into a group hug, as L'Abbé Lamourette had once suggested they do. The opposing team looks on, poker-faced.

"By the way, Moka, we need to borrow your hearse."

"What for?"

"Nothing much. It's complicated. We need to make a couple of stops and then we'll be back to pick you up."

Moka shrugs his shoulders and turns back to watch the match. Such strange times are these! Now, grown men run around playing with balls and spend the rest of their time chasing after little children!

Ed and Jones exit Sainte-Pélagie Prison. They are forced to push through suppliers, lawyers, visitors, inspectors, all of them waiting outside in chaos. Ed and Jones proceed toward Moka's hearse. It looks even more ridiculous than they had remembered.

* * *

Marie-Antoinette does not dare look at Rosalie. The young woman has just entered the cell. In the half light, she stands silently before her, two steps away. From that distance, Marie-Antoinette can sense her body trembling. The dear heart is troubled. She cannot utter a single word. Her emotional state prevents her from admitting that the members of the Committee have not honored her request. *Madame, I beg you to believe me! I have tried everything!* So that's how it will be! Those miscreants will not allow the former Queen of France to wear a clean dress to her death! . . . *Do not be alarmed, my girl. I know that it is not your fault.* Marie-Antoinette feels the iron blade wounding her belly. She will not have the strength to demand fair treatment. Of what importance is the stain that they think they are forcing upon her as punishment? She will not add the additional stain of begging her executioners for clean linens.

The Queen resigns herself to this latest insult. She looks up at Rosalie. The young girl is drowning in the chagrin of her eyes. She is trembling, tense with worry. Facing the Queen with outstretched arms, she offers her a miraculous, white bundle. It's a beautiful, luminous, white mound neatly folded beneath its collar. A clean dress! Marie-Antoinette is suddenly overwhelmed with gratitude. She holds back her tears as she confronts the terror that suddenly appears in Rosalie's eyes. She must reassure this poor dear. My worried face has made her think that I am disappointed. But I am not! This dress is the most beautiful thing that I have ever received. The Queen smiles at Rosalie.

"Thank you, my dear girl."

"Madame!"

"Come now. Let us not express too much emotion. We must make our preparations."

Marie-Antoinette takes the dress from Rosalie's arms. How clean it is! She lays it on the bed. In the half light it looks like a decapitated body. A lump rises in the Queen's throat. She turns away and catches the gendarme's blank look. Marie-Antoinette had almost forgotten his presence. She thought that he had left the premises. That would have been a noble gesture on his part. With a firm flick of the chin she sends him away with her eyes. The man stiffens. He clenches his teeth. He defies her. That injurious fraction of a second would have gotten him a *lettre de cachet,* an order under the King's private seal, and a stay in the Bastille prison. She cannot reveal the reasons behind her feminine modesty to this man so that he might understand her situation. It would be of the greatest indecency. The Queen gives up but does not lower her eyes.

Where can she undress at the farthest distance from this shameless man? Rosalie suggests the narrow space between the side of the bed and the wall. The young woman shows her how she will then be able to stand between her and the gendarme in order to block his view. The Queen realizes that this dear heart has communicated all of this to her without even batting an eyelid. This is definitive evidence proving the existence of a secret language share by women alone. She had been severely criticized for her female friendships. She thinks of Madame de Polignac, so quick to flee, and of her dear friend Madame de Lamballe, too prompt to return. How had she been able to hide the secret of the child from her for so long? A son! The destiny of the kingdom would have been turned upside down. But why? What could be hiding behind a secret so terrible that she would believe that even a mother's love could not comprehend it?

In the narrow space beside the bed, Marie-Antoinette lets her black dress slide to the floor.

Dear Husband! Do not think for a moment that I am abandoning my widow's weeds. I have been told that I must die clothed in white. That the people would be angry to see me go to the gallows dressed in black. These days, we must not upset the people even at the hour of our death.

I am reconciled to this because white is the color of mourning for queens.

Marie-Antoinette looks down at her bloodstained shift. Dear Lord! My body, how you seem to resent me! The gendarme walks up to Rosalie and looks around the screen that she has formed with her body. The Queen catches the indiscretion.

"In the name of honor, Sir, allow me to change my linens without your witness."

"I cannot allow that. I am under orders to keep an eye on all of your movements."

To keep an eye on! That is truly a watchman's duty. He reminds me of how Madame de Tourzel used to run after Madame Brunier in order to stop her from blowing out the newly lit candles in my daughter's apartments. It was so comical. My poor little Marie-Thérèse had to move from room to room, book in hand, looking for the light, like a sunflower . . . *Are you not aware, Madam, that in this household, it is forbidden to relight a candle once it has gone out? . . .* No, she had not been aware of that. *Because an extinguished candle now belongs to the others who are also using this room, since it is being shared with an unimaginable ferocity.* She had not been aware of that. *Have you any idea of the value of this candle?* She had preferred not to know. And she had been blamed for so much.

The memory of her daughter Marie-Thérèse sitting in an empty salon at Versailles, reading by the waning light of day, is enough to make her pardon such mean-spiritedness. Oh, my dear fifteen-year-old daughter! I pray that your grown woman's blood will have a more sacred destiny than mine!

Marie-Antoinette removes her stained shift with such grace that her nudity is never noticed.

* * *

Seiffert is furious with Zamor. The Belhomme Clinic can go to the devil. For a good while now, the carriage horse has been trotting up the road toward the village of Charonne and Our Lady of Good Help. It is as though they were a hundred leagues from Paris. Finally! There's the gate. The trees in the park are naked and scarcely any of the shutters have been opened. Here, the morning is heavy, like that Belhomme woman. Here she comes now.

"Doctor Seiffert! Do I have an ailing intern I wasn't expecting?"

She welcomes him onto the terrace with the powerful handshake of a former washerwoman. Near the steps, a tableful of aristocrats is drinking tea, their pinkies lifted.

"Ailing? It is I, Madame, who have been ill from not seeing you."

"Flattery is the better part of valor, Doctor!"

She doesn't know the half of it. In a different era, the only thing they would have had in common would have been bloody linen and enemas.

"Have you come to give me news of our good Olympe de Gouges? I've been told that the dear angel sits in despair in La Force Prison. Some old matron is claiming that she's not really pregnant. Can't you help remedy that, Doctor?"

"Madame, I am called upon to help angels come into the world, not to impregnate them. For the moment, I am here to speak to your husband about an urgent and . . . clamorous affair."

"Come in, come in! He'll be happy to see you. You'll help him get rid of those two pretentious duchesses."

The Doctor proceeds to Belhomme's office. He hears peals of laughter coming from behind the door.

"Citizens! If you cannot pay your pension, I will regretfully have to file a medical report stating that you are in good health."

"In good health?"

"How awful! Monsieur Belhomme, you are trying to kill us!"

"A clean bill of health will send us straight to the gallows!"

"Citizens, I am running a clinic here, not a sanctuary."

"Some clinic, Sir! Here you have to pay to be sick!"

On the other side of the door, Doctor Seiffert finds the topic worthy of consideration. However, he is in a hurry. He knocks loudly on the door, enters without waiting for an answer, nods curtly to the two ladies, and goes straight up to the desk.

"Doctor Belhomme, I have an urgent matter to discuss with you. But I see that you are busy."

"We have just finished. Citizens, you have been warned. If in two days you do not pay for this month and for the next trimester in advance, I will have to sign those medical reports."

"If that's the way it is, then we're at death's door."

Appalled, the two women rise and leave the office.

"Who were they, Belhomme?"

"The Duchess of Châtelet and the Duchess of Gramont. But that's over and done with. What have you brought me, dear colleague?"

For Seiffert, being Belhommme's "dear colleague" is unbearable. But tonight, he must bear it.

"I have brought you the Countess du Barry!"

"Damn! That's your best catch yet! Let's drink to that! How

about a glass of vermouth? I make it myself from absinthe and Tokay wine."

A vermouth at nine o'clock in the evening? Seiffert declines the bombshell.

"But be careful, Belhomme, the Countess du Barry comes with strings attached. I need transfer orders to get her out of Sainte-Pélagie, and an internment authorization notice from you. And I need it now."

"Right now? Just what makes you think that Fouquier-Tinville is going to sign those papers at this hour of the night?"

"Come now, dear colleague. You have the blank forms right here, and we've already used them before now."

Belhomme ponders the idea. Getting the Countess du Barry on credit is still a good deal. Except that Fouquier-Tinville would be hard-pressed to let her go. He wants her head and is likely to be even hungrier than usual. No matter. There will still be enough to eat. The lion's leftovers are better to eat than those of the jackal. Especially since two duchess spots will be opening up soon.

*   *   *

Pobéré enters the back room of Sweet Victory and goes straight to Dame Catherine's table.

"Mother! I've got good news!"

"Sit down first! You're dripping with sweat, Son!"

She strokes his head and dabs at his neck with the edge of her sleeve.

"I've been pounding the pavement in order to alert our partisans."

"Well, let's hear the report!"

"The Queen will go to the guillotine at noon!"

"Well, well! This calls for a celebration. Barmaid! Two pints!"

They shake hands, looking like they've just won the Royal Lottery. The Boss snaps her dishrag against a bench. They should be ashamed of celebrating the death of a woman and with that kind of glee! They won't be getting any Réveillon wine from her!

"Lower your voice, Son!"

Pobéré moves closer, right up to her ear.

"The execution is set to take place at noon. I got the news from the clerk at the Grande-Chambre. That gives us two more hours in which to call up our men and to take our positions."

"So we've won!"

The Boss shoves the pints in their general direction. There's no mistaking her attitude. The shine boy takes a sip and scowls.

"That harpy's trying to slip us some sour wine!"

"Calm down, Son! Don't get excited! Did you find a wheelbarrow?"

"Yes, Mother. But I don't see how you plan to 'play queen' with that!"

"Come with me. You'll see."

* * *

At the Sainte-Pélagie entrance gate, the Commander pushes a wad of documents through the bars to the guard.

"Civil Administration Commission! Police and courts!"

"Your Commissioners have already been here."

"Citizen, we must be ever-vigilant in our efforts to unmask the conspirators who would destroy our freedom and lead the nation astray. Are you part of that scum that thinks it can hinder the National Convention's relentless efforts to eliminate these conspirators and their followers?"

"You've got the wrong idea, Citizen! I'm extremely patriotic!"

Especially when he sees all of those orders, stamped, signed, and sealed.

"The other members of my surveillance team will confirm that I'm as good as anyone at denouncing conspirators."

"Glad to hear it, Citizen. Keep it up! Because of men like you, liberty will prevail over the land. Let me see your prison register."

"Er . . . I'm not supposed to . . ."

"Would you stand in the way of progress, Citizen?"

No, he would not. Not, that is, in the form of a six-foot, six-inch man who talks like a commissioner. The Commander scans the list of names and notations in the index: "rebellious'; "suspicious"; "son of an émigré"; "federalist"; "suspected of being suspicious."

"*This particular Citizen is known for not responding at roll call.* What is the meaning of this?"

"It's those French Theater ladies. They were all shouting at the same time. *What! Madame Raucourt is supposed to respond 'present' at roll call? Look at me, everyone! I'm supposed to show up at roll call? Well I don't have to! I am Madame Rau-*

court! Present and accounted for! Everyone started clapping. That was even better than having a front-row seat!"

The Commander smiles to himself. That makes . . . twelve, thirteen, fourteen, fifteen! Fifteen women to save. When the time comes, there won't be a trace of them left. Hmm . . . Du Barry! Former courtesan . . . Cell number five on the second floor. The Commander ditches the door guard, climbs the stairs to the second floor, and proceeds down the corridor. There is yelling. There is howling. There is singing. Nobody pays him any mind. All eyes are riveted on a ball game being played down in the courtyard. That will make things easier. Here it is. There's a gendarme in front of the door. The Commander goes straight up to him and accosts him with all of his height, waving the orders in his face.

"Civil Administration Commission! Is this the cell of Jeanne du Barry?"

"Yes it is, Citizen Commissioner."

"I am here to interrogate the prisoner."

"That's impossible, Citizen Commissioner. I have my orders."

"And these are mine."

He waves the papers and their tricolor ribbon in the air.

"Citizen, my orders are even higher and more strict than yours."

The Commander moves in closer and growls.

"There are no stricter orders than these."

The gendarme can feel the point of a knife sticking into his ribs.

"Open it!"

"Wooo! Gendarme! What's going on out zere?"

It's the Countess's voice from behind the door.

"A Commissioner has come to interrogate you, Citizen! But I have my orders."

The Countess trembles in her bath. This Commissioner is Zamor's envoy. He's come to inform her of her impending transfer to the Belhomme Clinic. The gendarme fiddles with the lock. The noise is frantic. That tenderfoot is going to break the key. The door swings open. The Countess glimpses the high stature of the Commissioner in the doorway behind the gendarme. Her savior! In his hand, a gleam of light. A knife flashes at her breast. Her heart bursts. She falls backward.

The Commander strikes again, but that idiotic gendarme has made it his business to interfere. He resists. The Commander grabs him by the nape of the neck and pushes him into the cell. Dagger in hand, he casts a sweeping glance over the meager space of the brig. The bathtub, the straw mattress, the window, the coffer. Completely empty.

La du Barry has vanished!

A formidable furor suddenly arises outdoors. What's going on? The Commander drops the half-strangled gendarme and leaves the cell. There is yelling at the windows and in the courtyard. At the end of the hallway, the Commander sees a tall, thin girl and a pockmarked black man running toward him. They've seen him. It's all over. He'll have to throw in the towel.

The Commander makes it to the stairway without lengthening his stride. His heart is in a much bigger hurry. The girl and the black man have disappeared. They weren't coming for him after all. The Commander would have had time to finish the job. Better luck next time. He descends the staircase, forcing himself to appear calm and self-assured. Once inside the entrance hall, he can hear sharp cries echoing above his head.

"Guards! There's been a murder! Someone's escaped!"

Things are in an uproar. There's a commotion. The prison's main gate is just a few steps away. He hears the gendarme's rapid footsteps in the stairwell.

"Civil Administration Commission. Open the door!"

"Leaving us already, Commissioner?"

"Hop to it! I'm in a hurry!"

The door guard opens the first gate. They're in the vestibule now. Just one more gate to get through and he'll be outside. The gendarme's hobnailed boots pound the floor behind him.

"Guard! Guard!"

"What does the Citizen want?"

Busy with his keys, the door guard turns around. The Commander urges him on.

"Thou shalt not hinder!"

That line helps him find the right key. He finally inserts it into the lock.

"There he is! Guard! The suspect is escaping!"

The gendarme points at the Commander. He unsheathes his sword, runs toward the gate, and thrusts it through the bars. The Commander seizes the door guard by the throat and uses him as a shield.

"You blackguard! You'll pay for this!"

The Commander escapes the stabbing, but the door guard isn't so lucky. He turns the key, opens the door, and rushes out of the prison. God, the air is refreshing! Even in the middle of this loud-mouthed mob of commoners milling around in front of the gate. He runs to his horse, mounts up, and drawing blood, spurs him on hard toward Rue de la Clef. He can hear barking behind him. A bullet ricochets off a windowsill. But he's far enough away now.

Near Sainte-Geneviève, the Commander slows to a trot. He eases up off his horse's back and rubs his neck. By what miracle did that harlot du Barry vanish from her cell? Bah. No matter. Doctor Seiffert must be intercepted. He must be with his informant, that Zamor clown. It shouldn't be too hard for him to track them down.

* * *

Suddenly a formidable roar rises up from the courtyard. The Sainte-Pélagie Blue Shirts have just scored. Ninon, the water bearer, and Moka run down the corridor. The young woman had come looking for him as he was watching the football fanatics play. Come quickly! It's Aurore Devey. If anyone can, you're the one who'll be able to say the right words . . . Come quickly! Does this beautiful child realize that even a Living Memory can get old and out of breath? No, she doesn't. Her legs were made for running after much younger men. Ninon and Moka run down the Ideas corridor. Nothing going on there. Everyone is at the windows. Down the hallway, Moka notices a tall man who is much too calm. He is walking out of La du Barry's jail cell. The man possesses that all-too-familiar masterful bearing.

"She's in here!"

The young woman points to Aurore Devey, who is standing on a chair in front of an open window. She looks like she is enjoying the spectacle of the match, except that she has a look in her eyes that extends far beyond the courtyard, and a length of cloth around her throat that looks like a scarf meant to hide an aging neck. Instead, it's a sheet whose other end is tied to the window handle. Nobody in the vicinity seems to have noticed her. Moka moves toward her.

"Madame, please . . ."

She turns her face toward him. It is made up to look like a young girl's. She stops Moka with a tired smile and swings out of the window and into the void. Aurore Devey's body rocks peacefully above the courtyard. All eyes are drawn to a tightly curled blond wig clutched in her hand.

* * *

"Hear that, Spike?"

"Hear what?"

"The silence."

Groundhog comes out of the cell. In the corridor, everything has come to a standstill. People are hanging out of the windows. The entire prison seems to have gone missing. Groundhog motions to Spike to come and see for himself.

"Take a look! That's how you spell 'escape.' C'mon!"

Even the sentry box is empty. Spike finds his pike and Groundhog recovers his sword. In the courtyard of the castigated there are no more castigates, just the little girl swinging on her swing next to the covered well, reading a book. Groundhog's heart starts swinging too. No doubt that's due to the long, blond-but-not-too-blond hair and the big blue eyes. But it is especially due to the dog that she is holding in her arms.

"Coco!"

The poor thing looks seasick. His tongue is turning green, his snout is dripping, and his eyes are weeping. The girl on the swing looks at them without a trace of surprise.

"Hello, my name is Belle-de-Nuit. What's yours?"

"He's Spike and I'm Groundhog. We're trying to escape in the right direction."

"How did you know my dog's name?"

"Because before, he used to be ours."

"Really? 'cause my father just gave him to me. He requisitioned him from a former somebody, along with this book, which is kind of disgusting. But I like the story."

Groundhog can't make out the title. The cover is spattered with dark spots. He wonders how he's going to get the pug back from Belle-de-Nuit.

"How do you like the dog? He's kinda small. If you want, I could trade ya for him."

"Trade him for what?"

Spike and Groundhog search their pockets and line their treasures up on the edge of the well. Two figurines and two bits of paper.

"A Voltaire! . . . A Rousseau! And some really rare wild words we caught ourselves in the street."

"I don't need those! I already have a pile of them in this story, even though I couldn't read the beginning because of the bloodstains."

She shows them the first pages covered with brownish spots that have consumed the print.

"What book is this?"

"*The Journals of Captain Cook.*"

"That's too bad, 'cause the beginning is the best part. Especially the part that comes before the beginning."

"You know the story?

"By heart! It's my favorite book! . . . Hey, how 'bout I trade ya the beginning of *Captain Cook* for that puny little pug?"

"OK."

Groundhog stands up tall like a town crier and begins his oration.

"First, the title page: *An Account of the voyages undertaken by order of His Present Majesty, for making discoveries in the Southern Hemisphere . . .*"

When Belle-de-Nuit widens her sea-blue eyes, Spike wants to become a sailor and Coco isn't so seasick any more. Groundhog continues, with a deep voice and a mysterious air.

The geography of half of the globe was covered in darkness when the immortal doctor Cook set out on his voyages . . .

Groundhog proclaims: *First voyage! Voyage from England to the Pacific by way of Cape Horn.* At that point, Belle-de-Nuit leaves the swing and hands him the pug.

"Here. Have your dog back. He'll travel more with you than he would by staying here. When you get to the other side, if you still want to escape in the wrong direction, you can come back and see me. I'll stay here and read until I get to Tahiti."

Groundhog mumbles, "Sure thing!" He'll be back. Slightly irritated, Spike pushes him to the top of the wall and drags him over it.

"Hey, Groundhog! What's the use in knowing how to read if you already know everything by heart?"

Groundhog doesn't hear him. He's thinking of Belle-de-Nuit, who has now set sail toward Tahiti.

"Me, too, Groundhog. I want you to read to me from the books you know by heart. You told me you have a pile of them in your cellar under the Capuchin monastery. How 'bout we head over there right now?"

"I have to take this pug back to Pretty Sidonie first. Then we'll go over there after that. I swear."

They hitch a ride on the back end of a fine cabriolet, slung low on its high wheels . . . *October 16th: A slight breeze is blowing. Skies are cloudy. Sailing due north toward the Rue des Moineaux gang.*

* * *

Zamor turns around to make sure that no one is following him. He never goes straight home. After Doctor Seiffert left for the Belhomme Clinic, he took a couple of detours before entering his building. Zamor climbs the stairs to the fifth floor. The stairway shakes like a suspension bridge hung over the humidity and mephitic odor of a latrine. Zamor makes certain that he is quite alone before groping for a key and finding it hidden in a hole above a window on the landing. Still no one around, except some skinny, resident rats. Zamor approaches a door. After scanning the area with a couple of extra wary looks, he turns the key and enters.

The door to his room hasn't been closed more than a minute before the parrot Petit-Louis begins to screech the words to that little ditty from the Antilles:

"Mé zami, mvê tadé: Baré!"

Zamor mutters "quiet!" in Creole. This has the immediate effect of making Petit-Louis shriek out an even louder translation: "My friends, I hear someone yelling, stop thief!"

Zamor passes through a finely beaded curtain that never fails to remind him of a waterfall in Martinique near L'Anse-à-l'Ane. He approaches the white parrot's cage and pushes his index finger through the bars for the parrot to bite. Petit-Louis calms down immediately. Zamor removes his turban and his frock coat. He cleans the cage, supplies clean water, and serves some millet, all the while engaging the parrot in the kind of conversation often exchanged by old married couples. "How are you? Did you have a nice day?" "And you? Did you know . . . ?" All of it in their own Creole language.

La du Barry used to find the couple highly amusing. She also used to enjoy dressing Petit-Louis in a tailcoat identical to Zamor's, entirely covered in faux-precious stones. *Look, Petit-Louis is shinier than thou!* The tailcoat hangs on a hanger hooked underneath the cage, as though Petit-Louis were ready to attend a gala.

Zamor contemplates his palace. It's a garret whose only piece of furniture is a rope hammock hitched to either side of the room. The walls are completely covered with clothes hung on hooks: liveries, frock coats with tailored Brandenburg cord and knot closures, doublets, his Saxony green tailcoat with gold braid . . . Like Petit-Louis! On the floor a row of shoes runs around the room like a coquettish skirting board. In a corner above a pile of books, a poster advertises a play: *December 18, 1789. Performance of L'Esclavage des Nègres Zamor et Mirzha ou L'Heureux Naufrage, Drame en 3 actes, The Enslavement of the Negroes Zamor and Mirzha or, the Happy Shipwreck, Drama in Three Acts by Olympe de Gouges, Woman of Letters. The play will begin at five o'clock sharp. The room will be heated by stoves that will not inconvenience the public.*

Zamor thinks of Olympe with sadness. He had so enjoyed the time he had spent with her. She had loved him all day long and hadn't stopped except to dictate a tragedy, a pamphlet, or a diatribe. You're my nègre, my ghost writer! she would say. She had told him all about Gorée Island. The acrid odor of the stones, the ocean, and the nappy blue waves. These days, she doesn't want to see him even in her prison cell. *You sold out to La du Barry! You sold out to your master!* How could he ever explain that it was all for her? The jewels, the Black Pearl, the leopard boy, the safe-conduct passes. All of it. How can he make her understand that with her he had felt like a real man for the first time? It would have been so easy, this summer, to help her escape from the Escourbiac nursing home. Innocence doesn't run away! Too bad, he'll just have to save her in spite of herself.

Zamor goes to his garret window. He opens it onto a small glass compartment, a greenhouse wedged into the space between the window and the guardrail. Inside it is a white flower. Zamor strokes the blooming flesh of the anthurium lily. Each time he does this, he thinks he can smell a woman's scent concealed inside. He stretches out onto his hammock and gazes at the flower as he swings back and forth.

Suddenly, Zamor jumps up, closes the window, and kneels before a pair of patent leather pumps. He moves them to the side and slides a floorboard back. The best hiding place is also the most obvious one. He probes the cavity with a long boot-pull and pulls out a brown leather bag tied at the top. Zamor goes to the door and presses his ear against it. Perfect. He throws the fake jewel-encrusted tailcoat over the top of Petit-Louis's cage.

"Sorry, but you are just too nosy."

"Di kwa?"

"Hey, birdie! You coulda learned French by now, you been here so long!"

The parrot speaks and understands it perfectly. But only when he wants to. Zamor gets undressed and stretches out naked on his hammock. He unties the leather bag and empties it onto his belly. An enormous black pearl shaped like a pear rolls into his navel. The Maréchal de Saxe's Black Pearl! Ah, no, Doctor Seiffert! La du Barry doesn't have it, I do! He makes the black pearl oscillate like a pendulum. This pearl alone is enough to save Olympe. But to do that, he'll have to go and feed that tiger Delorme without getting devoured himself.

Zamor gets dressed and goes out. He likes this moment when Haarlem is empty. At this hour it smells like croissants, coffee, and chocolate. A newspaper vendor yells, *Marie-Antoinette! Execution Immanent!* Zamor snags one. He's not even happy to hear the news. Even though he has never forgotten that night on a Versailles garden pathway when she called him an ape as he was holding La du Barry's train. In just a short time, he'll be watching her go by. He would like to be carrying a little baboon on his shoulder just to make her remember what she'd said.

Zamor passes the Church of Saint-Zita, cutting through the rectory garden. He steals past the Laughing Negress, an abandoned fountain whose enormous stone mouth still hovers over the crumbling basin. Zamor descends a staircase that plunges below the church. Once through the entrance gate, a metal bannister makes it possible to proceed through the darkness. Hold on tight and don't let go. Ever. When the bannister runs out, you have to stop and wait. It can take awhile. Delorme likes to generate fear in those who've come to see him. Zamor stops and waits. Someone is coming to get him.

"Follow me, Brother."

The man with the hoarse voice leads him along as if he were a blind man. The ground is spongy. Usually this passageway is dry. Strange. Still in darkness, they climb a steep set of uneven stairs cut directly into the rock.

"Stay here, Brother."

The man deserts him. Zamor is left teetering at the edge of a chasm. He can feel it falling away behind him. All they have to do is push him and he'll go crashing to the bottom.

Someone does push him.

Zamor screams and his body is thrown to the ground. He rolls over and comes to a stop on his back. A flash of light blinds his eyes. Roars of laughter slam into his ears. His eyes adjust. He can distinguish a circle of men hovering over him.

"Brothers! May I present the Grand Maharajah of Haarlem!"

The men who are mocking him look like soldiers on a pillaging rampage. They are dressed in the remainders of a green and gold uniform and a scruffy assortment of personal effects probably stolen on random occasions.

"Get up. The Master of Us All has agreed to receive you."

They blindfold him. Someone leads him firmly by the arm. When his blindfold is removed, he is disoriented at first. He finds himself in a vast limestone grotto in which a church has been carved. It is not yet finished but seems to have been designed to form a Latin cross with a central nave, choir, and transept. Halfway up the walls, a gallery runs around its sides. Zamor is impressed by the size of the construction site. Dozens of men are at work on it. The first thing he notices is a leopard skin hung from a balcony in the gallery. Even more surprising is the presence of a ship at least twenty-five cubits in length, under construction in one of the side aisles.

Amazing! A ship washed up inside a grotto! In the middle of the nave is a raised platform draped in emerald-green cloth upon which a wooden armchair reupholstered in white takes itself for a throne. Suspended above it is an immense painting that swings ever so slightly in its gilded frame. It represents the Maréchal de Saxe and his guard of black uhlans in ceremonial dress and on horseback.

"Admire it, Brother! That was at the Château de Chambord. The tallest one in the middle there is my father!"

Delorme! He lounges on his throne, whip in hand. His huge

head serves as his crown and his gapped teeth make him look like he has just devoured someone. He is surrounded by men who seem to have stepped straight out of the painting. Same colossal stature, same green and gold uniform, same helmet with its horsetail crest, same fierce bearing.

"Step forward, Brother! Welcome to Slave Route History Park!"

Someone pushes Zamor toward the platform in the central nave. His feet splash in the milky water puddled on the stone pavement.

"Brother, we will soon open the very first Site of Memory and Understanding consecrated to the Slave Trade."

Delorme lays out his vision. He explains how the visitor will, in just two days! and in real-life situations! experience slave life firsthand, from the point of capture all the way to the plantation! How, for the same price, he will be able to be captured in a raid, placed in chains, sold, branded, and finally sent to work on a plantation in the West Indies. All incredibly re-created! The visitor will also be able to sail aboard *The Slave Ark,* a faithful reproduction of the famous British slave ship, the *Brooks.*

"Take advantage of this opportunity, Zamor! For the moment, it's still free of charge, but not for long. This project costs a fortune, Brother."

"I've already paid my dues, Master of Us All."

"How true. You are a generous brother. But so many others have forgotten where they came from. Have you brought me the object of our agreement?"

"Where is the boy, Master of Us All?"

"Right over there!"

Delorme points to an old-fashioned sedan chair stationed in the transept. With its curtains drawn, it seems to be waiting to be borne away by wigged lackeys.

"I need to see him."

"First give me the Black Pearl that was stolen from my father."

He points to the painting.

"Delorme! You know that I don't have it on me. Your men already frisked me. Who would be fool enough to come in here with that?"

"We've seen a few!"

Delorme laughs. His enormous face lights up around his gapped teeth. Those gaps are a sign of good luck. His own!

"So, Zamor, what now? Do I hand you over to my henchmen so they can burn your feet, skin you alive, and break every single bone in your body?"

"That would be pointless. I've taken my precautions. Believe me, if I don't get out of here in less than an hour, the Black Pearl will disappear forever."

Delorme leaps up from his throne. He shouts as he smacks the arms of his throne with his whip.

"The Black Pearl belongs to me! It was stolen from my father just to satisfy the whims of that syphilitic du Barry! I should not have to ask for it back. I should be able to just take it!"

Suddenly Delorme calms down. He sits down again, crosses his legs as if he were engaged in polite conversation, and smiles. This makes him seem even more unpredictable.

"So, what do you propose, Zamor?"

"I take the kid with me and put him in a safe place. At a prearranged time and place, I'll give you the pearl."

"No deal! That kid isn't leaving here!"

"You're afraid of getting tricked, Master of Us All. You think I'm going to run away with the kid without paying you. Nothing leaves Haarlem unless you say so!"

Delorme looks down at his whip as though asking it for advice. What is there to worry about with this drawing room maharajah? That's what he thinks, too.

"Very well, Zamor. You can see the kid and take him with you."

Zamor walks over to the sedan chair. He hesitates before slowly opening the door. The leopard boy! There he is, right there, seated in a sweet-smelling half light. The boy turns his head and looks straight at him.

* * *

Ed parks Moka's hearse in front of the Marquis d'Andençon's mansion. He is satisfied. Since leaving Saint-Zita, he has hardly crushed, stomped, overturned, or shoved anything. Hardly. In the Rue de Viarmes, a teeming tangle of wagons, porters, and pushcarts converges and circles around the covered wheat market. This circular street resembles a roundabout where artisans hawking their wares stamp the trademarks of their guilds with their voices and attempt to attract customers. Jones admires a milkmaid who ambles about waving a red apron and shouting, *Milk! Milk for sale! Get your fresh milk! Sweet teats! Two bits a suckle!* His face set, Ed examines the façade of the Anderçon mansion. Jones can tell that Ed is in a bad mood.

"Watch it, Ed. You can't be too rough on the Marquis. He's our Lieutenant."

"Right. But we're going to warn him that we'll be dropping this mission if he doesn't reveal the true identity of the boy we're trying to find."

Ed and Jones exchange a look. Why do they have the feeling that the mansion is empty? The exterior door is closed. No one answers the bell. Ed climbs up onto the driving seat of the hearse and backs it up to the wall. The horse is obedient. He knows his job. Jones understands what's needed. He climbs up on the vehicle and jumps from the top of it over into the courtyard. Ed flashes his blue badge to the anxious public.

"Police, Citizens!"

This doesn't seem very reassuring, but it's enough to get people to go back to work. *Knives! Scissors! You own 'em, we hone 'em!* Jones opens the front door. Ed joins him. They enter. Empty. The entryway and blue drawing room are deserted. They go down to the crypt. Empty. Ed and Jones climb to the upper rooms. All of the doors are hanging open. The Marquise's room has been completely upended, the mattress thrown to the floor and the vanity mirror broken. As for the Marquis's chamber, it is intact.

Ed and Jones rifle through the household like a couple of thieves, with a brutality intended to hide their worst fears. There's been a struggle. There's no blood. But sometimes that's even worse. They speculate to keep their hearts from jumping to terrible conclusions. Ed thinks of the Marquise. You get a helpless feeling when you find nothing but an empty house! What if they've left? What if they've emigrated? That word has been lurking ever since they entered the house. These days, empty houses are becoming commonplace. One or two valets get left behind to make people think the house is occupied, giving the proprietors time to reach the border before anyone notices they're gone.

"Ed, what do you think happened here?"

"Anything could have happened. Robbery. Looting. Kidnapping."

"Shhh! Ed! What's that?"

There's a noise coming from the narrow panel next to the window. A scratching sound. Ed and Jones draw their .38s. They move in. It's loud and clear. Maybe it's a rat. It must be in there. Jones remembers the movements the Marquis had made. He slides his hand, feels the molding. Clack! The panel opens onto a cabinet holding a collection of volumes bound in red leather. In the lower part is a cubby hole. And curled up in the cubby is . . .

"Thomas!"

Ed pulls him out and unfolds him.

"Edmond and Jonathan! You've saved my life. Without your help I would have gone from being alive to *très pâle*."

"Trespass would suffice. You're already *très pâle*."

"That is to be expected, since I was reduced to enduring a suffocation deficiency in that dungeon dark."

Ed and Jones wonder what Thomas's sentences would be like if he weren't oxygen-deprived.

"What happened, Thomas?"

The valet stretches up to reach a height that he has never attained.

"Right after your precipitous departure, a mob of men immediately came to see my excellent master, Monsieur the Marquis."

"Thomas! Why don't you just say, 'Following your sudden departure some men came to see the Marquis.' Then we would ask you, 'what men?'" And you would say . . ."

"The kind of men you don't want to meet in a dark alley without a lantern, Mr. Edmond."

"Very good! That's much better."

"Did you recognize them?"

"I've never seen them before."

"Not even through a keyhole?"

"Well, maybe. It is true that I do know a lot of people by that intervention."

"What were those men and the Marquis talking about?"

"About a boy!"

"About what boy, Thomas?"

"About a boy to either kill or rescue."

"When?"

"Today."

Ed and Jones now miss Thomas's long, garbled sentences.

"What did the Marquis say?"

"He was defending himself. The men were accusing him of being a traitor and were saying that it was his fault if the boy was in danger and if the others were looking for him."

"What others, Thomas?"

"Can you recall any names, places, details, or anything at all?"

Thomas ponders on anything at all. He is usually asked for the opposite.

"I remember that they often spoke about a doctor or a physician who was supposed to be German."

"German! Did you get his name?"

"There were never any names."

"So who were the men talking about, again?"

"Some Commander. A Creole! I remember that word because Madame the Marquise explained it to me once, but I forgot what it means. Do you know what a Creole is?"

"It's complicated!"

Thomas thinks that the Marquise gives better explanations than Ed does.

"And you, Edmond and Jonathan, what are you?"

"Kettle Black and Charcoal Gray."

Jones isn't any better at giving explanations than the Marquise.

"Can you remember anything else besides the German doctor and the Creole commander?"

"No. I was starting to suffocate. Oh, yes! They were also talking about a pug dog."

"A pug!"

Ed and Jones think they'd better find Groundhog. But they've known that for awhile now.

"And then what happened?"

"It was dreadful! They got into a terrible argument. The men said that my master had told the Marquise too much. That she was the one who would bring down the entire operation. That they had to find her and get rid of her."

"Get rid of her?"

Ed butts the bookcase with his head. Thomas feels for it.

"The Marquis fought back. I thought they were going to kill him. They had to knock him out and take him away. After that, I didn't hear a thing. Until you got here."

"And the Marquise? Where was she all that time?"

"She had left just before that. I carried a torch for her all the way to a back door that opens onto Rue Mercier."

"Thomas, do you know where the Marquise went?"

"Madame did not want me to accompany her. All she told me was, I'm going to get some apples and blood sausage. Even though I'm always the one who does the shopping."

"Blood sausage and apples! Thomas, you the man!"

Ed and Jones leap at the valet. They hug him and congratulate him, almost suffocating him. Thomas heaves a sigh. What's the use of saving him, if they're just going to slay him in the next breath!

"Let's go, Ed, there's no time to lose! We need to get to Sweet Victory and the Boss on the double!"

Through the window, Thomas watches Edmond and Jonathan depart in their strange hearse. He returns to the secret bookcase and randomly chooses one of the books bound in red leather. Théveneau de Morande. *The Secret Memoirs of a Public Woman*. Time to start using shorter sentences.

* * *

Groundhog watches Coco lick Pretty Sidonie's face. He whimpers plaintively as he scampers around her. She remains motionless, impassive. The pug can't decide which part of her to lick first. That's because there is a lot of blood to clean up. One entire side of her face is covered with it. It has run down from her skull. That's where they must have struck her, with that skillet or this big copper pot. They killed her in her kitchen. Maybe she was baking those little stuffed pastries of hers. She still has flour on her hands and apron. Why would anyone want to kill a woman who knows how to bake cakes? Her body is lying on its side, her head pressed against the fireplace door, as though she had tried to escape through it. Groundhog would have helped her, if he'd been there. Coco gives up trying to clean up so much blood. He lays his head on Sidonie's shoulder. Maybe she'll wake up pretty soon.

"Where shall I put him, Groundhog?"

Spike is dragging the bodyguard's corpse down the hallway. He has been stabbed in the back. Nothing has been taken from him, not even his two pistols with grips shaped like pigs' feet.

Spike sits him up against the wall under the portraits of the ancestors whose faces are turned to the wall. He looks like he's going to start snoring. Groundhog doesn't dare close Sidonie's eyes. He's afraid that she'll be stone-cold. Cold in a way unlike any other and like what he's already felt on a cadaver on the banks of the Seine. He fishes the red apple and the walnuts from the folds of his cape. He places them next to Sidonie's face. That's what you do when someone has a long road to travel.

"Groundhog, we gotta get outta here. They might come back."

Spike is right. "They" might be the Viscount, the Doctor, the Commander, or someone else.

"Let's go to your cave now, Groundhog. You promised."

That's true, although he's wondering what to do with Coco now. There's only one person left to give him to. The Dauphin. It won't be easy to enter Temple Prison. Especially not today. Spike unhooks one of the paintings hanging in the entryway.

"What are you doing?"

"I'm taking an ancestor."

"What are you going to do with him?"

"An ancestor is always a good thing to have. I've never had one. Have you?"

"Nope, don't think so."

"You take one too. We can decorate your cave. From now on they'll be useless here, anyhow."

* * *

Doctor Seiffert pats the safe-conduct passes tucked under his coat. Belhomme had balked at leaving them blank, as Zamor had wanted. But he had finally given in. The idea of having La du Barry as an intern is much too exciting. Nevertheless, the Doctor still thinks Zamor's request is strange. From his carriage, he sits watching the entrance to the Jack of Diamonds. That's where he and Zamor were supposed to meet. There he comes! He's alone. Seiffert waves to him from his carriage.

"Well?"

"I have the boy, Doctor. He's safe and sound. What about you?"

"I've got the papers. But I want to see the child first."

"Show me the papers first, since we're right here."

The Doctor hesitates, then he takes the two thick pieces of paper from his coat and unfolds them. *Transfer Order. In the name of the People, it is hereby ordered that . . . be transferred . . . and Internment Authorization Notice . . .* Zamor cracks a smile. The orders are quite blank. These papers are worth the most beautiful of jewels. It's freedom worn around the neck. Zamor thinks of Olympe. This time she cannot refuse to be saved.

"Follow me, Doctor."

Zamor takes him up 125th Street until they meet a bottle-green carriage backed in under the vaulted ceiling of a porch.

"He's in there. Don't do anything to jeopardize our plans, Doctor. The driver is under orders to take off at the first sign of trouble."

Zamor cracks the door. Seiffert glimpses the boy. His bearing is distant, almost cold. Zamor watches for the Doctor's reaction. The child turns his head. Seiffert bows deeply.

"Your Majesty!"

* * *

Marie-Antoinette slips a white cotton gown over her fresh, clean shift. Rosalie helps her straighten it at the shoulders and at the waist. Her touch is light and steady. How sweet her face is. Following two attempts to tie her muslin shawl below her bosom, Marie-Antoinette decides to tie it across her chest. The young girl would have preferred the first option.

"Rosalie, this is the only point of disagreement we shall have ever had."

When it comes time to adjust her white linen bonnet, Rosalie acts like a mirror, moving her head impishly as she adjusts its angle. This Rosalie has many talents. Marie-Antoinette takes off her mules and slips into flats. This is her raiment. Her milliner, Madame Bertin, would have had no trouble assigning an extravagant name to such an outfit and would have had a bill of five thousand pounds sent over for payment.

Suddenly, Marie-Antoinette turns pale. On the floor, in the narrow space between the bed and the wall, she can see a little crumpled pile of cloth that is the stained shift she has just removed. The gendarme seems to have had enough of these female frivolities. He pulls on his boots and yawns. Rosalie understands. She moves into position. The Queen slips into the narrow space, retrieves the shift, and rolls it around her wrist like a sleeve. Marie-Antoinette shudders. She looks around the cell. Where can she hide it? She doesn't want anyone to find it, when they come looking for what she'll have left behind. They'll exhibit her shift as they would display the gown of a newly married virgin. She can just hear the obscene mockeries. Looky here, friends and neighbors! It took forever for Capet to get her cherry popped, but it was well worth the wait!

Marie-Antoinette's heart jumps. She has just discovered a small cavity behind the torn tapestry. She slides the shift all the way inside, hiding it completely. The half light is her ally in the successful accomplishment of the act. At first glance, no one would be able to find it. Perhaps no one will ever find it.

Rosalie and Marie-Antoinette exchange a smile for the ages. The young woman can take her leave now. She doesn't dare say a word, so fearful is she of uttering *adieu* by mistake.

The Queen watches Rosalie leave the cell with her usual timid step and slight bow of the head at the moment of crossing the threshold, as though she were afraid of hitting her head. I wish I could have at least given her my powder puff of swan's down. It would have been fitting. I hope that my remaining friends will look after her.

The door closes. The next person to enter will be the executioner.

She doesn't have long to wait before the lock on the cell door starts to rattle. A man in black comes into view. Is that him? He seems rather inconsequential for an executioner. And to think that I was afraid of him.

"Madame, I am Father Girard."

She almost bursts into laughter. How could she mistake a priest for an executioner, even in this gloom? That's putting the cart before the horse. My God! And what if she bursts into hysterical laughter?

"I have come to offer the services attendant to my ministry."

"Sir, you are a juror priest who's sworn allegiance to the Civil Constitution, are you not?"

"Yes, Madame. But . . ."

"Say no more. While I do not wish to offend you, I cannot recognize you as a representative of God."

"But, Madame, what will people say when they hear that you have refused religious succor?"

"You will inform those who speak of it that in His mercy, God provides."

"May I accompany you, Madame?"

"As you wish."

This is a priest who is satisfied with very little. At least he will act as a meager rampart, if anyone should attempt to cast a spell on her.

"Gendarme! Do you think that the people will allow me to reach the gallows without tearing me apart?"

"Citizen, one hundred gendarmes on foot will surround you, men with pikes will follow them, and thirty thousand men at arms will be posted along the route."

That's all she needed to know. Discreetly, she will be ready. The Red Porch after Robespierre's house. One thing worries her, though. She still does not know where they will expose the boy along her route. Has her poor little Coco been able to do his duty? And that Larivière, who still hasn't arrived. Just what is her lawyer up to? Finally, he comes in.

"Larivière, you do know that I have been sentenced to death?"

By the look on his face, she can see that he finds the question unsettling and even worrisome. Perhaps he thinks that I am losing my mind. He must not know about the escape plan. So, just where will this savior come from? How will she recognize him amid the multitudes?

10

THE MARQUISE

Kneeling at the foot of her bed, Marie-Antoinette closes her eyes. She is trying to keep the image of Rosalie's face fresh in her mind. The young woman has barely left the cell, and yet her features are already fading. How forgetful her mind is! It has abandoned this dear heart, so attentive to her, and now it is already busy listening to the noises on the other side of the door. Secretly, she had so enjoyed listening to the voices in the women's courtyard, listening to the conversations of the prisoners by the fountain! They have no idea how much their laughter or their intimate conversations made her want to join them. To pour water from the same jug, to share a piece of soap, or a hairpin. Dressed in the white piqué gown she is now wearing, she could be like them. What useless daydreams! She is the Queen. That is how it is. Everybody rushes to remind her of that fact, in order to better strip it from her. How could these people, mere human beings, even harbor the illusion that they can take her God-given right away from her? How inconsequential they are! If she is nothing now but a citizen, then they should allow her to say her good-byes as a commoner would. They must allow her to go to the courtyard gate in order to hug and kiss her loved ones.

Instead of that, she is forced to say her final prayers in the company of this contrite juror priest. Poor old priest who is sulking just because she won't allow him to hear her last confession. He offers her a pillow for her legs instead of a sacred host for her soul.

The prison door suddenly swings open, revealing a somber pack of hatted men. Marie-Antoinette makes the sign of the cross and stands up. She recognizes Hermann in the lead. He stops, facing her. He intends to wear a solemn expression on his face, but he merely looks mean. Two judges stand on either side of him. One of them is Donzé-Verteuil, the one who sat through the hearing rolling bits of paper into tiny balls, and the other, Foucauld, who kept dozing off. Where is the executioner? She looks to see if he is behind the judges. He is not. The Tribunal must have opted for leniency and decided to pardon her! That is what the clerk of the court has come to announce. The one with that picturesque Marseilles accent. Fabricius. He is standing behind the judges and holds a piece of paper in one hand.

The four men in black wait for the silence to settle in. Then Hermann addresses Marie-Antoinette.

"Listen carefully. We are now going to read you your sentence."

Her heart starts to pound. Read me my sentence! Again! She stands up tall. Do they think that the guillotine blade rises and falls like a yoyo? This is not a game. Is this how they've come to inform a queen that she will be put to death?

Without consulting anything except the Queen's bearing and the look in her eyes, the four men remove their hats. They seem ill at ease. They would have preferred that there be a bit more dread in her eyes in order to bolster their confidence. The victim's fear is the executioner's pardon. With a single stroke of a pen, Fabricius knows that he will obliterate this thought from his mind and these hats from the record. In this windy season, some heads also get blown way out of proportion.

Marie-Antoinette looks them up and down.

"Reading my sentence over again is completely pointless. I already know it all too well."

"No matter! It must be read to you a second time."

Marie-Antoinette decides to forgo confrontation. She cannot even see who has just spoken. She is often thankful for the myopia which exempts her from the company of men. For her dear Louis, it was worse. It exempted him from having to face the world. While her destiny stutters in the mouths of her judges, she must take back this short period of time and reverse its course. Outside, at the Red Porch, behind Robespierre's house, people now stand ready to help her. Marie-Antoinette has only just now understood the image of an hourglass being turned over. Her destiny can only be reversed because there is so little of it left.

Therefore it shall be for her a great reversal.

Father Girard turns to one side and discreetly checks his watch. Why does she find it unbecoming for a priest to be checking the time?

* * *

Zamor cannot keep from reading and rereading the two safe-conduct passes that Doctor Seiffert gave him in exchange for the leopard boy. The steps leading up to his rooms now feel like a magic carpet to him. He dreams that he is rescuing Olympe on a sweet-smelling horse. Suddenly, Zamor stops in his tracks. An unusual scent lingers in the hallway. You think about Olympe too much. Now you think you can smell her everywhere. As a precaution, he goes to the window on the landing and slips the safe-conduct passes into the window gutter.

He enters his lodgings. In crossing the threshold, a strange urge makes him stand stock-still behind the beaded curtain. Something is not right. He draws his knife. The fear that some-day his lair will be discovered never leaves him. Relax. You have the safe-conduct passes, the jewels, and the Black Pearl. You're almost there. Soon you'll return to your native land dressed like a lord. With big trunks, and ten mules to carry them all the way to your white house with Olympe standing in the doorway. Zamor smiles. He sheathes his knife and walks through the curtain as the fine beads flow over his face. The waterfall at L'Anse-à-l'Ane! A violent blow stops him. Someone grabs his throat. He is suffocating. It's not the memory that's choking him up, but someone's hand. A powerful "something is not right" hand. It slams him up against the wall.

"Don't even think about touching that knife!"

Zamor doesn't even think about it. The man holding him back is huge, with leathery skin, a freshly shaven head, and a machete on his back. His hand could crush him in an instant.

"Listen here, Zamor. I'm in a hurry. I'm looking for the leop-ard boy and I want you to tell me where he is."

At least things are clear. Careful, this guy knows his name.

"And don't lie to me!"

The man talks like a slave master with a whip in his boot. The bloodhounds, the whip, the torches, and the fearsome chase—he holds all of it in his eyes. Lifting him up, the man half-drags, half-carries him into the room. The jewel-encrusted tailcoat has been thrown over the parrot's cage. That's what was wrong. Petit-Louis did not cry, *Stop thief!* when Zamor came in.

"I know that you have been using the leopard boy as a pawn in your deals with Doctor Seiffert. I am the Commander. Did he mention my name?"

"No. He never mentioned you."

"You'd better tell me the whole story, or else . . ."

THE MARQUISE

The Commander lowers a shoulder so that Zamor can see the machete strapped to his back. Zamor has already seen it. Keep cool. You must save your life. And more than that if you can.

"Can I feed my parrot?"

"Go ahead, but don't try anything funny."

Zamor pulls the tailcoat off the cage and casually tosses it onto the hammock. The Commander does not notice that he has just secured several million pounds worth of emeralds, diamonds, and rubies. *The most obvious hiding places are the best ones.* Zamor cleans the cage. He is trying to think. Who is this Commander? How did he manage to find him?

"How did you find me?"

"How dare you ask me questions before you've answered mine?"

The Commander lashes his face with the whip. Zamor had forgotten all about that particular kind of burn.

"Now then. The leopard boy. Where is he?"

"With the Doctor."

"Where is he taking him?"

To attempt escape, even over the rooftops, would be futile at this point. Just a few moments ago, Zamor had imagined himself as the master of his domain, owner of a white house. Now he just wants to stay alive. Zamor pours water into the parrot's dish.

"He's taking him to the residence of some marquis who lives near the Wheat Market."

"The Marquis d'Andeçon! The one who gave his name to a slave girl from back home. I should have known. I'll add him to the list of people that I need to pay a visit to. And where are you from, Boy?"

"From L'Anse-à-l'Ane plantation in Martinique."

So why do you go around dressed like a maharajah? You ashamed of your people?"

The Commander points to the turban and the matching outfit. Zamor prefers not to look.

"L'Anse-à-l'Ane! So you're one of Mr. Belair's niggers!"

"I'm nobody's nigger! I'm a free man! I'm the intendant of the Louveciennes estate by decree of his Majesty Louis XV. I have the documentation if you wish to see it!"

"Don't bother. And don't move, Milord!"

The Commander snickers and takes a deep bow.

"Yes, Commander. I am free and my father is . . ."

"Right. I know. You were going to tell me that Mr. Belair is your father. All mulattos are the sons of their masters. That's a well-known fact."

Zamor watches as a dark cloud drifts into the Commander's eyes. He shuts them and becomes agitated. Now he's going to get killed because of a dark cloud. Never mention mixed-blood relations to a Creole. Zamor knew that.

"Can I water my anthurium?"

"An anthurium? You have that flower here in Haarlem? I don't believe it! Show me!"

Zamor goes to the window and opens it onto the miniature greenhouse. The Commander pushes him forward and bends down on one knee. He raises a glass panel.

"Incredible! An anthurium lily! How did you do it?"

Zamor points to the chimney pipe. Commander strokes the edges of the petals. He inhales the scent of the flower's deepest recesses. This gives Zamor the impression that he, too, is seeking a woman concealed within.

"I want this anthurium lily."

"Well, you can't have it!"

The Commander grabs Zamor by the hair and forces him to bend low to the ground.

"You dare to disobey me! When I want something, I take it!"

"OK, go ahead and kill me, then. But why do you want to kill the flower? She hasn't done you any wrong."

On bended knee, the Commander inhales the scent of the anthurium lily. He thinks of the Queen. Of the scent that she would leave on the back of his hand, so that he could carry it with him back home. The Commander releases Zamor. He makes the sign of the cross, stands up, and places his hat on his head.

"I'll let you go, Zamor. But you'd better look after this flower. You owe your life to it. And don't cross my path again. You won't get a second chance. And one last piece of advice. If you want to live a long life, find a new place to buy bird food. The shopkeeper talks too much."

* * *

"Halt! This area is closed to the public!"

The peace officer shakes his white stick in Pobéré's face.

"Just where do you think you're going with that rig, young man?"

The man points to the cart in which Dame Catherine is seated, facing backward, "playing queen" with a burlap bag across her legs.

"Citizen, I am taking my poor, crippled mother home. She is blind and her legs can no longer carry her."

"Where do you reside?"

"Rue Honoré!"

Dame Catherine answers the question. The officer bends over her, his hands cupped around his mouth.

"See here, now, good woman! You'll have to take a detour on Rue Baillette and go by way of the quays!"

There's no need to yell. What an annoying habit it is to think that blind people are deaf! As if withholding that particular misfortune in the general distribution of afflictions constituted an additional hardship.

"Citizen, the route is much more direct for me if I take Rues de la Monnaie, le Roule, and Honoré all the way . . ."

"I'm aware of that. But that's the route that the Widow Capet will be taking one hour from now. That's why no one can come through here. So go on! You'll have to turn back now."

"But Citizen . . ."

"Do as I say, old woman, or I'll have to arrest you."

She gives it some thought. To turn back would mean yet another wasted hour, and the final signal would be lost. The entire plot now risks failure because of this white baton.

"Very well, Citizen, I will obey. But before that, I wish to ask a favor of you on behalf of an old, infirm patriot."

"What is it?"

"Let me see your baton."

The officer looks at her suspiciously. Pobéré encourages him to give in to the whims of an old woman. The officer hands the baton to the blind woman, who touches it and beams.

"I knew it! Your baton is smooth and solid. I can tell that it isn't battered from beating the heads of the people with it. Tell me. Is it inscribed with the motto, *The law shall be enforced . . .?*"

"Yes, my good woman. And engraved on the knob of the baton is the eye of patriot vigilance, *See without being seen!*"

"Ah! To see without being seen . . . How I would love to have your motto, and your baton, so I wouldn't have to shout about who I am."

Dame Catherine bursts into tears and buries her face in her

hands. Ill at ease, the officer shifts from one foot to the other. He looks around. If people think he's mistreating a disabled person, there will be a riot. He slaps the baton against the palm of his hand, as if to soften his heart line.

"All right! All right! Go ahead!"

The wheelbarrow carrying Dame Catherine and pushed by Pobéré continues on its way.

"Mother, you were magnificent! I hope I'll grow up to be like you one day!"

"Never say that, my child. Do not be in a hurry to reach the age where people pity you. Try to be feared for as long as possible. And every time that you are forced to bow down, may a spring be wound within you."

"I'll remember that."

"Above all, remember our plan. This white baton means that the partisans who haven't yet taken their positions will have a hard time reaching their posts without attracting attention."

"They'll all be there, Mother!"

"Well, then, roll on, Child. That is why I wanted a cart. To make my way like the Queen will. From now on, I want you to tell me about everything, and to do it in color."

* * *

"Whoa, whoa, now."

Ed pulls on the reins with all his might. He is proud of himself. Moka's hearse has come to a stop just two buildings down from where he had intended it to. He maneuvers the vehicle and jumps down from the seat, right in front of Sweet Victory's busted sign. The Boss rolls a barrel out the door, singing, *The Vivandière is in love!*

"The Despicable Duo! Health and Prosperity! So, now you've gone into business as peddlers! *Moka, rex Moka!* You certainly won't go unnoticed in that circus wagon!"

"All the same, Citizen, it's thanks to this circus wagon that we were able to get through."

"There sure is a lot of commotion around here!"

Jones points to a line of national guardsman marching toward Saint-Honoré, guns to their shoulders.

"Well, hell's bells! I have a front-row seat to see the Austrian's carriage roll by!"

"They've already closed off the entrance to the Pont-Neuf. To get through, we had to tell them that we were making a delivery to Robespierre."

"And they fell for it! Even though everybody knows that Robespierre drinks only blood, not coffee."

"Citizen, be careful of what you say. There are lots of pigeons out roosting on stools today."

* * *

Jean-François Mourard, tinsmith in the neighborhood of Saint-Eustache, residing at number three, Impasse Fosse-Repose, has big ears. He very clearly heard what citizen Marie Moureuil, proprietor of the tavern formerly known as the Revolution Lunch Bucket, currently known as Sweet Victory, located on Rue de la Monnaie, directly across from number thirty-seven, said to two citizens with negroid features . . . "Robespierre doesn't drink coffee, only blood!" "Are you sure about that, Citizen?" He had repeated the information and reaffirmed his faith as a patriot . . . "Very well," the captain of the police had said. "We'll check it out."

* * *

The Boss stands her barrel up on one end and slides it into position in front of the window of her saloon. Ed and Jones give her a hand.

"If I climb up on this, I might be able to see something. With this crowd, it'll soon be rowdier than a dance at the Ramponeaux Cabaret. Come on in, my Two Terrors, it'll be more intimate inside!"

Ed and Jones follow the Boss inside. If they were looking for intimacy, they got intimacy. Emptiness itself must have slept here. She secures the door with an iron bar.

"Well, have you found your leopard boy yet?"

"You got anything to eat?"

The Boss knows the drill. Eat first. Talk later.

"How about a three-apple omelet?"

"Why three apples and not two?"

"Because, Jones, I'm the heart apple. The Queen of Hearts! I'm just that good. I get peeled, bitten to the core, and then thrown away. Right, Edmond?"

The Boss retreats to her stove, leaving Ed on simmer. A clattering of pots and pans, the sharp sizzle of Isigny butter, a wafting aroma, and she is back with a bottle of Réveillon wine and an omelet formed and folded into the shape of a pocketbook. Ed and Jones dig in.

"This is delicious!"

The Boss cracks a smile. Grunting, Ed devours the omelet. But this doesn't fool her. Once satiated, they'll get back to asking about the leopard boy. Ed doesn't even wait until then. He tackles the topic with his mouth full.

"Citizen, we need to talk about the Marquise."

"We know she's here."

"Right. She's upstairs, in my room."

Ed touches the Boss's hand lightly.

"Glad you told us."

Jones didn't think that Ed was capable of such a tender gesture.

"Tread lightly! The Marquise is as fragile as a flower. If you do her any harm, I'll grab Sanson and chop you into four equal parts."

The Boss doesn't even raise her voice. She just takes a quick swig from her cask. That makes it worse.

"What'd she tell you, Citizen?"

"Only that the Marquis has been abducted. But you probably know that already. Before they took him away, he had time to give her two letters that she was supposed to pass on to you."

"What letters?"

"One from the Marquis and the other from the Princess de Lamballe."

Without saying a word, Ed and Jones stand up, leave the table and head toward the stairway that leads up to the Boss's bedroom.

"Wait! There's one more thing. The Marquise is worse off than I said she was. Tried to commit suicide."

* * *

Zamor waits patiently at the base of the platform. Seated on his throne, Delorme is getting his boots shined by a chocolate-colored boy dressed in livery.

"That's good, Brother. Right on time. You got the Black Pearl?"

Since returning to the grotto, Zamor has been intrigued by

the water that has gradually risen and that is now covering the central nave. A legion of laborers toils near the Slave Ark. They labor away, their feet in the mud. It's as though the boat had run aground in a cove. A network of planks placed on boulders forms a series of passageways inside the church. Men, naked from the waist up, are at work installing the rudder. The wooden part swings softly in the air, suspended from a system of ropes.

"So, Zamor! What of the Black Pearl?"

"Here it is!"

Zamor dangles a leather pouch on a strap. The guards didn't bother to search him this time.

"Come closer!"

Magnanimously, Delorme beckons him to step onto the platform. Zamor obeys.

"Give it here!"

Delorme snatches the pouch from his hands. He unties the knot and takes out the Black Pearl. He gazes at it for a moment with empty eyes and suddenly raises it up like an offering before the enormous painting of the Maréchal de Saxe and his guard of black uhlans.

"Father, your pearl!"

A roar echoes through the grotto in response.

"Zamor, you have just rectified a great injustice."

Eyes closed, Delorme inhales the scent of the Black Pearl.

"Ahh. It still smells like the Countess! Did you know that the king was in the habit of hiding this pearl in her every nook and cranny? Can you believe that Louis XV played hide-and-seek with the Black Pearl on du Barry's body?"

Delorme's laugh uncovers the shreds of fat that have lodged between his teeth. Zamor does not wish to hear about the Countess's intimate games.

"As for my end of the deal, I've allowed your Doctor Seiffert to leave Haarlem. I put two men on his tail to follow him and to find out what my leopard boy is up to."

Zamor thinks that maybe Delorme will be the one to rid him of Seiffert and the Commander.

"Don't forget, Brother, that, in spite of the great sentimental value that it carries for me, the Black Pearl is only worth the rental of the leopard boy until noon."

"I know. That was our agreement."

"If for some unfortunate reason the leopard boy does not return, you will have to pay me for him with all the jewels that you stole from La du Barry. That's a minimum."

Zamor attempts to appear outraged.

"Hey, now, Brother, don't get offended. Those jewels constitute a fair reparation for the slavery that syphilitic whore made you endure. Those jewels that you have hidden so well . . ."

Zamor feels it coming. A line of sweat slithers between his shoulder blades. Suddenly a cry of terror fills the vault. Zamor jumps. Delorme reassures him.

"Don't worry. We're just doing a demonstration in the Cabin of Comprehension. Come with me, Brother, I promised I'd show you. It'll be a nice surprise."

Delorme rises from his throne, dismisses the shine boy, and leads Zamor to the back of the church. There is much to be surprised about. The transept is filled with slave cabins. Zamor feels like he's been transported to a plantation in the West Indies. Except for the muddy waters that are slowly rising. Delorme leads him into the apse and stops in front of a circular bronze door.

"This was the conduit that used to funnel water to the fountain of the Laughing Negress, which was an insult to the suffering of our brothers. So I blocked it off."

Suddenly, Delorme pushes Zamor inside a stone cabin. It's a working forge. Two bellows-shaped men seize him, strip off his coat, and force him to sit on a stool. A brazier full of red-hot coals glares menacingly at his feet and several branding irons glow, ready for use.

"Here we are, Brother, in the Cabin of Comprehension. This is where visitors will get their very own brands. There are a variety of shapes and sizes available."

Delorme pulls an iron from the coals and blows on it.

"Isn't it funny how this turns ruby red? By the way, Brother, in all those jewels, did La du Barry by chance have any . . . rubies?"

Delorme grabs Zamor by the hair and waves the glowing branding iron in Zamor's face. He spits on it. The resulting sputter sounds like it is already making his skin sizzle. Zamor doesn't fight back. He knew what he was in for as soon as he saw the hot coals. But this dog named Delorme won't get to feed on his fear. Yes, he'll scream all right. At the top of his lungs and until his heart bursts.

"Brother, I will do you the honor of marking you with a *D* for Delorme. Unless you tell me where you hid those jewels that you got from your syphilitic countess whore."

"You ain't gettin' nothin' from me! I'd rather die first."

"The choice is no longer yours, my brother. Hold him down!"

The two blacksmiths pin Zamor's arms back and hold his head up. Delorme rips off his shirt, uncovering his chest. He recoils in horror. The branding iron falls to the ground. He cannot take his eyes from the gnarled scar on Zamor's skin. Near his heart, his left breast is marked with a brand: dB.

"Well, I'll be damned, Brother! Delorme, Master of Us All, had the same idea as that syphilitic whore of a Countess du Barry!"

Delorme whips Zamor and spits in his face.

"Throw this bastard nigger outta here!"

The blacksmiths drag Zamor out. In the transept, they pass two booted hulks, a lout with kiwi-colored skin, and a mustachioed man with a ring in his ear. They run back and forth to the jingling music of their own spurs.

"Master! Master of Us All!"

Zamor is expelled by the smiths. He has just enough time to hear them.

"The leopard boy has gone missing!"

* * *

Inside the carriage, the leopard boy is jostled by jolts and bumps. He is silent, his head bowed and hidden beneath the hood of his cloak. Doctor Seiffert is watching him. He hasn't moved a muscle since leaving Haarlem. He appears calm. How can he explain what he is expecting the boy to do in the next instant? He will have to act fast and with agility. Will the kid be able to do it? Especially since he's wearing handcuffs. The Doctor had to use them. Otherwise he would have escaped. Seiffert glances back. The two black men on horses who've been following him since he left Haarlem are still there. He'd better get rid of them, or he'll end up at the Marquis d'Anderçon's with them in his medical bag. The Doctor calls to the driver through the trap door.

"Excuse me, my friend! Are you familiar with the dead-end street formerly known as Le Chat-Blanc?"

"You mean the one behind the Grand Châtelet stronghold across from the Jetaillerie depot, Citizen?"

THE LEOPARD BOY

"That's it. Now listen up."

The Doctor hands him a bag of money that would restore the hearing of a deaf man. You need a good ear to be able to hear his plan through the clattering hooves and the rollicking cab.

The two black horsemen have now launched into a full gallop. The cab they were following has just disappeared. It has taken a sharp turn and sped into Rue de la Vieille-Place-aux-Veaux. The Master of Us All will kill them if they lose sight of the leopard boy. They crack their whips. Two chattering chimney sweeps are just crossing the street. The excited horses graze their shoulders and knock them down, ropes, ladders, and all. They shout at the offending vehicle, drawing a crowd. The horses stumble, the hands holding the reins falter, and iron-shod hooves slip on the rotting straw lying in the gutter. But men and beasts get up, pull themselves together, and dash off after the cab. They do this just in time to see the contraption headed back toward them. They've run into a dead end! Not only that, but that moron of a driver has turned the cab sideways so that it blocks their way.

"Well done, my friend!"

From his hiding place behind the panel of a carriage door, the Doctor is unable to curb his enthusiasm. Now that's a bag of money that's been put to good use. The planned maneuvers in the dead-end street were executed perfectly. The kid was able to jump from the cab at exactly the right moment. He's light on his feet and not the least bit worried. Seiffert listens as the cab rattles off. Before the two horsemen even realize that the cab is empty, he'll be inside the Marquis d'Andeçon's mansion.

* * *

At Sweet Victory, the Boss's bedroom is lit by the flame of a single candle. Next to the bed, Ed and Jones watch the Marquise d'Andeçon as she sleeps. They are worried. What if she doesn't ever wake up? She tried to commit suicide . . . That's all they let the Boss say before rushing up here. Why would anyone so beautiful want to kill herself? . . . She feels guilty. Guilty of what? . . . Ed looks at the letter from the Princess de Lamballe that he is holding in his hand as if it held the answer to that question somewhere between its lines. Ed and Jones read and reread it until they have it memorized. Now they know the whole story of the leopard boy. They should be happy now, or at least relieved, but they can think of nothing but the Marquise.

Ed monitors her breathing, the rising and falling of her chest, the fluttering of her closed eyelids. They like the danger and worry that allow them to study her face under a candlelit glow.

"Well, Ed, we can't wait around for too much longer. The Boss will take care of her. We found out what we wanted to know."

"What about the Marquis?"

"What about him?"

"I don't get what he's trying to explain in this letter. Do you?"

Ed points at the folded piece of paper lying on Jones's knees.

"I got one thing. The Marquis is ruined, thanks to the huge sums of money he poured into preparing his expedition to discover the Northwest Passage. We knew he was obsessive, but not to this point!"

"I get that, Jones. I even get that he tried to obtain funding by means that were more and more risky. But then what happened?"

"What happened is that a savior comes on the scene and lends you money until the day comes when he asks for a little favor you just can't refuse. That savior was Doctor Seiffert, and the little favor he just couldn't refuse was . . . the leopard boy, who had to be located for the common good. But then the Marquis realizes that the Doctor is not interested in saving the boy but wants to kill him off instead. Only then it was too late. Doctor Seiffert was hot on his trail."

"That's when the Marquis called on us to find the leopard boy before this Doctor Seiffert did."

"That's why he only gave us twelve hours!"

Ed's face is full of worry.

"In my opinion, Ed, she's the one who gave Seiffert the name of a contact in Haarlem."

"Zamor?"

"Yes, Zamor . . . Because of him, she thinks it's her fault for putting the leopard boy's life in danger . . . not to mention ours!"

"You got that right, Jones!"

The Marquise! She's awake! How weak her voice is! She sits up in the bed, wearing nothing but a man's shirt, and it's half-open . . . God, she's beautiful! . . . Ed wishes he could find another way to say it, and Jones doesn't even make the effort.

"I still have one or two things to tell you about the Princesse de Lamballe's letter. What you have already read is true. The leopard boy was born of Her Majesty Marie-Antoinette's first pregnancy, on December 19, 1778. He is Marie-Thérèse's twin brother. Because of his appearance, the decision was made to eliminate him at his birth, but the Princesse de Lamballe saved him and was raising him until her murder last year. Read the line at the top of the page . . . *La Force Prison, September 2, 1792* . . . The day before she died! Without a doubt, this letter was meant for the Queen, but the Duc de Penthièvre never delivered it to her. Even worse, Delorme discovered its contents by way of a prison informant. On that dreadful Monday on the third of September, for four straight hours, Delorme and his accomplices tortured the Princess de Lamballe as they tried to force her into telling them where they could find the leopard boy. For four hours straight, she suffered in agony but said nothing. You know what happened after that. Thanks to Zamor, Delorme ended up getting his hands on the leopard boy. The Queen only learned of his existence during her imprisonment in the Conciergerie. She probably found out about him through Doctor Seiffert, who used the fact to exact revenge against Marie-Antoinette. She who had separated him from his beloved Princesse de Lamballe, and whom Seiffert holds responsible for her death, wants to see her child. So he hatched his nefarious plan whereby he made the Queen believe that he was going to save her son, just so that he could punish her all the more. As for the rest of the story . . ."

The Marquise lies back, exhausted. Ed has an urge to blow out the candle so that she can go back to sleep. Suddenly, down below, the Boss is screaming.

"Help! Ed and Jones, help!"

* * *

From street level, Doctor Seiffert is studying the windows of the Marquis d'Andonçon's mansion. Something is not right. Two men stand talking behind the draperies of the weapons room on the first floor. This was not part of the plan. The Marquis was supposed to be alone at the moment when he was to hand the leopard boy over. The Doctor delays entering since the men are still in there. He buys a glass of almond and barley syrup and a candy apple to keep the boy happy. The vendor is intrigued.

Seiffert adjusts the hood shielding the leopard boy's face and the edges of the cape that cover the handcuffs chaining them to one another. It would be a pity to be found out at the last minute.

* * *

From the threshold of the weapons room, the Commander gazes with curiosity at the miniature lackey outfitted in blue livery who stands perched on a chair. What kind of idiot would pose in front of a window and talk to himself? The lackey's interlocutor appears to be a decrepit suit of armor that has been placed directly across from him.

"I am not in accordance with you, Sir Rustbucket, concerning the Duke of Brunswick and those emigrés. Our army will eventually defrock them."

"You mean defeat them!"

Thomas jumps. His heart has barely settled down inside his chest again before he spies the huge hulk of a man who has just corrected him. He's even more intimidating than that suit of armor! Fear and surprise throw Thomas for a loop as he and his livery part ways. Everything topples over backward, the chair slides out from beneath him, and in his downward plunge, he snatches at the drapery, pulling the fabric, rod, hooks, and rings along with him. The lumbering suit of armor staggers and weaves before finally collapsing into a metallic heap on the floor. Pauldrons, visor, cuishes, tassets, and sollerets career across the room. They sure did wear a lot of vocabulary back in the day!

The Commander seizes Thomas's brachial extremities.

"Why were you talking to that suit of armor while standing in front of the window?"

"I was keeping the window busy, sir. In case anyone in the neighborhood would mistakenly think that I'm all alone in here."

"Well? You are all alone here, are you not?"

"Yes, but nobody is supposed to know that."

"Your mind seems quite addled. Where is your master?"

The Commander is holding him at arm's length.

"Sir, please do put me down. I beg you, I am subject to vestiges!"

"You mean vertigo!"

"That's just as high up."

"I'll ask you again. Where is your master?"

"Excuse me, Sir, I cannot hear you very well. Whom shall I say has come to call?"

By way of an introduction, Thomas is thrown to the floor and pinned on his back with a knee shoved into his stomach. The Commander draws his machete.

"See that broken armor? That's exactly what you're going to look like if you don't start talking. I'll start with the gauntlet."

"Not that one, Sir, I'm left-handed!"

The Commander strikes. There is a dull thud. Thomas screams. The machete blade is now lodged in the wood a hairsbreadth from his fingertips.

"How clumsy of me! Let me try that again!"

"No, don't!"

The scattered suit of armor pops into Thomas's mind as he recalls the incredible number of parts that can be removed from one single body. Even a little one like his.

"Tell me what's going on here!"

"Well, uh . . . the house is empty, and I'm all alone, so I've been standing up here putting on a show for the neighborhood in order to avoid being pilloried."

"You mean pillaged."

"That too. There's almost nothing left to take."

"You still haven't told me where to find your master."

"He emigrated!"

The machete lands next to his ear this time. Thomas can hear the metal vibrate as it tells him . . . *don't be stupid. Steel is stronger than you are.*

"Uh . . . What I meant to say was that my master isn't here anymore. He was emigrated by a group of men who were in for it."

"You mean they had it in for him. You use the masculine pronoun to talk about trouble."

"And sometimes you need the masculine plural!"

"Stop joking around. I believe what you're saying about your master. You're too much of a coward to be able lie three times in a row."

Or even twice in a row, thinks Thomas.

"Tell it to me straight. Has the Doctor been here with the boy?"

Thomas does not even dare to ask, What doctor? What boy? It sounds too much like he's been practicing his lines. Especially since, for a spineless valet, he knows a little too much about the boy in question.

"I haven't the foggiest idea, Sir, about that of which you are speaking."

"That, I have a harder time believing. I've never met a valet who doesn't stand listening behind closed doors or peeping through keyholes."

"Sir, I have an excuse. I'm just the right size for the job."

"So you saw the negress?"

"Sir, I believe you are referring to Madame the Marquise?"

"She was a negress before she became a Marquise. Still is."

"Sir must be right, given that he weighs one hundred pounds more than I do."

The Commander brutally slams Thomas's head to the parquet. The disadvantage of this particular position is that his ear is most viciously crushed. The advantage of it is that he can very clearly hear that someone is now climbing the stairs leading up to the room.

* * *

Pobéré is pushing the cart with his mother in it. He ascends Rue Saint-Honoré toward the Palais-Royal.

"Go on, my boy, tell me! Are there many soldiers?"

"There are more gendarmes than soldiers, mother. They are cordoning off the area."

"The colors, my boy! Tell me about the colors!"

"Blue. There's a lot of blue, and white on the breeches, and also gold on the braids."

"And red? How about red? I like red."

"There's a whole bunch of red on the wine seller's sign! And look! Here's a servant girl carrying a basket of tomatoes."

"Tomatoes? On a sixteenth of October? She must be coming from that American hotel. You can find springtime in the dead of winter in that establishment. Look closely, Son, the maître d' can't be too far off."

"That's right, Mother. His cheeks are all red and he looks worried."

Pobéré has just painted his own portrait. He looks and looks and looks again, but he doesn't see any of their partisans in the positions they should have taken by now.

"I'll bet you the man is worrying about his dinner menu. A fifteen-course dinner that includes two varieties of potage, two different dishes served in sauce, eight different entrées, two whole roasts, two pièces de résistance, and eight side dishes. Did you know that I served at the table of the Duc de Penthièvre when I was just a girl?"

"No, Mother, you never told me that. What would they be eating these days?"

"Want to hear what'd be on the menu?"

Pobéré sure does. He'll do anything to avoid having to describe what he is really seeing. Soldiers popping up everywhere, partisans missing from their predetermined positions, informants dressed up like informants, faces that are simply indifferent, women arguing over some nasty-looking sausages out in front of a butcher shop, and the Red Porch coming up quick.

"Come to table, my boy. We'll start with a Brunoy veal and vegetable potage, followed by a skewered Bayonne ham in savory sauce. For the next course it's Mirepoix quail. A Rhine River carp au bleu follows that as the main dish, and then two roasted wild Garenne rabbits."

"Mother! Please have mercy!"

Pobéré shudders. That's what the condemned beg of the executioner. Do they guillotine fourteen-year-olds? They are nearing the Red Porch. He looks around in vain. Jean-Baptiste is nowhere in sight.

"Don't worry, my boy, this is the point in the dinner when a blond young virgin will pour some Swiss absinthe into a crystal glass to tone the fibers of your stomach."

Pobéré doesn't see Merlin in the prearranged spot. The chickens may soon come home to roost.

"It's drunk down in a single gulp, my boy. It's called the Mid-Dinner Shot."

Pobéré could use one of those. A Mid-Dinner Shot and crack! Straight to the heart, just like what Sanson will be getting in his pretty soon. Unless something goes wrong with the knife. Elisabeth has taken her position. Hands on hips, she's flirting with two gendarmes. But Guillaume isn't there either. He's the one who's supposed to carry the knife until the very last minute. He wanted it that way out of concern for his wife. They were worried about her, but he's the weaker one.

"Stop here, Son. I'm sure of it. We are near the Red Porch, are we not?"

"How do you know, Mother?"

"I could feel you slowing down. You wish to take it all in. You wish to inhale the smell of this place where we are soon going to save the Queen. You are right. This pavement smells like freedom."

* * *

"Help! Help! Deadly Duo report to duty on the double!"

The Boss is yelling to them from Sweet Victory's back room. Ed and Jones rush from the room where the Marquise is resting.

They hurtle down the stairs, tromping on the landings and slamming into doors. The wooden staircase echoes their charge. They rush into the tavern's back room. The situation is immediately apparent. Four neighborhood militiamen, or a facsimile thereof, have seized the Boss and tied her hands behind her back. They are trying to drag her outside, but she has wrapped her legs around a pillar and won't let go. Her chest heaves under the strain. They'll have to pull the whole thing down on top of her before she'll let go. The arresting party is joined by a man dressed in informant gray who points an ink-stained index finger at the Boss.

"This is the citizen who said that Robespierre doesn't drink coffee, just blood."

The group is joined by one more man in epaulets who stands holding an accusatory piece of paper. Four plus one, plus one more makes six, which is divisible by two. To prove it, Ed and Jones take on three each with nothing to carry.

There ensues a more or less brutal series of multiplications, additions, subtractions, divisions, and extractions raised to each and every power. The militia is taken by surprise. It was not expecting a mathematical revolt. This is a first. It gives in.

Once the Boss has been liberated, Ed and Jones display their blue badges. There are salutes, heels click, the Boss pours drinks, and toasts are raised to patriotic zealousness. From behind his glass, the informant wonders whether this inferior wine may be watered down. The Boss looks gratefully at Ed, who turns a shade darker at the edges of his scars. Ed and Jones take the Boss aside.

"We'll leave the Marquise with you, Citizen. She's in great danger."

"You must not let anyone near her."

"What about the boy?"

"We know where to find him. We're on our way there now!"

* * *

Spike raises the lantern hanging from the end of his pike in order to illuminate the walls of books that surround him. The top of the stack disappears into a vaulted ceiling illuminated by the blue glimmer of stained glass.

"So this is your house, Groundhog? It's like we was in the belly of a whale."

"This used to be the Church of the Capuchins."

"So your house is a whale that swallowed a church. Where's your book fort?"

"Come with me and I'll show you."

Groundhog and Spike advance through a labyrinth of narrow gorges formed from piles of books. The passageway is encumbered by wheels from hackney cabs, Berlines, cabriolets, vinegar vending carts . . . My wheel collection! . . . Due to the trophy collection, Groundhog and Spike do not make much headway. This is also because each of them is already struggling to carry the portrait of an ancestor under one arm.

"How do you find your way around here, Groundhog?"

"Easy. It's all laid out in streets. Over there is Science Street, here on the right is Geography Street, and that one going off at an angle is History Street. And I live up there. That's my cave!"

Groundhog points to an area cut into the side of Book Mountain. They climb the stairs cut from the volumes, cross a scree formation of *in-quarto* editions and finally reach a sort of cavern paved with capitulary ordinances. Spike's eyes grow ever wider. Now he understands why Groundhog said that he lived inside books. They leave the ancestor portraits to stand guard at the door and enter. Inside, Groundhog lights an enormous Easter candle. Spike takes a look around.

"Your bed! Your bench! Your table! All of them made out of books! Where's your favorite one, the one you know by heart?"

"*The Journals of Captain Cook*? I put it right here."

Groundhog shows him a volume imprisoned beneath the vise of a large printing press.

"What's it doing under there? You're punishing it. Are you afraid the story'll run away?"

"No. It's to stop me from reading it all the time."

"By that you mean that when you love something too much, you have to set limits. It's the same with people. That's why I don't want us to like each other too much. Promise?"

"Promise."

Groundhog and Spike slap each other's palms in the manner of stockmen sealing a deal at market.

"Groundhog, you promised to read me your book by heart."

"OK. Which part do you want me to read?"

"The beginning. Not the one for girls, but the real beginning. The one where you get on the boat and it smells like the sea."

Groundhog and Spike sit cross-legged around the Easter candle. Groundhog begins his narration.

Friday May 27th to Friday July 29th. Moderate and fair weather, at eleven a.m. hoisted the Pendant and took charge of Ship agreeable to my Commission of the 25th Instant, She lying in the Bason in Deptford Yard.

Eyes closed, Spike listens, gripping the shaft of his pike, his face covered with sea spray.

. . . The transactions of each day . . . are inserted in the Logg Book and as they contain nothing but common Occurences it was thought not necessary to insert them here.

"Groundhog, I like stories where they tell you that they haven't told you everything. That way, there's something left to tell."

Groundhog and Spike carry on. They round Cape Horn at fifty-five degrees, fifty-three minutes latitude South, sixty-eight degrees, thirteen minutes longitude West and weigh anchor in Royal Bay. Groundhog thinks of Marie-Antoinette. The cart carrying her to the guillotine will pass right by here, on Rue Saint-Honoré. He unfolds a map . . . *First Voyage of Captain Cook (1768–1771)* . . .

"Where are we, Groundhog?"

"Right here!"

"Where are we going?"

"Over there. To Temple Prison. To give the little dog to the Dauphin."

"It's a good thing that it's not too far from here."

Groundhog is sad. He would like to have kept Coco for himself. He would have fashioned a doghouse for him out of an oversized atlas. But he mustn't. The Dauphin will be so happy to have the dog, to hold it in his arms, to breathe in the scent of his mother.

"We'll come back here, won't we, Groundhog? You're gonna tell me the rest of the story, ain'tcha? Was Captain Cook really real? Was he English? Doesn't his name mean, "someone who prepares food?" Wasn't he devoured by cannibals in the Sandwich Islands?"

Spike suddenly stops talking.

"Hey, just how do you think you're going to get into the Temple? You're not even a prisoner."

* * *

The Commander hasn't relaxed his grip. He continues to hold Thomas down, crushing one cheek against the floor and pushing one ear down into a crack between the wooden floorboards. The position is uncomfortable, but it allows Thomas to clearly hear the footsteps of the person who is coming up the stairs toward the weapons room. The Commander hears it too. He quietly slips a blade from his belt, stiffens, and concentrates on the doorstep. A form fills the doorway. The Commander dives, rolls, and launches his dagger. It lands planted in the doorframe next to Doctor Seiffert's shoulder.

"What the . . . ! That's one helluva welcome, Commander!"

The Doctor possesses the assurance of a man who knows he's packing a powerful pistol. He advances on the Commander, with the leopard boy still chained to his wrist. Thomas takes the opportunity to sneak out.

The Commander eyes the boy.

"So this is he!"

He removes his hat and bows in a manner that is intentionally bombastic and maladroit.

"Sire!"

In the same movement, Commander throws his hat into Seiffert's face. Caught off guard, Seiffert swerves and takes a random shot. The bullet splinters into the woodwork. The Commander launches his mass into the Doctor, who takes the chained boy down with him. Commander raises his machete.

"Don't kill me, Sir! Don't kill me!"

The boy begs, crouched at the Commander's feet. The Commander rips off his hood, grabs him by the hair, and pulls him up to standing. A white patch has devoured the skin on half of the boy's face. From the eye to the chin, it forms a kind of dolorous island.

"Don't kill me!"

"Shut up! You don't even exist!"

"Oh, but yes, Commander. Yes, he does indeed exist!"

The Doctor pushes the pointed end of a knife into the Commander's impassive neck.

"What are you after, Seiffert? You want to fight me? You want me to take the other sword down from the wall and fight a duel over the life of an heir to the French throne? How chivalrous!"

"I wouldn't stand a chance against you."

"Right you are, Seiffert. I would've cut that boy's throat before you'd even've had time to make a scratch on me. What difference does it make to you, since you were going to do the same thing anyway?"

"Certainly not like that, I wasn't."

"Ah. So you leave the dirty work to your associates. And who are they, by the way?"

"Commander, it's not hard to guess which parties would not wish to see a new pretender to the throne, and a young and healthy one at that!"

"You dare to embroil yourself in such an enterprise, Seiffert?"

"It's an enterprise that's just as ignoble as the murder of a child whose existence reveals the black blood that flows in your own veins."

"You return to the Viscount's insinuations. He didn't get away with them, and neither did an old Italian surgeon who I'm thinking of right now."

The Commander once again sees Norcia's smile. He's heard enough about his black blood! He roars, and as one removing obstacles from a path, he pushes the sword and the child aside. His machete slices the air with a backhand aimed at the abdomen. The Doctor sidesteps it and leaps back, dragging the boy with him by the wrist. He tries to hold the Commander at bay with his sword, but he stumbles over a piece of armor and lets down his guard. The Commander rushes him and strikes at his belly like a fang ripping into flesh. Seiffert emits a dry cough and falls to the floor on his seat in disbelief. He hadn't even seen the blow coming.

"The old man I mentioned earlier, Doctor, died in this very same way and with surprising courage. I wanted to see if you were anything like him."

Seiffert is trying to stop the bleeding with his hands.

"I hope that Sidonie will be able to sew me up as prettily as she did Her Majesty's pug."

Half-conscious, Seiffert raises his resigned eyes to the Commander, who towers massively above him. All that's left now is to finish him off. And yet, the Commander remains immobile, petrified.

"A scar! Damn it all to hell!"

He rushes at the terrified boy, who is huddling next to the Doctor.

"Don't kill me!"

The Commander seizes the boy's shirt and tears it off. He uncovers the abdomen, searches, frisks, and palpates. Nothing. The Commander stands tall, raising his hands to the heavens. He rails at the gods as when there is no stopping a wildfire raging through a field of sugarcane.

"This isn't him. This isn't the leopard boy! Wake up, Seiffert! Look at his belly! There is not the least little scar! The one we are looking for was castrated. This one is not!"

From far way, the Doctor can hear the Commander railing at the boy.

"You are going to tell me the whole story. I need to find the real leopard boy. If you lie to me, I'll be back to cut out your tongue and gouge out your eyes!"

The boy starts to tremble. He says his name is Zoé, as if that were enough to protect him. Then he starts talking. When it's over, the Commander points an index at him.

"I believe you. You better not be lying, because if you are, I'll be back to keep my promises."

The Commander leaves a pale Doctor Seiffert in Zoé's arms, who is rocking him, singing. He leaves the weapons room. From the top of the stairs, he can hear the brouhaha of clambering boots.

* * *

Ed and Jones charge up the white marble staircase, their .38s drawn and ready. Thomas whispers behind them from one of the landings.

"They're up there in the weapons room. They're fighting a duel!"

Above their heads, Ed and Jones can see the impressive silhouette of a man in black. Leaning on the balustrade with one hand, he leaps over it out into the void. His cape billows behind him in his downward drop. Ed and Jones feel a strong breeze ripple in the wake of this powerful body. He crashes, the ground shakes. He rolls, rights himself, doffs his hat to them, and disappears.

"What object hath just plummeted?"

Ed and Jones would like to answer Thomas's question. They know of few men able to survive a fall like that. They would really like to know "What object hath just plummeted" because they sense that they will soon run into this archangel again.

* * *

Marie-Antoinette looks on as the clerk of court flips the page from recto to verso and verso to recto. He seems surprised not to find anything written on the recto of verso. What was he expecting? They have just read out her death sentence a second time. She has nothing left to offer them. The judges seem to be at a loss.

The cell door opens. Everyone makes way. A man enters. God, how huge he is! It's the executioner.

11

BLACK DELORME

Marie-Antoinette looks up at the executioner. He is standing right in front of her. Although the man occupies the entire cell, he seems far away, almost inaccessible. How young he is! Is it the man's size or his boyish face that is most terrifying? With such smooth skin and such a gentle gaze, how could he wish to kill her? She is old enough to be his mother. Henri Sanson. That's what her lawyer had told her. Henri! She is surprised that such a position even has a first name.

"Hold out your hands!"

The executioner extends his own. They are holding a rope. The Queen shies away and shrinks back. What? They intend to tie her up? Where is that abbot with his watch? He must inform them of the sacrilege that they are about to commit. She is the Queen! They are planning to tie her up like an animal. Like a wolf, or a hyena, or a . . . crane. The words end up pronouncing the people's nickname for her.

"Are my hands to be tied?"

The executioner nods his head in the affirmative. It is in proportion to his large size.

"The hands of Louis XVI were not tied!"

Young Sanson's gaze wavers. He was not expecting a dressing down regarding points of etiquette. Especially not at this moment. The executioner turns and queries the president of the Tribunal with a flick of the head. Hermann is caught off guard. Marie-Antoinette is watching his face. With just one word from him, she will be able to touch the black mourning ribbon tied around her wrist, cross her fingers, or press her hands against her belly in order to reassure it when it is overly frightened. Hermann feels that his second-long hesitation is already too long. This could attract criticism. He barks out his orders.

"Do your duty!"

Sanson obeys and steps toward her.

"Oh, my God!"

Marie-Antoinette makes a defensive gesture. Suddenly, the

young man seizes her wrists, makes her pivot, joins her hands behind her back, crosses them, binds them with the rope, and gives it a brutal tug. The Queen feels the pain tear at her elbows and shoulder blades. In just a few seconds they have reduced her to the state of an animal tied to a stake. But they are unable to extract a single tear from her. She senses that everyone here is observing her, already sharpening a quill in order to later recount the scene.

She stands tall, arching her back. One must keep up appearances! Appearances at any cost! She hears her mother's strong voice. Marie-Antoinette obeys her, but she senses that her already heavy breast is reluctant to emulate that particular bearing.

Sanson turns her around to face him again. How vigorous he is! He smells faintly of lavender. The young man avoids her gaze, as if in amorous play. With a quick gesture, he removes her bonnet. And she had adjusted it so carefully! What would Rosalie say! Marie-Antoinette would like the entire world to know how women are treated in these moments. Yes! My errors, my mistakes, my crimes! I have already confessed. Why add more crimes to the ones I have already committed?

A gigantic blade flashes in the executioner's hand. Marie-Antoinette shudders. They have betrayed her. They are going to cut her throat right here, in her cell. It was all a lie. Axel, my knight, part the waters, open the earth! Save me! She is ready to fall to her knees and close her eyes. So as not to see the blade coming toward her. Sanson answers her plea. Firmly, he turns her toward the bed. She stares at the place where she hid the bloody shift. Behind her back, there is a metallic sound.

The executioner grabs Marie-Antoinette by the hair.

* * *

With .38s drawn, Ed and Jones run to the top of the main staircase at the Anderçon mansion. Thomas stands frozen on the lower landing. He peers over the balustrade and wonders how the Commander was able to make the thirty-foot jump into the void. Thomas envies him. He'd give everything he doesn't have in size, weight, and courage just to know, if only for a moment, what it would be like to be strong and to fly like an angel.

Ed and Jones stand outside the door to the weapons room. They lean into the frame and listen to what is happening inside.

Jones signals to Ed. Ed goes in first. With a quick scan of the room, they take stock of the situation. The picture comes into focus. It's the Pietà. A boy with an afro is cradling a man whose side has been pierced and who is stretched out on the floor. Ed rushes forward. Jones is right behind him. Transfixed, Thomas stands on the threshold, staring at the darkening pool of blood.

"Uh, I'll go fetch a cordial!"

He rushes away as though he were running off to vomit.

The pallid Doctor begins to laugh, but a hacking cough immediately cuts him off.

"A cordial! That's exactly what I need, Gentlemen. A cordial. What I really need is the first-aid kit in my medical bag."

Jones brings it to him, opens it, and rummages through it, looking as though he is planning to bandage the wound. Seiffert stops him.

"No, don't! I know only too well the kind of damage that a bad doctor can do. Because I'm one of them."

With his free hand, the Doctor pulls a long and pointed pair of scissors from the first-aid kit and cuts the bloody cloth covering his stomach. He winces.

"And whom do I have the pleasure of meeting, Gentlemen?"

"Ed Coffin and Gravedigger Jones, police officers! And you are . . . ?"

"It all depends on the diagnosis, Gentlemen!"

The Doctor exhibits a scrap of cloth on which hang shreds of flesh. He examines his wound and screws his face into a pessimistic frown.

"Let's just say that following this preliminary examination, I am authorized to tell you that I appear to be Jean-Geoffroy Seiffert, citizen of Germany, First Pill Dispenser of France, adventurer, hunter of dowries and of children. Former first physician of the Duc d'Orléans, former personal physician of the Princesse de Lamballe, sent away by the Queen, and most lately the victim of a Haarlem maharajah's deception."

"Zamor?"

"Ah. I see that you know him too. That must be because you have also been searching for this boy."

The Doctor looks up at the boy with the afro who is still gripping his shoulders, his face hidden in the Doctor's neck. Since entering the weapons room, Ed and Jones have not yet dared to look at him. They cannot imagine that the heir to the throne of France lies behind this ball of frizzy hair. And a handcuffed Dauphin at that.

"How about removing those, Doctor Seiffert?"

"Do as you like, Inspector, the key is in my vest pocket."

Jones takes it out and frees the child's wrist. He looks at Ed as if to say, *We've done it! We've located the leopard boy! Mission accomplished. And in twelve hours or less!* And yet, they seem disappointed. To think that a night like this is ending with the simple turn of a key. Ed and Jones remain pensive, looking as though they were watching a herd of cows from Ohio amble past. Look out! One of the calves is straying! The boy has jumped up. He has pushed past Jones and crossed the weapons room by jumping over pieces of armor, as one would hop on the rocks in the middle of a torrent in order to cross. Stunned, Ed and Jones have been left on the opposite bank. The boy has already reached the door. So has Thomas. He appears in the doorway with a glass on a tray.

"Your cordial, Sir!"

The impact is that, and a whole lot less. Too much speed. Not enough forward motion. The impact in the ribs is full on. Thomas is propelled into a backward flip. The glass follows, the tray flies up, falls, rolls, spins, and finally comes to rest among the debris of the armor as it tries surreptitiously to look like a fin-de-thirteenth-century shield. Caring not a whit for antiques, the kid steps over Thomas, who grabs one of his ankles in midair.

"Just where do you think you're going? You have to stay and help me clean up!"

Ed steps in, seizes them both, tucks them under one arm, and carries them back across to Jones and the Doctor.

"Gentlemen, now you know why I handcuffed him."

Ed is holding Thomas and the boy apart as one would do with two stubborn children who must be stopped from fighting.

"Bravo, Gentlemen. But you're out of luck. That isn't him."

"What do you mean, Doctor?"

"The boy that you have just captured is named Zoé. He's not the leopard boy. He's a fake! See for yourselves. Here. Wipe his face."

Seiffert hands Ed a wad of cloth that has been soaked in a bluish liquid. The child's head is lowered. Jones gently raises his chin. He does not resist, as though he were used to being examined. Ed dabs softly at the child's cheek. The skin on his face begins to appear. Ed and Jones both begin to feel painfully ill. The skin has been burned with acid.

"You see, makeup was applied to the area after somebody mutilated his face with who knows what kind of etching fluid. This kind of thing is often done to children to make them into beggars or sideshow freaks."

"Doctor, you suspected that this wasn't the leopard boy."

"I didn't just suspect it. I knew it."

Ed and Jones look at each other, taken aback. While caring for his wound, Doctor Seiffert tells them the story of his stay in England, in the city of Brighton. It was back in '87, and he was with the Princesse de Lamballe and the leopard boy. The Princess was taking a cure. There was swimming in the waves, galas with the Prince of Wales, London, the famous fencing match between the Chevalier de Saint-George and the Chevalier d'Éon dressed as a woman, their love affair, and the furor at court.

"So when Zamor brought him to me, I knew immediately that it wasn't him."

"And yet, Doctor, the child must have changed since you last saw him six years ago!"

"Certainly, Gentlemen! But when you meet him, you'll understand that no person or thing can replace him. I had to pretend to be fooled so that I could come back here and settle up with the Marquis d'Ançerçon."

Given the look in the Doctor's eyes, Ed and Jones can easily imagine the kind of settling up he had in mind.

"As for the other people who have taken an interest in the leopard boy, they don't know anything about his appearance."

"Speaking of which, Doctor, just who are these other people?"

"What difference does it make to you whether I was hired by the King's two brothers, the Comte d'Artois or the Comte de Provence, or by Robespierre, or even by the Duc de Penthièvre? I approached all of them. But I failed. Even as we speak, the Commander is galloping toward Haarlem, hell-bent on killing the real leopard boy."

"That should make you happy!"

"But it doesn't. The Commander wishes to erase a stain. But I had a love to avenge. There is more than one way to carry out a killing. Gentlemen, today is the sixteenth day of October. It was on the sixteenth of October 1787 that the Princesse de Lamballe left Brighton to return to France as she was ordered to do by Louis XVI, who had been manipulated by Marie-Antoinette. The date remains engraved right here."

Seiffert taps his forehead. Ed and Jones wish he had pointed at his heart.

"Do you mean to say that you were going to kill the leopard boy in celebration of that anniversary?"

"Try to imagine, Gentlemen, that one day you are separated from your one and only love after first being humiliated and insulted. What would you do?"

They would rather not think about it.

"The Queen wanted to keep the Princesse de Lamballe all for herself. Hers is the passion of a jealous hyena!"

"That does not justify killing a child!"

"Gentlemen, for the moment, it is you who are the killers. Rather than interrogating a man who is already pouring his heart out, you would be better off leaving and taking Zoé with you. He's the only one who will be able to take you to the real leopard boy."

It's funny how a man who is losing blood suddenly gains credibility.

"Take my handcuffs, Gentlemen. You are going to find out what it's like to put another person in chains."

Ed and Jones toss the chains and call heads or tails. Ed loses.

"One last thing, Gentlemen. If you miss the leopard boy, go to the Red Porch on Rue Saint-Honoré, near number 400. You will find that area to be of great interest to you."

Seiffert quickly explains how to get there through a tunnel that runs underneath the Tuileries Palace. Ed and Jones listen, preoccupied. Now it's the Doctor who is holding them up. They are in a hurry.

"OK, Doctor. OK . . . You want us to send someone to help with your wound?"

"There's no need, Gentlemen. Thomas is going to bring me a cordial."

* * *

Zamor lets a roll of coins fall into the gatekeeper's hand.

"I have to get back in to see La du Barry. But this time, I have to meet her in the women's quarters, and in person."

"In person! That will be difficult, Citizen. They transferred her from her cell to the infirmary following the assassination attempt. She's with Citizen Roland."

Zamor gets the lowdown. From the description of the knife, he recognizes the knight in question. A giant. Tall, shorn, with weathered skin. It's that Commander who let him live for the sake of an anthurium lily. That fiend was able to get inside with his weapon, make it all the way to her cell, make an attempt on her life, and then get away. Zamor feels a shiver of admiration run through him. He tries to understand. Why kill La du Barry? Never mind. You'll just have to stop worrying about the Commander and Seiffert. Come on, Zamor! Go ahead and do what you were going to do! The gatekeeper begins to gripe.

"Try to see it my way. Prices have gone up. And now I have a pug to feed."

Zamor drops a little more gold into his hand. Suddenly, seeing La du Barry up close and personal just got a little easier.

Zamor enters the infirmary. La du Barry is there in person all right, and she's stark naked! Citizen Roland is there too. They are making a racket. The two women are shouting at each other from either side of a screen that divides the infirmary in half. Zamor steps back and admires the show. Hairbrush in hand, the Countess is standing in her bathtub. Her anatomy trembles with rage. Madame Roland is sitting on a straw mattress and is busy writing on sheets of paper spread across her knees. Her long black hair flows loosely to her waist. She never raises her eyes from her work, but her voice is loud and clear.

"A perverted despot's ex-mistress can't teach me any new tricks!"

"Look w'o's talking! You're ze wife of a conspiring ex-minister and you're cheating on 'im with a Girondin deputy w'o's run off!"

"Yes, I am! And I'm proud of it! He and I are conspirators in the cause for liberty!"

"Liberty! Liberty! She's nothing but a good lay, zat's what I think! Oh, Liberty, what crimes are committed in zy name!"

The Countess, who is now even more naked than before, brandishes her hairbrush above her head. It's the Statue of La du Barry lighting the world.

"Fortunately, some people stand up for liberty while others bed down with tyranny."

La du Barry's hairbrush whistles over the top of the screen and lands on the wall next to Madame Roland. She ignores it and keeps on writing. La du Barry sticks her head around the edge of the screen.

"Go on, compose your memoirs. Zat's all you know 'ow to do. Use up all of your ink. And don't forget your pen when you go to see Sanson!"

"That's exactly what I'm going to do! I'll cry out even when I'm up on the scaffold! For the sake of writing just one more line, I'll beg Sanson! *One more minute, Mr. Executioner! Just give me one more minute!*"

"You turn my stomach! Where's your dignity? And you are called the Muse of the Girondins!"

"Yes, Madame, that is correct. I am called. You are summoned!"

Fortunately, La du Barry no longer has her hairbrush, powder compact, perfume bottle, scissors, curling iron, or box of beauty marks. Nevertheless, one gets the distinct impression that they are airborne in the infirmary.

The Countess finally notices Zamor.

"Oh, my sweet caramel candy, 'ave you been 'ere ze whole time? 'ow is Petit-Louis? Well? You are keeping 'is cage clean? Did you 'ear that someone tried to kill me? Luckily, I sunk my 'ead under ze water."

He recalls that she used to beat him at that little game. One day she almost drowned him. It had been just good, clean fun. Madame Roland lays an eye on him, even as she continues to write.

"Sir! I hope you have come here to right an injustice. This woman has managed to procure a bathtub, while they took away the pianoforte the concierge was keeping for me. Does Liberty fear music?"

La du Barry begins to laugh.

"Au contraire! Ask Marat. If 'e 'ad been able to play ze piano, 'e would still be alive. Zamor, my sweet bon bon, do not pay 'er any mind. Come over 'ere and let us discuss our affairs."

Zamor moves to the other side of the screen. He admires the sinuous history of a half century of seduction. She motions to him to keep his voice down so that Madame Roland cannot hear them.

"Do you 'ave my papers?"

Zamor rustles them.

"Due to ill health, you are ordered to be transferred to Dr. Belhomme's clinic, where you will have a view of the gardens!"

"'ow I love you, my sweet caramel candy! Give zem to me! Give zem to me now!"

"First tell me where the money and jewels are hidden at Louveciennes."

"Never! What would I 'ave left to my name if I did zat?"

"Everything that is now hidden in London and that the Committee would like to know about. That's my price. Or else I leave and take your transfer papers with me."

Zamor enjoys the look of fear that removes the makeup from La du Barry's face. Suddenly her body shows the wear and tear of fifty years of abuse. Zamor feels he has obtained satisfaction, but of what he is not quite sure.

"Fine. Ask for some paper and a pen from ze pen pusher. I, too, shall write on be'alf of my liberty. Pass me my inkwell. It's in ze trunk by my mattress."

La du Barry writes. Zamor imagines a cascade of diamonds and pearls trailing from the end of each sentence. The Countess folds the paper several times over. The letter is long. There are many hiding places in Louveciennes!

"We are agreed, zen, Zamor. As soon as you find what you are looking for, you will come back and give me ze papers."

"You have my word."

"Tell me. What is 'appening with ze leopard boy?"

"The Commander is out to kill him. And nobody can stop him. Not even Delorme."

"And you, Zamor, what are you going to do for ze boy?"

"Me? Why, not a thing. He is no longer my concern."

"If you say so. But read my letter closely, Zamor. And take care of Petit-Louis. Don't forget to clean his cage thoroughly."

Zamor shrugs his shoulders and walks out of the infirmary. La du Barry shivers as she stands naked and in her tub. Her entire body is trembling. Madame Roland crosses to her side of the screen and hands her a towel.

"Countess, that man won't ever come back."

"I know zat, Madame."

"What? He betrays you, condemns you, and you have nothing to say?"

"All I will lose is my life. But 'e will cease to exist."

"You should write that down, Countess."

"Zat's what I just did, Madame. And believe me, what I 'ave written will 'ave an impact!

* * *

The Commander eases his way through a brick conduit. It finally opens into a ruined hall scattered with broken columns, capitals, arches, and the ribs of ceiling vaults. Up to this point, Zoé's directions have been exact. That little nigger has a good sense of direction. And yet, one thing troubles the Commander, and that is the rising water inside the pipe that he had to crawl through to get here. In less than one hour this passageway will be impossible to use in case he decides to retreat. But does he really wish to turn back?

The Commander slips behind a series of vertical support beams that stand in a corner of the hall. He reaches a wooden box that reeks of incense and squeezes into it. According to the kid's directions, he'd then have to go in through the sinners' box.

From inside the dark confessional, the Commander can hear shouting, singing, barking dogs, the issuing of orders, the cracking of whips. He doesn't even have to close his eyes in order to see himself back on his plantation with his men as they all work together to lift the trunk of an old tree blown down in a hurricane. He parts the curtain. Gangs of bare-chested men stand ankle-deep in water as they pull on a series of ropes. They are hoisting a thick wooden platform upon which is perched a ridiculous-looking armchair.

"You dirty rats! Watch what you're doing or you'll tip my throne over!"

Delorme! The Commander knows that voice. The leopard boy can't be too far away.

* * *

"The passageway is right here, Boss!"

Zoé shows Ed and Jones a conduit half-filled with a torrent of milky-looking water.

"You call this a passageway?"

"There didn't used to be any water in it, I swear, Boss!"

"I told you not to call me Boss!"

Ed and Jones exchange a questioning look. They've followed Zoé all the way through this flooded tunnel, and they're not going to turn back now. The Commander's been here. That's reason enough for them. Neither of them can remember the last time they'd gone swimming. Maybe it was back in that Virginia river when they had ambushed a bunch of British soldiers. Their oil-cloth slickers had effectively protected their clothing, arms, and gunpowder. They would have to do the same in this situation.

"Zoé, we want you to repeat all the details concerning this passageway that you told us about earlier."

In the meantime, Jones removes his clothing and carefully rolls it into his coat. Ed does the same thing after handing Zoé, still tied up, over to Jones.

"It's your turn to deal with the kid now."

Although bare-chested and in long johns, Ed and Jones feel more naked without their .38s than they do without their clothes.

"You too, Zoé. Take off your clothes."

"No, Boss. I not go Guinea with Mandrâ! He angry! Master Us All command him take me away."

"Stop talking like an idiot and don't say Boss! Mandrâ doesn't exist."

"Drop it, Ed. Delorme must have scared him with the legend of the black savior who welcomes black people into a magical land under the sea. He'll calm down in a minute."

"We don't have time for that, Jones."

Ed strips Zoé of his clothing. The kid is shaking. He's wearing nothing but a pair of silk underwear. His back carries a maze of scars left by repeated lashings. Ed regrets having upset him. In an effort to drown his rage, he dives with no warning into the opening of the conduit.

"Edmond!"

The torrent sucks him down. The water holds his body in its icy grip. He pushes against the side of the drainpipe in order to avoid being carried away by its violent current. Zoé had mentioned an airshaft. There it is! Ed grabs it, wedges his bundle into it, and shouts back to Jones.

"Come on! Let the water take you. I'll stop you!"

Jones gets the message. He drags Zoé toward the opening. The two take a deep breath, dive in, and are pulled down by the raging torrent. Jones feels as though he has just been shot from a cannon. He slams into Ed, who grabs him and pulls his head up out of the water.

"You all right?"

Just as he is about to respond, Jones is pulled under again. He is completely submersed. Ed snags his hand. Jones can feel Zoé pulling on the other end of the chain as he tries to drag him away. Jones resists and attempts to gulp a lungful of air before going under, but he is torn between Ed and this devil of a boy. His lungs explode, his brain boils, and Ed's grip begins to slip. He'll just have to give up and let himself be taken away, or Zoé will drown him.

Jones can feel his brain turn molten. He can feel his body being invaded by a gentle heat. Strands of algae and shells glowing red dance in the water around him. Jones gives up. He'll just follow the boy down to that magical land that doesn't exist.

Zoé gives the chain a final yank. It breaks. Ed pulls Jones's head above the water. His mouth gapes as he gasps for air and gulps at it wherever he can get it.

"Mandrâââ!!!"

Zoé cries out the name. It bounces off the vaulted ceiling as he is carried away. Ed drags Jones from the brick conduit and lays him out on the flagstone floor in the ruined hall. Ed recognizes the place from Zoé's description. He checks inside the bundles. Everything is safe. Sprawled on his back, Jones slowly recovers his wits.

Dogs!

Ed can hear them barking. An old fear makes him recoil and prick up his ears like an animal. They are not far away and are getting closer. Ed shoves their belongings behind a chunk of broken column and rushes toward Jones, who is still in a fog.

"Come on! The confessional can't be too far from here!"

Too late. A couple of howling mastiffs surge into view. They are pulling a twerp by the leash. A torchbearer keeps him company. With a satisfied look, he shines a light on their catch.

"Two more caught trying to escape. Too bad you boys didn't make it. Now get back to work."

The invitation is sent by whip lash.

* * *

Zamor opens his window wide. Breathe. He must breathe. His entire being is smothering in rage. He fans himself with the letter that La du Barry wrote in the infirmary. That Countess! He'll kill her with his bare hands! She tricked him! Zamor reads two random passages. Perhaps he just doesn't understand the letter. *In two separate holes that have been dug to the left of the garden entrance you will find, in the first one, six bags of silver, one silver-gilt cup, nine louis in six pound écu pieces, one gold louis, one guinea, a golden half-guinea, one hundred emblazoned coins . . . biting his lip, he continues to read . . . one silver crucifix, one silver-gilt chalice and paten, one box filled with twelve golden teaspoons, striated and emblazoned . . .*

Furious, Zamor crumples the paper into a ball. The Countess has made a royal mockery of him with her junk-store inventory list. There is no mention whatsoever of a jewelry cache, no mention of any deeds, nor of any paintings. And what does the rest of the letter mean? . . . *in one of the outbuildings, underneath a cot you will find two fringed velvet seat covers, embroidered with gold and silver. Take them out and bring them to me for my departure from Sainte-Pélagie Prison. My position requires that I not travel unadorned in a simple cart. As for the bearskin, that is my gift to you. It is said to be a fool's coat. Above all, take good care of Petit-Louis. Keep him quiet. He knows too much about you and could get you knocked off your perch. Finally, tread carefully during the light of day. It kills secrets. Signed Countess du Barry, born in Vaucouleurs, August 19, 1743, soon to die in Paris.*

Zamor hurls the ball of paper at the cage from which the parrot is now scolding him in Creole.

"Take good care of Petit-Louis! Take good care of Petit-Louis!"

In a fury, he takes the cage in his fists and shakes it. The parrot flaps its wings and squawks in terror.

"Silence! I've had it with you and your mistress. I've fed you, cleaned you, taken care of you, and this is what I get for all my trouble!"

Zamor slugs the cage and knocks it to the floor. The door opens, the bottom falls out. Petit-Louis is ejected, surprised at having to fly. Something falls to the floor. Zamor picks it up. It's the parrot's perch. A piece of paper protrudes from one end of the thin section of bamboo. Zamor pulls on it. A roll of paper follows. He unrolls it. It contains the handwriting of La du Barry.

Zamor, what follows is an incredible confession. But I swear to God that it is the complete truth. Do you recall the carnival of 1778? That wild night at the Princesse de Lamballe's Italian festival? You were wearing a mask and were dressed in the guise of the Swedish Ambassador . . . Zamor has no memory of that. There had been so many parties and the Countess had loved to dress him up for the fun of showing him off as though he were her pet monkey . . . *I got my revenge while I watched as with your virility, you honored a mysterious woman in a blue domino mask. The woman was drunk on Amarone wine that had been spiked with a powder that I had added to it* . . . Zamor remembers the wine that had numbed his mind and stiffened his body . . . *From this union were born two children: a boy and a girl* . . . What! Now this whore is telling me that I'm a father? If she thinks I'm going to pay child support, she is mistaken . . . *That mysterious woman was Marie-Antoinette, Queen of France* . . . Zamor drops the roll of paper. He begins to shake violently from head to toe. He! He is the father of the leopard boy and of Marie-Thérèse! He pinches himself.

"If my son is the Dauphin, then . . . that makes me the King!"

His Majesty is too preoccupied with his newfound glory to notice the miserable parrot Petit-Louis flying away over the rooftops with the bejeweled tailcoat in his beak. There go thousands of pounds, right out the window!

"Come back, Petit-Louis, come back!"

Zamor knows that the parrot will not obey. He watches as his dreams glisten in the gray skies of Haarlem. Oh, well. Now he's got something much better in the form of this rolled-up piece of paper. But for it to be of any use, he must now save the leopard boy. The real one. The Dauphin . . . His son! The one that Delorme is holding in the grotto below Saint-Zita's.

* * *

From behind the confessional curtain, the Commander watches with an overseer's eye as the men maneuver the platform that hangs from their ropes . . . What a bunch of clumsy oafs! . . . Never mind. He must get his bearings in this strange underground church. According to Zoé's directions, the leopard boy's abode is just above the confessional. He has decided to take his position there. To lie in wait. To destroy him.

"It's going to tip over! Pull! Pull, you lazy bastards!"

With a loud crack, a rope snaps, the platform falls to one side, dragging the ropes with it and tipping the heavy platform over to the vertical plane. Delorme's throne is catapulted into a column, men fall over backward, others are jerked up toward the ceiling. There is shouting. Men run to the rescue from all quarters.

The Commander sees that this is his chance. He slips from the confessional, climbs on top of it, jumps up to the gallery balustrade, takes hold of it, steadies himself, and leaps over. All around him men are running in every direction. The leopard boy's abode is nigh. It is a kind of pavilion with an observation deck that juts out over the nave. Two guards dressed in the uniform of the uhlans stand guard at the entrance. Down below, Delorme's voice is menacing.

"My throne! . . . I'll curse you all if it falls! I will skin each of you alive, one by one. I want to see everyone right here! Right now!"

The two uhlans on guard duty in front of the pavilion cannot decide whether to abandon their posts or to be skinned alive. They take a little too long to make up their minds. The Commander skins them before they've even had time to feel alive. He drags their bodies into the pavilion. The Commander is stunned by the unusual beauty of the place. It is as though he had entered the den of a wild animal. The walls are covered in such a way as to give the impression that a leopard's skin has grown directly over the stone. The room is illuminated by a single torch driven into the wall above two crossed swords. The square room is topped with a cupola held by four columns. The wall facing the entrance opens onto the deck overlooking the nave. The Commander slides along toward it with his back to the wall. He is now able to see the scene playing out below him. A group of men pull on the ropes in a desperate effort to right the platform that now hangs in midair. Impossible to right it using this method.

Amid the ropesmen, Ed and Jones take note of their positions. By luck, after being discovered by the guards, they were taken for slackers, brought back here, and put to work with a couple of lashes of the whip.

Delorme's wardens are getting ever more agitated and aggressive. First there's this platform that threatens to fall, then there is an enraged Master of Us All, but especially there is this water! It has suddenly risen higher inside the church. The men are up to their knees in it. The water is muddy. It has overflown the central nave and is spreading. Bits of wood and debris float in it at random. The Slave Ark is almost off its moorings. Panic is beginning to take hold. Standing upright on a sedan chair borne on the backs of men, Delorme shouts and stabs at anything that comes near. A white-haired old man throws himself before him.

"Master of Us All! Mandrâ is angry. You must call on Lého to appease him."

Delorme kicks him out of the way.

"You crazy old bastard! That's an old wives' tale! There is no deity waiting for you under the water. There is no need to bother Lého for a few overflowing sewer pipes! It is I who am your savior!"

A murmur rises, and the crowd stands stock-still. Faces turn to stare at Delorme. He gets the message. Ed and Jones glimpse the look in the eye of the predator who senses that his prey is about to rebel. Delorme is only a few steps away. It would only take one swift stroke of the knife to cut his throat into a clean, two-lipped grin.

"All right, Brothers, all right! I will ask Lého to intervene in your favor."

Delorme commands the men to carry the sedan chair to a place just below the observation deck. He raises his arms.

"Lého, child of man and child of leopard. You whose skin bears the variegated colors of humanity. I implore you! Help us now!"

From inside, the Commander can hear Delorme's rising imprecation. What a joke! How can they believe this charlatan?

The leopard boy is watching the Commander. The torchlight delineates his wary face. This man has come here to kill him. It is not just the machete that says so, it is his entire body. This man is on the prowl!

The Commander feels a presence nearby. Delorme's plea means that the leopard boy is here, somewhere in this room. He scrutinizes the place and hums the Caïman's song. *Huye que te coge ese animal. Y te puede devorar.*

Lého steps out from behind a pillar and drops the leopard-skin coat that had kept him hidden and walks out to the balcony without worrying about the man behind him. Lého must always respond when his name is called.

THE LEOPARD BOY

He appears. Dressed in white from head to toe.

Down below, Ed and Jones catch sight of him. They remember the words pronounced by Doctor Seiffert at the Marquis d'Andersson's. *When you meet him, you will understand why he is not like anyone or anything else.* The Doctor was right. Lého walks toward the balustrade. All eyes are upon him. The church is suddenly so silent that the only sound is the rumbling water at work in the chancel. The leopard boy gestures with an open hand as though to wipe fear from a face.

Suddenly, a black shadow surges forward and attacks him from behind. The church is overcome by collective revulsion. Ed and Jones recognize that dark shadow. It's that flying black angel, the Commander!

"Someone is trying to kill Lého!"

The cry shatters the church. There is indignation, anger, and chaos. Men run toward the deck. They drop the ropes. The platform falls through the air like a guillotine blade, hits the ground, stands on its edge for a moment before slowly tottering to one side. It belly-flops and sends a huge wave of water straight into the side of the Slave Ark. Ed and Jones take advantage of the chaos and leap to cover beside the confessional.

"Jones, you get our clothes. I'll start climbing."

Ed points to the observation deck, where Lého and the Commander are now locked in a swordfight. Ed grabs a floating piece of wood and hits an uhlan over the head with it as he is running by. He grabs the cavalry saber and dagger for himself before shoving the body into the confessional with a sign of the cross for absolution.

Ed grabs one of the ropes that hang from the ceiling.

"Jones! Help me reach the upper deck!"

There is no need for signs here. Jones knows the kind of swinging motion that Ed has in mind. He propels his partner into the air with a mighty push. The first pass is not high enough to reach the balcony, but Ed gets close enough to Delorme to be recognized.

"Ed Coffin! You're back, you mangy dog! En garde! I want this rat for myself!"

Ed salutes the use of the possessive pronoun with his sword and uses a pillar to launch himself in the direction of the deck where Lého is defending himself with surprising agility.

The Commander shares this thought as he finds himself obliged to battle to the best of his ability.

"My compliments, Sir, to your master-at-arms. Your skill carries the unmistakable imprint of the Chevalier de Saint-George."

Lého acquiesces as he lunges into an attack at the heart, a move that the Commander counters with an ungraceful parry. He excuses himself.

"I suppose that the Chevalier de Saint-George has also taught you his dancing skills along with his excellent musical talents. I admit that I don't fancy all of his concertos, which are a bit too French for my taste, but I often find the Creole languor which accents all of his compositions most touching."

Lého provokes a brief corps-à-corps with the Commander to signal that he finds the expression "Creole languor" offensive. At this very moment, Ed, saber in hand, swings up and over the balustrade, still wearing nothing but his long johns.

"Police Officer Ed Coffin, here!"

He brandishes a nonexistent blue badge and turns to face the leopard boy. Lord! What majesty! A very old and very pure emotion rises up to his eyes. Ed feels naked and tormented. He regains control of himself.

"Citizen, I have my orders. You must come with me."

Lého experiences a moment of doubt. Who is this man? The Commander seizes the moment and disarms the leopard boy. He grabs him from behind and points his dagger straight into his chest.

"This 'citizen' isn't going with you. In fact, he's not going anywhere. This citizen is going to die and he knows it. But for the moment, he'll be my passport out of here."

The Commander drags Lého toward the entrance. Rushing footsteps echo along the gallery. He moves back to the balcony and considers his options. Down below, the church is completely flooded. A strong current is rushing up against the bronze door in the apse. The village cabins that had been set up in the transept along with its Cabins of Comprehension have been carried away. Men and women are swimming in the turbulent waters amid all sorts of debris. The Slave Ark has broken loose from its moorings and is floating aimlessly toward the chancel. Its central mast has skewered the painting of the Maréchal de Saxe and transformed it into a black flag. It will be impossible to escape by way of the balcony. The Commander shoves Lého out of the pavilion and into the gallery. He runs toward the choir. Ed falls in behind them. But uhlans and guards rush in from every direction and surround them. Ed is immobilized. Delorme arrives. He parts the ranks and punches Ed in the stomach as though it were an afterthought. He is focused on Lého. Nobody dares to approach the leopard boy. The Commander is still aiming his dagger at the boy as he straddles the gallery balustrade.

"Gentlemen, it's up to you. I can either pierce his heart or drown him."

Faking it, the Commander threatens to jump and take the leopard boy down with him. Everyone steps back. Suddenly Ed sees Jones swing into view, hanging from the end of his rope. He'd know the soles of those worn-out boots anywhere. And those soles land squarely on the Commander's back, launching him straight into the arms of the guards. In the same forward arc, Jones snags the leopard boy, and the two of them swing away together and out into the void. With a lovely swaying motion, Jones and Lého alight in the gallery on the opposite side of the nave.

Delorme reacts immediately. He drags Ed over to the balustrade, the blade of his sword pushing against Ed's throat.

"So, Gravedigger Jones, take your pick. Who dies? The boy or your friend?"

Groundhog would think of it as a dilemma. Jones thinks it's a dirty deal.

"Don't listen to him, Jones! Save the kid! And that's an order, Soldier!"

Delorme slugs Ed to shut him up. Jones looks at Lého. The boy answers him with the same kind of nod that his partner makes to say, *Just do it! Go in for the kill!* He rifles through Ed's gear, takes out the .38, hands it to Lého, and tosses the bundle into the void where it comes to land on the poop deck of the Slave Ark. Gripping the rope, Jones and Lého take a flying leap and lay down a line of fire that takes Delorme and his men by surprise. Ed takes advantage of the distraction to break free. They set to work in the gallery, exchanging punches with their adversaries. There's a head count. Ed, Jones, Lého, and the Commander. That makes four. No barroom brawlers here. Nothing but fine swordsmen. The guards are retreating, the uhlans are overwhelmed, and Delorme is flailing his sword, outmatched. He has the shortness of breath of a man who has been sitting on a throne for too long. The four storm the pavilion. Jones thinks they should jump from the balcony to the ship's mast and execute an emergency descent. The Commander issues a warning. After that, Gentlemen, it's a free-for-all. Every man for himself! May the best man win! They swear by their swords. It's a sight for chivalry's sore eyes, but they're now being inundated with as many uhlans as they can run their swords through.

Covered by the others, Jones leaps from the balcony to the mast. Lého follows suit. Ed and the Commander argue over who should have the honor of going last. In the end, it's age before beauty. Down below, Jones and Lého take turns hacking at the base of the mast with the ship's axe. The mast wobbles and snaps. The Commander has waited just a little too long to join them. Now it's too late. The mast gives way and crashes onto the bridge, taking the black flag down with it. Ed saws through the remaining moorings. The Slave Ark is cut loose as the current draws it toward the choir. Ed, Jones, and Lého look up at the balcony where the Commander is battling Delorme with his back to the balustrade. They have no time to see much more than that. The boat has just rammed into the monumental bronze door at the back of the apse, knocking it off its hinges. The tide is rushing in. Ed, Jones, and Lého jump into the water, allowing the current to take them. Ed has just enough time to see the Commander throw himself from the balcony and to hear Delorme's final promise.

"I'll catch you later! I know exactly where you're headed!"

* * *

Anyone hiding by the fountain in the Saint-Zita of Haarlem rectory gardens would swear that they had just seen the Laughing Negress spit out three men, who then proceed to jump into the driver's seat of Moka's hearse and gallop away. They would also think they had seen a gigantic fourth man follow, yelling in their general direction.

"Remember, Gentlemen! It's every man for himself! May the best man win!"

From his hiding place behind a clump of trees, Zamor is happy to see that the leopard boy is still alive and that he has escaped from Delorme. Above all, he is proud that his son is so handy with horses. He follows behind in hot pursuit and does not hear the formidable laugh that issues from the stone mouth as it shakes Haarlem to its core.

* * *

Spike is waiting for Groundhog at a prearranged location near the Enfants-Rouges Market. From where he is standing, he can see only one of the Temple Prison's four large towers and pointed turret. He has not been to this neighborhood in a long time. Not since before the construction of this high wall. Spike is worried. Groundhog hasn't come out of the prison yet. It was a bad idea to return Coco to the little Dauphin. Dogs were not meant to live in prison. And what if Groundhog can't get back out!

In order to calm his fear, Spike rummages through his game bag. He examines a couple of words, feeling that he is able to recognize their physiognomy. Some of them seem pleasant, and some even smile at him. Like this one, for example. He is almost certain that he recognizes it. Others scurry away like notary publics in the rain. Ah! Here's that friendly one again, all warm and round, looking like a tiny pennant. "Bread." Right. You are "bread." I'm Spike. Now we're friends. Stay here! Don't move! Don't run away! I'm going to write your name down.

"Spike!"

It's Groundhog. He is panic-stricken, and still holds the little dog in his arms. He is crying. His tears mix with the snot running from his nose as they drip onto his heaving chest.

"Who made you cry, Groundhog? Just tell me. We'll go back in and, bingo! I'll run him right through. Like we did with that other one. Remember?"

"C'mon Spike. Let's get outta here."

"You sure you don't want me to skewer one for ya? What about Coco? And the little Dauphin? Wait up!"

Groundhog takes off, hugging the little pug to his chest. Spike looks like a streetlamp that hasn't been lit yet.

"Wait up, Groundhog! Tell me what happened! You know I can understand anything when it ain't written down!"

No, he'll never be able to understand. Nobody could. How can he explain what he heard? A son singing disgusting songs about his mother, drinking wine and dancing in front of the guards while they laugh and clap their hands! That's what he just saw and heard in the courtyard as he was hiding near the gate. He had covered Coco's ears. Groundhog would like to be able to run fast enough to smash the paving stones into his head so that he can no longer hear the Dauphin. A son who disrespects his mother! He who is lucky enough to have one. He will never play hoop-and-stick with him again.

"Come on, Groundhog, let's show Coco to the Queen. That will warm her heart and yours, too."

* * *

Marie-Antoinette closes her eyes. She is ready. Let the executioner cut her throat. It's her destiny. If this is what God wills. At least she will be saved from the humiliation of being executed amid the hatred of . . . *Shlik!* . . . *Shlik!* She recognizes that sensuous sound. Scissors! Of course, it's scissors. The terrible blade in the executioner's hand was only a pair of scissors. These tiny resurrections, how sweet! She opens her eyes. Clumps of thick white hair fall around her feet. Are these her beautiful blond curls? Those reddish blond locks that made La du Barry call her *that little redhead*?

Why had she so hated that woman even before she had even become queen? She simply had not been able to accept that every single night, her husband's grandfather was paying her homage in a way that her own husband could not. And yet, if it had not been for La du Barry, it would have been her dear Madame de Lamballe in her stead, since she had been promised to His Majesty, Louis XV. How different some destinies would be today! And where would the child be now?

Marie-Antoinette watches as the final locks fall to the floor in clumps. Why is she having these thoughts at this moment? When preparing to die, does a man count his mistresses and a woman her lovers? What strange a winter is the end of a life!

Marie-Antoinette can see Sanson stuffing his pockets with her hair, as a child would do with stolen candy. She hopes that the locks that she has secretly given to her lawyers will reach their intended destinations. She prefers not to think about it in case just doing so would be enough for them to get caught. The executioner places her bonnet back on her head. Goodness! How awkwardly he's done it! He's trying to make her look like a fishwife! She feels the cool air on the back of her neck. The slight breeze pinches her heart. That is where the blade will fall.

People make way before her. It is this movement that reminds her that she is not completely alone with the executioner. And yet, where are her judges, her lawyer, the abbot, and the aides? She can hear nothing but the rustling of fabric, footsteps, coughing. She feels surrounded by ghosts who are embarrassed to be here. Well, then, leave! At least have the courage to do that. Nobody is forcing you to be present! The quick, dry sound of the lock startles her. The door opens. It will be for the last time. She cannot imagine not being able to feel the paving stones beneath her bare feet, not being able to inhale that fragrance of dried roses that lingers in the tapestry. She almost forgot about those flowers that are so kindly being delivered here. In gathering her strength, she moves a bit too abruptly toward the door. A sharp pain runs through her spine. Sanson is still holding the rope that pulls her elbows up and behind her back. He's keeping her on a tight rein. As one would do in taming an animal.

Marie-Antoinette steps across the threshold of her cell. They turn her to the right. Her gaze falls upon a solid wall of uniforms lined up in the prisoners' gallery. Gendarmes. A double row of them with faces that remind her of Varennes. Such as it is, she is having difficulty recognizing the area. To the left must be Rue de Paris. The street where the executioner lives. This Parisian man whose immense presence is palpable through her back. She brushes by a place of regret. It's the gate of last good-byes. It's the final stop before the ultimate departure. These are the bars that separate the women's yard from those who are going to their deaths. These bars have been polished by hands that grip and tears that weep. How she would love to feel the light touch of fingertips on her face. She would leave traces of lipstick and rouge with her beloved.

She walks on, looking straight ahead, without slowing. Where is she? Is it the front desk, or the clerk's office already? There are so many bars and doors! She now realizes the size and number of obstacles that had to be overcome by those who had tried to save her. If only she hadn't been so fearful and so worried about her children. There's the clerk. She recognizes him from that lingering odor of urine that hangs about him. They open two more doors and she enters a small courtyard. Beyond that is a gate.

Marie-Antoinette feels faint. She regains control of herself. Sanson has just tugged on her rope. The pain helps to keep her legs from collapsing. A cart! She cannot take her eyes from it. A horrible cart. A tumbrel! So they will be taking her to her death like a load of manure! It's too much for her body as it gives way. She can feel the warm heat of renunciation in her lower extremities. Marie-Antoinette turns and implores Sanson.

"Sir, I beg you, kindly untie me. It is a question of female modesty."

He understands and unties her hands. She walks over to the drainage ditch, and like a child urinating by the side of the road, squats and goes beneath her skirts.

Marie-Antoinette stands up. She feels like shouting to everyone present, *Go ahead, gentlemen! You can kill me now!* But what's the use? She extends her hands to Sanson but is incapable of smiling at him in thanks.

She walks through the small courtyard. It could be that the weather is nice with a fine myopic mist and a temperature of about fifty degrees on her arms and neck.

Marie-Antoinette looks at the stone arch that leads to the Cour de Mai, where the cart stands waiting. She knows that beyond that point nothing belongs to her. But she must remain the Queen, now, even more than before.

She steps through the archway.

12

MARIE-ANTOINETTE

"Place your foot there."

The executioner points Marie-Antoinette toward the second rung of the short ladder that rises into the cart. The tumbrel is mud-covered and filthy. Perhaps they've fouled it just for her! The two cart horses have received better care than she has. Animals before humans. Sanson takes her by the arm and helps her hoist herself up. It seems so high! Careful! She must not trip, stumble, or get tangled in her black skirts. Behind her, the abbot groans under the effort.

They want her to sit on this crude plank! She was not expecting a cushion, but there should at the very least be a cloth of some kind! Nothing of the sort. Let us be seated.

"No, Madame."

Sanson stops her from stepping over the plank. She must sit facing backward. This is yet another measure intended to offend the conventions of royal etiquette. Marie-Antoinette takes her place, her back to the horses. A prediction once made by Madame de Lamballe comes to mind. Madame, you will enter the Temple backward. She had been right. And yet, at the time, she had mocked her dear Marie-Thérèse, who had been playing at being the Grand Mistress of the Masons with her mysterious pronouncements. *You shall be pushed into darkness and you shall have nothing to guide you but a Flaming Star.* Today she shall seek out that star in order to muster the same courage that the Princess had found at the hour of her own death.

The cart jerks forward. Marie-Antoinette sits up straight. Only at this moment does she realize that she is surrounded by gendarmes and pikesmen. She hears the creak of the gate over the noise of the wooden wheels and the clattering of hooves on the paving stones. The procession is leaving the Cour de Mai.

Now, the mob!

It had been standing in wait on Rue de la Barillerie. Marie-Antoinette comes upon it. It is silent. But she only retains the image of a single face. It is that of a young woman wearing a white shawl draped across her shoulders. Her expression holds no joy, no hatred, only weariness. Marie-Antoinette shivers. The road ahead will be long.

The cart starts to cross the Pont-au-Change. The rumbling echoes through the arches below. What a good idea it had been to raze those hideous houses that had blocked the view of the Seine. Suddenly, the wind comes up. She can feel it rifling her bonnet. What would happen if it blew off? Would a pikesman spear it in midair as if he were capturing a butterfly? How many hearts have been pierced using that same method! Why not hers? Oh! There are the three towers of the Conciergerie! She tries to see whether any of her judges are watching from behind its narrow slotted windows. She lifts her chin. Don't rejoice too much, Gentlemen! I am merely preceding you on this road.

"Do you know, Gentlemen, why one of these towers is nick-named Bonbec?"

"Uh, to tell you the truth, Ma'am, it's from when they used to torture the inmates. Their mouths gaped wide as they cried out."

"Thank you for telling me that, Sir."

She herself had often wanted to cry out. But one simply does not do that. One holds one's head high. One looks ahead of one! One must not allow oneself to look over at the spectacle being played out on the river below. Apparently, there is sailing and water jousting.

* * *

Dame Catherine and Pobéré stop in front of a small boat moored at the Port aux Huîtres below the Old Louvre palace. Pobéré climbs aboard.

"I'll hoist the sail. Even if there is very little wind, the current will be strong enough to carry us along. No one will think of looking for us on the Seine."

Pobéré grasps his mother's arm, holding her back. With a grave and worried face she turns to face her son. This is his first moment of hesitation.

"Listen, Mother. You should wait here. Things are going to get ugly. What would become of you if I lost you in the crowd?"

"What would become of me? I would make my way home. I'm not helpless, just blind! Did you know that on days when there's a thick fog over Paris, it is the patients from the Quatre-

Vingts Hospital for the Blind who lead the wealthy bourgeois to their homes?"

"Don't get angry, Mother! I'm just saying that . . ."

"Come here, my son."

Dame Catherine pulls her son into her arms. He resists, and then gives in, his head on her shoulder. She strokes his red hair. She whispers in his ear, as he had done earlier in hers.

"I know full well why you want me to wait here. I know you. You are my son. You are the best shoeshine boy in Paris. With your brushes, you could convince the roughest piece of leather that it is made of kidskin. But you are no good at lying to your old mother. You think I can't hear in your voice that a good number of our partisans haven't shown up?"

The boy begins to cry, sobbing against his mother's breast. He hugs her waist, almost to the point of suffocating her.

"What are we going to do, Mother?"

"What are we going to do? We're going to save the Queen! Just the two of us. Along with Guillaume, Jean-Baptiste, Elisabeth, Merlin, and the other partisans who have remained loyal to our cause. We're better off with fifty dedicated men than with five hundred fainthearted ones. I just know that you'll soon be taking your Queen for a sail in this little boat! Now dry your eyes!"

The boy stops crying. They will save Marie-Antoinette, he's sure of it now.

"Son, before we return to the Red Porch, I have a favor to ask you."

"Anything at all, Mother."

"Before we go to see the Queen, I want you to make my shoes look like the slippers of a princess."

And there on the bank of the Seine, in the late-morning light, a red-haired boy kneels before a blind woman whose shoes now shine as if ready for a special occasion.

* * *

Ed, Jones, and Lého disembark at the Quai du Louvre. They had had to abandon Moka's hearse on the opposite bank of the Seine. All of the bridges have been closed to vehicle traffic and are now guarded by cordons of soldiers. It had not been easy to find a boatman, even at a hefty price. They had heard that the Queen's

convoy had left the Conciergerie. They had had to act fast in order to get Lého to Sweet Victory, where they would place him on
her route. During their hearse ride from Haarlem, Ed and Jones
had had time to explain everything to him.

As soon as their feet hit the ground, Police Sergeant Ed reports
to duty and spurs Jones and Lého into a dead run. They all turn
the corner at the Church of Saint-Germain-l'Auxerrois and reach
the tavern, entering through its back door. They are barely a
quarter of a league's distance from the Quay. From where they
are now standing, they can just make out the Queen's procession,
already moving up Quay de la Mégisserie. She is coming straight
toward them.

* * *

Marie-Antoinette draws a deep breath, inhaling the odor of the
river. Her gaze is drawn to a little black boy perched on a stone
post. He is showing her something that is hidden beneath his
cape. It's a dog. It's Coco! Her pug! How is this possible? She
had left him . . . Just where had she left him . . . ? No matter.
It's him, no doubt about that. Marie-Antoinette would recognize
him anywhere. Dear God, that little black boy has disappeared
already. Ah! There he is again. He seems to have decided to follow her.

* * *

Groundhog jumps from his perch in excitement.

"Did she see him, Spike? Do ya think she saw him? Did she?
I think she saw him. I think she musta seen him. What do you
think?"

Spike picks up his pike and thinks it over.

"Sure she saw it!"

"I knew it! What about you, Boy? Did ya see your mistress?
Huh? Did ya see her?"

Groundhog repeats his questions to the pug, who responds by
curling up and going back to sleep under the cape.

"Com'on Spike. Let's go to the corner of Rue Saint-Honoré
and Rue du Roule and show her Coco there. That's where I
found my wheel with the yellow spokes on it."

"How many times are we going to show him to the Queen?"

"As many times as we can! Just as many as we can!"

* * *

Marie-Antoinette feels her cheeks burn in anger. She has not seen one single familiar face in this entire crowd that is now lining her route. Not one former courtier, not a single servant girl, not even a single woman friend. But her dog is there! How absurd! Where are those who, with just one word from her, had obtained a name, a title, a tract of land? All that remains now is her little barking pug dog. This is indeed a miserable Te Deum! Marie-Antoinette thinks of Mozart. Poor Amadeus! Soon they shall be reunited. They had wanted to marry. She had been fourteen years old. It had been summertime. Six months later, she had been married off to the future King of France.

This thought alone would have made her shoulders droop in despair. But Coco's presence means that somewhere along the route there must be something afoot to help her escape. Up to that point she hadn't given the idea much credit except to use it to help her hold her head up high. But now! My God! What a disaster! She can no longer remember the message that had been delivered by that woman in heavy makeup. The one who had brought her some bouillon. There had been something about the color red in the secret message.

The cart enters Rue de la Monnaie. The street is very narrow. What an unusual sign . . . Sweet Victory . . . Sweet Victory must surely be that beautiful buxom blonde standing on that barrel. Strange how she holds her red axe so tenderly in her arms. As if she were cradling a child! . . . Red! A Red Porch! That's what the heavily made-up woman had said! There would be a red porch, after Robespierre's house . . . She is saved! Thank you, Madame Victory, for that axe.

* * *

Ed sprints through the back door and into the tavern's back room. He gives it a quick inspection. There is no one at the tables or near the ovens. He signals to Jones and Lého to join him. Ed rushes to the front door. It is closed and must certainly be barricaded from the outside. He pushes on it. It won't budge. Ed looks around for the axe, but Sanson has gone missing.

"Listen! The cart is approaching! Quick, Jones! The window!"

Jones opens it, but a barrel is blocking the view. Nothing

doing. Someone is standing on top of it and the populace has crowded in from all sides. They'll never be able to see the cart pass now. Enraged, Ed bangs his head violently against the wall.

"We almost made it!"

Jones flops onto a bench. Suddenly, the floor begins to shake and they can feel a rumbling reverberating with increasing intensity. Lého cocks an ear. The three men stand stock-still. The Queen! There is not a single shout, not a single murmur from the street. The silence is deafening. There is nothing but the heavy hoofbeats of the horses and the sound of the ironclad wheels crushing the pavement. They begin to breathe again. Ed, Jones, and Lého follow the convoy as it moves along the tavern's outside wall. The Queen is passing at this very moment. They've engaged in hand-to-hand combat with their enemies and cut the guts out of their adversaries. They've almost died just to reach this moment. And here they are, prisoners caught for no good reason in a jail that stinks of cold grease.

Ed and Jones look over at Lého. The leopard boy is crying, his face turned toward the open window. It's as though he were standing before a broken pane of stained glass. His head is angled in a manner that makes the others ashamed to look at him. Jones tries to fathom this onyx face. Tries to understand how the colors of his skin mix and fade and define his features. Why the tears from his eyes only seem to run like dark veins through marble.

The cart carrying the Queen has now passed. It is moving off into the distance.

In its wake, the procession has left a trail through the room that runs right over the three men. The look in Lého's eyes is one of devastation. From the foot of the staircase that leads to the upper rooms, the Marquise d'Anderçon is watching him.

*　*　*

Marie-Antoinette glimpses a black spot moving at the very edge of her field of vision. She thinks that she knows what it is. To make certain, she could simply turn her head and pretend to ask the abbot a question. He is still huddled over his crucifix. The poor man! He must be thinking about how he will respond when he is asked, *Well, what did the Queen ask you?* Never mind. The black spot has stopped moving.

The Commander!

His eyes meet those of the Queen. He is in position in front of this tavern, convinced that he will find Lého there. *Meet up at Sweet Victory!* That was the cry that had gone up as the four of them had fought with Delorme and his uhlans on the observation deck. Strange how it had brought together on the same side two black police detectives, a mixed-race leopard boy, and himself, a Creole from Saint Domingue. He had enjoyed it. But that had not been enough to make him change his mind. *Every man for himself. May the best man win.* He will destroy the leopard boy at the moment when they show him to Marie-Antoinette. This is how he will respect the Queen's wish to see the boy, without also breaking his personal promise to kill him. But Lého had not appeared when the Queen passed by Sweet Victory. The Commander stares at Marie-Antoinette. He removes his hat. For the last time, he uses their secret code to ask whether her decision is final.

* * *

Marie-Antoinette is on fire. The Commander was there. Praise be to God! This means that he must have decided not to follow through with the unspeakable act that he had announced to her at the Tribunal. He would kill a child! When their eyes meet, he removes his hat and places it over his heart. How careless! Nobody salutes the Queen any longer. To do so is to put one's life in danger.

What happened to his silky black hair? He looks like a penitent. His fingers play along the brim of his felt hat. But Marie-Antoinette is too far way to be able to decode the message. And how to respond with her hands tied behind her back? The Commander must certainly be trying to tell her that her child is alive and that he will be placed so that she will be able to see him, as she had requested.

Marie-Antoinette has just caught sight of the little black boy carrying Coco in his arms. He sneaks behind the gendarmes and Commander. My, how agile, how dear he is! He is simply adorable!

* * *

"Watch it, you dirty peasant!"

The Commander has just been jabbed in the back by a tall

beanpole toting a pike. The clumsy oaf begs his pardon. The Commander recognizes his acolyte as he is sneaking away. It's Doctor Seiffert's little nigger boy! He's carrying the Queen's pug. The Red Porch! Now he remembers. That's where they'll all meet up. He must catch that boy. He'll lead him straight to the leopard boy.

* * *

The Marquise d'Andercon curtseys deeply before Lého, who returns the gesture with a surprisingly elegant bow. For a moment, grace reigns in the tavern's back room. Ed and Jones suddenly see a shimmering Bohemian crystal chandelier in place of the wagon wheel that hangs from the ceiling. The Marquise approaches Lého and takes his hands in hers.

"Sir! How I wish you were my son! Unfortunately, that is not the case. But thanks to you, I have been able to tell my husband a secret that had been stifling my heart and had taken away my reason."

Ed moves toward the Marquise. He does not wish to hear anything further. The expression on his face says it all.

"Madame, if you need an arm to escort you home, I am at your service."

"Thank you, Edmond. I value your attentiveness. But I already have an escort."

She nods. The Marquis appears. Ed and Jones salute him as regulations require, but do nothing more. He moves toward the Marquise and stands near enough to have slipped his arm around her waist. The skin on Ed's face throbs as his heart tries to find a place to hide somewhere down in his chest.

"Men, I understand your worries. I just want to add to the letters that you have read that I have not fallen short of honor or of friendship. You have my word as an officer and as a brother-in-arms!"

The Marquis might just as well have announced, *I'm buying the next round!* The tavern door swings wide open and a horde of thirsty drinkers pours in, pushing the Boss before them and shouting, *Did you see that conceited look on Crane Face! The Austrian will soon be looking straight through the neck hole!* Ed glimpses the devastation on Lého's face. He leaps into the middle of the room, draws his .38, and fires at the ceiling.

"Line up!"

"Count off!"

Jones joins him. Silence falls like a spent bullet. Ed issues a warning.

"From now on, whoever wants to drink in here will pipe down or scram!"

The Boss gazes at the noisemakers, who now sit as meekly as church mice. It looks like the place just got itself a Boss Man. Sweet Victory gives him a wink. Ed winks back. But first and foremost, the mission must be completed. The Boss decides to up the ante. She joins Ed, who is standing with the Marquis and the Marquise. That makes four even.

They would all like to revel in this moment and to make it last. But the cart is still moving toward its final destination, and they are painfully aware of that fact.

Ed takes the Boss aside and asks for a candle and a lantern. She gives him a coy look.

"Wanna come down to the cellar and take inventory with me, Edmond?"

"I can't. I already have a date with a tunnel."

The Marquis and Marquise d'Anderçon go back upstairs together. There is still so much they must tell each other! The Boss watches Edmond leave with Jones and Lého. She had never dreamed that one day she would be jealous of a tunnel.

The three of them run along the Seine, on the Quai du Louvre. Direction, Tuileries Palace. Seiffert had mentioned the existence of a tunnel running underneath its gardens. It must lead somewhere. Upon inspection of the second gate blocking their way, they discover a chain that has been cut and clumsily camouflaged. Ed rubs his face. It has suddenly started to itch.

* * *

The cart comes to an abrupt halt at the entrance to Rue Saint-Honoré. The Queen feels a moment of panic. What new torment will they inflict upon her now? A child held aloft in a woman's arms blows her a big kiss. Marie-Antoinette feels faint. Her entire body begins to tremble. No! That cannot be him. Today he would be fifteen years old. She almost breaks down. When will she cease to allow even the tiniest of hopes tear at her heart? The cart suddenly jerks forward again. The Queen's body starts to pitch forward. Sanson snaps her back with a sharp tug on the rope.

"Ha! No more Trianon Palace seat cushions for you!"

There is a collective snicker at the agitator's jibe. The whole crowd begins to shout as if on cue.

"Death to the Austrian! Death to the Austrian!"

Marie-Antoinette is not afraid of these sudden slings and arrows. They scarcely surprise her. The silence that had reigned until now had been much more bewildering. For a moment she thinks that the crowd will storm the cart, pull her down, and tear her limb from limb. The beat of the horses' hooves and the jostling of the cart reassure her. And yet, as she proceeds up Rue Saint-Honoré, this very same street that used to take her to the Opera in her royal coach, she can see nothing but hostile eyes and insulting signs hovering below tricolor banners that fill the sky.

Marie-Antoinette feels as though she has never seen this street before. A carriage can be such a hindrance! For their royal upbringing, princes should be made to ride on the roof rather than inside.

* * *

Dame Catherine and Pobéré cross the Red Porch and step onto Rue Saint-Honoré. Dame Catherine is wearing her princess shoes. Pobéré is relieved. He's just caught sight of Merlin, who is standing on the other side of the street behind a row of gendarmes. He is carrying his lamb across his shoulders, as though he were planning on showing it the Queen. Pobéré counts fewer than one hundred partisans at the meeting point. But the cart is still at the opposite end of Rue Saint-Honoré, almost a league away. The others will come. Dame Catherine squeezes her son's arm.

"There's no point in saying anything, Pobéré. I can tell. But there will still be enough of us to save her. You we're right. I'm going back to the boat. I'll be more useful back there. It'll be ready when you get there with the Queen. You'll see. I'm sure she'll be jealous of my shoes."

* * *

Marie-Antoinette allows her gaze to fall on the abbot's shoes. Did he choose the ones he thought would go best with the execution of a queen?

* * *

Zamor leaps from his horse. He ties it to a hitch ring behind the Church of Saint-Germain-l'Auxerrois and begins to talk to him. Wait here. I'll be right back with my son. The horse lays his ears back. He doesn't want to hear any more secrets. Zamor unfolds La du Barry's letter. The one in which she informs him that he is the father of the leopard boy. He reads with difficulty. The ink has become even more faded. That lowdown Countess! She tricked him! As he rereads the last sentence, it all begins to make sense. *Be wary of daylight. It erases secrets.* The letter had been written in one of those magical inks that she once used in her secret correspondence. The ink fades by the light of day. The more it is exposed, the faster it vanishes. Zamor jumps up and down and stomps his feet. The sole proof of his paternity is disappearing before his very eyes! There go his fortune, his glory, his house overlooking the sea, all of it slipping through his fingers like so many grains of sand. You'll pay for this, Countess! You'll pay for this with your life! I swear it! She's probably sitting in her bathtub laughing about it right now. *Zamor. Father to the heir of the French throne. The Crane and the Ape got together and made a Dolphin!*

But, whore, you forgot that you used to send me to fetch your ink from that famous apothecary in Rue Saint-Honoré. He's a real magician! That's perfect. He'll just cast a spell and bring my son back.

* * *

They're shouting at her!

They're shouting at her as she passes! In spite of her attempts to shut them out, the cries explode inside her head with every lurch of the cart. Oh my God, it's Axel! He's standing by the front door of the apothecary shop. That's his back. *My sweet Fersen! I knew that you would dare! That you would not abandon me. Even though you swore that you would not put your own life in danger.* Her heart sinks. No, that man is not Axel. Her mind is playing tricks on her. It's because of that shop! That's the shop where Axel used to procure his violet-colored ink. The ink that had kept their secrets safe from prying eyes.

The man standing outside the apothecary's shop seems anxious. That cannot be Axel. He is pounding on the locked door in an apparent frenzy. What terrible illness would make him need to seek help with such urgency? A gendarme orders him to stop. He gives up and turns around. How could she have taken this mulatto, albeit a good-looking one, for Fersen? Marie-Antoinette is suddenly, overpoweringly, inebriated. Her head begins to spin. A wild carnival whirls vividly through her brain. A masked ballet dances through a party of dominoes. There are crystal goblets filled with powerful wine. My God, what is happening to her?

* * *

Zamor feels panic course through him and settle into the area between his thighs. He'll shatter the window of this shop if someone doesn't open this door immediately! He must have that antidote! The ink has probably turned invisible by now. But how will he tell? On the wall there is a sign, mocking him. It reads, *Manufacturer of essential essences designed to evaporate when exposed to steam or to vanish into thin air.* Vanish into thin air! That's all that will remain of his son. They have just got to open up!

Zamor looks up to find that the Queen is looking straight at him. He could swear that the sight of him has troubled Marie-Antoinette. Does she recall that Italian soirée at the Princesse de Lamballe's, as La du Barry described it in her letter? Zamor can recall nothing but the Amarone. He watches as the rough cart carries the Queen away. Zamor sniffs his hand. He is trying to recover the scent of the woman who reminds him of the anthurium lily. Is it the Queen's scent? A firm hand grips his shoulder.

"Citizen, you're coming with us!"

* * *

Marie-Antoinette slowly sobers up, thanks to the acrid odor rising from the Seine. Her mind is unable to untangle the images that dance before her eyes. Fersen's face, and the face of her daughter. What could they possibly have in common with that seemingly desperate mulatto who had been outside the apothecary shop? Memory is a deceitful matchmaker. Her belly is in full rebellion. She is trying to make sense of it all. But the cart keeps moving forward.

Coco! There he is again! Now he is right below a boot maker's sign. The little dear is putting on an outrageous act in order to erase some of the wrinkles from his mistress's worried face. He has extended his horribly long tongue on purpose, although she had always forbidden him to do so. How droll! The little black boy who is carrying him in his arms has such a loving face. How soft to the touch his hair must be! Suddenly, his big eyes make her want to cry. My God, what is happening to her heart! Where is the flood of emotions coming from? She hopes to find out before she dies.

* * *

Groundhog threads his way among the crowd. He is carrying Coco so that she can keep a constant eye on him. But he is small. Spike had suggested hooking him to his pike. And why not put a candle in his mouth too? That would make a fine Chinese lantern of him! Spike had sulked for a couple of houses or so. Groundhog had had to reassure him after that. Yes, he knew where they were going. *The Red Porch? Where's the Red Porch?* "It's just past the Feuillants Monastery." *I want you to write "feuillant" for me!*

* * *

In the darkness of the sewer pipe that runs beneath the Tuileries Palace, Jones carries the lantern, followed by Lého and Ed. The light of the candle is too feeble to illuminate the colonies of rats that they are now disturbing. But there is enough light to make out the crosses that have been traced in chalk on the walls. Ed had been right to trust his itch. It's this way!

* * *

Spike's forged iron rosette hovers above the bellowing mob as it berates the passing cart. Then the rosette moves on, bobbing above the heads in the crowd. The Commander follows it from a distance. He would never have expected that one day he would find himself following the banner of a *sans-culotte*.

* * *

This section of Rue Saint-Honoré suddenly seems very familiar to Marie-Antoinette. That gable. This window. She has the pleasant sensation that someone is expecting her. She straightens her back. Grand Mogol. Mademoiselle Rose Bertin's clothing and hat boutique. She hears herself asking the dressmaker about her latest creations.

"Madame, what have you invented to tempt me now?"

Twice a week, the ritual was the same. The stylist would ask everyone present to bear witness to her innocence. This would be followed by the Queen's next question.

"And what is La du Barry's latest order?"

But under no circumstances would she ever give her the time to respond.

"They say, Madame Bertin, that with the Countess, you must have two different tastes in style. In fact, it is said that if she leaves your boutique with a white riding habit sewn from raw silk, she will immediately run over to the Trait Galant, Mademoiselle Pagelle's boutique, and have bouquets, garlands, fur collars, tassels, and who knows what else added to it. How patient you are! However, it is also said that La du Barry's account with you shows a balance of nearly one hundred thousand pounds! The price of a regiment!"

That is exactly what it cost to purchase the command of the Royal-Suédois Regiment, Madame. The command that you yourself offered to Count Axel von Fersen!

Those are the kinds of snide remarks that the pretentious little dressmaker probably made as soon as she left the boutique. And she had been right! Look at yourself! Here you are riding in a cart on your way to the guillotine, and all you can think about is your dressmaker! It is time to come to terms with reality. The people are insulting you. They want you dead. Take a good look at these women. Do you think that they have come here to see you go by? Of course not! They have been standing in line outside that bakery since five o'clock this morning, just so that they can buy a bit of bread! Even the smallest amount on one of your payment slips would have been enough to feed all of the people lining this street!

But Mother, I was the Queen!

A loose paving stone makes Marie-Antoinette bounce up off her wooden plank, joggling her breasts.

She leans over to speak to the abbot.

"Tell me, Sir. Under the new system of measurement, how much are three feet six inches?"

The question surprises Father Girard, but he is happy to do

something more than stare down at his shoes. He calculates the conversion, tapping it out on his crucifix.

"Six hundred centimeters, Madame. Or, one meter, six centimeters."

Marie-Antoinette pulls her shoulders back slightly. Madame Bertin had been correct about the size of her chest. It was truly of royal proportions.

* * *

In front of the Red Porch, Pobéré searches the crowd for his partisans. The gathering on the corner of Rue Florentin has not grown any larger. Luckily, his mother is safe. Pobéré is nervous. The cart is only half a league away.

* * *

"Citizen Commissioner, I can assure you that I was not blowing a kiss to the Queen!"

"Well, what were you doing, then?"

Zamor tries to think of something that would explain why he would be sniffing his hand. He'd better come up with a good answer or he'll soon be receiving the kiss of Sanson. The two tough guys who've brought him into the station don't seem to be in a joking mood.

"I, I uh, . . . was uh . . . casting a spell on that . . . demon-possessed bitch. That's how we take care of their kind back home in my native Martinique."

"Ah, so you're a sorcerer, are you?"

How stupid of him. Now he's jumped from the scaffold and into the fire.

"And what would this be, Citizen?"

One of the tough guys holds up the letter from La du Barry, fished out from between his Carte de Sûreté guaranteeing his allegiance to the Republic, his Civics ID Card, and other papers spread out on the table. He's in for it now. When they find out that the father of the Dauphin of France is an adulterer, a liar, a sorcerer, and black, they'll reinvent the rack just for him.

* * *

"Where do you think we are right now, Jones?"

"We're somewhere below the Tuileries Gardens. We're right below Rue Saint-Honoré."

"Can you believe that Marie-Antoinette's cart is probably right over our heads?"

Jones decides not to look up. That would be like looking up the Queen's skirts, right in front of Lého. All of a sudden, he stops and blows out the candle.

"What's going on, Jones?"

"Shh! Look straight ahead. There's a light coming toward us. Don't move! It's a lantern!"

* * *

Marie-Antoinette hears a roll of thunder pulse into her back. The cries are becoming more virulent. *Death to the Austrian!* Those are female voices. *Put the Crane to the blade!* Throughout her ordeal, these women have been the most ferocious. *Madame Arch-Tigress, you will kiss the basket when your head lands in it!* The cart continues to advance. Marie-Antoinette can see them now. Her skin begins to prickle. It's the terrible tricoteuses, those fierce market-women! When they are present, the end is near. The women have gathered on the steps of Saint-Roch, coiffed in red revolutionary bonnets and rosettes, and armed with spikes. They shake their fists at her and gesture obscenely. *You'll get cut too! Just like your dear Louis!* These are the same women who had squeezed together behind the courtroom balustrade at her trial.

"Tell me, Sir? Who was Saint-Roch?"

The abbot does not have time to respond. The liaison dressed in the uniform of the national guard who had been trotting his horse at the front of the procession falls back to the side of the cart.

"Here she is, the infamous Marie-Antoinette! She's done for, my friends!"

Standing in his stirrups, he points his sword at her and flails it for the benefit of the fishwives. Marie-Antoinette recognizes him. It's that common actor, Grammont! Lately named Chief of Staff. He denounced the Duc de Biron. Her heart aches. Dear Lauzun! He would have found something witty to say about this grotesque creature. What glory does he think he will gain from this masquerade? Marie-Antoinette casts her gaze elsewhere. *Workshop for the Manufacture of Republican Armaments Made for the Annihilation of Tyrants.*

Marie-Antoinette thinks of Robespierre. He must like the

message written on the sign. His house is quite nearby, as is the Red Porch, and her final deliverance. Exhaustion suddenly overtakes her. This street just won't stop bouncing her around. The cart creaks as though it were about to break in half and it addles her brain. She had imagined a different sort of trajectory. One that would have been more dignified, more majestic. Marie-Antoinette would rather have been assaulted by her own inner peace and elevated thoughts. Nothing more. But the pavement and the wheel have decided otherwise.

The crowd grows ever larger and its anger ever more intense. Let it be done. She is tired of this spectacle. She is ready to join her unfortunate children in limbo and her poor unfortunate Louis on his endless hunting expeditions. They lied to her. Nobody will intervene. Everyone has abandoned her. Up in the sky a scintillating white bird flies. He is like the bird of her personal motto: *Tutto a te mi guida*. Is this bird the Flaming Star that Madame de Lamballe had promised her?

* * *

"Groundhog, do you see that big white bird flying overhead?"

He has seen it. It's a parrot. It is flying just above their heads, as though he were showing them the way. Can he see the Red Porch from on high?

* * *

Jones is right. The glimmer of light from the darkness of the sewer pipe is coming from a lantern. They press hard against the sewer walls, gripping their .38s. Lého is quiet. The approaching footsteps are calm and sure. The person is familiar with the premises and seems to be completely alone. This is indeed the case. At a distance of three steps away, the lantern-bearing shadow becomes immobile. They've been discovered. The shadow holds the lantern up to their faces.

It's the blind woman!

She sniffs the air in their general direction. They stand stockstill, not breathing. Suddenly she laughs and, pfft! No more lantern. Only complete darkness and the noise of her footsteps running off in the opposite direction.

"Quick, Jones! After her!"

"I have to light the lantern first!"

MARIE-ANTOINETTE

"Don't bother! If she can run in the dark, so can we!"

Ed, Jones, and Lého break into a run, using their hearing to guide them. Ed's declaration is their only star. After an inaugural night flight complete with oaths and a jumbled landing, they decide to light the light. A big pool of viscous black liquid is stares back at them. It's not so easy being blind.

* * *

Riding backward, Marie-Antoinette senses Robespierre's house looming. Where could he be at this moment, he who had so desired her death? This porch, is it his already? Marie-Antoinette senses that he must be standing behind his door, listening as she passes by.

* * *

"Down, Brount, down!"

Maximilien Robespierre tugs on the leash attached to his Labrador retriever, but this has little or no effect. The animal is on its hind legs pawing at the door handle and whining.

"No, Brount! I told you! You'll go out once the Queen has passed by."

But the dog has no regard for propriety. He has to go, and he has to go now. His master refuses to let him out. Consequently, Brount raises his hind leg as high as it will go and vigorously inundates the door with a bright and abundant liquid.

"Brount, no! For the love of God, stop it!"

Robespierre pulls on the leash but the dog pulls back.

Maximilien gives up. Apparently distracted, he glances at the lamp. His wig is straight and his stockings are pulled up tight.

* * *

Dame Catherine cannot be sure that she has outrun the three men whose scent she had detected inside the conduit. They must be spies. Maybe they fell into the sinkhole. That hole doesn't forgive anyone. She must warn her son and the others that the route through the conduit has been cut off. The Queen's escape is now out of the question. Dame Catherine crosses over the Red Porch and steps onto Rue Saint-Honoré. Over the shouting in the street, she can hear the cart as it rolls nearer.

"Citizen! A poor, blind patriot needs assistance!"

A sergeant takes her by the arm.

* * *

Groundhog sees the blind woman being taken away. The plot to rescue the Queen at the Red Porch must have been uncovered. He'd better make himself scarce, or they'll think he did it. Spike does not agree.

"Just because nobody else is coming to save her don't mean we have to save ourselves."

He's right. They've come this far. There's no sense in turning back now. They'll stick with the plan. Groundhog and Spike go over it again, step by step. Step one. Make it look like Coco has run off when he jumps into the cart. Step two. He lands on the Queen's lap. Slurp! Slurp! He licks her neck and cheeks. Step three. The Queen is happy and starts to laugh. She gives them a queenly look with her queenly eyes. Coco jumps back into their arms. They take off and run all the way to their Book Mountain hideout so that they can read *The Journals of Captain Cook*.

Step One. Groundhog picks Coco up.

* * *

Down at the station, Zamor notices a sudden flurry of activity.

"Now listen up! I need all available men to follow me to the corner of Rue Florentin and Rue Saint-Honoré! Some birds who were plotting to save the Queen are gonna get a new nest. They're probably just a bunch of wigmakers!"

The men trade jokes as they suit up.

Zamor is now sitting alone behind the table strewn with his papers.

"What do I do with the warlock?"

One of the cops picks up La du Barry's letter and waves it in the air.

"Get him outta here! We're gonna need more room in here!"

Zamor is thrown into the street. He takes a deep breath. The Conspiracy of the Wigmakers has just saved his life. He'll think more about that when he takes his own wig in for powdering. As soon as he has put some distance between himself and the station, Zamor unfolds La du Barry's letter in a fever. It's blank! Completely blank! He flips it over. In vain. The ink is now completely invisible. Zamor looks around as though the boy were somewhere nearby. La du Barry got him this time, but that cutpurse will pay for this! Zamor returns to his horse and whispers in his ear.

"My jewels are gone forever and so is my son. But I can still save Olympe."

* * *

The Commander watches the little nigger boy and his friend with the pike. They've stopped near a door the color of dark red wine. So that's the Red Porch! The place where they're supposed to meet the blind woman. This is where it's supposed to go down. He positions himself so that he'll be directly across the street from the kid. From this distance, there's no escape. It'll be a clear shot.

* * *

The hole full of murky water in the underground tunnel kept Ed, Jones, and Lého from catching the blind woman. But they hadn't needed her after all. They immediately recognize the Red Porch that Doctor Seiffert had told them about. Ed, Jones, and Lého rush forward, their hearts pounding as if they were charging into battle. They stop to listen from behind a carriage gate. The insults being proffered in the street tell them that the crowd hasn't yet had its fill.

Suddenly they feel the ground vibrate below their feet.

The Queen has arrived.

* * *

The Red Porch!

Marie-Antoinette can feel it looming over her shoulders. Her heart begins to pound wildly. She prepares herself. She anchors herself more firmly on her plank, widens her gaze. Any moment now, a group of men will come running toward her. The cart rolls on at a snail's pace. This part of the route is particularly narrow. It must be here. She had been told not to put up a fight. Let them take her, grab her, carry her off! There's no need for modesty when it's a question of life or death for her and her loved ones. Oh, my dear children! Mon Chou d'Amour! Sweet Mousseline! I cannot wait to hold you close to my heart and ask forgiveness for the torments that I have caused you. There, there! It's all over now. We'll hug each other and cry together. We'll pray for your poor father, who is looking down on us from heaven and rejoicing. Come here and let me hold you tight. It was all a bad dream. I'm here. Soon, everything will be as it was before.

Marie-Antoinette readies herself. From which side will her savior appear? And the child, when will they show him to her? How silly of her! She will not be able to see him. Why would they place a child in harm's way? Soon she'll be safe and then she'll be able to meet him and dry his tears. She is angry at the impatience that devours her reason. Fortunately, those about to save her are more sensible. The honors that she shall bestow upon these brave men will never equal the nobility of their fearless acts. She vows that they shall be handsomely rewarded.

* * *

On a street corner, a man in black raises his hat high above his head. The partisans, some fifty strong, are immediately surrounded by a cordon of police dressed in civilian garb. They rush out from among the crowd. They work without raising a single alarm and without the slightest resistance. Pistols are aimed, wrists are bound, and the entire group is taken to a line of waiting police carriages. The crowd hasn't noticed a thing.

Near the Red Porch, two men slip behind Merlin and lock him in a chokehold. He lets out a roar, breaks free, puts his head down, and rushes them. In return, a short sword stabs him clean through the stomach. The men drag him into an entryway and leave him lying in a wine-colored pool. They reassure a worried citizen. It's no big deal. He drank to the health of the Austrian and now he's sleeping it off. The frightened lamb bleats forlornly next to the slumped body. Guillaume tries to retreat. He gets bashed in the head with a gun butt and his bloody body is taken away. Elisabeth is dragged by the hair like a common harlot. They struggle to wrest her knife from her grip. Jean-Baptiste looks around. He must get home and burn their papers.

Pobéré saw the snitch raise his hat. He saw him, but by then it was too late. The partisans are caught like sparrows in a trap. Pobéré moves back toward the Red Porch. Mother! What is she doing here? Why did she come back? A gendarme has her. Pobéré draws his knife. Too bad about the uniform. *Thank you for your kindness, Citizen Sergeant!* Pobéré leans over and whispers in the blind woman's ear.

"Why did you come back here, Mother?"

"I ran into a group of men in the underground tunnel and I wanted to warn you. What's going on here?"

"They've captured all of our partisans. All is lost."

"Calm down now, Son. Think of the Queen. All is lost for her. But we still have the boat."

"But the tunnel has been taken. How will we reach it?"

"You forget that your mother is blind. Watch!"

Dame Catherine takes Pobéré's arm. She pulls them both into the crowd.

"Make way! Make way for a poor blind patriot! Make way!"

* * *

Marie-Antoinette is distraught. The façades begin to crumble, the narrow sky collapses. What's happening? Men have been apprehended. A woman, too, and harshly. Where are the partisans who are supposed to save her? All around her Marie-Antoinette can see nothing but pandemonium, hear nothing but shouting and insults. There is only this little boy. He presents Coco to her. The poor animal is terrified. So these are the only efforts that will be made on behalf of the Queen! Her woman's belly gives way beneath her. And her child? And her son? Where is he? They must have been mocking her. How shamefully have they toyed with a mother's emotions! Have they only made her raise her hopes just so that they could better destroy her? They will not succeed.

* * *

Behind the entrance to the Red Porch, Ed stands with one ear pressed to the door. The street roars just on the other side. He turns to Lého.

"Are you ready? When I make the signal, step through the door."

Jones cracks the door. The cart is right there. It fills the space in front of the porch and seems to be floating above the crowd. Jones catches Marie-Antoinette's haggard look as she searches the crowd.

"Get ready, Lého. It'll be any minute now!"

The boy is crouched and ready to spring. Suddenly, Ed grabs Leho's arm and pulls him back. The Commander! He has just caught sight of his great height towering directly across from them on the other side of the street. At the very same moment in that very same instant, he spies Groundhog and Spike standing with their backs to him. They are waiting in front of the Red Porch. What are they doing here?

Ed and Jones have no time for speculation. They jump on them, snatch them, and pull them to safety under the porch, where they roll together in pairs. It's an odd reunion! With his Sunday-best tongue lolling, Coco gives each face an earnest lick. Lého goes to stand in the doorway. He dares to look at the Queen. His entire body recognizes her. May she turn her gaze toward him! It will only take a second. But the Queen passes by without seeing him.

As for the Commander, he has just caught sight of the leopard boy.

Lého wants to howl. He wants her to hear him roar. He knows that she would recognize him. Then she would know that he was right by her side. That he had not abandoned her. That he would never abandon her.

* * *

It's over. The moment has flown by. The luminous white bird rises high above her. Marie-Antoinette knows that from now on, she will be completely alone. She has barely left Rue Saint-Honoré behind her before the cart is inexorably drawn toward Rue Royale. Nothing will stop it now as it rolls on relentlessly toward the scaffold. Better to go quickly. She no longer has the heart to hope.

* * *

"Hurry!"

Ed spurs his small troop onward. It didn't take long for them to decide to catch up with the Queen's cart on Place de la Révolution. Nobody has dared to utter the word "guillotine." The underground tunnel is the only route possible. With Ed in the lead, the little troop is running beneath the light of a lantern hung from the end of Spike's pike.

"Watch out for the black hole!"

They carefully avoid it and start running again. There is no time to lose. They must cross the Tuileries Garden once again, travel up the quay to Place de la Révolution, cut through the crowd, and reach the scaffold before the blade comes down. They can hear its slick descent as it falls just above their heads.

* * *

Cloaked in darkness, machete in hand, the Commander follows the sound of pounding footsteps echoing through the obscurity before him. The Commander was able to cut through the jumbled crowd and slip through the door of the Red Porch once the cart had passed. He had gotten through just in time to see someone enter the garden shed covering the entrance to the underground tunnel. He'll never give up now. He knows that Lého is with them. The way he had looked at the Queen was unbearable. Look out! A light has just turned to the right. In the darkness, the Commander lengthens his stride. He tracks them, using his hunter's instinct. He can hear the song of the Caïman in his head. Its jaws are right here. *Huye que te coge ese animal. Y te puede devorar.* Arggh! The ground gives way beneath his feet. He is swallowed up. Water floods his mouth, his nose, his lungs. The water is acrid and thick. He has the presence of mind to plant his machete into the tunnel wall, pulling himself up just enough to be able to cry out. But the water puts a weight like lead in his boots. He cannot hold on.

The Commander's cries echo through the tunnel. Lého stops dead in his tracks. The others stand still. Ed reaches him and takes his arm.

"Come on! There's nothing we can do. We have to keep going, or we won't get to the Queen in time."

Lého breaks free. He runs back toward the sound. Spike follows him with the lantern. The hand of the Commander still gripping the machete handle is all that rises above the surface of the viscous water. Lého rushes forward, grabs the machete handle, and pulls the Commander up. His head emerges. He sputters and spits. His face is spattered with filth.

In the aura of the lamplight, the Commander has trouble distinguishing the face of the man who is pulling him up. The light moves. Half of the face is now illuminated. The leopard boy! It is his hand that is keeping him from falling back into the cesspool. How they must resemble each other at this moment! The Commander wants to scream. No sound comes out. Too bad. He'll grab the boy and pull him down with him. Then this show will finally be over. The Commander looks deep into the leopard boy's eyes as they seem to be saying, *Come with me, Sir, please!* The Commander smiles at him.

"No, thank you!"

With a flick of his fencer's wrist, he breaks free. His hand slips. The Commander allows himself to be swallowed up. There is nothing left of him now but the blade stuck into the lip of the black hole.

* * *

Marie-Antoinette thinks that she can hear bells ringing noontide from somewhere far away. The bells toll slowly.

At the first strike of the bells, the Countess du Barry opens the pinewood coffer that sits at the head of her straw mattress. She picks up a red bead but hesitates before inserting the needle and thread. Her hand is shaking. The Countess feels that her own days are also numbered.

* * *

"Citizen Biron, remove that white flag from your window!"

"That's no flag—it's a shirt that I've hung out to dry."

"Are you kidding? That shirt has neither sleeves, nor collar, nor buttons!"

"It's not my fault that the Republic took everything from me. Even my Queen."

Saint-Zita is humming. Moka leans over the billiard table. He places the figure of Marie-Antoinette on the mockup, at the center of Place de la Révolution. He waits, holding the leopard boy in his hand.

Through the barred gate of La Force Prison, the gatekeeper hands Zamor the sealed envelope containing the safe-conduct passes.

"Citizen Olympe de Gouges told me to tell you that she doesn't want anything from you. She would rather die. That's what she said. I held up my end of the bargain, Citizen. Now I'm keeping the money."

Thomas hands the mirror to the Doctor. Seiffert inspects his face. He is disappointed. He sought vengeance and lost. And all he got out of it was a close shave. Although the Princesse de Lamballe certainly had enjoyed stroking his cheeks.

"Voilà, Sir. You are now freshly disbearded."

"And most handsomely disbearded, even if I do say so myself."

Sadly, Thomas tells himself, if nobody else needs his services he'll just have to be put upon to learn to talk better.

With Delorme in the lead, the uhlans charge through Haarlem at a gallop. Just when they are about to cross through the stone gate, Delorme suddenly pulls his horse up. The horse rears. Why risk going in to get the leopard boy now? He'll be back. They won't want anything to do with him anyway.

* * *

Marie-Antoinette thinks that she has just heard noon strike somewhere off in the distance. She who had been ready to die just a second ago now suddenly feels a ferocious desire to cling to every single one of these twelve strokes. She wishes they were that many more hours to live.

Ding! It's midnight again. The debates surrounding her trial are just ending. *This hearing is adjourned!* Marie-Antoinette is sitting on a chair. Please let them forget that she's here. Reverse the hours, the days, the years. Let the hands on the clock wind back to that precise moment when everything changed. When had it happened? Was it at the storming of the Tuileries Palace? After the flight to Varennes? Was it because of Necker? Or because of the scandal surrounding that diamond necklace? Can someone tell her what she should have done so that today the crowd would be cheering for her instead of throwing their hats in the air for joy at her impending death? Can someone explain what should have been done so that instead of being forced to ride in this tumbrel, she and her children would instead be riding in a carriage upholstered in crushed velvet? So that Louis would be at the window, greeting his subjects? The cart rolls over a bump and shocks the Queen out of her daydream. The chief examiner's bell rings again.

Ding! The hearing is back in session. Her heart aches. The last twelve hours of her life have disappeared in the space of a single jolt. The crowd is shouting. Death! Death! Death!

* * *

Jones, Groundhog, Spike, Lého, and Ed come out on the Quai des Tuileries. The sight of the Commander deciding to say *Thanks, but no thanks* still lingers before their eyes. They run past stands vending sausages, oranges, and *oublies* waffles. *Bli, bli, bli! Come and get an oublie!* The vendors prepare for the crowd's return. It will soon be hungry. Jones points at a small boat descending the Seine with the wind in its sail.

Dame Catherine and Pobéré let themselves be carried away.

"Poor boy! Instead of the Queen, you've set sail with your old mother."

"Never mind, Mother. You're my queen."

"Bah! Instead of your sweet talk, why don't you just describe the river?"

"Maybe you should be doing the talking now, Mother."

"Doing the talking about what?"

"The Duc de Penthièvre. Why has he been so good to us? And don't forget to tell me in color."

* * *

Ed and his little troop run up against the crowd. It spills out from Place de la Révolution and flows down to the Quai des Tuileries. They'll never be able to part this mass. Ed and Jones each assume an authoritative air, pull out their .38s, and try to muscle their way through the crowd. But people only move grudgingly aside. A spot has to be won. Only the sight of Lého seems to have the power to move some people. The guillotine is still far away. Over there, on the other side of the Place, they can follow the cart as it moves up Rue Royale thanks to the hats that fly into the air like fireworks.

* * *

Marie-Antoinette turns her head toward the Tuileries Palace. The palace looks as though it is again under siege. People have even climbed up into the trees. My God, how small people look at this distance! So this is all that the people could see of her when she stood on the terrace and waved. They had been cheering for a dwarf!

How much suffering has been left behind here! But they don't give her the time for that. The crowd is devouring her! Oh God!

The cart pushes its way into the square. Her gaze can do nothing but ricochet off the sea of faces like a pebble tossed by a child. The sky is the only refuge for her eyes. The luminous white bird flies above her. The Flaming Star is there as promised. It will follow her.

The cart pulls up in front of the scaffold.

* * *

Lého pushes through the crowd without taking his eyes off the guillotine blade. Marie-Antoinette rises from her seat atop the cart. Let us perform our duties as Queen! She will not give her body the time to be afraid. It must obey her. It is her last subject. No! She does not want any help. Marie-Antoinette uses the short ladder to descend from the cart. Her legs are devoid of strength. The smell of horses reassures her. She turns to face the guillotine. There it is! A wave rolls through her belly.

Lého continues to advance. The crowd pushes him back. He is still some distance away. He is too far away for her to be able to see his face.

Groundhog calls out to Dame Guillotine, trying to catch her attention. *Madame! Madame! It's me! Remember? Remember the night when I asked you to be nice to someone? That's her. I wrote you that letter. Maybe you didn't have time to read it.* On the contrary, child! Don't worry. Trust me, I'll help her. *Thank you, Madame!* Take care of yourself, child. And cover up!

The white parrot has just landed on the wrought-iron scroll atop Spike's pike. He is holding the bejeweled tailcoat in his beak. It shimmers strangely.

Marie-Antoinette climbs the scaffold steps. Her back is straight. Her stride is firm. She uses her heels to make the wooden steps reverberate. *Bravery banished the big bad wolf.* When she was a little girl, this is what she used to tell herself to chase her fears away as she walked through the gardens at Schönbrunn Palace. As she stomps on the final big bad wolf, her foot slips and her shoe slides off. Now she has lost her shoe. She limps as though bedeviled. Fate is against her, even in her final moments. It likes to remind her that she is not worth more than the rotten tooth that was pulled from her mother's mouth on the day of her birth. Dear God, that was only . . . thirty-seven years ago.

Lého can see the Queen's silhouette as it climbs the steps. He is still too far way. He will never reach her.

Marie-Antoinette steps onto the platform. The crowd is limitless. It reaches beyond what her eyes can perceive. For her eyes are completely filled with a brilliant flash that has just appeared before them. Her Star!

"I beg your pardon, Sir. I did not mean to do it."

Blinded by the light, she has just tripped on Sanson's shoe. Perhaps this is all that anyone will remember of her. She will forever be known as the Queen Who Stepped on the Executioner's Foot. No matter. She offers up all of her glory in exchange for this brilliant light.

He is there. Facing her.

Lého can see the Queen. She is looking in his direction. He fervently wishes that he could raise his voice above the mob. But his body is paralyzed. Chills run across his skin in waves. Men approach, ready to seize her. He must save her. He must stab them and deliver her, even if he loses his own life. Lého rushes forward. Ed and Jones have read his mind. They hold him down. Paralyzed with impotent rage, Lého never takes his eyes off the queen.

Marie-Antoinette sees the executioner's assistants come at her. She knows what their next move will be. No! They will not remove the Queen's head covering. This fine linen bonnet is her final crown, and she will remove it herself. With a flick of her head, Marie-Antoinette tips it off. The crowd groans. That's one less miserable humiliation that it will get to witness. The assistants seize her and pull her to the body board, now set at the vertical. Where is her special star? They push her up against the bascule, face-first. Her pelvis scrapes against the rough wood. This cradle of unborn lives shall forevermore be sealed. Time speeds up. They begin to tighten the straps across her back. They raise her chin. Their movements are quick and brutal. She is no longer a being worth cherishing. She is undone.

Ed and Jones struggle to contain the fury that erupts from inside Lého's body. Meanwhile, Spike is tracing letters on a scrap of paper taken from his game bag. They are holding hands and are starting to look like words. Groundhog hides Coco's muzzle under the cape. He doesn't want the little dog to see that he is crying.

MARIE-ANTOINETTE

From her vertical position on the bascule, the Queen can see her special light shimmering beside a young man dressed in white. Brilliant rays hide his face. These executioners certainly are making sure that the straps are tight! As they bind her body, she has time to examine the young man. She notes his fine wrists, his svelte waist, the line of his shoulders. Could that be him?

The board swings her down and into the horizontal position. The movement wrenches her womb and injects her entrails with the heat of an overwhelming emotion as her throat presses down on the lower half of the wooden collar. It's him! Her entire body screams it as it tells her that it's so. They tighten the wooden collar around her neck. She senses the looming menace suspended above her head. If it's you, I beg you, tell me so in a way that only I would understand! Tell me now!

Lého presses his hand against his abdomen. He reaches deep down inside, tearing at his throat and chest. From deep within him a scream makes its way to the surface. He can feel it rising. But his mute body holds it back. Soon it will be too late.

There is a metallic snap. The blade has been released. Its sharp edge plummets downward. The luminous white bird has taken flight. *Tutto a te mi guida.* The Flaming Star flies high. Marie-Antoinette can see the young boy's face distort under the pressure of a terrible eye-penetrating pain. Suddenly, a long wail escapes him. It is at once infantile and animal-like, expressing the infinite pain of abandonment that she had once heard from the other side of the curtain. It is the sound of inconsolable grief. Of submerged tears. Marie-Antoinette runs her hand through Lého's hair. Wipes a tear from his cheek. The Queen's face wears the smile of a mother who has finally found her child.

AFTERWORD

I believe in the power of fiction.
—DANIEL PICOULY

Rocambolesque. In French, the adjective is used to describe a genre of popular fiction whose plot is woven around a series of fantastic and extraordinary adventures. *The Leopard Boy* is just such a book, and perhaps the only one like it to appear in the CARAF (Caribbean and African Books in French) series at the University of Virginia Press.[1] Set during the Reign of Terror (1793–94), that period during the French Revolution when more than forty thousand people were executed on the guillotine,[2] the plot of the novel is driven by the search for a mysterious mixed-race "leopard boy" whose mottled black-and-white skin gives him his nickname.[3] Rumored to be the son of Marie-Antoinette and a black man, the search for the boy over a twelve-hour time period is punctuated by Marie-Antoinette's brief trial on October 15, 1793, her swift condemnation to death, her humiliating trip to the guillotine, and her beheading on October 16, 1793.[4] Much of the action moves between two Parisian prisons, the Conciergerie and Sainte-Pélagie,[5] and a fictional Parisian Haarlem that pays homage to the African American detective novelist Chester Himes's idiosyncratic portrayal of Harlem, New York.

Given this context, *The Leopard Boy* may at first seem to have little to do with the Caribbean or Africa. However, by combining the genres of historical fiction and detective fiction, Daniel Picouly creates a popular adventure novel that uncovers the historical roots both of racism and multiculturalism in French society while reminding readers that France was also heavily involved in the slave trade until its abolition in 1848.[6]

Thus, when asked in a *Paris Match* interview whether *The Leopard Boy* "violates history" in this story where the French monarchy, the origins of the French Republic, and slavery intermingle, Picouly explains, "Genetics are on my side. In my family, I am the only one who is this dark; my twelve brothers and sisters have light hair and blue eyes. The fact that Marie-Thérèse [daughter of Marie-Antoinette and Louis XVII] is white and her brother born ten minutes later has mottled skin is the story of my life" (5).

As Daniel Picouly explains, he himself is of mixed descent. His father was Martinican, and his mother was a white home-maker and mother of thirteen children, of whom Picouly is the eleventh. However, because Daniel was the darkest-skinned of his siblings, he was often called upon to justify his "origins," while his siblings were not. As a result, much of Daniel Picouly's fiction interrogates in some way skin color, race, class, ethnicity, and their relationship to French history and society. This is how Daniel Picouly explains his interest in the figure of the leopard boy. As Picouly puts it:

> There are seventeenth-century paintings of children suffering from vitiligo, a skin disorder that makes one look like a leop-ard. This is a formula that I find metaphorical [because] the mixing is obvious. The person is not mixed in the sense that the two colors are not blended. The two origins are visible. You are black and white. When I was a child, I used to love black-and-white Paint Horses. This is what interests me in the figure of the leopard boy. He is a person of mixed descent whose two origins are visible.[7]

In 1995, Picouly's humorously entertaining autobiography, *Le Champ de personne,* won the highly regarded Prix des lectrices d'Elle, awarded by *Elle* magazine to the "best and most imagina-tive prose work of the year." While Picouly's love for his mother and siblings is evident in this book, the image of his father, who was employed by Air France as a boilermaker, is downright heroic. In reference to the comic-strip character Mandrake the Magician, Picouly nicknames his father "Chaudrake," evoking his father's profession as a *chaudronnier.* When he is called to help in the construction of the first nuclear-powered commercial airplane, the Caravelle, Picouly describes his father as a kind of black sorcerer in a manner that may remind some readers of the description of the supernatural powers of Camara Laye's father in *L'Enfant noir (The Dark Child).* In preparation for his mission on the construction site, his father "aligns the 'tools that obey only him.' A collection of steel sledgehammers made to fit his hand and of hammers with heads shaped like magical animals and sculpted handles. He performs his black sorcerer's magic over the bag" (61).

Picouly further develops the story of his mixed-race parents in *Paulette et Roger*, which won the Prix populiste in 2001. This prize recognizes a work of fiction that portrays working-class people in an engaging and humanistic light. In addition to these two prestigious prizes, Picouly also won the coveted Prix Renaudot in 1999 for *L'Enfant léopard*.[8]

When I asked Daniel Picouly in an interview whether he had a specific target audience in mind for the work that is translated here into English for the first time, he replied that he never intends for his work to be read by any one group in particular. However, he explained, "in my fiction, what I'm trying to do is to bring people who never existed to life . . . who stand in for those who did exist and who are never discussed . . . [A]t first people would say, 'you are inserting black characters into history [even though] there weren't any.' And I say, 'oh, yes, there were.'"[9]

In chapter 6, the author reminds us that René-Auguste de Chateaubriand (1718–1786), father of one of France's most illustrious nineteenth-century writers, François-René de Chateaubriand (1768–1848), was the commander of the slave ship *Apollo*, where the fictional Moka, a former slave turned black entrepreneur, had been taken captive. Having gained his freedom, Moka visits the Chateaubriand estate in Brittany, making the point that the city of Saint-Malo is "rich" and "clean" "a little because of us." In revolt against the slavery that had contributed to French wealth, Moka decides to begin making figurines of important blacks in French history so as not to forget the past. Moka's experience reminds readers that French prosperity was partially generated by slavery and the triangular trade, in full swing during the eighteenth century. It also demonstrates that slavery and interracial mixing, or *métissage*, were an integral part of mainstream "French" society rather than being confined to the colonial periphery alone.

Thus, through Moka's passion for making historical figurines, Picouly astutely (re)introduces the somewhat forgotten eighteenth-century mixed-race General Alexandre Dumas-Davy (father of the novelist Alexandre Dumas) and the Chevalier de Saint-George, alongside more iconic figures of eighteenth-century France such as Rousseau and Voltaire.[10]

AFTERWORD

In dedicating *The Leopard Boy* "to Christian Mounier who spoke with such elegance of Chester Himes's elegant style," Daniel Picouly alerts the reader to be on the lookout for references to Himes, whose intertextual presence in a novel about the Reign of Terror may at first seem completely incongruous.[11] Nevertheless, references to Himes permeate *The Leopard Boy,* and it is even possible to surmise that the man with "mottled brown skin" and "cold yellow eyes" (5) who appears on the first page of Himes's *For Love of Imabelle* may have something to do with the genesis of Picouly's leopard boy.[12]

Daniel Picouly discovered Himes's work through his father, and went on to publish his first detective novel, *Nec,* in Gallimard's Série noire crime series in 1993. According to the journalist Thierry Gandillot, Picouly's father would come home from work, open a Série noire detective novel, and devour it with his dinner. Unfortunately, writes Gandillot, "Papa Picouly never got the chance to read *Nec* . . . over his beef and carrots: on the day of its publication, he was dead. So Daniel placed one of the black and yellow covered copies on his grave."[13]

In *The Leopard Boy,* Himes's two black vigilante Harlem detectives "Coffin Ed" Johnson and "Grave Digger" Jones (known for ordering people to "straighten up" and "count off") become Edmond Cercueil (Edmond Coffin) and Jonathan Fossoyeur (Jonathan Gravedigger).[14] As their names imply, these two former soldiers are now employed disposing of the many dead executed under the Reign of Terror. As in a Himes detective novel, the two of them report to a white lieutenant. But in Picouly's version of events, Himes's Lieutenant Anderson becomes the "Marquis d'Andercon," leader of an unnamed expedition to Virginia (possibly the American War of Independence) in which Ed Coffin and Jonathan Gravedigger had served. They had also belonged to the "real-life" "légion Saint-George" a regiment under the command of the Chevalier de Saint-George. The regiment was formed in 1792 and was called the Légion nationale des Américains et du midi; it counted among its members Alexandre Davy de la Pailleterie, father of the novelist Alexandre Dumas.

In 1792 and indeed, in 1793, "Américains" referred to residents of the West Indies as well as to people from farther north. In *The Leopard Boy,* in addition to Ed and Jones, Zamor, the Commander, the voodoo-practicing Marquise d'Andercon, and

Black Delorme all have roots in the Americas. Zamor hails from L'Anse-à-l'âne in Martinique, while the Commander and Black Delorme are from the French colony of Saint-Domingue.[15]

Further allusions to Himes include the character La Marmotte (Groundhog), whose name recalls events in Himes's novel *All Shot Up,* translated into French by Jeanne Fillion as *Imbroglio negro* (1960). The action in *All Shot Up* begins at 11:30 p.m. on Groundhog Day, translated as "la nuit de la chandeleur" or "la Nuit des Marmottes" (7). The automobile tire that is stolen in *All Shot Up* and that rolls and bounces uncontrollably through several of its chapters on that night eventually shows up as a runaway cartwheel that lands in the Sweet Victory tavern in chapter 4 of *The Leopard Boy,* where the Boss turns it into a chandelier.[16] Excepting the scenes focusing on Marie-Antoinette, this kind of slapstick humor à la Himes informs *The Leopard Boy* and contributes to its "rocambolesque" character.

According to the critics Edward Margolies and Michel Fabre:

> Himes had an eye for the grotesque and slapstick . . . His thrillers feature runaway hearses, headless motorcyclists, exploding houses, brotherhood street fights, men walking the streets of Harlem with daggers through their foreheads, bodies tumbling from tenement windows, corpses in breadbaskets, and bodies soaring through the air after being hit from behind by trucks. His Haarlem demimonde consists of juvenile delinquents, pimps, pansies, political hacks, quacks, femmes fatales, addicts, pushers, numbers racketeers, black "nationalists," prostitutes, stool pigeons, and bizarrely costumed religious charlatans of every ilk. Some of his characters are throttled, mauled, sliced, stabbed, shot, or garroted, and they themselves commit similar kinds of violence against others. (100)

In *The Leopard Boy,* it is the violence of the Reign of Terror with its looming guillotine, its dank prisons, its hulking executioner Sanson, its pike-toting *sans-culottes,* and the cruelty of slavery that stand in for Himes's Harlem violence. The obligatory detective-novel femme fatale is incarnated by the Countess du Barry,[17] the runaway hearse turns up as Moka's coffee-delivery wagon, and the corpse in the breadbasket is mentioned in chapter 5 in the scene where Ed and Jones violently interrogate the clownish King Mac.

In order to differentiate between his fictional neighborhood and Harlem as it is portrayed in the fiction of Chester Himes, Picouly's Haarlem retains the double *a* of the Dutch spelling. As he explains in his interview with *Paris Match:* "While studying a map of the Paris of that time by Verniquet, I realized that behind the Luxembourg Gardens near rue Denfert, there existed a sort of no-man's-land where I located this quarter. This area was structured like Harlem, with thoroughfares laid out on a grid. This allowed me to number my streets and my avenues the way they are in New York" (4).

Picouly's fictional Haarlem thus constitutes a literary response to Himes's equally fictional Harlem. According to Margolies and Fabre: "Himes wrote with an awareness of a French readership for whom denizens of Harlem were exotic jazzy creatures who sometimes blustered in stereotypical dialect. Frequently, these characters first appear before the reader almost as cartoon figures" (100–101). This element was not lost on Picouly. In fact, the short story "prequel" to *The Leopard Boy,* "Tête de Nègre," was also published as a two-volume comic-book album.[18]

Indeed, Picouly's Haarlem is peopled by a number of Himes-like characters. These include the gold-toothed King Mac and his buxom wife, Félicité. King Mac is the creator of the *en-bourgeois* (hamburger) and includes figurines of eighteenth-century notables like Voltaire and Rousseau in his sandwich meals, while Félicité runs a scam operation using "animal magnetism."[19] Her previous scheme involving cooking *assignat*[20] notes in a wood stove and turning them into gold louis is a direct reference to a similar scheme in *For Love of Immabelle.*[21]

As is evident from these examples, Picouly's "rocambolesque" fictions are partially grounded in historical fact. For instance, while Marie-Antoinette never conceived a mixed-race child, she did snub the Countess du Barry at court.[22] In recalling the famous snub, Picouly also reminds us of the existence of Zamor (1762–1820). Known as "le nègre de La du Barry," Zamor was given to the Countess by Louis XV. Although portraitists painted him with African features, Zamor was apparently born in India, possibly in the French colony of Pondicherry. This is perhaps why Zamor dresses as a maharajah in *The Leopard Boy.* Picouly places Zamor's origins in Martinique, that other (West) "Indies" where people of European, African, Amerindian, and East Indian descent mixed to form a new creole culture. In a clever twist, Picouly's Zamor is in love with the feminist abolitionist playwright Olympe de Gouges (1748–1793), author of the abolitionist play inspired by Zamor entitled *Zamore et Mirza*. In *The Leopard Boy*, Olympe de Gouges playfully calls Zamor her "nègre à plume," literally, her black man with a pen. "Nègre" is the French term for ghostwriter and implies that Zamor actually helped her write her famous play.[23]

Picouly further tweaks history by sidelining Marie-Antoinette's historically documented Swedish lover, Count Axel von Fersen, and replacing him with the murderous Commander.[24] However, the encounter between the castrating Dr. Norcia da Lecce (based on a stock character from the Italian Commedia dell'Arte) and the machete-wielding, limb-chopping Commander foregrounds the dehumanizing practices of eighteenth-century European civilization. While Norcia da Lecce explains that he had castrated the leopard boy in order to retain his singing voice, the Commander feels justified in using corporal punishment on "his" slaves because the Code noir, that set of laws regulating slavery, officially allowed him to do so.[25]

As the evil counterpart of the Commander, Black Delorme re-enacts the dehumanization of blacks when he threatens to brand Zamor. Known in French as "Le Nègre Delorme," he was a cartwright by trade who was born in Port-au-Prince, Saint Domingue, in 1758. He became an entrepreneur who served in the French National Guard and furnished the French army with materiel. Like Alexandre Dumas, Delorme was the son of a soldier. But his father was a black uhlan in the service of the Maréchal de Saxe.[26] Because he reputedly participated in the killing and mutilation of the Princesse de Lamballe,[27] Picouly has chosen to cast him as a megalomaniac ("The Master of Us All") who is building a theme park dedicated to "the first site of memory [lieu de mémoire] and understanding dedicated to the slave trade" (235). In using the term "site of memory," Picouly reminds readers that, at the date of publication of the novel in 1999, the memory of French involvement in the slave trade had only just begun to emerge from a collective amnesia. As Christopher Miller points out in *The French Atlantic Triangle*, the monumental seven-volume *Lieux de mémoire* (translated into English under the title *Realms of Memory*), edited by Pierre Nora and containing essays by prominent scholars on places (sites) important to the French national consciousness, "contains not one essay about the slave trade or slavery—both being, in effect, *lieux d'oubli* [places of forgetting]" (xi). Indeed, it was not until the 1990s that a monument commemorating slavery in France was erected in Nantes.[28]

In fact, Picouly declared to Jérôme Béglé of *Paris Match* that, in addition to being highly entertaining, *The Leopard Boy* constitutes "an inquiry into the role of skin color in the history of France. History textbooks only mention white people. Blacks do not exist. Strange. Hence an extremely important figure during the eighteenth century, the Chevalier de Saint-George, has vanished from memory. Who is aware that Dumas is of mixed descent? . . . It is often said that the archives are in black and white. I personally find them to be rather monochromatic" (4). In the same interview, Picouly further declares that he would tell Alexandre Dumas not to forget that "you are a mulatto. There isn't much color in your stories" (4).[29]

Given this context, it could be said that alongside explicit references to the writings of Chester Himes, *The Leopard Boy* is also in part a rewriting of Alexandre Dumas's historical novel *Le Chevalier de Maison-Rouge*. First published in 1845 and set in 1793 during the Reign of Terror, the *Chevalier de Maison-Rouge* is based on the historically documented attempt by the Marquis Alexandre Gnosse de Rougeville to save Marie-Antoinette and to warn her of the impending (but failed) rescue attempt by way of secret messages sent to her rolled into the petals of a carnation. The plot is known as the "Affair of the Carnation," or the *complot de l'oeillet*. After receiving the messages, Marie-Antoinette returned a response by using a pin to prick her words into a piece of paper.[30]

As the literary scholar Sylvie Thorel-Cailleteau explains in her preface to Dumas's work, *Le Chevalier de Maison-Rouge* grew out of an earlier short story entitled "Blanche de Beaulieu ou la Vendéenne," and involved the following constellation: "the color red, a flower, the guillotine, a doomed love affair between an aristocrat and a republican—all of which are associated with the evocation of that Herculean mulatto . . . who is none other than General Dumas, father of the novelist" (14).

AFTERWORD

Le Chevalier de Maison-Rouge retains most of that constellation, with the exception of Dumas's "herculean mulatto" father, who makes no appearance in the novel. The only "black" remaining in *Le Chevalier de Maison-Rouge* is Marie-Antoinette's pug, whose real name was "Black." In Dumas's tale, the chevalier, or knight, of Maison-Rouge takes the dog in his arms in chapter 48 and exhibits him to Marie-Antoinette as she is driven to the guillotine in a cart. In *The Leopard Boy*, the little black boy known as Groundhog carries the pug, here named "Coco," and holds him up so that Marie-Antoinette can see him. Rather than the carnation flower, the pug becomes the vessel for secret messages, and it is the charming and comical combination of a little black boy and his exuberant dog that drives some of the action and suspense in Picouly's novel.

In another transformation, the *maison rouge,* or "red house" that constitutes the name of Dumas's title character becomes the "Red Porch" in *The Leopard Boy*. In Picouly's novel, the Red Porch is located across from number 400, Rue Saint-Honoré. Maximilien Robespierre resided at number 398, Rue Saint-Honoré, from 1791 to 1794, in a house belonging to the woodworker Simon Duplay, said to be Robespierre's personal secretary.[31] In 1794, Robespierre was the victim of a bloody assassination attempt at the location of the so-called Red Porch. Like Marie-Antoinette a year earlier, Robespierre was taken to the guillotine in a cart on July 28, 1794. The cart stopped in front of the house where the fictional Red Porch is located. This event is briefly foreshadowed in chapter 12 of *The Leopard Boy* when the Red Porch becomes the place where the final action of the novel unfolds before Marie-Antoinette recognizes her son just prior to being beheaded.

In the final scene of the novel, Picouly once again reminds readers that ethnic mixing as well as the refusal to acknowledge it, or the desire to forget about it, is an old story. As the Boss reminds us in chapter 4 of *The Leopard Boy*: "Tales of hidden black children are a dime a dozen. If you ever took the time to read the newspapers, you would know that the tales start with Anne d'Autriche, and continue with Restif de la Bretonne, not to mention the American ambassador to Paris, one Thomas Jefferson . . . [I]n Paris, he went everywhere with his slave Sally . . . They had a bunch of babies together, but she wasn't the only one he . . ." (63).[32] By recognizing her mixed-race son, Marie-Antoinette, the foreign-born "scapegoat queen" who was blamed for France's political and economic difficulties, reminds contemporary readers that a French "multiculturalism" with roots in the eighteenth century isn't as "rocambolesque" as it may at first have seemed. In exclaiming, "If my son is the Dauphin, then . . . that makes me the King!" Zamor comically underscores that fact.[33]

Notes

The epigraph comes from a personal interview with Daniel Picouly. All translations of this interview, of Daniel Picouly's interview with *Paris Match,* and of other passages from the French texts cited here are mine.

1. I first learned of Daniel Picouly's work when he was the special guest of the twenty-fifth annual Conseil International d'Etudes Francophones conference, held in May-June 2011 in Aix-en-Provence. When I arrived at the lecture venue, the room was already packed, and Mr. Picouly was in the middle of a humorous explanation about how his personal experience as the darkest-skinned child of a mixed-race couple had influenced his prolific writing career. His story inspired me to inquire whether he had yet been translated into English. Astonishingly, he had not. In this translation, I have endeavored to re-create Daniel Picouly's quick popular style (except for the passages where Marie-Antoinette speaks in a formal and queenly internal monologue) and flavor it with a Himes-like hardboiled detective pugnacity.

2. Once the National Convention (Convention nationale), the first French assembly to be elected by universal male suffrage, had enacted the Law of Suspects, anyone thought to be a counterrevolutionary was considered guilty of treason and sentenced to death. The parliamentary Committee of Public Safety (Comité de salut public) and Committee of General Security (Comité de sûreté général) oversaw the Reign of Terror (1793–94). The Committee of Public Safety constituted the executive branch of the revolutionary government, while the Committee of General Security had the authority to refer suspects to the Revolutionary Tribunal. Many suspects were tried and then executed on the guillotine. King Louis XVI de Bourbon was guillotined on January 21, 1793. The descendent of Hughes Capet was given the nickname "Capet" by the revolutionaries to emphasize the abolition of the royal title and the monarchy along with it. Similarly, Marie-Antoinette was nicknamed the "Widow Capet" following her husband's execution.

3. Mottled skin is a symptom of vitiligo, a condition that causes uneven variations in skin pigmentation.

4. Archduchess of Austria Marie-Antoinette (baptized Maria Antonia Josepha Johanna) was born in Vienna on November 2, 1755. She was the fifteenth child of Holy Roman Emperor Francis I and Empress Maria The-

resa. She married the future Louis XVI in 1770, became Queen of France and Navarre in 1774, and was deposed in 1792. She is thought to have been suffering from uterine cancer at the time of her imprisonment. In addition to being called the "Widow Capet," she was nicknamed "the Crane" (la grue) because of her long neck. These were just two of many derogatory nicknames given to her by the French people after her fall from popularity. Her last words before being guillotined on October 16, 1793, were, "Pardon me, Sir, I did not do it on purpose," when she accidentally tread on the executioner's toes. Recent portrayals of Marie-Antoinette include the films *Marie Antoinette* (directed by Sophia Coppola) and *Farewell, My Queen* (*Les adieux à la reine*) directed by Benoît Jacquot, which was adapted from the novel of the same name by Chantal Thomas.

5. The Conciergerie Prison was known as the antechamber to the guillotine because it was the final stop for more than two thousand prisoners before they were executed. Wealthy prisoners could purchase improved "accommodations." In *The Leopard Boy*, this system is at work in the Sainte-Pélagie Prison (whose first female prisoner was Madame Roland) and in the Belhomme Clinic (Pension Belhomme), which eventually became a haven for rich prisoners who cohabited with the clinic's mentally ill patients.

6. The slave trade is also known as the triangular trade because slave ships would travel from France, to Africa, to the West Indies and back to France again. The trade began in the 1600s and reached its heyday during the eighteenth century. Although it was officially abolished in 1848, slavery continued until well after that date.

7. Personal interview.

8. The bibliography here lists nineteen of Daniel Picouly's books, and this does not include all of his works. Indeed, Daniel Picouly, who always seems to be at work on his next book, also writes for children and young adults. He also has his own television show, *Le Monde vu par . . .* (The world as seen through the eyes of . . .); see www.franceo.fr/emissions/le-monde-vu-par. For Picouly's complete bibliographical and biographical information, see www.picouly.com.

9. Personal interview.

10. In fact, in the late 1950s, the Mokarex coffee company began placing toy figurines in its packages of coffee. As Picouly explains, among them were the models for some of the main characters of *The Leopard Boy*. As a boy, Picouly played with toy models of Marie-Antoinette, Robespierre, Danton, Marat, Louis XVI, Madame du Barry, the Princesse de Lamballe, and Count Axel von Fersen, but not of Dumas-Davy or Saint-George. The Chevalier de Saint-George was a knight and musician highly favored at the court of Louis XVI. Born on a plantation in Guadeloupe, his mother was slave from Senegal, and his father was a white planter. Picouly further develops Saint-George's story in *La Treizième mort du chevalier* (2003) volume 2 of the trilogy formed by *L'Enfant léopard*, *La Treizième mort du chevalier,* and *La Nuit de Lampedusa* (2011).

AFTERWORD

11. Chester Himes (1909–1984) began writing while doing time in the Ohio Penitentiary for armed robbery. Once released, he made his way to France; he was the contemporary of James Baldwin and Richard Wright, who were also living and writing in Paris at the time. It was Marcel Duhamel, the founder of Gallimard's detective Série noire, who encouraged Himes to begin writing hard-boiled detective novels. The books were immediately translated into French. Himes eventually won France's Grand Prix de Littérature Policière in 1958. For a fascinating study of the ways in which Chester Himes influenced Francophone African detective novelists, see Pim Higginson, *The Noir Atlantic: Chester Himes and the Birth of the Francophone African Crime Novel*.

12. In *La Reine des pommes*, Minnie Danzas's French-language translation of *For Love of Imabelle*, the man in question has "un oeil jaune et froid" (cold, yellow eyes) and is "brune de peau, le teint brouillé" (brown-skinned, with mottled tones) (9).

13. In my interview with him, Daniel Picouly compared his father's elegant appearance to that of Chester Himes, thereby reaffirming the connection between Picouly's literary practices and genetics.

14. In *For Love of Imabelle*, Himes writes: "Grave Digger and Coffin Ed weren't crooked detectives, but they were tough. They had to be tough to work in Harlem. Colored folks didn't respect colored cops. But they respected big shiny pistols and sudden death. It was said in Harlem that Coffin Ed's pistol would kill a rock and that Grave Digger's would bury it" (59). Their "specially made long-barreled nickel-plated .38-calibre revolvers" (*Imabelle*, 52) appear in chapter 2 of *The Leopard Boy*.

15. Saint-Domingue, located on the Caribbean island of Hispaniola, was under French control from 1659 to 1804, the year of the founding of the Haitian Republic. Inspired by the events of French Revolution, the Haitian Revolution began in 1791. The formerly enslaved rose up, defeated the French army, and declared independence.

16. In chapter 10, the Boss refers to herself as the "Queen of Hearts," which translates as "La Reine des Pommes." This is a reference to the French title of Himes's *For Love of Imabelle*, also published under the titles *The Five-Cornered Square* and *A Rage in Harlem*.

17. Madame du Barry (1743–1793) was born Jeanne Bécu. She acquired the title of countess as the last official mistress of Louis XV, grandfather of Marie-Antoinette's husband, the future Louis XVI. The Countess was famous for having attempted to buy her way out of her death sentence by revealing the hiding places of the jewelry that she had received from the King. In *The Leopard Boy*, she is variously known as Citizen, the title that the revolutionaries used to replace (and efface) more traditional forms of address, or "La du Barry" (literally, "the" du Barry), and more rarely as "Countess," because, like all members of the nobility, she has been stripped of her title. In chapter 11 of *The Leopard Boy*, in the scene where Madame du Barry and Madame Roland get into an argument, Picouly has the two

women switch famous last words. Madame Roland (imprisoned because as a "girondist" she was not against the monarchy) pronounces the Countess's famous last words to the executioner, "One more minute!," while Madame du Barry pronounces Madame Roland's, "Oh Liberty, what crimes are committed in thy name!"

18. In *Tête de Nègre*, Ed and Jones recover the severed head of the Marquis and Marquise d'Andreçon's blue-eyed son.

19. The theory of animal magnetism was first developed by Dr. Franz Mesmer in his 1766 doctoral dissertation, "De planetarium influxu in corpus humanum" (On the influence of the planets on the human body) and was later elaborated in his *Mémoire sur la découverte du magnétisme animal*. Animal magnetism was later referred to as "mesmerism" and eventually became linked to the practice of hypnosis. As in chapter 6 of *The Leopard Boy,* patients were seated in a wooden tub called a *baquet* which was filled with water, glass, and magnetized iron filings with protruding iron rods. Patients were treated in groups and were instructed to touch the rods simultaneously to facilitate the flow of a healing magnetic energy among them.

20. *Assignats* were paper currency issued by the French National Assembly between 1789 and 1796, and were based on the value of confiscated church properties. The currency became overinflated because the amount printed exceeded the value of the confiscated properties. It was not until 1803 that Napoleon introduced the franc as a replacement for the then worthless notes.

21. In the Himes novel, a con man named Hank convinces a sucker named Jackson that he can turn "fifteen C's" (6) into fifteen thousand dollars by rolling one-hundred-dollar bills in sheets of chemical paper and placing them inside a gas oven.

22. Because she was from the common people and had gained notoriety as a courtesan, Marie-Antoinette famously refused to speak to her. One day, the future Queen finally uttered the famous phrase, "There are many people at Versailles today."

23. According to the literary and cultural critic Dominic Thomas, "the term or label *nègre* was interchangeable with the word 'slave.' *Noir* became common as early as the eighteenth century, when it was adopted in 1788 by the abolitionist *Société des amis des noirs*, and 'black' has been in usage in France since the 1980s" (12). The derogatory term *nègre* has been translated here as "nigger," "black," or "slave" according to the context in which it is used. For instance, the Commander, as well as the sailor who attempts to castrate Groundhog in chapter 1, are virulent racists in whose mouths the derogatory word acquires its full racist force. Olympe de Gouges's joke is significant because, as Dorish Kadish writes, Olympe de Gouges herself "constantly had to mediate between the official use of the French language and her own regional use of Occitan . . . [H]er works were typically dictated rather than written" (32). In this connection, Alexandre Dumas, whose work constitutes an intertextual reference in *The Leopard Boy,* was also

famous for using a "nègre" named Auguste Maquet. Maquet would carry out Dumas's research and wrote certain passages of Dumas's novels.

24. The Commander is a character whose name is also a title. As such, it resonates differently according to context. First, the name refers to the well-known character in Molière's play and Mozart's opera *Don Juan*. In these works, the Commander, a member of the Spanish nobility, is killed by Don Juan as he tries to avenge his daughter's honor. He returns as a statue and pulls Don Juan into hell. Given that in *The Leopard Boy,* he is a virulent racist from Saint Domingue who lives in denial of his own possible mixed-blood heritage, his name also refers to the West Indian use of the term to designate a plantation overseer. The Commander's mission to undermine and exterminate the mixed-race leopard boy can also be understood as an effect of the Haitian Revolution.

25. The Code noir was drawn up by Jean-Baptiste Colbert and ratified by Louis XIV in 1685. Indeed, Article XXXVIII of the code stipulates that "the fugitive slave who has been on the run for one month from the day his master reported him to the police, shall have his ears cut off and shall be branded with a fleur de lys on one shoulder. If he commits the same infraction for another month, again counting from the day he is reported, he shall have his hamstring cut and be branded with a fleur de lys on the other shoulder. The third time, he shall be put to death."

26. The Maréchal de Saxe (1696–1750) was Count of Saxony. As a French marshal, he commanded an army which defeated the Duke of Cumberland at the Battle of Fontenoy in May 1745. He was naturalized as French in 1746. As a reward for his military exploits, Louis XV gave him the Château de Chambord. According to Louis Susane, "Le Maréchal de Saxe. . . wanted to have, for his personal guard, a company composed entirely of blacks mounted on white horses" (32). In the novel, this company of hulans, or uhlans, appears in a painting in Delorme's possession that formerly hung in the Château de Chambord. The uhlans were light cavalry in the Austrian, Prussian, and Russian armies.

27. The Princesse de Lamballe (Maria Teresa of Savoy-Carignan, 1749–1792), confidante of Marie-Antoinette, was married to the Duc de Penthièvre (1725–1793) at age seventeen. The Duc de Penthièvre was the grandson of King Louis XIV. His father was Alexandre de Bourbon, an illegitimate son of the King who had been recognized by the King and named Count of Toulouse. Following her arrest during the Reign of Terror, the Princesse de Lamballe refused to swear an oath against the King and Queen. She was thrown into the street, where she was mutilated by a mob. Her head was exhibited on a pike below Marie-Antoinette's window. See www.lepoint.fr/c-est-ar rive-aujourd-hui/3-septembre-1792-l-effroyable-depecage-de-la-princesse-de-lamballe-par-les-egorgeurs-sans-culottes-03-09-2013-1720457_494 .php. See also Raymonde Monnier, *Le Faubourg Saint-Antoine 1789–1815,* where Delorme is mentioned on pages 143–44.

Delorme also appears in Alphonse de Lamartine's *Histoire de girondins.* In that work, Delorme is described as "infatigable au meurtre" (a tireless murderer) who massacred more than two hundred people. Lamartine sees him as a "symbole du meurtre et vengeur de sa race . . . le crime extermina-teur punissait l'Européen de ses attentats sur l'Afrique" (symbol of murder and the avenger of his race . . . the crime of extermination punished the Eu-ropean for his attacks on Africa) (137).

28. According to the website of the Mémorial de l'abolition de l'escalvage (Memorial to the Abolition of Slavery), located in Nantes: "Slavery is part of our history . . . [F]or a long time, Nantes looked away from this past until the 1990s when we decided to face it head on" (http://memorial.nantes .fr/le-memorial/une-volonte-politique). In *Bordeaux, port négrier* (1995), a meticulous study of the "forgotten" history of the slave trade in the French port city of Bordeaux, Eric Saugera writes:

> It is not certain that the city and its inhabitants have anything to gain by recalling a system that depended upon the deportation and exploitation of individuals for the profit of others. It is not certain that this exhumation will not tarnish a reputation that is held dear. Humanism, liberty, elegance, *art de vivre:* can they co-exist with what is now commonly recognized as a crime against humanity? To associ-ate Bordeaux with the slave trade . . . is not gratifying. But it is not gratifying for anyone. How many cities have finally accepted this lu-gubrious past and opened up about it to the world? Le Havre (1985), Liège (1989), Nantes (1992), Liverpool (1994) have exposed this past in order to go beyond it and to mourn over it. (22)

See also "In Bordeaux, a Struggle to Face up to a Slave-Trading Past," an article by Edward Cody that explores continuing struggles to foreground this history in Bordeaux (www.washingtonpost.com/wpdyn/content /article/2009/09/25/AR2009092504013.html).

29. Alexandre Dumas was the son of Thomas Alexandre Davy de la Pailleterie, known as General Dumas-Davy, the first West Indian of African descent in the French military. General Dumas-Davey was born on March 25, 1762, in Jérémie, Saint-Domingue (Haiti), and died February 26, 1806, in Villers-Cotterêts. Technically, the French term *mulâtre* in English is "mu-latto." Currently, the term used in French to designate a person of mixed black and white ancestry is *métis*. In English, I use the term "of mixed de-scent," or "mixed."

30. In *The Leopard Boy,* Marie-Antoinette uses a pin to prick a message sent out in the body of her pug that tells the Commander, the Viscount, and Doctor Seiffert that she wants to see the leopard boy.

31. Maximilien Robespierre was one of the most influential figures of the French Revolution. Thought to be "incorruptible" (indeed, this was one of his nicknames), he was also bloodthirsty and intransigent. He insisted that Marie-Antoinette stand trial, that her son the Dauphin be imprisoned, and that her husband, King Louis XVI, be beheaded.

32. Indeed, one such "hidden black child" was the cloistered Louise Marie-Thérèse (1664–1732), the so-called Mooress of Moret. Rumored ei-

AFTERWORD

ther to be the daughter of Louis XIV and an unknown mother, or of his wife, Queen Marie-Thérèse (1638–1683) and her black slave and constant companion, a "dwarf moor" named Nabo, the existence of this "black nun" is documented, although her exact lineage remains a mystery. In any case, she was hidden away in the convent of Moret-sur-Loing, near Fontainebleau. The portrait of Louise Marie-Thérèse hangs in the St. Geneviève library, 10, Place du Panthéon, 75005, Paris.

33. "Dauphin" was the title of the heir apparent to the French throne and refers to the dolphin that appears in the royal coat of arms.

BIBLIOGRAPHY

Beaglehole, J. C., ed. *The Journals of Captain James Cook on His Voyages of Discovery. The Voyage of the Endeavour 1768–1771.* Cambridge: Cambridge University Press, 1955.

Béglé, Jérôme. "Picouly se la joue aristo." *Paris Match,* October 7, 1999.

Blanchard, Pascal, Nicolas Bancel, and Sandrine Lemaire. "La Formation d'une culture coloniale en France, du temps des colonies à celui des guerres de mémoires." Introduction to *Culture coloniale en France: De la Révolution française à nos jours,* edited by Blanchard, Bancel, and Lemaire. Paris: CNRS Editions, 2008. 11–64.

Burrows, Simon. "A Literary Low-Life Reassessed: Charles Théveneau de Morande in London, 1769–1791." *Eighteenth-Century Life* 22, no. 1 (1998): 76–94. https://muse.jhu.edu/login?auth=0&type=summary&url=/journals/eighteenth-century_life/v022/22.1burrows_s.html.

Cabanés, Augustin. *La Princesse de Lamballe, intime. (d'après les confidences de son médecin: Sa liaison avec Marie Antoinette, son rôle secret pendant la révolution.* Paris: Albin Michel, 1922. https://archive.org/details/laprincessedelamoocabauoft.

Cody, Edward. "In Bordeaux, a Stuggle to Face up to Slave-Trading Past." www.washingtonpost.com/wp-dyn/content/article/2009/09/25/AR2009092504013.html.

Coppola, Sophia, dir. *Marie Antoinette.* Columbia Pictures Corporation, 2006.

Deveau, Jean-Michel. *La France au temps des négriers.* Paris: France-Empire, 1994.

Dumas, Alexandre. *Le Chevalier de Maison-Rouge.* Paris: Gallimard, 2005.

Fabre, Michel, Robert E. Skinner, and Lester Sullivan. *Chester Himes: An Annotated Primary and Secondary Bibliography.* Westport, Ct.: Greenwood, 1992.

Gandillot, Thierry. "Un Picouly Sauce Chester." *L'Express.* www.lexpress.fr/informations/un-picouly-sauce-chester_634625.html.

Garane, Jeanne. "Playing with the Past: How and Why Daniel Picouly Rewrites Chester Himes." In *Afropean Cartographies,* edited by Dominic Thomas, 82–96. Cambridge: Cambridge Scholars Press, 2014.

BIBLIOGRAPHY

Guédé, Alain. *Monsieur de Saint-George: Le Nègre des lumières*. Paris: Actes Sud, 1999.

Higginson, Pim. *The Noir Atlantic*. Liverpool: Liverpool University Press, 2011.

Himes, Chester. *All Shot Up*. Chatham, N.J.: Chatham Bookseller, 1973.

———. *For Love of Imabelle*. Chatham, N.J.: Chatham Bookseller, 1973.

———. *Imbroglio negro*. Translated by Jeanne Fillion. Série noire no. 601. Paris: Gallimard, 1960.

———. *La Reine des pommes*. Translated by Minnie Danzas. Série noire no. 419. Paris: Gallimard, 1958.

Jacquot, Benoît, dir. *Les Adieux à la reine (Farewell My Queen)*. GMT Productions, 2012.

Kadish, Doris, and Françoise Massardier-Kenney. *Translating Slavery: Gender and Race in French Abolitionist Writing*. Vol. 1. 2nd ed. Kent, Ohio: Kent State University Press, 2009.

Lamartine, Alphonse de. *Oeuvres complètes de Lamartine. Histoire de girondins*. Paris: Chez l'auteur, 1847. www.googlebooks.com.

Laye, Camara. *L'Enfant noir*. Paris: Plon, 1954.

Lenotre, G. *La Captivité et la mort de Marie-Antoinette: Les Feuillants—Le Temple—La Conciergerie*. Paris: Perrin et compagnie, 1908. https://archive.org/details/lacaptivitetlaoolenouoft.

Monnier Raymonde. *Le Faubourg Saint-Antoine 1789–1815*. 1981. Paris: Société des études robespierristes, 2012.

Nora, Pierre, ed. *Les Lieux de mémoire*. Paris: Gallimard, 1984. Translated by Arthur Goldhammer as *Realms of Memory: Rethinking the French Past*. New York: Columbia University Press, 1996.

Miller, Christopher. *The French Atlantic Triangle*. Durham, N.C.: Duke University Press, 2008.

Peabody, Susan, and Tyler Stovall, eds. *The Color of Liberty: Histories of Race in France*. Durham, N.C.: Duke University Press, 2003.

Picouly, Daniel. *Un Beau jour pour tuer Kennedy*. Paris: Grasset, 2006.

———. *Le Champ de Personne*. Paris: Flammarion, 1995.

———. *Le Coeur à la craie*. Paris: Grasset, 2005.

———. *Le cri muet de l'iguane*. Paris: Albin Michel, 2015.

———. *La Donzelle*. Paris: Le Rocher, 2004.

———. *L'Enfant léopard*. Paris: Grasset, 1999.

———. *L'Extraordinaire voyage de Lulu*. Paris: Magnard jeuness, 2011.

———. *La Faute d'orthographe est ma langue maternelle*. Paris: Albin Michel, 2012.

BIBLIOGRAPHY

———. *Fort de l'Eau*. Paris: Flammarion, 1997.

———. *Les Larmes du chef*. Paris: Gallimard, 1994.

———. *La Lumière des fous*. Paris: Le Rocher, 1991.

———. *Nec*. Paris: Gallimard, 1993.

———. *Nos Histoires de France*. Paris: Hoëbeke, 2011.

———. *La Nuit de Lampedusa*. Paris: Albin-Michel, 2011.

———. *Paulette et Roger*. Paris: Grasset, 2001.

———. *Personal Interview*. June 5, 2012.

———. *68 mon amour*. Paris: Grasset, 2008.

———. *Tête de nègre*. Paris: Librio, 1998.

———. *Tête de nègre*. Vol. 1. Illustrations by Jurg. Paris: Emmanuel Proust/La Martinière, 2002.

———. *Tête de nègre*. Vol. 2, *Le Casse du siècle*. Paris: Emmanuel Proust/La Martinière, 2007.

———. *La Treizième mort du Chevalier*. Paris: Grasset, 2003.

Ruggieri, Eve. *Le Rêve de Zamor*. Paris: Plon, 2004.

Saint-Jean, Raymond, dir. *Le Mozart noir: Reviving a Legend*. Media Headquarters, Canadian Broadcasting System, 2003.

Saint-Loup, Gérard de. *Zamor, le nègre de la du Barry*. Paris: L'Harmattan, 2006.

Saugera, Eric. *Bordeaux Port Négrier: XVII–XIXe siècles*. Paris: Karthala, 1995.

Susane, Louis. *Histoire de la cavalerie française*. Vol. 3. Paris: Librairie Hetzel, 1874.

Thomas, Chantal. *Les Adieux à la reine*. Paris: Seuil, 2002. Translated by Moishe Black as *Farewell My Queen*. New York: Touchstone, 2004.

Thomas, Dominic. *Black France. Colonialism, Immigration, and Transnationalism*. Bloomington: Indiana University Press, 2007.

Tulard, Jean, Jean-François Fayard, and Alfred Fierro. *Histoire et dictionnaire de la Révolution française. 1789–1799*. Paris: Robert Laffont, 1987.

Verniquet, Pierre. *Paris de 1789 à 1798*. http://picpus.mmlc.northwestern .edu/mbin/WebObjects/Picpus.woa/wa/displayDigitalObject?id=1102.

Zweig, Stephan. *Marie-Antoinette*. Translated by Alzir Hella. Paris: Grasset, 2003.

Recent Books in the Series

CARAF Books
Caribbean and African Literature Translated from French

Yanick Lahens
*Aunt Résia and the Spirits and
Other Stories*
Translated by Betty Wilson

Mariama Barry
The Little Peul
Translated by Carrol F. Coates

Mohammed Dib
At the Café and *The Talisman*
Translated by C. Dickson

Mouloud Feraoun
Land and Blood
Translated by Patricia Geesey

Suzanne Dracius
Climb to the Sky
Translated by Jamie Davis

Véronique Tadjo
Far from My Father
Translated by Amy Baram Reid

Angèle Rawiri
The Fury and Cries of Women
Translated by Sara Hanaburgh

Louis-Philippe Dalembert
The Other Side of the Sea
Translated by Robert H.
McCormick Jr.

Leïla Sebbar
Arabic as a Secret Song
Translated by Skyler Artes

Évelyne Trouillot
Memory at Bay
Translated by Paul Curtis Daw

Daniel Picouly
The Leopard Boy
Translated by Jeanne Garane